Since his first p established him and promising horror. He has b anthologies, and <del>prize-winner of the</del> <del>ters of the</del> Future Contest. *Metal Fatigue* is his debut solo novel.

Sean lives in Adelaide and, when not writing, works in a specialist CD shop.

METAL FATIGUE

SEAN WILLIAMS

HarperCollins*Publishers*

HarperCollins_Publishers_

First published in Australia in 1996
by HarperCollins_Publishers_ Pty Limited
ACN 009 913 517
A member of the HarperCollins_Publishers_ (Australia) Pty Limited Group

HarperCollins_Publishers_
25 Ryde Road, Pymble, Sydney NSW 2073, Australia
31 View Road, Glenfield, Auckland 10, New Zealand
77–85 Fulham Palace Road, London W6 8JB, United Kingdom
Hazelton Lanes, 55 Avenue Road, Suite 2900, Toronto, Ontario M5R 3L2
and 1995 Markham Road, Scarborough, Ontario M1B 5M8, Canada
10 East 53rd Street, New York NY 10032, USA

National Library of Australia Cataloguing-in-publication data:

Williams, Sean, 1967 - .
  Metal fatigue.
  ISBN 0 7322 5633 X.
  I. Title.
A823.3

Cover illustration by Greg Bridges
Cover design by Darian Causby

Printed in Australia by Griffin Paperbacks, Adelaide

7 6 5 4 3 2 1
99 98 97 96

"Each culture casts its own shadow, a shadow which is a perfect description of its own form and nature. The shadow which our technological civilisation casts is that of Lilith, 'the maid of desolation' who dances in the ruins of cities. Now that we have made a single polluted city of the entire world, she is preparing to dance in the ruins of our planetary megalopolis."

William Irwin Thompson
The Time Falling Bodies Take To Light

In memoriam
Harold Alwin Schiller
1903–1983
David John Williams
1942–1995

The author would like to thank the following people for their help during the preparation of this novel: Bill Congreve, Shane Dix, Bill Gee, Jeff Harris, Phillip & Jo Knowles, Kelly Manison, Peter McNamara, Sputnik, Nick Stathopoulos, Jonathan Strahan, Louise Thurtell, Damien Warman and Juliette Woods.

Some sections of this novel are loosely based on the short story "Robbery, Assault and Battery", published in *Nemesis* #17 (March, 1992).

PART ONE:
THOU SHALT NOT STEAL

PRELUDE

Friday, 14 September, 2096, 11:15 p.m.

"I am Lucifer," said the voice.

He woke with a start, and opened his eyes.

The room was lit by second-hand streetlight, an indistinct, yellow haze which spilled through the curtains and lapped at the damp-stained walls. The curfew had not yet fallen, which placed the time at before twelve o'clock; still, the faint electric light was not quite enough to fully dispel the night. Shadows crowded about the bed, whispering black secrets in the distant voice of the city.

He sat up, letting the sheet slip from his shoulders to his lap. The humid air, stirred by the sudden movement, brushed the rigid bulges of his muscles with the electric caress of an approaching thunderstorm. The woman beside him snuffled to herself and rolled over. There was a subtle tension in the air, an expectant pause, a moment waiting to be filled.

He listened . . .

People stirred in the buildings around him: someone screamed, another laughed, a third raised her voice in anger. A nearby couple made love with abandon, oblivious to his prying, sensitive ears. Far away, the languid tongue of the river licked its lips and tasted the rotten teeth of Patriot Bridge.

When the voice spoke again, it did so without sound or expression. It whispered directly into his mind a second time, "I am Lucifer," then fell silent again, waiting.

He closed his eyes, concentrated, and visualised a reply, parcelling the soundless words into a bundle of electric thought and hurling it outward into the night.

The response was instantaneous: "Remember your duty."

He slid from beneath the sheet and stood upright. In profile and near-darkness, his naked body was sexless and smooth-skinned. His chest and shoulders were massive, and his limbs gifted with both power and grace. His poise balanced, trembling, on the brink of blinding motion.

He remained that way for some time – frozen, indecisive, reluctant to commit himself to any course of action – until movement through a part in the curtains caught his pinprick eye. Leaning closer to the window, he peered out and down at the empty street below. As he watched, a shadow moved, stepped onto the littered roadway and into a wash of streetlight.

The man stood a full foot shorter than he, with wide shoulders and a wrestler's build not yet soft with age. Receding mouse-brown hair exposed a high, proud forehead and generous ears. A thick moustache bristled beneath the snub nose, lending the man an air of familiarity that defied the best efforts of his memory. He might have seen this man somewhere before, although he wasn't sure where.

It didn't matter. The man, whoever he was, was irrelevant. Curiosity had been carefully bred out of him, replaced with an inescapable compulsion to obey orders.

There was something about the man's silent watchfulness, though, that made him nervous. Something indefinably wrong. The man was so still, he hardly seemed to breathe . . .

The woman stirred again, not quite awake. Her voice was muffled by sleep. "Cati?"

He turned away from the window. The blackness of her hair formed a puddle on the pillow, a pool of darkness deeper than the shadows. Reaching down with one massive hand, he touched her reassuringly on the shoulder. The trembling of his fingertips eased as he gently caressed her soft skin, even when the voice called a third time. She was Sanctuary in a world he could not begin to understand, queen of a haven called Peace; he would protect his Sanctuary every way he could, even if it was his own nature that threatened her.

Slowly, her breathing deepened, became more regular, until she finally returned to sleep.

He went to the bathroom, where he would not disturb her further, and opened his mind to the insistent touch of the one who called himself Lucifer.

When curfew fell at midnight, he was leaping from rooftop to rooftop high above the streets, hunting. And the silent man who had stood on the street under his window had long since disappeared.

CHAPTER ONE

Saturday, 15 September, 1:25 a.m.

From the outside, it looked like an empty warehouse: its doors had rusted shut; its windows were broken and boarded up; its roof was slowly caving in.

Kennedy Polis had many such buildings. Once, six decades past, swift, solar-powered ferries had shunted back and forth along the river, bringing with them trade goods from nearby towns. The warehouses had been full, then, and business brisk. Kennedy had shone like a jewel in the North American Model City Project's crown. Completely free of petrochemical fuels, self-sufficient except for a few basic raw materials and equipped with the latest reclamation technologies, it had symbolised the new, cleaner lifestyle promised by politicians for decades – a harbinger of the NAMCP's utopian dream.

The War, however, had killed the dream, and the Dissolution that had followed had killed most of the dreamers. Now the warehouses stood empty, rotting slowly in the moist air drifting off the river. Some had become temporary homes for refugees, others were taken over by the Mayoralty; the remainder simply awaited the reopening of the city's self-imposed walls, if such ever happened.

The years rested heavily upon Kennedy, and upon its warehouses in particular. But it had not died.

Not yet.

This warehouse was located on a deserted cul-de-sac not far from the slosh and tumble of the river. A white, electric vehicle slid to a halt by a rusted phone booth at the end of the street. The letters "RSD" were painted in bold black down each side of the car and on its trunk.

The younger of the two people inside the car, a woman in her mid-thirties with shoulder-length blonde hair and strong laughter-lines, peered sceptically through the rain-spattered windscreen.

"You're sure this is the right place, Phil?"

The man beside her nodded. With a slightly receding hairline, a thick moustache and a body that was past its peak without being infirm, he looked to be only a few years older than his companion; perhaps in his mid-forties. He was in fact much older. It showed sometimes in his voice.

"This is it, Barney. Trust me." He smiled, teasing. "You wanted to come, remember?"

"Only because you promised to buy me a drink." She pouted mournfully, and he knew she was ribbing him in return. Barney Daniels and Phil Roads had been close friends for most of her life, especially since her father's death, and knew each other's games well.

"Best bar in Kennedy, you said," she continued, nodding disdainfully through the window at the derelict warehouse, no different from the scores of others within spitting distance. "Doesn't look like much to me."

"Nevertheless." He locked the dash with his thumb-print and keyed the car's security system. Thirty seconds. "Coming?"

"Do I have a choice?"

They stepped out of the car and into the street, pulling coats closer to protect their bodies. The rain was heavy and thick, falling in a warm sheet from the dark sky, a solid mass only slightly less dense than the nearby river. Their clothing consisted of the standard casual uniforms of the city's Regional Security Department: grey synthetic fabric, recycled aluminium buttons and thick greatcoats. Roads' genuine leather boots were a rarity in Kennedy, and allowed him to walk through puddles with greater comfort than Barney.

"This way." He led her down a narrow flight of stairs between two buildings. Paint peelings from the crumbling brick walls littered the asphalt path. A left turn took them to a steel door, which slid aside on smooth-oiled runners as they approached. The passageway on the other side was gloomily lit, but at least relatively clean and dry.

As they passed through the entrance, Roads noted the tingling, skin-crawling sensation of security scanners, electromagnetic fingers that reached through their clothes to search for the telltale shapes of concealed weapons. Barney, beside him, was far too young to remember the technology that had been available, if not commonplace, before the War, and nervously rubbed the suddenly erect hair of her forearms.

Roads didn't break his stride; the security-sweep was just the first of many technological traps designed to unsettle the unwary or the ignorant, and he didn't want to stop each time to bring her up to date. Besides, she was canny enough. If he looked like he knew what he was doing, she would follow his example.

He only hoped he *did* know. It had been so long since he had last come this way . . .

The door at the far end of the corridor remained closed. A panel slid aside in the wall to the right of the door and a gender-neutral voice spoke:

"Please disarm. Your weapons will be returned to you when you leave."

7

"Phil?" Barney's voice betrayed her nervousness.

"It's okay." He opened his coat and removed his belt. The pistol – loaded with plastic bullets, lead being another rarity – and its holster vanished behind the panel; hers followed after a slight hesitation.

The door slid open.

They stepped through into a muffled riot of noise. Somewhere nearby, removed by only a wall or two, a very large, very noisy party was taking place. Roads smelled smoke and liquor in large quantities, and a general miasma of damp flesh.

Two large bouncers awaited them behind a low counter. "Names?" asked one without looking up from a neon-bright video screen. His left eye was covered with what looked like a simple leather patch. Roads didn't doubt that it hid more than an empty socket.

"Phil Roads." He pressed palm to scanner and waited for confirmation. "I still have access here, I believe."

"That is correct, sir," said the bouncer, his manner formal once the ID was approved. He waved Barney forward, and she likewise subjected her handprint to the machine's scrutiny.

It beeped a negative: as far as its files were concerned, she did not exist. That wasn't necessarily a problem; at least she wasn't a known threat.

"Ms Daniels is my guest," explained Roads. "We're here to see the Head. He's expecting us."

"I'll notify him of your presence." The bouncer listened to an earplug's whisper for a moment, then said: "He'll meet you shortly. This way."

Barney hesitated again, and Roads patted her on the shoulder, nudging her forward.

"After you."

"Will I regret it?" she asked.

"Probably."

She grimaced. "If you insist, then."

He smiled in return, and followed her inside.

The bar was full of half-seen, vaguely demonic shapes that twisted and writhed in the smoke of a hundred lit cigarettes, thrown into sharp relief by irregular strobes. Music blared from towering wall speakers as Roads and Barney headed in the general direction indicated by the bouncer. An expansive, horseshoe-shaped counter draped with bodies lay across their path. Short but solid, Roads used his weight plus the occasional elbow to clear a way through the crowd. Barney followed close at his heels.

The cubicle awaiting them was the only empty space in the entire venue, one of ten similar cubicles raised half a metre above floor level. Containing nothing more than a table and two leather-bound chairs, it was tucked into an anonymous corner opposite the entrance. A yellow lamp provided its sole illumination.

Roads shrugged out of his damp overcoat and slid awkwardly into the cramped enclosure, noting with relief that it was acoustically shielded. Behind them, the bellow of the crowd diminished to an irritating rather than painful mumble. Barney settled into the seat across the table from him, looking bedraggled and slightly stunned.

"Drinks?" asked a woman via the booth's intercom.

"Water, thanks." He glanced at Barney. Drinking on duty was forbidden, but she looked like she needed it. "And a Scotch."

"Any preference? We have –"

"Something from the cellar. Glenfiddich, if possible. No ice."

"Certainly. Your drinks will be with you shortly."

He leaned an elbow onto the table and smiled at his assistant's expression, waiting for her to speak. She seemed to be having trouble choosing one question out of the thousands she obviously wanted to ask.

"Where's your friend going to sit?" she eventually managed.

"He'll cope."

"I guess he'll have to." She looked around. "Are you going to tell me where we are, or –?"

He hushed her with a finger to his lips. "Wait until he arrives. Then he can explain."

They scanned the room to pass the time. Kennedy no longer boasted a decadent social set, but this crowd wouldn't have been part of it even if it had. Roads recognised a number of people, several matching records in the city's Most Wanted datapool. It was almost as if all the riff-raff of Kennedy Polis had gathered for a quick drink before venturing out into the night to pursue their regular activities. A disconcerting number were young – from teenagers to mid-twenties – reflecting the city's growing youth crime problem.

"If only I had my gun," whispered Barney. "Isn't that Danny Chong, the bounty-hunter?"

Roads nodded. "It is, but forget it. This is neutral territory. No-one has jurisdiction in here."

"Except 'the Head'?"

"Right. And I shouldn't have to add that we're outnumbered as well."

"Point taken. As long as the restriction works both ways, I'll keep quiet."

"It does." He was glad she understood. Barney wasn't stupid, but she was still young. At his age, he tended to forget about justice and aim for workable compromises instead.

He was about to point out another celebrity of the underworld when a third voice from within the cubicle cleared its throat and spoke:

"Would you care for a conversation?"

They turned to face a holographic image of the head of a man in his late forties. The head was bald and angular, somehow twisted from true; the nose in particular was obviously crooked. Its lips curled with wry amusement.

The head floated in the air one centimetre above the tabletop. Barney's gasp of astonishment was clearly audible.

"The cost for my time is negotiable," the head continued, radiating dubious goodwill. "It can be debited from your R&R account or settled in cash. Whichever you prefer."

"Really?" Roads settled back into the chair. He doubted that the first option was accepted very often; the Rations and Resources transaction could be too easily traced, for both patron and establishment. Although the alternative, cash money, had only recently reappeared in the city, as a result of the latest downgrade of the R&R commerce network, unofficial currencies had always circulated through the underground economy.

Barney reached out to touch the hologram, as though she couldn't believe what she was seeing. Her hand passed through it unimpeded.

"What is it?" she hissed to Roads.

"I am a computer-generated psychogenic template," said the hologram before he could reply. "A simulated personality, if you like, provided for nothing more than your entertainment."

"But –"

"My existence is highly illegal. I can assure you of that." The head grinned, obviously enjoying her discomfort. Hardware sophisticated enough to generate real-time holograms hadn't been used in decades for anything as frivolous as entertainment.

Roads leaned forward to butt in. "Quit playing games, Keith. I haven't got all night."

The head froze in mid-expression, caught between a frown and the beginning of a word, like a movie in mid-frame. An instant later it returned to life. Although its grey features hadn't changed, Roads detected a subtle difference, a nuance of facial tension that suggested another, quite separate personality.

"Ah, yes," said the head, tilting in acknowledgment. "I apologise for the previous personality. A simple ruse to affirm your identity."

"And you are?"

"Tut-tut, Phil. It hasn't been that long, has it?"

"No, but it pays to be sure."

"Quite so, for both of us."

Roads felt the pressure of eyes upon him, and belatedly turned to his companion.

"Keith, I'd like you to meet my assistant, Barney Daniels. Barney, this is Keith Morrow."

Her eyes widened.

"Pleasure," said the Head, bowing at the neck. Not just 'a head', but *the* Head.

She stared at the hologram, then at Roads. "*The* Keith Morrow?"

"At your service."

"Oh my God."

Roads knew what Barney was thinking. Keith Morrow was on the city's *other* Most Wanted list, the one the general public didn't see. There was no physical description for anyone on that list, just a tally of suspected crimes against the city – including conspiracy, murder, and resource misappropriation. Standing orders were not to arrest, but to 'decommission'. In Morrow's case, in all the years Barney had been on the force, no Regional Security Department officer had come close to doing either.

Barney's hand slipped down to the radio in her pocket.

"Don't." Roads reached across the table to stop her. Out of the corner of his eye he saw the bouncers hovering. "This isn't a bust."

Her eyes flashed. "Then what is it?"

"A very bad pun," said Morrow, looking pained. "I am a businessman, my dear, not a petty criminal. Ask Phil. Just a smuggler with connections, I swear."

"Hoarding is still illegal," she protested.

"It is, yes, for the moment. These are desperate times. I do what I can to survive, and no more, until the day when I am no longer considered to be a criminal."

"On those charges only."

"On all charges. I do not prey on the weak; only the strong."

She hesitated, but her hand remained in her coat. "Phil?"

"Trust me," he repeated. "I'm not bent, if that's what's worrying you."

"Alas," rued the Head. "How true."

"And besides," Roads went on, "we couldn't arrest him if we wanted to."

"Why not?"

Morrow smiled. "Because I'm dead, my dear, that's why not. I died over fifty years ago."

"That's impossible –"

"'Impossible' is a ridiculous word." Morrow rolled his eyes. "You children of the Dissolution are all the same. You have difficulty accepting the fact that the present is not representative of the past. Many things that once could be done cannot be done now. That is all, my dear."

Barney still floundered. "I don't understand."

"No," said Morrow. "And therein lies the difference between us."

"I'll explain later," said Roads, leaning over the table to place a hand on her arm. "We've got more important things to talk about at the moment."

Barney nodded dumbly, casting a *What the hell have you got me into?* look back at him.

Their drinks arrived at that moment via a trapdoor in the rear of the cubicle. Roads put his in one corner of the table, away from the flickering hologram. Barney drank half of hers in one gulp.

Roads reached into a pocket, produced a cigarette and a lighter. He lit up and took a deep, sour breath.

"I need your help," he said to Morrow, getting down to business.

"I guessed as much." The Head rotated to face him.

"How much do you know?"

"That you have a serious problem. I'm glad it's you and not me, no offence."

"Thanks. Are you going to help me?"

"That depends. Are *you* going to help *me*?" Morrow countered.

"If I can."

"How?"

"I don't know. Put in a good word, perhaps."

"That won't be necessary. I have something more concrete in mind."

"Tell me."

"First, the problem," said Morrow. "You've got a thief to catch. And a killer too."

"How much do you know?"

"Enough. Since the first of August, there have been thirty break-ins and eighteen political assassinations within the city – all of them unsolved. The bulletin boards think that both series of crimes were performed by one and the same person, although RSD is treating them as separate matters entirely. No-one has given the killer a nickname yet, but the thief has been dubbed 'the Mole'. What little evidence you have in either case is inconclusive. In particular, the identikit pictures of the Mole are ... how do I put this? ... *interesting*." Morrow smiled apologetically. "You can't blame me for having been suspicious of you, at first."

"No, I don't." In the six weeks the Mole had been operating, RSD had learned only one thing about him: that he looked exactly like Roads. After the first break-in, Roads had been on suspension until he could prove his alibi; he didn't like remembering the experience. "Is that all you've found out?"

"Absolutely not, my friend. I know that the murders were of highly placed officials who actively supported the Reassimilation Bill. Mayor Packard is down-playing the political motive behind the killings, but the thought of joining the Reunited States of America has obviously ruffled someone's feathers. I know security has been upped at Mayor's House, and another hundred officers have been drafted from RSD to help with the arrival of General Stedman on Tuesday." The Head winked. "I'm sure that's ruffled still more feathers downtown. Or have RSD and the MSA finally reached a consensus that I'm not aware of?"

Roads didn't dignify the comment with a reply, although it certainly hit home. RSD had evolved during the Dissolution from a small, privately-owned security company. Kennedy's former police department and a small Army garrison had been combined to form the Military Services Authority. While RSD officers patrolled the streets and maintained civil law, the MSA's main task had originally been to keep external forces out of the city. In recent years, however, the MSA's authority had been extended to cover many matters dealing with the city's internal safety – a fact many old-hand RSD officers, including Roads, resented.

Roads put aside the cigarette and leaned forward. "Go on."

"The thief is another kettle of fish," Morrow said, his face sobering. "And the one you're after in particular – the Mole, rather than the assassin. That's been your assignment for the last six weeks. But you've had no luck thus far, and I can well see why."

"Oh?"

"Of course. The thefts were not of valuable items that would reappear later, as the b-boards depict them, but of information concerning RSD resources, movements of the MSA, reactor status and population figures, among other things. Correct?"

"Yes." The MSA break-in tended to overshadow the other thefts, but Roads knew them all by heart.

Morrow went on: "It's hard to see why anyone would bother stealing this data at all. There's so much of it, for a start, and of such variety. Who could possibly find a use for it all?"

"That's what we've been trying to determine." Roads leaned back into the seat, away from Morrow's probing stare. "As you say, the evidence is nonexistent, and the few suspects we've uncovered all had alibis. Motive is all that's left, and it's getting us nowhere."

"So you've finally come to me for help," Morrow said, the suggestion of a grin at the corners of his mouth. "Do you suspect that I am involved, perhaps?"

"No," Roads said. "You could break into any system you wanted without sending in the heavies."

"Exactly. The computer sciences employed by this city are not what they used to be." A fleeting regret clouded the Head's face, almost as though he missed the challenge.

"They're still not exactly easy to break into," said Barney irritably. "Whoever the Mole is, he knows what he's doing."

"True," the Head conceded. "So it would seem."

"I'm hoping you might have heard something," Roads prompted. "A rumour, anything."

"If I had, I would tell you for free."

"Does that mean you haven't?" Roads tried to keep the disappointment from showing.

"Not exactly." Morrow hesitated. "But it's strange," he said. "I thought you would have guessed by now."

"What?" asked Barney.

"Let's study the Mole's behaviour, shall we? He works under the cover of darkness, often three or four nights in a row. He is a meticulous professional, and he works alone. He does not socialise or talk to others, for, if he did, someone would surely have seen him doing so by now."

"We know this, Keith," Roads said.

"Yes, but have you ever stopped to ask yourself what he *does* do on his nights off?"

He had, frequently. "I've got a feeling you're going to tell me."

"Exactly. And the time has come for me to ask for that favour in return."

"Go ahead."

"It's quite simple," Morrow said. "I too want you to catch the Mole."

Roads performed a mental double-take. "You what?"

"I want you to catch him, for even I am not immune to this invisible thief. On every night the Mole has not been robbing you, he has been locking horns with me. And winning, I should add."

Roads almost laughed at the Head's expression. It must have hurt Morrow plenty to even contemplate asking an RSD officer for help, albeit that Roads had come to him first.

Barney shook her head. "Shit."

"My sentiments exactly."

"What have you lost?" asked Roads.

"Not much. Invoices, inventories, securities, private records. I get the feeling the Mole is simply testing my defences, waiting until he's ready to pull off the big one."

"Have you kept a record of what he took?"

"Naturally, and of the time each break-in occurred. Like you, I have been unable to determine a pattern."

"Regardless . . . I need your data."

"And you shall have it. But only you, not the entire Regional Security Department."

"You have my word. They don't even know we're here."

"Good."

The trapdoor opened in the back of the booth, revealing a data fiche the size and shape of an old smart card. Roads gently picked it up and pocketed it, keen to study it but trying not to raise his hopes too high. The revelation, unexpected thought it was, might still lead nowhere.

Morrow had closed his eyes, and appeared to be thinking to himself. Roads looked at Barney, who shrugged. He waited as long as he could before breaking the silence.

"I don't suppose you have a card reader here, Keith?" he asked. "I want to get started on this right away."

Morrow's eyes snapped open. "Of course; you must be keen to explore the depth of my vulnerability. But not right now. I have other work for you to do."

"Oh?" Roads said cautiously.

"Yes. The time is two-fifteen. You are still here, which I take to mean that you have not received a report from RSD HQ regarding the latest robbery."

Barney glanced at her watch. "That's right. But that doesn't mean we won't. Sometimes it takes a while for a break-in to –"

"I have just had word from one of my subordinates," Morrow interrupted. "An entry alarm was triggered twenty minutes ago. Our friend has been busy."

Roads gripped the edge of the table. "Where?"

"One hundred and fourteen Old North Street. If you hurry, you might catch him on the way out."

Barney lifted her coat into her lap. "It'll take at least ten minutes to get there."

"I know," Roads said.

"And he has an annoying habit of triggering alarms when he leaves, not as he enters." The Head shrugged with his eyebrows. "Still, someone will meet you there. Call in the troops and see what you can find, but remember: I didn't tip you off."

"Of course not. Thank you." Roads clambered across his seat.

"A pleasure – and to have met you, my dear." Morrow smiled at Barney. "Do keep in touch."

The Head flickered once, and vanished.

CHAPTER TWO

2:45 a.m.

The rain had gone as suddenly as it had come, leaving nothing but dampness in the air and swirling water on the streets. In places, storm drains had been overloaded or blocked, and mirror-flat puddles shattered into spray as the RSD patrol car passed.

Roads drove while Barney arranged the rendezvous with HQ, using the secure phone in the dash rather than the radio. The duty officer confessed to being slightly overwhelmed with requests: more than just the Mole had been busy. It took five minutes to confirm that a footsquad and van would be dispatched to Old North Street as soon as possible, and that curfew would be lifted in the area once power loads could be juggled across the city to accommodate the extra demand.

When she had finished, Barney collapsed into the seat and slicked back her still-damp hair. The alcohol slowly dissolving in her stomach didn't ease the sensation that her world had suddenly been turned upside down. Watching Roads drive wasn't helping, either.

Kennedy Polis had been designed and built with an emphasis on new ways of managing resources, waste, and movement. The last, in particular, gave the city a unique shape. Instead of a complicated tangle of roads and freeways, Kennedy had boasted a massive twin-track personal rapid transport system arranged in seven concentric rings – designated A to G – spaced one kilometre apart, web-like, around the nominal heart of the city. Each elevated guideway, not much wider than a conventional sidewalk, had originally carried six- or two-seater cabs that could be summoned from numerous stops and junctions along the network. Powered by linear induction motors, the cabs had been computer-controlled, quick and safe, designed as a compromise between buses and taxis. Armed with a smart card, a commuter could have summoned a cab at any time from anywhere in the city – arrival within two minutes, guaranteed – and taken it wherever he or she liked.

The annual cost of regularly using such a service had amounted to little more than the cost of maintaining a private motor vehicle to travel the same distance, so patronage of the system – nicknamed the 'Rosette' – had been high. As an added incentive, the city's streets were deliberately narrow – with priority lanes given to bicycles and service vehicles rather than general traffic – and followed the path of the Rosette almost exactly. These long, curving maintenance roads provided the only relatively uninterrupted stretches of tarmac in the city, apart from radial freeways pointing the four directions of the compass.

Following the War and the enclosure of the city, private vehicle ownership had been banned and use of the Rosette rationalised. New outer sections, once intended as complete additions to the original ring structure, had been turned into loops connecting the inner rings with more distant sites, thus allowing commuters access to their workplaces. Little-used segments had been shut down completely, their reaction plates and control systems cannibalised to repair others. The only vehicles allowed on the roads were those performing the work of the Mayoralty.

The streets were, therefore, empty for the most part, maintained irregularly, and ill-lit at night. Rusting hulks left over from the old days had long since been recycled, but there were still plenty of other hazards. Where tarmac had crumbled, a new surface compounded from old rubber tyres filled the gaps. Traffic lights no longer worked at all. The motorist's only advantage lay in the assumption that all wheeled traffic was important, and therefore had right of way.

Roads, accordingly, drove as though he was the only person on the road. The harbour lay to the south of the city, with Old North Street perversely to the south-west, in an area that had fallen into disrepair after the deactivation of the nearest segment of the Rosette. Following maintenance roads along J loop back to G ring, he pushed the patrol car's small electric motor to its limit, growling around bends and accelerating across intersections without even pausing.

Along a relatively straight stretch, Roads fumbled with one hand inside his coat and handed her the data fiche.

"We'll have to decide what to do about this later," he said. "Until then, keep it safe for me."

"Will do, boss." She tucked it into the breast pocket of her shirt. The sharp edges of the card nagged at her. Accepting help from a known felon smacked of corruption, and contradicted everything she thought she knew about her partner.

"You really surprised me tonight," she said.

He glanced at her, then back to the road. "What do you mean?"

"Come on, Phil." She studied his face closely in the dashlight. "When the hell did you start dealing with Keith Morrow?"

"A long time ago," he said, his expression fixed. "But it's not as bad as it looks."

"Are you sure? For someone who swears he's not crooked, you keep the damnedest friends."

"Is that what's bothering you?"

"Well, you've got me worried, I'll admit."

"Don't be," he said. "I haven't spoken to him for almost twenty years, until tonight."

"But you *did* deal with him?"

"In a way. We helped each other out, once." He shrugged. "It's a long story, and not particularly relevant."

She wanted to believe him – and did for the most part – but the question had to be asked. He was so much a part of her life that the very thought of him betraying her made her stomach turn.

"Promise me you're telling the truth," she said.

"Easy," he said, and smiled. "You've never met a straighter cop."

Her doubts ebbed at that. They had been partners for long enough to know when they were telling the truth, as well as their games.

"I know," she said, returning the smile and adding a suggestive leer. "At least, that's what I've heard."

"So believe it."

"As long as you tell me the full story one day."

"Maybe." He returned his attention to the road. "But not right now, okay?"

She took the hint.

Roads directed the car along a cross-route between G and F rings. The headlights seemed to disappear into the gloom, sucked away from them by the night and returning only in brief reflections off broken glass. Whole blocks had been left to the elements, abandoned for more convenient locations closer to the Rosette. Decaying facades gaped back at her like mocking skulls, blank and impersonal yet eerily animated all the same. If buildings could look wild, untamed, then these did, as though the dead blocks resented the intruder that had so rudely disturbed their brooding, uneasy rest.

Then, as they neared the address Morrow had given them, Roads flicked off the headlights.

"What –?" she began.

"No need to let the Mole know we're coming," Roads said, his voice soft. "If he's still around."

Barney put one hand on the dash. Privately she doubted that the Mole would be anywhere near the address Morrow had given them: not because Morrow had lied, but because the Mole had an uncanny knack of slipping away well before anyone came close. That wouldn't stop her from trying, of course – but the possibility of crashing into something in the dark concerned her more. The road ahead was utterly dark.

"Jesus, Phil –"

"It's okay. I can see fine."

The car swerved to the left, and she clutched the dash hard. "Are you *sure*?"

"Positive."

Dark buildings loomed on her side of the car, and she flinched instinctively away. Roads had been RSD's champion marksman for more years than she could recall, but that didn't make her feel any safer.

Suddenly Roads spun the wheel and brought the car to a sudden halt.

Barney jerked back into her seat. "Now what?"

He pointed past her, through the window on her side of the car. "We're here: 114 Old North Street."

"How can you tell?"

"Would you believe I'm psychic?" He opened his door and stepped out of the car.

"Sure." She unclipped the holster of her pistol, grabbed a torch, and did likewise. "And I'm General Stedman."

"Pleased to meet you." Roads indicated the low, iron fence that separated the tangled yard from the pavement.

Barney's eyes slowly adjusted to the darkness. Now that she looked, she could see a corroded brass plate on the fence with the building's number.

Not psychic, then. She cursed him under her breath, feeling stupid and resolving to be more observant in future.

One hundred and fourteen was large, forbidding, and seemed to have been carved from a solid lump of stone two storeys high. The ground-floor windows were boarded shut, like the warehouses of the harbour; its facade was similarly weathered. Someone had painted "RUSA OUT!" across one wall. An open gate leading to a short flight of steps granted access to the yard. The main door of the building was ajar.

"What now?" she whispered.

"We go in."

"Okay. But after you, this time."

He led the way through the gate and up the steps. At the entrance, he nodded her to one side, then nudged the door open with his foot.

Barney clicked on the torch she had brought with her and swept the beam across the rubble on the floor. The light revealed old food cans, empty; rotten cardboard boxes and a pile of yellow newspapers; a sofa that had seen better days, half a century ago. The house had obviously escaped the usual scouring for recyclable resources. The next room was similar. Roads pointed to split up and edged into the darkness of the building, torchless.

The ground floor was empty. They met at the base of the stairs and headed upward. The first floor was empty too, and the second.

"Cellar," said Roads, his breath thick with dust-laden air. They found the entrance in a closet off the unused kitchen. The door was locked.

Barney took position on one side as Roads kicked it in. The lock splintered with a loud crack. She pointed the torch through the open doorway.

Dim light cast faint shadows at the bottom of a flight of stairs, its source out of sight. Movement in the shadows coincided with the sudden cessation of sound, as though someone had quickly moved for cover.

"Who's there?" she called.

"You tell me," floated back a voice.

Roads gestured for her to cover him as he went down the stairs. She moved to another position, juggling torch and gun in both hands, trying to get a better angle. From the top of the stairs, she could only see two or three metres across the room below, and Roads obscured much of that. When he had descended a half-dozen steps, she dropped to her knees and aimed over his shoulder.

"Morrow sent us," Roads said. He stopped as something moved out of Barney's line of sight.

"What a coincidence," said the voice in return. "He sent me too."

Barney saw Roads' shoulders tighten as someone stepped out of the shadows and into the light. Roads' pistol snapped up, ready to fire. She craned for a better view, but could see little above the waist of the person confronting him.

"I'm your consultant," said the man. "And you must be Phil Roads. Come on down and I'll show you what I've found so far."

Roads didn't respond immediately. His posture remained tense, as though he had seen something that bothered him. But just as Barney was about to ask what was wrong, his pistol slowly fell, and he took another step down the stairs.

Then the sound of a vehicle pulling up outside the house reached her. She listened briefly, until she recognised the familiar whine of an RSD engine.

"Phil," she hissed into the cellar. "The squad's here."

Roads stopped on the last step and looked up at her. "You go," he said. "Have them seal the house and set up a cordon – you know the drill. Just talk to me before letting anyone else down here."

"Are you sure?" She frowned at his concerned expression. "I can –"

"No." He cocked his head. "I'll be okay. Git."

The squad had already begun unloading equipment from the van by the time she left the house. Komalski, the officer in charge of the footsquad, greeted her warmly, despite the hour. Cleaning up after the Mole was a familiar job for both of them, and under normal circumstances she would have responded in kind. But the fact that Mole might be only minutes away – plus her misgivings about Roads being alone in the cellar with one of Keith Morrow's gangsters – dispelled any pleasantry she might have attempted.

She briefed Komalski as quickly as she could. As soon as she was sure he knew what to do, she hurried back into the house.

The cellar door had swung shut since she had left, but no attempt had been made to seal it again. It opened easily, and she craned her neck through the doorway to listen for movement. Voices floated up at her from the pitch-black space below, too faint to be understood but not indicative of trouble.

"Phil?" she called.

The voices stopped for a moment, then he replied: "Barney?"

"Are you okay?"

"Fine. Come on down."

With the aid of the torch, she negotiated the narrow flight of steps. The wall to her right vanished as she descended. She swept the light across the cellar. It seemed to stretch forever into the shadowy distance, cluttered with benches and inactive computer terminals. A hurricane appeared to have blown through the room, emptying filing cabinets, searching through cupboards and opening boxes at random.

Roads was sitting on a stool in the middle of the room. The tension she had sensed in him earlier hadn't gone, but he had it under control. Opposite him, a tall black man leaned against one wall. The man was totally bald and, beneath a black skinsuit, economically muscled. His eyes glittered oddly in the torchlight, sparkling like jewels. As he raised a pair of dark glasses to cover them, Barney realised they were artificial.

"This is Raoul," said Roads. "Morrow sent him."

The man grinned a mouthful of gold teeth and offered his hand. Barney hesitated, then shook it, hoping her nervousness didn't show.

"I haven't touched anything," he said. "Just locked the door on my way in and waited."

"No-one else has been here?" asked Barney, forcing her clenched jaw muscles to move.

"Not a soul. I've confirmed that the Mole triggered the alarm deliberately when he left. The team sent in to investigate had only been in the area a few minutes when the Head ordered them to leave and contacted me."

"Why you?"

"Until a week ago, I ran this operation. I can tell you what's missing."

Barney walked across the room to peer at the debris – anything other than him. "But can we believe you?"

"Implicitly." Raoul grinned. "At least, as far as this room is concerned. On anything else, you'll have to take your chances."

"And why's that?"

"Why do you think?" Raoul's smile only widened. "When you work for the Head, you don't speak freely with RSD. Not without his permission, anyway."

"Thanks, Raoul," Roads broke in, standing. "Barney and I will go up and talk to the team while you get started. We need a complete inventory of everything in the room, plus a list of anything missing – although it looks like the usual story, so far. If you'd like some help, just ask."

"A couple of officers for the grunt work. That's all."

"I'll send them down."

As Roads and Barney climbed the narrow stairs, the black man seated himself before a terminal and began tapping into the system. When they had reached the kitchen, Barney let free the breath she had been holding.

While she and Roads had been busy, the footsquad had deployed itself throughout the streets and alleys around the house, sealing the area from what little traffic there was at that time of night. A request to Power Central had not yet been answered, and the night was still pitch black. Until the lights along Old North Street and its tributaries returned to life, the scene would remain shrouded with shadows, like the frieze of an empty tomb.

Roads sent four officers down into the cellar: two to help Raoul, two more to go through the motions of fingerprinting and photographing. He obviously didn't expect any new evidence to emerge from the procedure, but they had to try regardless. Barney was already dreading the report she would have to file later that morning with Margaret Chappel, head of RSD.

"You know what I think?"

Roads was leaning up against the car, deep in his own thoughts. "That you'll be glad to catch this bastard and get back on day shift?"

"No. That we're in over our heads, and getting deeper by the second."

Roads looked up at her. "You mean Raoul?"

"Yes."

"Well, I can understand that. Unfortunately, if we want Morrow's help –"

"But *do* we?" Barney broke in. "I think he's hiding something."

"And I agree."

"Can we trust him, then?"

"What Keith said about himself was true, Barney. He's a modern version of the old junkyard men, collecting gadgets for the rainy day that may never come. Hence his position on the Most-Most Wanted list: the distributors in R&R don't know what he is, but they know what he's got, and they'd love to get their hands on it." Roads shrugged. "No-one's managed to get close because he'll fight when he has to."

Barney absorbed that in silence, until the question that nagged at her most finally broke free:

"That trick with the hologram . . . is Morrow *really* dead?"

"He sure is." Roads's gaze wandered as he replied. "His mind was transferred to a neural net just before the War, shortly before his body died of a motor neurone disease. Now he fits into a crate about half the size of an ordinary coffin, and weighs twice as much."

"Doesn't that make him vulnerable?"

"Only if someone knows where that crate is – and he makes sure no-one does. It could be on the other side of the city, for all it matters."

"How?"

"Because he can use communication links to transmit data, just like a computer. All he needs is the right hardware and he can 'be' wherever he likes."

It was this that bothered Barney most of all. "You talk like he's a machine, and yet he reckons he's human. Surely he can't have it both ways?"

"Unfortunately, he can." Roads looked sympathetic. "He explained how he works, once, but I'm not sure it makes a lot of sense."

"Try me."

"Serious?"

"Why not? You said you would back at the bar."

He shrugged. "All right then. Have you ever heard of something called 'syncritical path analysis'?"

"No."

"How about the Boss Voice theory?"

"Never," Barney said.

"Well, neither had I until Keith explained them to me." He smiled. "It helps if you imagine the brain to be a collection of many parts working in concert rather than a coherent whole; more like the organs in a body or the species of an ecosystem than the components of a machine. Some parts keep you breathing, others monitor your use of language or memory recall; there might be thousands of individual parts in your head, each evolved to perform a particular function, and they all interact: a portion of one will play a role in the function of another, and vice versa. With me so far?"

Barney nodded. "I think so." She had taken a term of basic psychology back in high school, and the general principle rang a bell. "The whole thing is moving, right? Even when we're asleep?"

"As I understand it, yes. Everything in the brain is cyclic and chaotic. You have oscillations that appear regular, but arise purely by chance; if the parts – the pattern generators – were rearranged in even a slightly different way, the end result would be quite different. So the closest you get to stillness is when you meditate and reveal the standing wave, the holding pattern, beneath the mess. But the sum of this 'mess', not the holding pattern, is what we call consciousness; if you add all the processes together, in other words, what you get is 'I', the Boss Voice in our heads."

Roads glanced at Barney to confirm she was still keeping up. She nodded, although less certainly than before.

He went on: "Researchers back in Morrow's day apparently knew how the brain uses chaos to encode and transmit information along neurons; that's how they built the implants used in berserkers. Decoding the parts of the brain and the way they interact involved similar principles. It was the sum of the interactions between the parts – the syncritical path, as they called it – that Morrow's pet scientists set out to measure."

"Like brainwaves?"

"No, although there is a relation. Electrical and magnetic activity of the individual parts could be measured, and their relation to the whole could be approximated. Apparently."

"So . . ." Barney prompted. "They copied the parts?"

"They copied the chaotic way Keith's parts *behaved* – the functions governing their behaviour, at least – onto an enormous neural net, an electrical analog of a human brain. This was much easier than building a virtual model of his entire brain, neuron for neuron. Even though they often didn't know what the individual parts did, they in effect made a copy of his consciousness in the process. As long as the parts were there, with their strange attractors and their links to each other, the whole thing worked. And is still working today."

"But what about his memory?" Barney broke in. "That's not a process, is it?"

"Some memories were, mainly the ones that related to sensory perception. Those that didn't were supplemented by notes he made before he died. Otherwise, he's exactly the same as he ever was – except that he's potentially immortal, and far better off than he ever was. Or so he says."

Barney shook her head. "I think I'm going to have to take your word for it."

"Don't. Look it up one day. I may not have it right myself, or Keith might've been bullshitting me." Roads half-smiled. "But whatever they did, I'm betting not many people tried it. It was an expensive and revolutionary experiment, and only someone rich and desperate would have tried it. Keith may be the first and last of his kind, anywhere in the world – a unique relic from the old days."

Barney understood what Roads was saying there, at least, but didn't think that was a good enough reason to let a known criminal remain free. Relics had proved to be highly dangerous before.

Although she was too young by twenty years to remember the Dissolution, Kennedy's schooling system had made certain she knew the reasons why it had occurred. In individual conflicts, the reasons for going to war had been territorial, but overall the cause was people: eight billion of them by 2040, and only a minority satisfied with their lot.

A burgeoning population may have caused the War, but it was a new minority that contributed to the severity of the Dissolution. Although the nuclear phase of the War had lasted only a few days, it set a dangerous precedent of mass-murder that overshadowed less visible and more efficient means of killing. One of the greatest threats was to be found on the ground, where soldiers armed with the latest mechanical and biological weapons created havoc on the battlefields.

Berserkers – the most ruthless caste of the many biomodified combat soldiers created by the US Army – killed at random for decades after the War. Just one could decimate a small city in a matter of weeks. They were unstoppable, implacable and utterly unwilling to negotiate. Their motives were hard to fathom; although some were genuinely insane, it appeared that others had been given explicit orders to kill civilians – which they did with all their genetically-honed combat skills. This parting gesture from the military lingered for forty years until the last known survivor was hunted down and killed in Kennedy.

The United States might have pulled itself together after the War, had it not been for the berserkers and other creatures like them. That was the lesson Barney had learned – both in high school and from her father's death – and the reasoning behind the city's Humanity Laws: biomodification had resulted in the suffering of millions, and would no longer be tolerated at any level of a sane society.

It was no wonder, then, that Keith Morrow made her nervous. He was obviously different from the berserkers, but that didn't stop him being *more than human* – and if he had broken the Humanity Laws, then it was her duty to turn him in. That they needed his help to gain information about the Mole only made her more uneasy.

And then there was Raoul, with his artificial eyes – tangible, clear evidence of biomodification. Who knew how deep his inhumanity ran, or what dark motives his appearance concealed?

"I don't think Keith felt threatened by us, so we can probably take everything he said to be the truth."

Barney looked up at Roads. "But what about what he *didn't* say?"

"Yeah, I don't know."

She tapped the heel of one boot to the toes of the other. She hated that she had no choice but to go along with the situation. It was wrong in principle, if not in the details as well. Maybe later, when things were back to normal, she could reconsider and take appropriate action.

"What are you going to tell Margaret?" she eventually asked.

"I'm not sure yet." Roads grimaced. "An anonymous tip-off, probably."

"Well, let me know so our stories'll match."

"I will."

The radio crackled and Roads pulled his receiver from his pocket.

"Roads."

"Sir?" It was Komalski. "Something just went by us, but we're not sure what. It looked like it was heading your way."

Roads was instantly alert. "Where was it?"

"Corner of North-East and Murdoch Lane. Barker and Stilson saw something pass over their heads. They think it might have been someone on the rooftops."

"Okay, we'll keep an eye out. Thanks for the warning."

Giving the receiver to Barney, Roads signalled to the three officers in the van and relayed the information. The five of them spread out in an expanding circle from the car.

Barney touched the reassuring weight of her side-arm and studied the darkened street. Windows stared blindly back at her; narrow alleyways gaped like open pits.

Behind her and to her left, Roads turned slowly in a full circle, peering into every shadow. The seconds ticked by, until Roads suddenly froze.

"There!" he hissed, pointing.

Barney caught a flicker of movement in an alley twenty metres away. Roads took off toward it, and she followed him, the other officers not far behind. Fumbling for the radio, Barney shouted orders while she ran.

Roads was halfway up the alley before she even reached it.

"Shit." Nuggets of fallen concrete threatened to trip her. "Phil – wait!"

But Roads had already turned left at the end of the alley and disappeared.

When she reached the intersection, he was gone altogether. Even the sound of his footsteps had faded.

The three officers burst from the alley behind her.

"Split up," she told them, and picked a side street at random. She could see no-one, nor anything to suggest that Roads had been that way recently. The streets, still damp after the rain, were empty.

Reinforcement arrived, in the form of Komalski and two other men, and the search widened. Barney chose another side street and followed it to its end. Apart from a feral cat looking for food scraps in the gutters, she found nothing. Stony-faced houses stared solemnly back at her, any one of them potential harbour for a fugitive. The clicking of her soles echoed on cracked pavement as she followed another lane back to Old North Street. The flashing light of a second RSD van strobed the area in blue: more back-up had arrived. She thought of Raoul's cold eyes reflecting the blue from the safety of 114, and repressed a shiver.

Heading back into the maze, she recalled the officers assisting her.

"Anything?" she asked when they had regrouped.

"Not a trace," said Komalski. The heavy-set cop was sweating. "Of Roads, or anyone. Any idea who he was after?"

"No, I only caught a glimpse." She glanced nervously at her watch. "Where the hell *is* he?"

"Should we buzz HQ, get another squad? If we quarter the area –"

"No, let's give him a little longer. He'll have to come back this way. Four of you, go back to the house and keep an eye out. Komalski, Vince, stay here with me."

"Yes, sir."

The minutes crawled by. Komalski eyed the dark buildings that surrounded them.

"Do you think he's –?"

"No. He'll be okay," she said as much to reassure herself as him.

The other officer cocked his head. "Listen."

Footsteps approached. Barney tensed as the sound grew nearer. The steps were unevenly paced, not Roads' steady plod. She held her pistol at the ready.

A shadowy figure stepped out from behind a fence not far from them. She almost took a shot at it, then, turning the reflex into a wave, flashed the torch to attract its attention.

Waving back, Roads limped to join them. His breath came heavily, as though he had only recently stopped running. His trousers were torn, and a small amount of blood showed through the opening.

"Are you okay?" asked Barney.

"Been better." He came to a halt with an audible sigh. Barney offered him the receiver, which he put into a pocket with a sheepish expression. "Sorry to keep you all waiting. I'll take this with me, next time."

"Good idea. Where did you get to?"

"I lost him four blocks down. He went up a ladder and onto the roof. I tried to follow, but the ladder collapsed when I was halfway up." He winced, flexing his leg. "I don't think it was an accident."

"Should we try and go after him?"

"No. He'll be miles away by now. He's one fast sonofabitch, that's for sure."

"Was it the Mole?"

"No, someone else. Bigger." He tapped a button on his overcoat. "It's lucky I had this. Didn't get a good look at his face, but I managed to tag his profile a couple of times. If the shots turn out, we might be able to work out who it was, and if he's relevant."

Barney nodded. Roads had maintained a long-standing dispute with RSD supplies for the disguised camera. Miniaturised equipment was at a premium, of course, but he had argued that on occasions the right tools were a necessity, not a luxury. If he did get a good picture of the man he had chased, then the effort would have proved worthwhile.

"Could be a coincidence, you think?" she asked, following on from his last comment.

"Maybe." He glanced up and down the street, as though making sure they were alone. "Komalski, go back and help secure the cordon. Vince, go with him. I don't want anyone else getting in. Barney and I'll be at the house in a few minutes."

"Yessir." The two men jogged up the street and turned a corner.

When they were gone, Roads sighed again, this time in annoyance. "I was *this* close, Barney. I can't believe he got away so easily."

She studied him closely, noting the bunched crow's-feet and sweat on his brow. "You can quit playing the tough guy now. It hurts, doesn't it?"

He sagged. "Like hell. Want to have a look?"

She knelt and peeled back the ripped fabric. The wound was shallow but long, from the back of his knee to halfway down his lower leg. Blood seeped steadily from it. She brushed away dirt with her fingers and used spit to clean the rest.

Roads handed her a handkerchief without looking down, and she covered the gash as best she could. As strange as she found his phobia, she had to feel sympathy for him. A cop afraid of blood was like a surgeon afraid of sharp knives.

She stood, wiping her hands on her coat. "There. Nothing serious. All you need is a tetanus shot and you'll be right as rain."

"Thanks, Barney. I owe you one."

"One what?"

He smiled, obviously back to his old self. "That's up to you."

She was about to reply when the streetlights suddenly came on. Pale yellow light, too weak to dazzle but bright enough to illuminate, flooded the suburb. The road lit up as though it were a stage and the two of them actors frozen in a tableau.

Barney stood, her words forgotten. His eyes caught hers, and she stared back, fascinated by the grey swirls and patterns of his irises. Although he had the best eyesight of anyone in RSD – had she doubted it, the way he'd caught sight of the man in the alley would have convinced her – the orbs themselves were reassuringly human. Nice eyes, kind eyes, eyes a girl could fall for as an old friend had once said, but otherwise nothing out of the ordinary. They were even slightly bloodshot.

She shivered, remembering yet again the artificial lenses of Morrow's consultant. If Roads had had eyes like Raoul, Barney doubted that she would have liked him half as much as she did. Which was more than enough for the time being, maybe for both of them.

Roads broke the moment by reaching for a cigarette. The pale, short-lived flame sent shadows flickering across his eyelids and forehead. When he looked back at her, he smiled gently.

"Want one?" he asked, offering her the pack.

She shook her head. Anti-cancer vaccine bred into tobacco plants had effectively made smoking a safe practice, but cigarettes were prohibitively expensive due to short supply. Maybe that explained Roads' involvement with Morrow: nothing more serious than black-market smokes. The thought came as something of a relief after her earlier fears.

"Let's get back," he said. "We've got work to do."

"Yes, boss." She took a deep breath to gather herself. "A thief to catch, et cetera."

"And don't you forget it."

The short walk back to the house passed in silence.

CHAPTER THREE

6:00 a.m.

Dawn came suddenly, dissolving the claustrophobic thickness of the night and replacing it with a weak, orange sky. As it lightened further to yellow, then blue, Roads started to feel tired. The city was stirring at a time he was normally getting ready for bed. The thought depressed him, as it always did.

From his position by the patrol van, he watched as old solar sheets, most of them salvaged from abandoned buildings and passed from owner to owner down the years, unfurled from windows and rooftops like silver banners. Old North Street looked as though it was about to receive a ticker-tape parade for celebrity robots.

Roads had to remind himself that this greeting of the dawn was a photovoltaic phenomenon, not a poetic gesture – and that it was a symbol of the fight for survival, not of the love of life. For every two or three solar sheets there lived one person unable, or unwilling, to pay for power. It was, like Kennedy itself, a reminder of everything that had been lost.

Barney emerged from 114, where she'd been helping Raoul catalogue the wreckage, looking as tired and dirty as he felt. Her clothes and hair were rumpled, and there were bags under her eyes.

"You look like shit, Barney."

"Ever the smooth talker." She came to join him by the van. "Top of the morning to you, too."

"Any news?" he asked.

"None that I'm aware of. But that's hardly surprising. Morrow's little friend is having a ball down there – too busy ordering us around to actually tell us anything."

Roads grunted, understanding her resentment. It hadn't been an easy decision to make, to approach Morrow for aid, but he'd only made it when every obvious avenue had been closed. Just one set of new data would make the risk worthwhile – and justifiable, when the time came.

Even if Old North Street proved another dead end, there was still the data fiche Morrow had given them. Whether that proved to be a dead end too he wouldn't know until he managed to get access to a card reader. At the rate the current investigation was going, that wasn't likely to be until late that afternoon.

Roads wasn't by nature a fatalist, but on mornings like this, after a night of insufficient sleep, reality was sometimes hard to fight. There was no denying the past, no matter how hard he tried to avoid it; the present had its own perils, and the future promised nothing but uncertainty. He felt as though he had been trapped in amber for the last forty years – secure in the knowledge that nothing could get in, but increasingly conscious that he was unable to get out.

He grimaced. The metaphor was one that came to mind whenever he thought about Kennedy.

"Are you okay?" asked Barney, peering at him.

He nodded. "Just tired." *Like everything else*, he added to himself.

The War had been both vicious and sudden – yet many forecasters had been predicting it for decades.

Prolonged environmental disturbances early in the twenty-first century had led to crop failures and water shortages, exacerbated by pollution of what little resources there were available. As new diseases and old reappeared in countries barely able to feed their many millions, let alone heal them, many regimes had turned to violence in order to quell uprisings of people educated to expect better by the World-Wide Web. Internal distraction had become civil war, or encouraged invasion from without, while affluent countries had continued to pay lip-service to the United Nations. An already inequitable distribution of resources and justice had worsened – until finally the pressure became too much.

The first atomic bombs exploded in anger for almost one hundred years burst a symbolic dam. Fighting erupted overnight in South Africa, South America, Eastern Europe, Indonesia and China – the countries most in need of resources. United Nations peace-keepers were fired upon and executed in defiance of one last effort to restore order. Mediation was seen as intervention, and prompted violent backlashes. Fighting spread to the Middle East and Europe.

Soon, no continent was free from conflict. Refugees – and invaders – poured into the United States of America, Western Europe and Australia. The border between the United States and Mexico was pelted by missiles launched from the Alpha-2 Space Station – the first time war had ever been conducted from space – but sophisticated weaponry had little effect against sheer numbers. When Alpha-2 was finally shot down by a ground-based laser in Argentina, the southern defences of the United States began to crumble.

Around that time, five years after the beginning of the War, the Dissolution began. In the United States, it coincided with the recall of the Armed Forces to halt widespread looting in New York, Los Angeles, Chicago and a dozen other major cities. Whole battalions refused orders to fire on civilians, or simply rebelled against their superiors. Simultaneously, the internal revolt which had been building for a century reached flashpoint. Armed demonstrators stormed the Pentagon, and the new President disappeared in the process of evacuating – or, as some believed, retreating to a more secure stronghold to leave the fringes to battle it out among themselves.

The fighting lasted a further five years, in which time the army itself disintegrated. Local governments formed and fell in violent clashes that tore the Union to tatters. Gangs of predatory nomads spread from town to town, pillaging for food rather than working for it themselves. In the anarchic chaos that enveloped North America, anyone with even the slightest advantage was either a beloved ally or a feared enemy.

Kennedy had survived the Dissolution purely because it was designed to be as self-sufficient as possible. The city had remained able to feed, house and heal its million-odd citizens when crops failed or were left to rot unharvested outside, or when threatened by the many diseases that rocked the collapsing United States. At first the Mayoralty had welcomed refugees with open arms; later, with a population inflated to five million people and several million more storming its walls, it had been forced to adopt a harder policy. It had closed its doors, physically and metaphorically, purely to remain a viable enclave of civilisation.

Isolation had saved it from the worst of the Dissolution. Reversing that policy was not just a matter of writing a new clause in the Mayoralty's Constitution, but rewriting the entire city's psyche.

Roads himself felt it. Even though he agreed with the Reassimilationists – who believed that the arrival of an envoy from the Reunited States, six weeks ago, couldn't have come at a better time – the thought of living without walls around the city bothered him. He had become used to isolation, and the illusion of safety it gave. That was why the conservative members of the Council that had held the upper hand ever since the War had initially been reluctant even to acknowledge the existence of the RUSA. Only at the last moment, when it became clear that the envoy wasn't going to take no for an answer, had they backed down and allowed negotiations to take place.

And now, if one believed the rhetoric, all the city's problems would soon be solved. General Stedman and his convoy were due in a matter of days, and Kennedy would join the Reunited States of America within a month, at least as a partner if not as a member. Trade routes would open, allowing an influx of resources the city desperately needed. People would be able to leave and enter at will – maybe not at first, but certainly within a few years. And if all went well, within a generation or two the damage caused by the Dissolution would be erased forever.

If all went well . . .

Roads wasn't so naive as to believe that it would happen so easily, but he was certainly a long way from the assassin's point of view – who had killed, and would certainly kill again, in order to prevent it happening at all.

Eventually the vividness of the day became too much for him.

"My turn to help out, I guess," he said.

"Just get a straight answer out of him," Barney said, "and you'll have done well."

He entered the house and descended the steps to the cellar like a vampire returning to its crypt.

The scene was one of organised turmoil. Raoul, still wearing dark-tinted glasses to hide his eyes, sat on a desk and directed the efforts of the four officers he had been assigned. As they rummaged through boxes and cupboards, he wrote down the serial numbers of any parts they found. If the part had no number, he wrote a brief description of what it appeared to be instead. Once each part had been catalogued, it was returned to its original place. Without a genuine reason, RSD was unable to impound the contents of Morrow's underground operation.

"How's it going, Raoul?"

The black man looked up from his hand-held terminal. "Slowly. Give us a few more hours, and we'll have the first list ready for you. Then another hour to run it through the inventory."

"What about the data?"

"I've patched a link through to the Head. He's scanning the system now. An hour, tops."

"Good." Roads stepped gingerly to a pile of electronic components and studied them thoughtfully. "What exactly was this place?"

"None of your business." Raoul added another number to the list and looked away.

Roads didn't press the point.

"Phil?" Barney's voice floated down from the floor above.

"Yes?"

"Call from HQ."

"On my way."

He took one last look around before heading back up the stairs. Barney was waiting for him at the top.

"Can't help bad timing." She gave him a mobile phone. "It's Chappel."

"Oh, hi, Margaret," he said into the phone. "To what do we owe the pleasure?"

"Good morning, Phil." Her voice was crisp and freshly-ironed; he hated her for sounding like that. "This is more than just a social call, I'm afraid. We need you at the office."

"Now? I'm a little tied up –"

"The MSA has requested your presence for a meeting in half an hour. You don't have any choice, I'm afraid."

Roads cursed automatically. "Damned soldiers." He reached for a cigarette. "Always sticking their nose in."

"And meaning business, unfortunately," said Chappel. "Time's running out on us."

"Tell me about it." He dragged deeply on the smoke, pinching the bridge of his nose. "Okay, Margaret, I'll be there ASAP.

"Good. I'll make sure there's coffee ready," she replied, and cut the connection.

He gave the phone back to Barney.

"What is it?" she asked, noting the expression on his face.

"Some military bigwig wants a bullshit session. You're in charge until I get back – which won't be long, I hope."

They left the house, blinking in the razor-sharp daylight, and headed for the patrol car. Roads climbed into the driver's seat.

"If I'm not back by ten," he said, "I'll make sure they send you a replacement."

"That's okay. I don't mind waiting. Just keep the car-phone with you, in case I need you urgently."

Roads revved the engine and drove away, watching Barney recede in the rear-vision mirror. She stood alone, waving, silhouetted against the street-haze of the rising sun. He had a brief vision of her, the crowd, and him –

47

the parade of robots – being separated by a wash of yellow fire from the solar sheets . . .

And then he turned the corner.

The headquarters of the Regional Security Department lay in the green centre of the bullseye that was Kennedy Polis, a fifteen-minute drive from Old North Street. Along the way, Roads passed cyclists and pedestrians enjoying the first few minutes of the new day, while occasional flashes of light reflecting off Rosette cabs gliding along active tracks highlighted the movement of people on their way to or from work. He encountered only two other vehicles on the road: one RSD patrol car much like his own, and an Emergency Services clean-up squad heading back to the Works Depot. The latter, he assumed, finished patching yet another blot in the city's landscape; nothing major in itself, yet part of a series of similar band-aid fixes that amounted to a significant, and growing, problem.

The city was, for the most part, built on level ground. As he neared the centre, however, he crested a gradual rise that enabled him to see above the buildings around him and into the distance. Not far away was the innermost and therefore smallest ring of the Rosette, one and a half kilometres across. The city's heart served as a nexus for the radial freeways, and as a convenient location for various administrative buildings such as Mayor's House, the MSA Academy and RSD HQ. A green belt containing Kennedy City University, and a now defunct zoo and arboretum, echoed the shape of A ring, separating the centre from the suburbs.

Ahead and beyond the city lay a low range of ragged hills dotted with communication towers and scrub forests: the former acted as the city's northern line of defence, with spotters mounted on each tower to monitor and counter any inward movement from Outside; the latter had once comprised the city's obligatory carbon sink, but now provided wood and fibre for a variety of uses, plus medicinal and industrial compounds farmed from genetically modified tobacco, hemp and potato plantations. Between the hills and the edge of G ring were food and animal crops, tended the same way they had been for decades: with maximum efficiency. Little innovation had been added to the system since the Dissolution, and it still served the city well, complementing food factories elsewhere.

To the west, visible as a dozen large tank-like shapes looming in the distance, were the two-hundred-metre-high air towers that provided a large proportion of Kennedy's general-use power and helped clean the tainted air and water released as a by-product of industrial activity. Apart from turbines taking advantage of the nearby river's kinetic energy, the city's only other means of mass-producing power was also to the west: the Kennedy Prototype Fusion Reactor, a low blister situated midway along the arc of air towers. The facility had originally been a research centre designed to test the feasibility of kick-starting a small-scale fusion reaction by employing single bubble sonoluminescence and the cavity effect – or, as Roads understood it, using sound to create bubbles in water that collapsed at temperatures and pressures greater than those found at the centre of the sun. A working model had been built in 2036, with the space industry very much in mind, and power production had begun in 2039, just one year before the first outbreaks of the War. By the time the Dissolution had set in, KPFR had been running at full capacity.

Automatic gun emplacements atop the air towers protected the flatlands to the west, just as they did on the communication towers in the hills. To the south, the main defence was the river, wide enough to prove a deterrent to foot soldiers and blocked by locks along its length. On the far side were nothing but ruins; Patriot Bridge had once connected Kennedy proper with a few far-flung suburbs and an airport, but these had been isolated since the beginning of the Dissolution. On the near side were warehouses, docks and reclamation plants – the last performing essential treatment and recycling of water, glass, plastic, rubber, textiles, wood pulp, soil and paper. Most employed variants on "natural" techniques, using bioreactors and anaerobic digesters – mainly modified fungi or bacteria – to strip soil, water and solid waste of contaminants until they were fit to be re-used. Thirty per cent of the city's population was employed in the reclamation industry, if not in the plants themselves then maintaining the air towers and sewerage works; the rest worked in civil services – like RSD, Power Central, the MSA and Emergency Services – or tended the farms.

Sometimes, if Roads squinted hard enough from this angle, he could almost pretend that the War hadn't happened, that the intervening four decades had been nothing but a bad dream. *Almost*, though, and never for long.

To the east, like a long, black scar cutting a chord through the outer limits of the city, was the Wall – an artificial barrier fifteen kilometres long and five metres high. Its triangular backbone had been built from a black carbon alloy during the early years of the Dissolution, before the materials industry the city had been famous for had been diverted into other areas. Solar powered, electrically live across its entire surface and topped with a formidable array of sophisticated defences, it acted as a definitive barrier against intrusion. With only one break – at the Gate, midway along its length – its sole purpose was to keep people out, and it performed its task well. The Gate had been fully opened just once in the previous twenty years, and then only for the RUSA envoy. In the bad days, the Wall had never been opened at all, and had been constantly patrolled by up to a thousand MSA guards. This unending vigilance, plus the Wall's stark, geometric lines, acted as more than just a physical boundary: it reinforced the truth, that the city was isolated by its own choice.

Behind walls of stone, air, water and fire, Kennedy Polis sprawled like a vast stone starfish, languishing in its separation from the rest of the world. Not even radio could penetrate the barriers; all transmissions from the Outside were scrupulously ignored, having proved too often in the past to be fakes. Nothing short of actually arriving at the Gate and banging on it would result in it being opened – which is exactly what *had* happened, six weeks before . . .

Sunlight flashing in mirror-tinted glass brought Roads back to the present. RSD HQ, like all of the buildings in the centre of Kennedy, stood no more than ten storeys high and boasted lush roof gardens at its summit. Grey composite plastic wrap, manufactured from waste products by modified *E. coli* bacteria, kept its concrete from crumbling under the influence of the elements, and most of its lower-floor windows had been fitted with transparent solar panels. The environment within the building was maintained by passive measures in conjunction with air-conditioning, just as a large percentage of its daytime illumination came from lightwells rather than electricity. An absence of sharp corners and flat planes made it look half melted from the outside, although its interior was more conventional in design: pooled offices, open and flexible floor plans, and a generous illusion of space wherever possible.

Roads pulled into the welcome darkness of the underground carpark and found a recharge bay for the patrol car. Crinkling his nose at the stench of ozone, he left the vehicle and tapped his PIN number into the elevator keypad. The heat of the day was already building, now that the overnight storm had passed, and he rolled his shirt sleeves up to the elbows as he waited for the cab to descend.

PIN number . . . He scowled at the keypad, remembering the days when the lock had been keyed by either retinae or hand-prints. The old systems had been replaced two decades ago, their original components either malfunctioning or required elsewhere.

It sometimes seemed ironic that, after forty years of Dissolution, the greatest threat to the city's viability came not from the outside, but from within. Materials could only be recycled for so long without fresh input; streets and buildings were not built to last forever; metals had become scarce; complexity was being traded for longevity in a desperate bid to keep the city's computer networks running. It was only a matter of time before the situation became critical, and Kennedy was forced to do what it had resisted for so long.

The doors to the elevator slid open and he stepped inside. The rear wall of the cab comprised a full-length mirror. He studied his reflection gloomily, trying to coax a semblance of life out of his clothes and hair. Even his moustache looked limp.

A wave of giddiness accompanied his sudden ascent to the top of the building. When the doors opened again, he entered the floor that housed the senior administrative bloc, a region he preferred not to visit too often. His own office was on the fifth floor; not too far from the rowdiness of street level, but not too close to it, either. He had no aspiration to rise any higher, preferring quiet efficiency and anonymity to conspicuous success.

Margaret Chappel's private secretary spotted him the moment he stepped out of the cab.

"Officer Roads –"

"Hello, Michael. Where's the coffee?"

Michael handed Roads a cup. "If you'd like to go through, sir, they're waiting for you."

Roads was tempted to ask who, exactly, *they* were, but let it pass. Instead, he followed obediently to the main office.

Margaret Chappel was tall, thin and on the far side of fifty – an age she preferred to show rather than hide behind makeup. Roads had known her ever since he had joined RSD, and had both followed and supported her rise to the top. Their close friendship was well known, but he refused to confirm whether he had coined her unofficial nickname – 'the Mantis' – in order to enhance her already terrifying reputation on the lower floors. Just a glimpse of a scowl, accentuated by narrow cheekbones and grey hair worn habitually in a pony-tail, had been known to silence the most vehement protests.

When he stepped into her office, she stood, smiled and gestured at a seat. Two other men occupied the room. One – a wide-faced red-head with freckled, pale skin – was Roger Wiggs, head of the specialist homicide team assigned to hunt the assassin; he looked about as fresh as Roads, despite being in more formal uniform. The other was an unknown, dressed in a black, casual suit that matched his hair and briefcase. His features were narrow, but not disproportioned; even seated it was clear he was the tallest person in the room. Had Roads been asked to guess an age, he would have started at thirty and worked his way up – but not too far.

Margaret Chappel performed the brief introductions. "Phil, this is Antoni DeKurzak. He's acting as a special liaison between us and the Reunited States Military Corps, on behalf of the MSA and the Mayoralty."

DeKurzak stood and shook hands with Roads. "My job is to keep the Reassimilation as smooth as possible," the liaison officer said, his voice mild and unassuming. "We don't want any mishaps along the way, do we?"

"Naturally not." Roads collapsed into a chair and felt his bones creak. He wasn't in the mood for pleasantries. His reaction to meeting the MSA officer consisted of annoyance, mixed with surprise that his superiors hadn't sent someone more senior. "You'll have to excuse the blood and sweat, folks. One of our little 'mishaps' kept me busy all morning."

Wiggs raised an eyebrow. "That makes two of us."

"Oh? Who this time?"

"Jessica Yhoman of the Mayor's office."

Keen to pursue the distraction from his own misery, Roads encouraged the conversation. "How does this one fit in? She sounds pretty unremarkable."

"Outwardly, yes. Privately, no. She is – *was* – Senior Councillor Norris' personal adviser. He might back down at the last minute, without her."

"Really?" Norris was a mainstay of the Reassimilationist movement, not renowned for retreating from difficult situations. "It's a little late to change his mind, I would've thought."

"Maybe." Wiggs glanced at DeKurzak. "It's never too late in politics."

"If you say so." Roads took a sip of bitter coffee and pulled a face. "Agh. So she fits. The killer is sticking to his demographic. When did it happen?"

"One-thirty this morning. Yhoman's de facto came home not long after and discovered the body. Her neck was broken, like the others; a swift, smooth, and very clean job." Roads heard a note of awe in the man's voice; one professional admiring the work of another, he supposed. Although he had worked with Wiggs long enough to call him a friend, he still found his fellow officer's fascination with homicide unnerving.

Chappel pointedly cleared her throat. "Phil, I was telling Antoni about the lead you're pursuing, the latest break-in. It's not one of ours, is it?"

"That's right," Roads said, turning to face her. "One of my contacts tipped me off that a cowboy outfit had been done over shortly after two this morning. We're going over the scene at the moment, looking for anything new. If we find anything, we'll let you know."

"How do you rate your chances?" asked DeKurzak.

Roads thought of the man he had chased from Old North Street, and decided not to mention it. This wasn't the time to air hunches. "Not good, I'll admit, judging from previous experience. But we're doing our best."

"Do you believe that will be sufficient? It has been over a month, after all, and still these matters have not been dealt with."

Roads felt the hackles on the back of his neck rise. "What exactly are you suggesting?"

DeKurzak held up both hands placatingly. "I'm not questioning your capability, Officer Roads – or yours, Officer Wiggs. These are difficult cases that standard operating procedure has thus far failed to bring to light, and no-one is necessarily to blame. I am merely expressing the concerns of those above me that your methods might be at fault." DeKurzak looked from Wiggs to Roads to emphasise the point. "Perhaps SOP is no longer equal to the task."

"That's easy for you to say," Roads snapped. "Got any suggestions?"

"Phil." Chappel cast him a cautionary glance. "Let's look at what we have before we go any further."

"About the Mole?" Roads took a deep breath, tried to dispel the exhaustion that was making him so irritable. DeKurzak was talking sense, as much as Roads didn't want to hear it. "Almost nothing. He doesn't leave genetic fingerprints or identifying marks of any kind. He follows no fixed m.o., except that he works at night. He only sets off alarms when he wants to. And the one description we have is anomalous."

"He looks like you, in other words," said DeKurzak.

"Unfortunately, yes."

Chappel turned to the other officer. "What about you, Roger?"

"The killer operates at night, also." The burly redhead shifted in his seat. "We do have a sample of genetic material, but it doesn't match any in city records. We have no physical description, nor any other clues to his identity. Only his motive seems certain: to frighten the Council into backing down from the Reassimilation."

"Yes." DeKurzak steepled his fingers and pressed them to his lips. "I've read the reports, and they're not terribly encouraging." He shrugged. "One uncatchable criminal I could believe, perhaps, but two . . .?"

Chappel intervened before Roads could take offence. "We are treating each series of crimes separately partly out of practicality, partly because of the timing. Although the murderer and the assassin *could* be one and the same person, he'd have to be fast on his feet as well as practically invisible. Last night demonstrates that quite well. It therefore doesn't seem likely that one person working alone is behind both series of crimes."

"But it isn't impossible," said the liaison officer. "That's the point I want to stress. We're not in a position to rule out anything."

Roads shook his head. "We've been through this a dozen times before. You didn't interrupt our work to discuss profiles. Why don't you get to the point?"

DeKurzak nodded. "Fair enough. My superiors are determined to present as united and positive a face as possible for the Reassimilation. General Stedman will be in Kennedy in three days, and they want the cases closed by then. To put it bluntly, that doesn't look likely – does it?"

"I'm still confident," said Roads. "We are pursuing a number of possibilities –"

"Operation Blindeye being one of them?"

"Yes."

"And you, Roger?"

"We'll see what forensics find at the Yhoman site before we make any plans."

"I see. I will reassure my superiors that everything that can be done is being done. In the meantime, I have been given the authority to become actively involved in both investigations. Please bear in mind that, in less than a week, Kennedy may no longer be an independent state. If the Reassimilation goes ahead as planned, it's likely that either or both cases will be handed to the Reunited States Military Corps prior to then for further investigation."

"What?" Wiggs' face flushed with anger. "You can't –"

"They can," said Chappel, grim-faced. "The RSD charter allows the MSA to take any of our cases at any time if ordered to do so by the Mayor. The MSA can do whatever it likes with them from there. And after Reassimilation, who knows what will happen to local law enforcement?"

"We need results fast, to prove that we can competently handle our own affairs." DeKurzak did his best to look sympathetic; Roads wondered how sincere the effort was. "If combining our resources will help, then I think it makes sense to try. To that end, an officer specialising in law enforcement from General Stedman's staff, Captain Martin O'Dell, will be arriving in Kennedy later this morning to provide his own viewpoint. As an outsider he may be able to see something that we're missing."

"Great. That's just great," said Roads, draining the last of the coffee. "We need another army about as much as we need blindfolds and our hands tied."

Chappel stared him down. "They're only trying to help."

"Famous last words." As much as the city needed to open its doors, he rued the fact that it had been a military nation like the Reunited States that had made the first move. From what little information he had gathered about the RUSA, it seemed to be run entirely by its Military Corps. He had never heard mention of a President, or a similar non-military title. No wonder the MSA and General Stedman seemed to be getting along so well. Tarred from the same brush.

Roads glanced at Wiggs, who looked as pained as he felt. "I'm sorry to be blunt," he said, "but is that all you wanted to see us about?"

"I think so, for now," said Chappel.

DeKurzak agreed. "I understand your reluctance, gentlemen, but I'm sure we can work it out. If you have any questions later, don't hesitate to contact me. Margaret has my number."

"Good." Roads stood. "Then, if you'll excuse me, I have work to do."

Wiggs also rose, slicking his hair out of his eyes.

"I want reports by eighteen-hundred." Chappel rose to let them out. "And, Phil, we need to finalise Blindeye before then."

"I'll call you." As she closed the door behind them, Roads caught a glimpse of DeKurzak, still seated in his chair opposite Chappel. The liaison officer nodded farewell, apparently unfazed by the cool reception his announcement had received.

"What a load of shit," Wiggs said when the door was firmly shut. "This whole thing stinks."

"We need to get together soon, to swap notes."

"Agreed. I'd mail them to you, but you know what I'm like."

Roads nodded. Wiggs' lack of computer skills was renowned. An attempt to mail Roads the notes on the assassin could easily misfire, and result in sensitive RSD files landing in the lap of a bulletin board. Safer, and more productive, to talk in person.

At the elevator well, Wiggs leaned up against a wall and closed his eyes. "To be honest, Phil, this case is driving me crazy. I'll be glad to see the end of it, if it comes to that."

"At least you've got a geneprint." Roads forced a smile. "All you have to do is test everybody and find the one that matches."

"Yeah, right. Except the city'll be full of outsiders. People like this O'Dell, or whoever he is, marching in to 'smooth the way'. Give them a month and we'll be overcrowded again."

Roads feigned horror. "Don't tell me you're anti-Reassimilation, Roger."

"No, it's not that. It's just . . ." Wiggs sighed and ran his hand through his hair. "I was a child during the food riots, Phil. My parents weren't well off, and we were almost kicked out of the city. I remember what it was like – a little too well, sometimes."

"It wasn't pleasant, that's for sure." The elevator doors pinged open and they filed inside. "But I don't think it'll be like that this time. Outside's not so bad any more."

"It couldn't be." Wiggs glanced at his reflection in the mirror, grimaced. "Can't help but worry, though."

As the cage plummeted toward the carpark, Roads' phone buzzed for attention.

"Phil, it's Margaret."

"Christ, we haven't even left the building yet."

"Good. DeKurzak's on his way down. He wants to visit the scene on Old North Street."

"Great," Roads groaned.

"Lucky you," whispered Wiggs, with a smirk.

"It was my idea," continued Chappel. "I like the MSA about as much as you do, but we all have to live with it. And him. By letting him see the way we operate – and can cooperate – we decrease the chances of those above him taking the cases from us." Chappel paused, obviously waiting for a response. "Anyway, I said you'd give him a lift."

"Fine." Roads sighed. "It's not as if we've had much success on our own, I suppose."

"Exactly. When he's finished, lend him one of the cars so he can join homicide at the Yhoman place."

Wiggs' face fell.

"With pleasure."

"Good." Chappel's tone softened slightly. "Stay in touch."

"I will."

CHAPTER FOUR

10:30 a.m.

Roads would have preferred to drive the whole way to Old North Street in silence, but DeKurzak clearly had other ideas.

"You're not from here, are you, Roads? Not originally, anyway."

"What makes you say that?"

"Your accent, mainly. English? South African? I can't quite place it."

"My parents were Australian." Roads couldn't help but be impressed at the observation; few distinct accents remained in Kennedy, and only a handful of people of DeKurzak's age could distinguish one from another.

"Ah." DeKurzak nodded. "Expats?"

"No, on holiday when the War broke out. We were lucky to be staying near Kennedy at the time."

"Very lucky indeed. What happened to them?"

"Killed in food riots when I was a kid. I'd rather not talk about it."

DeKurzak smiled. "Of course. You don't have to."

Roads guided the car onto the south-bound arterial freeway. The road surface was rough after so many years without regular maintenance, but he preferred it to the Rosette routes when heading in that direction. As they drove, the ruins of Patriot Bridge dominated the forward skyline. Time was slowly pulling it down, piece by piece; Roads could see the odd gap-toothed hole where the road itself had fallen away, or been blown away by explosives. The old maglev track had been dismantled entirely.

He'd always thought the bridge had been hard done by, and privately hoped that the Reassimilation would result in its reconstruction – although he doubted it.

DeKurzak seemed to be reading his thoughts. Roads felt the liaison officer's keen eyes studying him.

"How exactly do you feel about the Reassimilation, Officer Roads?"

"Honestly?"

"Of course."

"Well, I can't see what all the fuss is about."

"What do you mean? This is the first contact we've had with anyone outside Kennedy –"

"No, what I mean is: it has to happen eventually, doesn't it? There's no point arguing about it, or putting it off any longer."

"That's the best way to think about it." DeKurzak nodded, waving one hand at the view before them. "Kennedy is like a tide-pool that has been isolated for so long it's forgotten about the sea. But the tide's going to come back in whether we want it to or not. The only question we have to ask ourselves is whether we let it in gracefully, or go down with a fight."

Roads looked at his passenger out of the corner of his eye. DeKurzak seemed to have missed the point entirely; Kennedy had to Reassimilate because it would die if it didn't, not because the RUSA wanted it to.

He cleared his throat, choosing tact rather than debate. "I would have thought the answer was obvious. If we send them away now, they'll only come back later, when they're even stronger."

"True. A lot of people feel otherwise, though."

"One in particular?"

"The killer? Yes, he – or she, of course – is an extreme case. But that wasn't really who I was talking about. I meant the Old Guard, the people who lived through both the War and the Dissolution. These people have seen terrifying things, and we can only sympathise with their reluctance to place themselves at risk again by reopening the city. But where do we draw the line? There are already enough of them in the Mayoralty to obstruct a move that the rest of us regard as being inevitable, even if it does make us all nervous."

Roads shrugged. "So? Politics and people have always been like that when it comes to change. King Canute wasn't the only one,"

"That's true." DeKurzak stared away from the river, at the distant glints of the city. "Would you count yourself among the Old Guard, Roads?"

Roads almost laughed. Either DeKurzak was extraordinarily clumsy at asking leading questions, or genuinely had no idea how his inquiries sometimes sounded. "I'm old enough," he said, "but, to be honest, I really don't give a shit. I just try to do my job. If you think I'm conspiring to wreck the Reassimilation, then you're barking up the wrong tree."

"I didn't say that." DeKurzak chewed thoughtfully on his lower lip. "What about Wiggs?"

"Too young. Haven't you checked his records?"

"Birth dates can be faked."

Roads glanced across at DeKurzak. The liaison officer's face was closed, serious. The urge to laugh abruptly vanished. "You're crazy."

"It's worth checking. And, what's more, if you stop to look at things objectively, it makes sense. The best way for the assassin to remain at large – and the thief for that matter, assuming they aren't one and the same person – is to ensure that the authorities don't want to catch him. Or to actually *be* the authorities."

"So you think I'm the Mole?"

"No. Your alibis check out. But the resemblance is uncanny, all the same."

Roads gripped the steering wheel tightly with both hands and tried to keep his anger at bay. Again he wondered if DeKurzak was deliberately trying to provoke him, or simply didn't realise what he was saying, what open nerve he had unwittingly probed.

"How old are you, DeKurzak?"

The liaison officer blinked. "Thirty-six. Is this relevant?"

"It might be. Anyone under fifty won't remember the War –"

"Obviously, but –"

"– and if you don't remember the War, how can you possibly understand what it was like? How can you speak for this 'Old Guard' of yours if you haven't been through what they have? Think about it for a moment. Doesn't it seem more likely that those who have seen the Dissolution first-hand would actually *want* the Reassimilation, rather than resist it?"

DeKurzak had his mouth open, wanting to break in, but Roads ploughed on: "The ones who remember what it was like to watch hungry people die rather than let them in and starve the city, who were forced to kill the beggars that screamed at the Wall for months, who had friends and relatives thrown out of Kennedy for fighting when there wasn't enough to go around . . . These people aren't your Old Guard. These people won't kill to keep Kennedy closed. They've seen enough death already.

"The ones you're looking for are younger. They've lived here all their lives, and regard Kennedy as *theirs*.

They don't want it invaded by upstarts from the Outside. If anybody's going to fight to keep Kennedy closed, they'll be the ones – not people like *me* . . . "

Roads took a deep breath, suddenly conscious of the fact that he was sweating heavily.

DeKurzak looked surprised; Roads' outburst had clearly startled him, too. "What exactly are you driving at, Officer Roads?"

"That it's not me, you son of a bitch. I'm not the Mole, or the assassin, and I'm not protecting anyone."

"But Wiggs might be."

"He's not. Jesus." Roads felt like banging his head on the steering wheel. "We're just trying to do our jobs."

"And no-one's stopping you." The liaison officer glanced away. "No-one's questioned the fine work you've done for RSD over the years. That's not the issue here. What is at stake is *this* case, at *this* moment, and how we're going to solve it. Given that it's not a simple whodunit, and that there's no keeping politics out of it, we have to consider every possibility."

Roads bristled at the 'we', but kept his mouth in check this time. "Just give me a little longer, DeKurzak. I don't believe in the uncatchable thief."

DeKurzak smiled. "Neither do I, as a matter of fact. But we've only got three days left before General Stedman arrives."

The turn-off for Old North Street appeared, and Roads swung the wheel to follow it, grateful for the distraction. As the scene of the break-in approached, DeKurzak broke the brief, tense silence.

"I'm only doing my job, too, Phil. Remember that, and our relationship will be a little less strained."

With daylight had come the spectators. A couple of dozen had settled in shaded doorways and windows for the morning, curious to see what had happened. Most were young parents with small children in tow, looking for entertainment. Although loitering was technically illegal, being a waste of human resources, none of the attending officers bothered to move the crowd along.

Barney was asleep in the van, stretched across the rear seat with her coat bunched up against the window, acting as a pillow. He felt like a bastard for waking her.

"What –?" She opened her eyes and rubbed her forehead. "Oh, it's you."

"Sleeping on the job?"

"Yes and no. HQ sent Rashid to relieve me not long after you left, but I thought I'd wait for you to come back." She glanced at her watch. "I only lay down ten minutes ago."

"This fanatical devotion to duty will get you places."

"That's a relief." She struggled upright and tugged at her clothes. The rear of the car was suffocatingly hot and her uniform damp with sweat as a result. "Are we going now?"

"Not yet. We have a visitor."

"Who?"

"The MSA have sent someone to watch over our shoulder. He's standing just over there and answers to the name 'DeKurzak'."

"Watch us why?"

Roads filled her in on the meeting that morning, content to let the MSA liaison officer wait a few minutes longer. By the time he finished, Barney had recovered a semblance of alertness.

"So they're giving us a deadline?"

"Seems that way."

"Bastards." She groaned as he helped her out of the van. "Okay, I guess I'm ready. As if I haven't already done enough for one day."

"I presume you went through this lot for eye-witnesses," Roads said, indicating the crowd with a nod.

"Yeah, not a one. Door-knocked, too." Barney raised a hand to point. "This is 114, right? One hundred and eleven, 113 and 115 are empty offices, haven't had tenants for at least ten years and haven't been converted to accommodation because no-one really wants to live in this area. One hundred and twelve and 116 are tenantable, but unoccupied. City records don't mention anyone ever moving in, so they've been empty since the War – just like 114 itself, supposedly."

They walked to where DeKurzak was standing, watching the squad move in and out of the house. Roads made the introductions. DeKurzak shook Barney's hand with an ingratiating smile, then suggested they move inside.

The cellar was cool but crowded, and considerably more ordered than when Roads had last seen it. The piles of components had been returned to their respective boxes; all the cupboards were closed.

Barney's replacement was talking earnestly with Raoul over one of the terminals. A short, dark-haired man, he had a large smallpox scar on his left cheek that Kennedy's utilitarian approach to medical care had not allowed to be removed. He looked up as Roads and company approached.

"Good morning, Phil."

"That depends. Have you got anything for me?"

"I'm not sure. We have the security check on the data system."

"And?"

"It looks like nothing was stolen."

Roads raised his eyebrows. "Run that by me again?"

"As he said," said Raoul, his dark skin dusty. He wiped his hands on a rag as he approached. "It's as clean as a preacher's prick down here."

DeKurzak looked curiously at the new arrival, and Roads explained as briefly he could: "Raoul ran this place. He can tell us what's been stolen."

"Which is nothing," Raoul repeated.

"But that's inconsistent," Barney said. "Why would the Mole go to the trouble of breaking in and then not take anything?"

"To prove he can?" DeKurzak suggested, obviously dissatisfied with remaining an observer.

"We already know he can."

"Then maybe he was scared off."

Roads shook his head. "The building was empty until Raoul arrived. Right, Raoul?"

"That's correct. He set off the alarm as he left. He must have finished what he came to do."

"Exactly. But what the hell was that?" Roads rubbed thoughtfully at his moustache. "How's the list of hardware coming?"

"Finished. We're about to check for discrepancies."

"Good. That might tell us something."

"Do you really think so?" asked DeKurzak, peering curiously into an open box nearby.

"Of course." Roads fought yet another explosive response, already sick of justifying himself to the liaison officer. "This is the first time the Mole hasn't lifted data in six weeks. If he took hardware instead, then that must mean something. And if he didn't, same again. Any break in the pattern, no matter how slight, is significant."

"I guess you're right." DeKurzak looked suitably chastised. "I wasn't thinking."

Roads, slightly mollified, turned away. "Rashid, this is Antoni DeKurzak of the MSA. When he's finished looking around, have one of the squad take him to see Wiggs at the scene of last night's homicide. HQ will give you the address."

Rashid mock-saluted. "Yessir."

"Meanwhile, I'm going to get some sleep. Have someone call me if you find something."

"Will do, boss."

"Okay. Ciao."

As they climbed the stairs, Roads felt DeKurzak's hurt stare at his back. The liaison officer knew he'd been dumped, but Roads wasn't going to let that bother him.

"He's keen, at least," said Barney.

"Yes, but a little on the paranoid side, too, if I'm any judge of character."

"Ain't that dandy."

"No, not really." They exited the building. The thinning crowd watched them walk down the steps to the sidewalk with mild interest.

They had hardly gone more than a few steps towards the car, however, when Barney stopped and squinted through the sunlight. "Hang on."

"What?" Roads followed the direction of her gaze. On the second floor of one of the neighbouring buildings, half-visible through a curtained window, something moved.

"That's strange," Barney said. "I checked 116 myself."

"Did you actually search every floor?"

"No. I just knocked where I couldn't get in, and left it at that." She squinted to see better, but the movement didn't return.

"Do you want to check it out?"

"Do we have to?"

"No." For once, he was glad to play devil's advocate. "Maybe it's time we called it a night."

"Well and truly." She didn't move on, however. "But I suppose we'd better have a look. *Fuck*."

Roads followed her past the van and through the cordon to the address next door. The building was narrow, two storeys high, and had obviously been much better-kept in years gone by; its stonework was now chipped and scarred, its glass for the most part broken. Like 114, it had a small yard and fence, with a flight of steps leading to its front door. From the street, its interior looked abandoned, and didn't welcome potential visitors.

Barney knocked once on the door, waited a second, then shouldered it open. Dusty silence greeted them, but both sensed the presence of an occupant, somewhere in the building.

"Squatters?" proposed Roads. Individual property ownership had been abolished in the first decade of the Dissolution, with housing dispensation resting in the hands of the Mayoralty. After the difficult years, however, the number of houses had gradually exceeded the number of tenants and the rules had been relaxed. Squatters presently had the right to move into any building, provided only that the building was officially listed as unoccupied. It was entirely possible that someone had moved into the house next door to 114 without registering the move with the Mayoralty.

Barney shrugged in answer to Roads' question. "Could be. Doesn't explain why they didn't respond when I came here earlier, though."

"I don't know. You can be fairly intimidating when you're short of sleep." Roads ignored the look she cast at him, and indicated the stairs. "Shall we?"

The first floor was empty. Roads' shout of "Hello?" echoed dully from stained walls and ceilings. He was about to suggest that they try the second floor when the sound of stealthy movement came from the stairwell.

He and Barney took positions out of sight on either side of the stairs, pistols at the ready. The slight sound became the creaking of steps as someone descended slowly into view. Roads peered at the indistinct form, obscured by the shadows: small in both height and mass, most probably female, hair long and in curls; clothing dark-coloured and loose-fitting. Her hands appeared to be empty.

The silhouette of the woman stopped on the last step. "Hello?" she called, softly. "Is someone there?"

Roads nodded to Barney in her hiding place. She holstered her pistol and stepped into view. "Hello," she said. "My name is Officer Daniels. I'm with RSD."

The woman visibly started at Barney's appearance. "What do you want? I haven't done anything."

"No-one is suggesting you have." Barney motioned for the woman to come down the stairs

She shook her head. "There's someone else here with you. A man; I saw him. Where is he?"

Roads stepped forward. "We're investigating an incident that occurred next door," he said. "Part of that investigation includes checking neighbours for possible eyewitnesses. I don't suppose you saw anything?"

The woman glanced between them before asking: "When?"

"Last night, early this morning."

She shook her head. "I wasn't here then."

"But you live here?"

"I came up here for the view."

"Why?"

The woman hesitated. "Because I was curious." She stepped down from the stairs. In slightly better light, Roads could finally make out the details of her face. She was older than her slight figure suggested, maybe early thirties. Her dark brown hair and eyes, full lips and olive skin suggested a distilled European ancestry. The way her hand gripped the bannister behind her betrayed her tension.

"Will you tell me what happened?" she asked. "Next door, I mean. What sort of 'incident'?"

Roads met her stare evenly. "If I tell you, will you tell me why you want to know?"

The woman hesitated again, but only slightly. "You first."

Roads passed the buck to Barney, who explained: "Someone broke into the building next door. No-one was hurt; we're not even sure if anything was taken. There's nothing to be concerned about, if you do live in the area."

The woman looked sceptical. "So why all the fuss?" she asked. "Houses are broken into every day."

"We're still looking into it," Barney explained, "but we believe this break-in to be the work of the Mole."

"The who?"

"The Mole," Roads echoed. "There have been notices on the b-boards. You've never heard of him?"

The woman shook her head. "I don't really follow the news very much."

"Maybe you should." Roads quickly outlined the history of the serial thief as it had been presented to the public, all the while watching the woman's reaction. As she absorbed the information, her face remained appropriately serious, but a slight look of relief was evident in her eyes.

"I'll keep an eye out," she said when he had finished. "Thank you."

"And that makes it your turn, I think." Roads kept his voice firm. "Why did you want to know?"

She shrugged. "It's kind of stupid, really. I live with someone, you see, and he didn't come home last night. I thought . . . I don't know what I thought. I was worried."

"Does he do this often?"

"No. He doesn't go out much at all these days, and when he does he's always home by dawn."

"Before curfew ends?"

The woman's eyes shifted. "No, after. He'd never break curfew, I'm sure of that."

"Where does he go, then?" Roads pressed.

"I don't know. He can look after himself, but I still worry." She paused, looked embarrassed. "When I saw the patrol cars on the street, I thought there might have been some sort of accident."

Barney broke in on Roads' automatic curiosity. "I'm sure he'll be okay," she said. "He'll come home when he's ready."

"I guess." The woman smiled weakly. "I'm sorry for wasting your time."

"That's okay." Roads smiled encouragingly in return; just like hers, and Barney's sympathy, he was sure it looked fake. "One more thing, though, um . . .?"

"Katiya."

"Thanks, Katiya. I don't suppose you know what went on next door, do you?" He pointed at the building, number 114. "If you live nearby, you might hear things occasionally, or see things . . .?"

She shook her head definitely. "I don't know anything about that."

"That's okay. Just thought I'd ask." Roads pulled out a card and gave it to her. "If ever you do see anything out of the ordinary, I'd appreciate you giving me a call."

"Maybe." She glanced at the card then tucked it into a pocket. "You don't mind if I keep watching, Officer Roads?"

"Of course not."

"Thanks." Katiya smiled half-heartedly and began to climb the stairs back up to the second floor, stopping only once to see if they were leaving.

"You shameless opportunist," said Barney when they were out of earshot.

"It's worth a try. You have to admit that." He grinned wearily. "Besides, I'll have Rashid send someone over in an hour or so, to pull her in if she's still there. Ten to one says she won't be."

"If she ever does call you, it'll be man trouble again for sure."

"And if it is, I'll threaten to book him with curfew violations. What else *can* I do?" He squinted as the daylight hit them. "Let's get you home."

Barney sagged against his shoulder. "Please, before something else happens."

They drove in silence. Barney and Roads both lived between B and C rings, within fifteen minutes' walk of RSD headquarters and not far from each other. Roads often dropped her home at the end of a shift, when they had access to a vehicle, rather than leave her to make her own way home from the office. He pulled the car to halt out the front of her building, certain that she had fallen asleep on the way.

"Hey, Barney," he whispered, nudging her shoulder.

"I'm awake." She opened her eyes, stirred sluggishly. "Do you want to come in? I'll make you breakfast, if you like."

He hesitated. The offer was tempting, but . . . "I'd better not, Barney. I've got work waiting at the office. Besides, people might talk."

"I don't give a shit about talk."

"I know." He winked. "Another time, perhaps."

"Okay." She smiled. "Make sure you get some sleep."

"I will."

He waited until she had unlocked her door before driving away. Only then did he realise that she had left

Morrow's data fiche sitting on the passenger seat. Thanking her to himself, he slipped the plastic card into his pocket and kept going.

CHAPTER FIVE

1:00 p.m.

Roads' office was small. All it contained was a desk and terminal, two chairs and one filing cabinet. Sparse and spotlessly clean, except for a dirty ashtray in the bottom drawer of the desk, it gave the impression that its owner was rarely present – which was, in fact, quite true. When not on the road, he preferred to work from the office pool one floor down, where Barney had her desk, or from home. The city's optical fibre network was still intact, and allowed someone with the correct facilities to telecommute; the fact that few people did any more was yet another indictment of the state of the city's hardware.

Perversely, the only item in his office to which Roads felt even remotely attached was the terminal. Externally, it had been his since his first day in administration, although now – many years and several overhauls later – most of its boards and chips had been replaced with others scavenged from broken machines or those made by the city's small cottage electronics industry. It was a battered but determined survivor – just like him.

The first thing he did when he logged in was check the bulletin boards. Everyone in Kennedy was theoretically connected to the city's information and entertainment networks; in practice computer terminals were limited by supply to those who needed them most.

Anyone who didn't have access to a terminal could borrow a neighbour's or friend's, or join a neighbourhood collective designed to share such scarce technological luxuries. Data-input and processing for the news services were performed by a small team of professionals or clerks in the Mayoralty. Roads couldn't remember a time when there had been so much to report – not in the last twenty years, anyway.

The headlines were mainly of Yhoman's assassination, both the act and its possible ramifications. Senior Councillor Norris had issued a statement to the effect that he would not allow terrorism to interfere with the planned Reassimilation. Known anti-RUSA activists had responded by decrying the violence, but warning that it reflected a genuine mood in the community. The imminent arrival of General Stedman and the RUSAMC dominated the rest of the bulletin's opening pages.

Neither story told him anything he didn't already know. There was no mention of Martin O'Dell, the RUSAMC captain assigned to the cases RSD was struggling with. Obviously that development was being kept quiet for the time being, possibly along with other sensitive details he was unaware of.

The Old North Street robbery warranted a brief column on the second page, below a feature article about a grey timber wolf that had been sighted several times on the streets of Kennedy. The species had been thought extinct in the area for many years, and the writer of the article was taking its reappearance as a positive omen. Roads, having glimpsed the animal a couple of times himself, wasn't so sure, but saved the article out of interest before settling in to work.

His report of the events of the previous twelve hours took an hour to write. In accordance with his agreement with Morrow, he made no mention of the meeting at the warehouse bar, nor of his guesses regarding the nature of the Old North Street operation. When he had finished, he mailed one copy of the file to Barney's home computer.

Then he shut down his terminal, rebooted, and loaded another program. He physically unplugged the leads at the back of the terminal and locked the door to his office. When he was sure that he would not be disturbed, he removed a web of contact electrodes from a drawer and placed them in position around the nape of his neck.

He closed his eyes, leaned back and concentrated. Slightly more than a minute later, he opened his eyes.

On the screen in front of him was a two-dimensional image of the unknown man he had chased from Old North Street – blurred and in vaguely unreal colour, but useful nonetheless.

The man was frozen in the act of turning to glance over his shoulder. He was wearing a large, grey overcoat and a wide-brimmed hat of the same colour. Dark glasses obscured most of his face, apart from a straight nose and a wide chin – not enough detail even to run a comparison against the mug shots in RSD's files. The only distinguishing feature was the man's size. He was *huge*.

Roads had never seen anyone that large in his life. If he had, he would have remembered.

There were four other tags in the file he had transferred. The first was the best. He printed two hard copies and added one of them to his report. The second he pocketed to await further consideration. Even if it was relevant, it wasn't terribly informative.

Then he inserted Morrow's data fiche into a card drive he had requisitioned from RSD supplies. The main menu listed twelve dates. Each described a break-in performed by the Mole: approximate times, the nature of the theft, and the results of any subsequent investigations. Similar to Kennedy's experience, the Mole had been given away by operating systems that automatically recorded when and which particular files had been accessed; in Morrow's case, however, the intrusions were noticed sooner, due to the Head's more frequent checks on his datapools.

There were no addresses on the disk, and no information as to the purpose of the individual establishments. Otherwise the information was complete. As Morrow had said, the thefts seemed to be of minor data, mainly inventories. That of the Old North Street residence was the only one explicitly identified; the Mole had obtained its address from another database three weeks before the actual break-in. This fact seemed significant, but Roads was too tired to think it through just then.

Morrow's fiche also contained a ten-minute video file. Curious, Roads loaded a video editor and settled back to watch.

The video showed a man walking along a hallway. He was dressed in grey garments from neck to foot with only a narrow-brimmed hat obscuring his features. Even if the man had been wearing a balaclava Roads would have recognised him. It was himself.

But, as he had never been in that particular hallway at any point in his life, he had to assume that he was watching the Mole in action.

The thought sent an involuntary shiver down his spine. Apart from identikit pictures pieced together from fragmentary security footage, he had never seen a true image of his adversary. The Mole, in six weeks, had not been captured in full by an RSD camera.

Morrow's facilities were considerably better-equipped. The picture was colour, and came complete with sound.

The Mole took a left turn and encountered a locked door. The angle shifted as the video switched to another camera. Roads watched as the Mole manipulated the simple lock for a second or two, opened the door and continued deeper into the house. The entrance to an expansive study was protected by a mesh of invisible laser beams, revealed only by the presence of tiny photo-voltaic detectors lining the frame. The occasional mote of dust twinkled as it passed through the beams. The Mole walked through the doorway without hesitating.

Roads waited for the sound of alarms, but none came. The beams had not been deflected.

"Shee-it."

The Mole walked behind an enormous mahogany desk, took a small painting off its hook and placed it gently on the floor. Behind it was – predictably enough – a combination lock. The Mole placed a palm upon the dial and went absolutely still.

The camera angle shifted to one hidden on the other side of the wall. After a moment, the lock clicked open. The camera angle shifted back to cover the study again. The Mole hadn't moved a muscle.

Roads replayed that scene, but remained just as dumbfounded the second time.

The thief came to life and pushed the wall open, revealing a hidden room on the other side. It contained a workshop similar to that on Old North Street, but smaller. The Mole sat in front of a terminal and began to tap at the keys, blindingly fast.

The video jumped, obviously edited in order to protect the guilty. When it continued, the thief had finished his work at the terminal, and deactivated it with a cursory flick of the switch.

The Mole left the room, locked the wall behind him and replaced the painting. Then he retraced his footsteps back through the laser beams and along the hallway.

The colours on the screen became lurid as the image switched to infra-red. The Mole vanished, except for five small spots of light in an elongated pentagon where his throat, nipples and hips had been. Someone had thoughtfully provided an outline of the man as he walked, otherwise Roads would have lost track of him immediately.

The spectrum shifted back through the visible, and beyond. The Mole appeared briefly as a flickering shadow in microwave, like a poorly-tuned television station, and then even the dots vanished. Back to visible again for one last glimpse of the thief, then the video image ceased.

Roads took a deep breath and dialled a number on his desk intercom.

Chappel uttered only one sentence throughout the whole video:

"How the hell does he *do* that?"

Roads said nothing, gestured instead that she should keep watching. When the recording had finished, he gave her the best answer he could.

"Well, the trick with the lock probably involves a magnetic glove of some sort. Not easy, but feasible."

She looked doubtful. "And the rest?"

"I don't know." He leaned back in his chair. "It's more than simple biomodification, which would be bad enough."

"So you don't think he's a berserker?" Chappel asked.

"No, he doesn't fit the mould; he's too methodical, less rampant. The Mole is something else – biomodified, yes, but armed with stuff I've never seen before. Either he has a means of making himself invisible that works on all frequencies of light outside the visible spectrum –"

"Which doesn't make sense. Or?"

"Or he's a ghost," said Roads.

"Unlikely."

He raised an eyebrow at her response. "Not impossible?"

"I'm getting so desperate I'll believe anything."

"That makes two of us."

She stood, walked across the room, and stared out the window at Roads' fifth-floor view. "How far can we trust Keith Morrow?" she asked. "Could he be involved in this somehow?"

He shrugged. She alone knew the complete history of Roads' ambivalent relationship with the Head, and her confidence was strict. "I don't think so."

"But you're not sure." She turned. "He could be feeding us false information, trying to put us off the trail."

"Maybe."

"What do you suggest, then? Do we cancel Blindeye? I mean, if the Mole is as invulnerable as he seems –"

"He can't be."

"– then we'll be pissing into the wind." She came back to the desk. "Phil, we don't have time to play games."

"I'm sorry, Margaret. I really don't know. A few thoughts here and there, but nothing coherent. Really."

She sighed again and sat down. "So. Do we go ahead, or not?"

"We go ahead, I guess. We might as well."

"Tomorrow night?"

He smiled. "To beat the deadline, right?"

She didn't smile back. "If we don't catch the Mole, then either the MSA or the Reunited States Military

Corps will take the case from us. And from there it's just a short step to dismantling RSD altogether."

"I know." It was a possibility he tried not to contemplate – not out of conservatism, but out of a basic disrespect for the military mind. He and the rest of the world had seen the damage it could cause in the past.

But he had to admit that the idea in principle was sound. Reassimilation would result in the closure of either RSD or the MSA. The city wouldn't need a defence force *and* a police force. Either both would be amalgamated into one unit, or one would become a local garrison of the RUSAMC and therefore no longer exist.

The current situation – with the MSA always the traditional favourite of the people, and RSD struggling to solve a string of major crimes – didn't look good at all for RSD. But no firm plans had been made, and with luck – and a couple of quick arrests at the right time – the situation could easily change.

"How ready are we?" Roads asked.

"We can do it. The Mayor has given us his blessing, and the complete set of access codes for every city department. With DeKurzak's support, we can start pulling data at any time."

"He *will* support us?"

"Yes. He agrees that it's the only decisive course of action left open to us."

"Good. He's not a fool, then."

"He shouldn't be. He comes highly recommended."

"By whom?"

"By the Mayor himself. And the head of the MSA. I get the feeling he's being groomed for promotion to the upper ranks; maybe even Councillor, one day."

Roads folded his hands across his lap. The position of liaison officer between the MSA, RSD and the

RUSAMC was one of tremendous responsibility; it certainly wouldn't be handed to someone who hadn't proved to be capable elsewhere. DeKurzak seemed a little wet under the collar to Roads, but perhaps he would improve with time, given the chance.

Roads forced himself to concentrate on the topic at hand. "I suggest we wait to see what the Mole does tonight, then start Blindeye first thing tomorrow morning. That gives us over half a day to get everything organised down at KCU."

"That should be long enough." She scratched her head. "But it'll be messy."

"You're telling me." Roads was almost daunted by the thought: shutting down the entire city's data network, transferring the information to the main banks of Kennedy City University, and erasing everything else would bring administration to a standstill – all to catch one thief. It would be worth it, though, if it worked.

Chappel stood. "Get some sleep, Phil. You look like you need it."

"So everyone keeps telling me."

"I'll put Jamieson on in your place. Take the night off." She winked knowingly. "Barney, too, if you like."

He groaned. "It's nothing like that, Margaret."

"I know, but I can still hope for you."

"Don't. I'm not . . . I don't know. I'm getting old, in case you hadn't noticed."

"Actually, just to look at you, I wouldn't." She smiled. "You haven't told her?"

"No." He studied his hands for a moment. His feelings for Barney were uncertain at the best of times, and his past didn't make it any easier. "I'm not sure I'm going to. But thanks for the break anyway, Margaret."

"That's okay. You've earned it."

She patted him on the cheek and left. He lingered for

a few minutes to shut down the computer and to gather a case full of files, then did likewise.

The streets were getting dark. At some point in the afternoon, Roads seemed to have lost an hour or two. He didn't remember having lunch. Or breakfast.

The evening was warm and the walk pleasant; the ache in his injured leg had vanished entirely. He stopped to buy some takeaway from an R&R vendor and ate it on a park bench halfway home. The inner city was extensively 'greened' in accordance with the original city plans, but the parks and nature strips had grown somewhat wild over the years. He remembered a time, not long ago, when they had been razed to the ground to kill a burgeoning rat population. The infestation had subsided in the city and reappeared not long after in the farms.

The hot dog was made from soya extracts and unidentifiable vegetable matter, but it tasted like meat. Almost as good as the ones before the War, back when they had seemed to symbolise everything the United States had stood for. All in all, given the city's limited resources, his diet was surprisingly varied. What couldn't be grown could be adequately imitated or synthesised. His only regret was a shortage of natural spices, and a deep boredom of all the places he had eaten many, many times before. He longed to go for a holiday, just to eat somewhere new.

When he had finished, he picked up his briefcase and moved on, feeling as though his body weighed a tonne. As he walked away from the park, he felt eyes watching him. Without breaking stride, he glanced over his shoulder.

Nothing. He was just imagining things.

He lived in a side street, on the first floor of an otherwise empty apartment building. The complex had been modelled on the stone architecture of the mid-twentieth century, with no yard and a sheer, box-like appearance. He had once had fellow tenants, but they had moved away over the years and RSD had seen fit to take the other rooms on his behalf. He preferred solitude and privacy to noisy neighbours. The people in the buildings to either side were close enough.

As he neared the main entrance, it opened and a uniformed RSD officer appeared.

"Hi, Charlie." Charlie Farquahar was Roads' official caretaker, assigned to him since the appearance of the Mole. Wispy white hair and wide, moist eyes crowned a scrawny body racked by age, overdue for retirement by almost twenty years. One of the few members of Kennedy's original security force to have survived the Dissolution, he dozed by day in an empty ground floor room, with one ear constantly alert for intruders; after nightfall he watched vigilantly from the doorway. If he minded the dull post, he never said; he rarely spoke in sentences longer than three words.

"Phil."

"Any problems?"

"Not today." Charlie shrugged. *Not ever*, the gesture economically conveyed.

Roads patted him on the shoulder as he passed. "Keep up the good work."

"Always."

Roads went up the stairs and unlocked the door to his rooms. His home environment was as comfortable as he could bear, but not overly so. His main extravagance was a small collection of watercolours by the two or three Kennedy-born artists that he considered talented. The unframed canvases, mostly of sweeping landscapes, lent the apartment a modicum of warmth; without them, it would have looked cold and heartless.

He stepped in slowly, scanning the lounge. Putting his coat and briefcase on a chair, he went through the familiar routine of checking each room, one after the other, looking closely at everything.

Then he found it: a kitchen stool stood out of place in the hallway. It hadn't been there when Roads had left that morning. He put it back where it was supposed to be without fuss, resigned to this sort of thing happening every now and again.

The mysterious break-ins had begun shortly before the Mole's first appearance, and Roads didn't doubt that the same person was behind them. The taunting visits only occurred when the apartment was empty, and no amount of passive surveillance had revealed how the thief gained entrance. Nothing was ever taken, but something was always moved, and gradually Roads had stopped reporting the intrusions.

He didn't have the heart to tell Charlie that his vigilance was fruitless. This was something he kept from RSD altogether. It was personal, between the Mole and him. As long as nothing was taken or damaged, Roads was prepared to tolerate the occasional intrusion. It was – he believed – simply the Mole's way of saying that he had been here, a reminder that there was nothing stopping him coming back any time he wanted.

He made himself a cup of coffee and went into the study. A message from Morrow, asking him to call, awaited attention on his home terminal's screen. Before he answered it, he sent a message to Barney telling her not to bother going to work that night, unless she wanted to. There was no response; he assumed she was still sleeping.

Then he tried Roger Wiggs, keen to swap information on the latest cases. The duty operator at RSD told him that the homicide officer was on duty and unavailable, still busy at the scene of the Yhoman assassination. Roads hung up and frowned. Still? It wasn't usual for Wiggs to remain behind after forensics had finished, which they should have by now. He made a mental note to try again in the morning.

Finally, he dialled Morrow's unlisted number. The Head appeared on the screen of his computer in full colour, looking much the same as he had earlier that day.

"We meet again, Phil."

"Yes." It seemed much longer than mere hours since their conversation in the bar. "I assume Raoul has kept you informed?"

"Naturally. As an observer, few are better qualified than he."

"Should I know him?"

"No. His, ah, field of expertise was not the same as yours."

Roads nodded, remembering his first sight of Raoul in the darkened cellar. The mutual recognition had been instantaneous – not of who they were, but of what they had once been. He'd hoped – and feared at the same time – that they might have had more in common.

Morrow's voice intruded upon his reverie. "I have some information for you."

"Go on."

"Raoul left Old North Street two hours ago to help me process the data he collected. It took us longer than we thought to check the list of hardware, but we made it in the end."

"And?"

"We found a discrepancy." Morrow's face shifted aside to make room for a text-box, in which appeared a single line of data:

EPA44210: 314, 315, 318

The numbers made little sense to Roads. "Explain, please."

"Serial numbers for three missing items, and one part number."

"Of what?"

"That I can't tell you, I'm afraid, although I can describe them. Each EPA44210 is spherical, three centimetres in diameter, made of a silver metal, and weighs two hundred grams. The serial numbers are physically inscribed, and cannot be removed."

Roads scrawled the digits on a sheet of scrap paper. "Why can't you tell me what they are, Keith?"

Morrow winked. "Because I can't, my boy. You'll have to find that out for yourself."

"Thanks a lot." Roads yawned involuntarily. "Is there anything else you wanted to tell me?"

"No. Nothing that can't wait."

"Good. Then I'll speak to you later."

"Sleep tight." The Head vanished from the screen.

Roads rubbed his eyes and tried to think. His instincts nagged at him, trying to tell him something, but he couldn't force it through the exhaustion.

He stared at the information Morrow had given him for five minutes before giving up. The numbers meant nothing to him.

He loaded the fiche containing the new data gained from Morrow. Cross-referencing each break-in with those he had already been aware of – involving 'official' datapools rather than Keith Morrow's – he arrived at a comprehensive calendar of the previous forty-odd days.

On every night, the Mole had plucked information from various places in the city, apparently at random. Hospitals, community services, the MSA and RSD itself had been raided, plus the establishments that Morrow had not identified. The stolen data concerned disease outbreaks, population figures, defensive capabilities, staff movements, production estimates, policy decisions, financial flows, and so on.

There was no obvious link from one night to the next, almost as though the Mole had been aiming for a random overview of the city's combined datapool, and the Mole's drunkard walk became even more confusing when Morrow's data was added to the list. The Blindeye strategy gained credence the more Roads thought about it: the Mole's path was unpredictable, so RSD had to force him to a specific location where they could be waiting for him.

If it worked, they would have him. But, if it didn't, the Mole would have *them*: the city's entire datapool – anything he wanted – at his fingertips.

But what, Roads asked himself, sensing he was getting close at last, did the Mole *want*?

Much of the stolen information was sensitive, but much wasn't. One night, the Mole gained access to confidential records that listed every piece of equipment owned by the Military Service Authority; the next, he contented himself with the relatively petty list of inventories from one of Morrow's secret hideaways.

It made no sense. Why would the Mole bother with small-scale stocktakes, unless . . . ?

Roads glanced higher up the list. The Mole had looked at the city's warehouses early, before checking the MSA and RSD stockpiles. At about the same time, he had lifted the first 'unofficial' inventory. A fortnight later, he had gained access to the records for the Old North Street residence.

From that point onward, no other small-scale inventory had been stolen.

Roads thumped the desk. He had it. The Mole had been looking for something specific among all the other data, something concrete. Then, as soon as he had located it, he had stopped looking. Three weeks later, he broke into Old North Street and took what he wanted without even a cursory glance at its data system.

But what, then, had he taken?

Roads' excitement faded rapidly in the face of oppressive tiredness. Five weeks of night shift were finally taking their toll. As he took out his contact lenses and stumbled to bed, he promised himself that he would look more closely at his discovery in the morning, if he could find the time among the preparations for Blindeye. He had yet to work out why the Mole had waited three weeks before taking what he wanted from Old North Street. If he had needed it so badly, why the delay?

One question turned constantly through his mind as he tried to sleep. It was a question he feared he would never be able to answer, let alone in the few short days remaining to him – but he knew instinctively that the success of his investigation hinged upon doing just that.

When he finally succumbed, he dreamed that a large man dressed in an overcoat and hat had given him an EPA44210 – and it was nothing at all.

INTERLUDE

11:45 p.m.

The night cooled rapidly. High above the street, among the wires and chimneys of the city, a subtle wind blew. It crept through clothing without being strong; it robbed warmth despite a lack of ice.

He drew his overcoat closer about him and thought of heat, waves of heat flowing from the core of his body. A long and uncomfortable night stretched ahead of him. The ledge upon which he lay was narrow and exposed to the wind, but also the only one which granted him an unobstructed view of the house below. He would be forced to rely upon abilities he had not exercised for many years to remain alert.

He had been designed neither to sleep nor to dream, and although experience had taught him that he needed both to function at optimal efficiency, he could still manage stretches of up to seventy-two hours without either. Sometimes he had micro-dreams – vivid, disturbing hallucinations that encroached upon his waking life until he could no longer function at all. But that only happened under extreme stress. At times like the present, when all he had to do was wait, a halfway state was sufficient: neither asleep nor awake: ready to act if anything changed below, but not wasting energy.

Unblinking, he watched. His pulse slowed; his fingertips began to tingle. Within minutes he was no longer cold, and he had entered a state not dissimilar to deep meditation.

As his thoughts stirred, sluggishly, one name recurred with regular frequency:

Roads: the moustached man he had seen entering the building next door to his; the same man who had chased him upon his return three hours later; the man he remembered to be a police officer, based on a news report he had glimpsed in a market some days ago; the man he had followed in turn from RSD HQ, and for whom he now waited, again.

Roads: the name by which the moustached man had referred to himself.

Roads . . .

He could not return home. The area had been swarming with police the last time he had tried. Had he been recognised at last, after all the years of Sanctuary? He couldn't risk returning until he knew for sure that he hadn't. The witch-hunts of his distant memories were a harsh but accurate reminder of what would happen if he did.

The wind grew stronger as the night deepened. Curfew came and the lights went out. This did not bother him; he could see just as well in infra-red as he could in other spectra. If anything, it relieved an ever-present concern. Had anyone looked up from one of the very few positions from which he could be seen, prior to curfew, they would have caught a peculiar sight. What they would not have seen lay beneath his disguise, of course, and was far more disturbing. But that he could have been seen *at all* made him restless; after so long hiding, it felt strange to be moving of his own will out in the open again.

The moon, half full, rode silently across the field of stars.

He waited.

At some point during his timeless meditation, a timber wolf paced the street below. Its fur shone in the moonlight; its bearing was proud and noble. Unaware that it was being watched, it stalked silently back and forth along the opposite pavement like a restless spirit, a passing visitor to the world of flesh.

The wolf disappeared before dawn, leaving him to his lonely vigil. Sooner or later, he knew, Roads would emerge, and only then would he have to decide what to do.

CHAPTER SIX

Sunday, 16 September, 5:45 a.m.

Roads woke before dawn feeling as though a truck had run over him during the night. Without quite getting up, he fumbled for his coat and found a cigarette. The smoke was acrid and thick, but had the required effect on his circadian rhythms: the various parts of his mind got their act together and allowed him to be *him* again.

Still, he waited until the sun had risen before climbing out of bed. The room was stuffy and stale, and the feeble light that ventured through the blinds did little to enliven it. He took a shower, only to be irritated by the water pounding his shoulders. Although pleasantly hot, it felt wrong. Not for the first time, he wished for sonics and a thorough dermal scrub. But he was stuck on the far side of the Dissolution in a shabby remake of the twentieth century. Only a few anachronisms remained to remind him of what had once been.

Anachronisms like Keith Morrow. And hot dogs. And Sundays. He'd been working a seven-day week for so long he'd quite forgotten that weekends had ever existed.

He shaved, dressed in a casual jumpsuit and made breakfast. Taking a cup of coffee with him, he succumbed to a nagging sense of duty and checked the computer.

There were two messages waiting. One was from Barney, asking him to call. He tried her home, but she didn't answer. The other was a short, encrypted file from Chappel. He opened it and scanned its contents.

The Mole had struck again during the night. Shortly before one, the thief had availed himself of data from the Kennedy Prototype Fusion Reactor; he now knew the design tolerances of the facility, plus a few relatively irrelevant details concerning the facility's chief administrators. Officer Jamieson's preliminary report had already been filed: no new evidence and no eyewitness accounts.

The latter alone was noteworthy. KPFR was staffed twenty-four hours a day by in excess of three hundred people. Quite apart from an extensive array of anti-intrusion devices – including pressure-sensitive pads in major hallways and a video camera network that was constantly monitored – the open spaces themselves must have been difficult to navigate without being seen.

Difficult, but obviously not impossible. Not one alarm had been triggered, and no-one had seen the Mole enter or leave. That the Mole had actually entered the grounds, and not accessed the data from elsewhere, was beyond doubt; the address the stolen data had been routed to lay within the main complex building.

Roads could see DeKurzak's point: it smacked of collusion somewhere along the security chain. The possibility could hardly be ignored that someone had prepared the thief's path by deactivating certain alarms or turning off cameras at prearranged times, or by erasing information after the fact. But, if such collusion existed, who was the Mole's silent partner? Or *partners*: the KPFR break-in was just one of many, and the security of each target must have been compromised. For such a feat to be possible, the Mole had to be part of a massive conspiracy.

But to what end? What would such a large organisation possibly hope to gain from such activities? And how had it managed to keep its existence a secret for so long?

He shook his head. The MSA liaison officer was getting to him. Before long, he told himself, he'd be believing in the mythical Old Guard as well.

His computer winked urgently to announce incoming data. He toggled for video and took the call.

It was Barney. In the background, he made out the blurred buzz and bustle of HQ.

"Morning, boss." She waved cheerily. "Deep peace of the running wave, and all that."

"Say what?"

"Philistine. How's the leg?"

He shrugged. It had healed cleanly during the night. "I'll live."

"Good. The Mantis wants you in here as soon as possible."

"Bully for her. Tell her I died peacefully in my sleep."

"Come on, Phil." She chided him with a motherly pout. "What else have you got to do?"

She had him there. He sighed, resigning himself to the fact. "Anything I should prepare myself for?"

"Ah, let's see." She skimmed through the files on her desk. "You heard about last night?"

"Yes. Margaret sent me Jamieson's report."

"Okay . . . How about Blindeye?"

"Yes again, but fill me in anyway."

"Well, the Mantis gave the word before I got here. We're going ahead. She's down at Data Processing supervising the transfer with a horde of Mayoralty nobs peering over her shoulder. You'll be glad to miss that, I'm sure. David Goss is getting things ready at the uni, at least as far as the security side of it goes. It looks like they've made you the night watchman."

"I thought they might." That meant he would have to find time for a work-out sometime during the day; a session of target practice wouldn't go astray either. It wasn't a matter of toning up, but a mental discipline he wanted to perform. If Blindeye worked, he would come face to face with his dark half within twenty-four hours.

"What about DeKurzak, Barney? Has he wandered in yet?"

"I haven't seen him, but Margaret told me to tell you that he'll be out of your hair for the day. Seems he's right into info management and all that shit, so he's down with her in DP."

"Any idea how he went at the Yhoman site?"

"No, but Roger's been in a foul mood all morning."

"That's a bad sign. I guess they didn't find anything, then."

"Safe bet."

"I'll try to catch up with him later, if I get the time." Roads scratched the back of his neck and yawned. "What else should I know?"

"Just one little thing." She smiled coyly.

"And this is . . .?"

"The States rep, Captain Martin O'Dell, has arrived."

He groaned. "Oh great."

"No, Phil. He's okay. I think you'll like him, if you give him half a chance. Not what I was expecting at all."

"What does that mean?"

"No horns, pointed tail, cloven hoofs, or the like. He looks just like everyone around here, except . . ." She leaned close to the screen, whispered conspiratorially: "Boy, is he cute!"

He couldn't help it; he laughed.

She leaned back in her chair and adopted a self-satisfied expression. "There, Phil. That didn't hurt, did it?"

"Not much, I'll admit. Are you really trying to make me jealous?"

"Maybe I am, maybe I'm not." She winked. "But he *is* cute, nonetheless."

"That does it. I'll be there in five minutes. Someone has to warn him of the terrible danger he's in."

She waved. "Mission accomplished. See you soon."

He cut the connection with a grin and went to get suitably dressed.

HQ was on the upswing of a busy day when he arrived. On top of the usual shift changeover, extra staff were on hand to assist with a few extra projects currently under preparation. One of them was Blindeye; another was the arrival of General Stedman and his entourage, scheduled for two days time. Roadblocks and security sweeps had to be organised. Mayor's House was already under surveillance to prevent the importation of assassins and potentially deadly weapons.

Roads entered by the ground-level foyer and was promptly brought to a halt by a pair of heavily-armed guards. They checked his hand-print in a portable scanner and waved him on, satisfied that he really was Senior Officer Phil Roads and not the Mole.

Security was tight, but that pleased him.

The fourth floor was a maze of partitions over which rose the combined chatter of fifty busy people. Roads negotiated his way to Barney's cubicle, nodding at faces he knew along the way. As much as he valued privacy, he enjoyed the communal environment of the fourth floor. It was vital and vigorously social. The lonely solitude of the higher levels was, by comparison, sterile.

He stuck his head into Barney's workspace, and immediately pulled it back out. She was deep in conversation with an attractive brunette from four desks down.

He "knocked" for attention and waited until she called him in.

"Oh, hi." Barney waved at a chair. "Shelley and I were just discussing the new arrival."

Shelley looked embarrassed. "Have you met him yet, Officer Roads?"

"No. Is he as cute as I'm told?"

"He's –" Shelley rolled her eyes "– simply fabulous, in a weird kind of way."

"Weird how?"

"Well, he looks normal enough – better than normal – but his accent, and some of the things he says . . ."

"I get the idea." Roads smiled reassuringly.

Barney tried to hide a grin. "Shell, do you know where he is right now?"

The brunette looked forlorn. "Last time I saw him, Angela Fabian was making him a coffee."

"Could you tell him that Phil is here?"

"With pleasure." The brunette left the cubicle and hurried off through the maze. Roads raised an eyebrow, but did not comment.

"He's been asking for you," said Barney. "He wants to go over a few things before Chappel takes him away."

"Fair enough." Roads shook his head. "Should I feel honoured?"

"If you like. He's really turned this place on its head, let me tell you."

"I can imagine. He's the first official Outsider in more than forty years."

"That he's here at all isn't public knowledge, yet. But you know exactly what I meant."

"All too well, I'm afraid."

Shelley returned with a sandy-haired young man firmly in tow. He looked freshly-tanned and superbly polished, somewhere in his late twenties or early thirties with a firm, athletic build. His uniform, a standard military khaki, was little different from those Roads was used to. O'Dell smiled cheerfully and with no small amount of bemusement upon entering the cubicle, as though overwhelmed by the hospitality he was being shown.

Roads, studying him, grudgingly admitted that he really was handsome, from his close-cropped hair down to the tips of his polished boots. His uniform on closer inspection was of a better cut and made of finer fabric than anything Kennedy had seen for years. The only flaw to his perfection lay in his left hand: the last two fingers were missing.

And he looked so *young* . . .

"Officer Roads," Shelley was breathless, "this is Captain O'Dell."

The young man stepped forward and held out his right hand. Roads stood and shook it, aware that he was being studied in return. O'Dell's grip was strong, his smile wide and sincere. An irresistible warmth radiated from the RUSAMC captain, and even Roads felt himself respond.

"It's a great pleasure, Phil." O'Dell's accent was a broad mutation of the old mid-west, altered by time. "I can call you that, can't I?"

"Why not? Martin, wasn't it?"

"That's right." He turned back to Shelley. "Thanks, um, Shelley. I think I can manage from here."

The brunette's reluctance was obvious, but she left.

Barney gestured that they should sit, and O'Dell settled back with obvious relief.

"Coffee?"

O'Dell nodded. "Thanks, uh . . . I'm sorry, but what was your name again?"

"Call me Barney. Everyone does."

"Why?" The RUSAMC captain's curiosity was both frank and disarming.

"My mother died giving birth to me," Barney replied with equal honesty. "Dad always said I looked like her, and I never fancied the name I was given. The idea that taking her surname would somehow bring me closer to her made sense when I was five. By the time I changed my mind, it'd stuck."

"Her name was Barney, too?"

"No. Barnace. Helen Barnace. I didn't even get it right." Barney smiled, then politely closed the subject. "What about you, Phil? Coffee?"

Roads noted that she had appropriated a brewing machine from one of the upper floors. Nothing but the best for their visitor, in a city where even instant coffee was a luxury. "Love one."

She poured three cups. O'Dell asked for two sugars and a generous portion of milk. Maybe that explained it, Roads thought to himself; it was possible to tell a lot by the way someone took their coffee. Roads himself preferred black and raw, as did Barney.

"I understand you've been sent to help us," he said, keen to get the real conversation under way.

O'Dell gestured dismissively. "As an observer only, and with access to the total datapool of the Reunited States Military Corps. I don't want to disrupt your usual procedures."

Roads indicated the door of the cubicle. "Judging by the impression you've already made, I'd say that's going to be unavoidable."

O'Dell's grin became wry. At least he wasn't naive. "My wife would kill me, if she knew. She didn't want me to leave Philadelphia in the first place. Our boy just turned three, you see, and . . . Well, let's just say that I'm keen to get this over with as soon as possible – without treading on too many toes along the way. I hope you don't mind."

Roads stared at O'Dell for a moment – thinking, *a father?* – then was amazed to hear himself say that he didn't mind at all, that another viewpoint could only be helpful. Barney covered her amusement with a cough.

The three of them clustered around the computer terminal and examined the history of the Mole in between questions about the RUSA. O'Dell had read summarised reports of the Mole's activities and had seen the identikit pictures of his face, but neither Barney nor Roads had had much access to information about the Reunited States. As recently as six weeks ago, no-one in Kennedy had even suspected its existence.

"We've been growing for about fifty years," O'Dell explained. "Slowly at first, but building up momentum. At this point, we cover most of the old north-west States, some of what used to be Ontario, and the east coast as far as South Carolina. An appreciable percentage of the old United States, all told, and growing all the time. The General hopes to have the west coast Reassimilated as well by 2100."

Roads nodded. One thing he *had* heard was General Stedman's desire to fast-track the reunification of the old US. "Do you think this is possible? There's only four years to go."

"If anyone can do it, he can," O'Dell responded. "He's a very powerful man, and the most intelligent I've ever met. I don't think it's cynical or disloyal to say that he's deliberately appealing to all the right emotions. By reinforcing the old state lines, for instance, he's tapped into a very strong pool of tradition. In most of the small communities we come across, the leaders still remember the horrors of the War and the old ways that led to it –

but the ordinary people, the children, people like me who weren't born until recently, we've only heard stories about the way it used to be. We don't feel the horror; we mourn for what was lost. The old United States is almost a legend now, and the chance to rebuild it, to become part of that legend, is very strong."

The echo of his own argument with DeKurzak made Roads wince. "But you're a military culture, right? The army runs everything, or so I've heard. Don't people feel threatened by that?"

"Some." O'Dell shrugged. "But we aren't aggressive by nature, unless we're attacked. The Military Corps offers a wide variety of community services apart from defence, including education, internal peace-keeping, community maintenance and so on. It was army discipline that founded the Philadelphia Accord in the first place, and helped it survive the Dissolution. Now the Corps is the glue that keeps the States together."

"Or a tide of molasses rolling across the continent," said Barney, "drowning everything in its path."

"If only it were that easy. We could just lean back and enjoy the ride." O'Dell returned her smile easily. "But there are troublemakers everywhere we go. Like this Mole you've got. Any guesses what he's after?"

"Very little," Roads said, uncomfortably aware that in making that admission he was exposing his own inability to solve the case. O'Dell listened patiently as Roads outlined the break-ins, declining to comment at all – let alone judge – until they had brought him completely up to date.

"A month ago," Roads said, "when we first realised that the crimes were a series, not just isolated incidents, we began looking for motives. Since some of the stolen information was extremely sensitive, extortion immediately sprang to mind. But we've never once had a demand for money, or anything at all. Sabotage was next on our list, possibly connected with the anti-Reassimilationist movement. But again we've had no threats, no warnings, and nothing has gone wrong to suggest that the stolen data has been used this way."

"How about suspects?" O'Dell asked.

"Apart from me, you mean?" Roads shook his head. "We have no evidence pointing to anyone: no DNA, no fibres, no fingerprints, no descriptions, no hearsay."

"Nothing circumstantial?"

"Not a scrap," Barney said, "apart from the fact that the Mole must have a large amount of technical know-how in order to get away with what he does. Every theft occurs in a different place and at a different time. There's no pattern that might give us some idea of the thief's habits. There's no pattern to the differences, either – such as thefts taking place at later times the further they are from a central location, which might be where the Mole lives or works." She glanced briefly at Roads, then back to O'Dell. "We've tried every permutation of the stats, and come up with absolutely nothing."

"The Mole is almost too clever, isn't he?" the RUSAMC captain mused. "I mean, not only does he have an uncanny ability to evade detection and penetrate defended datapools, but he's done his best to shift suspicion away from him to a prominent member of the local security force. It's ingenious, don't you think? Using something as simple as a rubber mask, I suppose, to confuse the enemy."

Roads remembered the video footage Morrow had given him. "It's not a mask."

"No? You think he really does look like you?"

Roads shook his head. He had considered this, briefly, but dismissed the possibility as too remote. "I had plastic surgery in mind."

"Seems a bit extreme."

"It depends how serious he is."

"I guess." O'Dell looked uncomfortable. "I'm sorry. The thought of cosmetic alteration disturbs me. I had no idea the practice still existed in Kennedy."

"It doesn't," Barney was quick to reassure him. "Unnecessary biomodification has been illegal for as long as I can remember. That includes plastic surgery."

"Good." O'Dell took a sip of his coffee and Roads was reminded of the captain's injury. In a perverse way, he seemed to wear the deformity like a badge of honour.

O'Dell, noting Roads' glance, put the cup down and flexed his crippled hand. "The States have outlawed all forms of biomodification," he said. "To become super-human is to lose one's humanity, and to be truly human is to suffer the imperfections of the form with dignity. I'm glad to see that the Mayoralty of Kennedy agrees with us, at least on this."

Barney nodded. "We had trouble with berserkers, too. One killed seventy-five people when I was a teenager. They had to destroy an entire block just to bring it down."

"I was a child when the last fell, but I've heard the stories." O'Dell's right hand caressed the stumps of his missing fingers. If he noted the sadness in Barney's eyes, he didn't comment on it. "I'd rather be crippled than allow the possibility of similar atrocities to occur in the future." He smiled self-deprecatingly. "Not that I'm handicapped by this, of course. I hardly notice it, most of the time."

Roads could contain his curiosity no longer. "How did it happen, if you don't mind me asking?"

"Nothing particularly dramatic. My brother slipped chopping wood when I was twelve." O'Dell put the hand into a pocket and glanced at the watch on his other wrist. "I have an appointment in a couple of minutes that'll last until later this afternoon. Perhaps we could meet afterward to discuss Operation Blindeye."

"Of course," said Roads, noting that O'Dell's watch was solar powered. On impulse, he added: "If I'm not here or in my office, I'll be down at the target range. You can join me there, if you like."

O'Dell nodded with a glint in his eye; he knew a friendly challenge when he heard one. "Four o'clock, say?"

"Done."

The RUSAMC captain stood. "Thanks for the coffee, Barney."

"Pleasure."

As he left the cubicle, the usual hubbub of the communal office ebbed for a split-second, then resumed slightly louder than before. Roads shook his head in amusement.

"So." Barney leaned against the desk and folded her arms. "What do you think?"

"He'll be fine. A little young, but okay, I think. He's obviously been around, and that will help."

The intercom on Barney's desk buzzed. It was Michael, Chappel's secretary, looking for Roads, with a call from David Goss at Kennedy City University waiting to be put through.

"No rest for the wicked," Barney whispered from out of the camera's field of view.

"In this town?" Roads edged toward the exit. "Not bloody likely."

"Before you go, Phil." She stood. "Am I invited to the old hand versus new blood showdown this afternoon?"

"If you like, but only you. I don't think he'd appreciate a crowd."

She nodded. "Yeah, and the Phil Roads fanclub would look pretty thin if he did, wouldn't it?"

"Sadly so." He tipped her a quick salute and made a dash for his office.

CHAPTER SEVEN

3:30 p.m.

Four o'clock came swiftly. While Chappel babysat DeKurzak elsewhere, Roads took charge of organising Blindeye. He didn't mind the extra work, but it meant that he had little time to follow up his vague thoughts of the previous night. Likewise, his promise to catch up with Roger Wiggs went forgotten until after twelve, by which time the homicide officer had finally gone off duty.

At half-past three, he checked out of his office and took the lift down to the basement. There he dismantled his pistol and cleaned it thoroughly. When he had finished, he signed for a box of plastic bullets and went to the range.

The long, underground chamber was empty. He chose one of the middle lanes, donned earmuffs and goggles, and fired a few practice rounds at an old-fashioned paper target. The familiar smell and grit of gunpowder quickly filled the air, sensations he had missed in the last six weeks, thanks to night shift. His aim was as good as ever, though. When he tired of static targets, he instructed the range simulators to begin.

The paper bullseyes withdrew into the ceiling and the lights dimmed. At the far end of the lane, a man appeared. He held a submachine gun in one hand and a torch in another. The torch came up, shining into Roads' eyes, dazzling him. Behind the glare, the submachine gun started to rise.

Roads snapped off a single shot. The torch went out and the man fell over. A diagnostic chart appeared on the screen by his side; the bullet had penetrated the hologram's forehead just above its right eye.

He grunted with satisfaction and cleared the simulator for another attempt. It was good to release some of the frustration that had built up in recent weeks, even if it was against an illusory opponent.

Three rounds later, he managed to put the bullet straight through the eye itself.

"Impressive," said O'Dell from behind him as the last hologram flickered and vanished. Roads cleared the screen and took off the earmuffs, assuming that the RUSAMC captain had been referring to the simulation, not the diagnosis of Roads' aim. O'Dell's uniform jacket was open, revealing a leather shoulder holster. He looked tired, less animated than before.

"A toy from the old days," said Roads. "Nothing special."

"But so much better for training than VR, which we use back home."

The two men faced each other in silence for a split second, Roads acutely conscious of O'Dell sizing him up, and aware that he was doing the same in return.

Barney stepped into the room at that moment, flustered. "Sorry I'm late, Phil. Have I missed anything?"

O'Dell turned; the bright-eyed grin reappeared. "No, we haven't started yet."

"Good." She handed him a set of protective earmuffs. "I brought you these. Do you need ammunition?"

He shook his head. "No. I'll be fine, thanks."

"Okay. Well, I'm a terrible shot on a good day, so I'll just stay up here and watch. Have fun with your toys, boys." She climbed a short flight of stairs to an observation platform and took a seat.

O'Dell chose the lane to Roads' left. "I get the feeling I'm being tested," he said.

"In a way, you are. It's not often I get to try out against someone new."

"I should warn you, then." O'Dell casually unclipped his holster. "I graduated first in marksmanship from my regiment."

Roads smiled. "And what would you say if I told you that I was RSD champion for ten years running?"

"Well, I guess I'd be forced to ask why you used the word 'was' in that context."

"Fair enough: I retired from the contest undefeated."

"Good for you." O'Dell reached between the lanes and they shook hands. "May the best shot win."

They adopted two-handed stances and waited for the simulations to begin. O'Dell felled nine of the first ten targets; Roads dropped all ten. They reloaded. The next round was an even ten-all. The third went to O'Dell, ten-nine.

"A draw." O'Dell bowed to Barney's applause. "Fancy a rematch?"

"If you like. But first . . . may I?" Roads indicated that he would like to see O'Dell's sidearm. The captain handed it over. The pistol was large but light-weight, and sported a laser-sight along the barrel which O'Dell had not activated. "I'm not familiar with the make."

"Hardly surprising." O'Dell folded his arms. "It's brand new."

"Really?" Roads had suspected as much, although he feigned surprise. That simple fact made the pistol even more remarkable. Kennedy's supply of weapons was severely limited, a fact he had come to take for granted. Once again, he realised how little he knew about the

RUSAMC – and was doubly glad he had invited O'Dell down to the firing range: how better to learn more about a potential opponent than by engaging in ritual combat?

"I had no idea the States were so advanced," he said.

"Not many people in Kennedy do, I guess." O'Dell accepted the pistol back from Roads. "Designs and technology have been preserved since the War, but until recently there existed no inclination to use them. It wasn't until the States were founded that the reconstruction of the past began. Not all of the past, of course; we've drawn the line firmly at biomods, as you know, and genetic manipulation. We've used just enough old science to rebuild a society that can manufacture sophisticated products, like this pistol."

"And your watch," Roads added. "Both more significant than anything we've made in the last thirty years."

O'Dell shrugged noncommittally. "The only difference between us and Kennedy is that we have resources at our disposal and you don't. That's why it makes sense for you to join us."

"I can't argue with that." Roads selected a different simulation. "But I must confess that I have trouble seeing the difference between machines of metal, machines of flesh, and machines that are a mixture of both."

Two identical targets appeared at the end of their respective lanes, but neither of them turned to aim.

"The difference," explained O'Dell, "is not so much the machines themselves, but the way they're used."

"I agree with you so far. Go on."

"Biomodification is dangerous because it gives one person superiority over others. This superiority can lead to a *sense* of superiority, which is something else entirely."

"So possessing a pistol with a laser sight is different, say, from having augmented vision – even though the end result of each modification might be the same?"

"Yes. We believe there's nothing that can be gained by biomodification that cannot be had by more orthodox means. For instance, a laser sight may act as a deterrent, whereas augmented vision can be used to invade privacy."

"It boils down to a question of intent, then. Not an intrinsic wrongness of biomodification."

"I suppose so, although it's widely held that biomodification offers greater potential for abuse than conventional technology."

Roads nodded. "Interesting." He gestured at the targets. "Shall we?"

The targets were simple: alternating red and white rings with a black centre. They both scored bullseyes on their first attempt. New targets appeared, ten per cent smaller. Bullseyes again, although the diagnostics asserted that Roads' was slightly closer to the absolute centre than O'Dell's. As the targets decreased in size, their performance worsened, until, on the eighth target, O'Dell missed altogether.

"Try again," offered Roads. His own shot had penetrated the third ring out.

When O'Dell's second attempt also missed, Roads suggested that the captain try a third time, this time using the laser sight as an aid.

"But doesn't that give me an unfair advantage?"

"Regardless." Roads waved at the target. "I insist."

O'Dell switched on the laser and aimed. The tiny red dot was almost invisible from the end of the lane, and the tremors of even a rock-steady hand were amplified enormously by the distance. Nevertheless, the shot went home – three rings out, like Roads'.

Two new targets appeared, smaller still.

"Before we go on." O'Dell leaned against the low wall separating the two lanes. He kept his voice low, obviously so Barney wouldn't overhear. "I happened to be scanning through some old MIA records before I came to Kennedy. There are a lot of people trying to trace their families back to the War, and we thought it would be interesting to see if any soldiers had died here during the Dissolution. The easiest way to do that is by cross-referencing with Kennedy's mortuary records."

"That makes sense."

"I thought so, too. It turns out, however, that the records we want are hard to obtain. All we could get were the results of a census taken two years ago."

Roads kept his smile steady to hide the sudden sinking in his stomach, and the cold feeling enveloping his arms and legs. "That's a pity."

"Yes, it is. There isn't much point scanning through the population of Kennedy to see if anyone has survived from that long ago, so the project has stalled." O'Dell's expression was bland, but his eyes were very much alive. "I have the MIA data with me, though, just in case."

Roads nodded slowly; he understood all too well what O'Dell was hinting at.

"I suggest we discuss this later," he said. "There might be something I can do to speed things up down at Births and Deaths."

"Thanks, Phil." O'Dell turned to face the target. "Now, where were we?"

Roads' shot just clipped the outer ring; O'Dell's thudded home on the second. The next target defeated Roads altogether; a slight tremor in his hands had betrayed him. He wondered if that had been the intention of O'Dell's little revelation. O'Dell's shot made it, although barely, onto the outer ring.

"What's your call, Phil?"

"It's not over yet, Martin." Roads cleared the targets and punched for another display. "Just one more, if you don't mind."

At the end of each lane appeared a single glowing point of light. "Try and hit it," said Roads. "You have three rounds."

O'Dell looked puzzled, but took aim anyway. Three shots rang out, and the diagnostics showed a trio of glowing red dots arrayed in an uneven triangle around the central point.

"Now, three more without the laser."

This time, O'Dell's aim was more dispersed, tending upward and to the left. He shrugged and holstered the pistol while Roads lined up and also fired three times.

Roads' aim was midway between O'Dell's two attempts; none of his shots landed closer than any of those aided by the laser-sight, but none further out than those aimed by O'Dell's naked eye. When the echoes of the last shot had faded, he turned to face the RUSAMC captain and extended his hand.

"I suggest we call it a draw," he said.

O'Dell looked surprised. "Why? I beat you."

"But that was with the laser-sight, don't forget."

"Well, given *your* unfair advantage –"

"Oh? Watch carefully." Roads turned back to the glowing target, raised, aimed and fired the pistol. Three shots split the air in rapid succession.

But only one dot – which was actually three combined – appeared on the diagnostic screen, centred precisely in the heart of the glowing target.

"Now *that*," said Roads, "is what I'd call unfair."

O'Dell just gaped in amazement.

Barney suddenly appeared, down from the stalls. "Who won?" she asked. "I didn't see the results of the last round."

Roads glanced at O'Dell. "It was a draw. Right, Martin?"

O'Dell met his eye, and nodded. "I'll go with that."

"Good." They shook hands.

"For now . . . "

Kennedy City University was a one-kilometre walk from RSD HQ. Roads and O'Dell, with a bodyguard of two, took their time on the way, stopping occasionally to study the city's landmarks. Barney had remained behind to complete her rostered workload.

Before leaving RSD HQ, O'Dell had changed out of his uniform and into more casual attire. Again, Roads was impressed by the fine cut of the fabric; not only were the materials natural cotton and wool, but the dyes used were more vibrant than the familiar, dull hues Kennedy produced. This essential difference negated the reason for changing in the first place. O'Dell's clothing, to a keen observer, marked him as different; he didn't need a RUSAMC badge to betray his origins on the Outside.

The few people they encountered, however, appeared to take no notice. Most were heading home from work, walking briskly to the nearest Rosette junctions as the day began to cool. In the centre of Kennedy, all employees in some way worked for the city; if not directly for the Mayoralty, then in a hospital, perhaps, or a Rations and Resources department. Although in theory the city guaranteed equal treatment for all of its citizens, in general such employees looked better-off than their counterparts in more menial fields. Roads had noted this inequality before, and that day was no exception. Similarly, the suburbs surrounding the route from the city centre to the Wall were home mainly to MSA staff, who lived near the Gate supposedly to demonstrate their constant devotion to duty. The fact that those same suburbs had always been more affluent than any other in the city was officially irrelevant.

Not everything Roads saw aroused the cynic in him, though. At one point, a group of school children crossed their path, forcing them off the sidewalk and onto the road. As the gaggle of tiny bodies swarmed past, with their teacher struggling to keep them under control, one young boy pulled a face at Roads. He waved back, and was rewarded with a cheeky grin. Instead of being annoyed, he smiled. It was just what he had needed.

A growing lack of resources was bad enough. Worse still was the fact that so many people like Barney, who had lost parents during the Dissolution, were now losing their children to another cause: teenage crime was on the rise, and youth suicide had tripled in the last ten years – the last a fact carefully glossed over by isolationist statisticians. Kennedy's second generation of citizens was losing the will that had kept the city alive for so long – and without that will, there was nothing left to fight for.

If all went well, though, by the time these children were teenagers they would be completely free of the prison that had confined their parents. No matter how bad the present looked – no matter that the children wore ill-fitting clothes and had to learn from books rather than the more sophisticated aids taken for granted in their grandparents' day – at least there was still hope for the future.

When the children had become just an echo of laughter far behind them, Roads and O'Dell resumed their conversation. In the presence of their bodyguard neither man had raised the matter of the mortuary records, although Roads would have liked to, if only to clear the air. He hated hiding, hated being forced to deny reality. The fact that someone might have discovered the truth came almost as a relief.

And therein lay the real reason for sharing target practice with O'Dell: not so much to learn about the RUSA, but to find out how much they knew about *him*.

"By concentrating the city's data in one location," Roads explained as they walked, "we hope to force the Mole to come to us, rather than the other way around. That's the essence of Blindeye."

"Logical enough," O'Dell replied, "but will he come?"

"If he wants to steal data, he will." Roads pointed in the direction of LaMont Hospital, a squat, white building to their right. "Say, for instance, he targets medical records tonight. He'll go through his usual routine of sneaking in and trying to lift data, except that this time he'll face an automatic message telling him that all the records have been transferred to the KCU library. There's no way he'll be able to take anything himself, because there'll be nothing *to* take and the land-lines to KCU will be down. So he'll come."

"Knowing it's a trap? He's not a fool."

"No, but we're hoping he'll try anyway. It's a challenge, if you like."

"So, he comes to KCU, sneaks in, and . . . ?"

"I'll be hidden inside, waiting for the word. We've put everything we've got into this, Martin, every surveillance system we can get our hands on. Should he still slip by, I'll be there for when the data-retrieval system starts operating."

"Just you?"

"Just me. And three dozen officers elsewhere on campus, keeping a low profile unless I need help. We don't want to scare him away too soon."

"Obviously not."

They reached the northern edge of the grounds of the university in good time. An iron fence separated KCU from the rest of the city, with entrance gained by a number of gates that would be locked after nightfall. The library, where the trap waited to be sprung, was a mock-Victorian edifice three storeys high in the very heart of the picturesque grounds. From that point, it was almost possible to imagine that Kennedy Polis and the rest of the outside world didn't exist.

Roads glanced once over his shoulder, sensing again that he was being watched. Then he chided himself for being foolish. Of course he was being watched; the area was full of RSD officers – although apart from a slight increase in pedestrian traffic there was little indication of the industry taking place within the university's grounds. The students had been given an unexpected holiday while the library's facilities were being used.

"It's a long-shot," O'Dell drawled, "relying heavily on the assumption that the Mole won't know you're in there."

"I know." Roads mentally added the possibility that the Mole might not move on an official datapool at all, in which case the entire procedure would have to be repeated the following night. "But it's our *only* shot."

A passing plain-clothes security guard checked Roads' ID and waved them on. They strolled toward the library.

"What do you plan to do, once you've got him?"

"Whatever it takes." Roads grimaced. "I don't want to kill him, but I will if I have to."

O'Dell seemed surprised by his reluctance. "I wouldn't hesitate, in your shoes. After all, this guy has made a mockery of your security forces. He deserves everything he gets."

"Maybe, but I don't like killing. There are better ways."

"And it'd feel strange, I guess, aiming for yourself."

The entrance to the library loomed before them, at the summit of a flight of wide, stone steps. They stopped there, on the threshold, where moss had attacked the composite protecting the stone and turned it a mottled green.

"But if you have to," O'Dell added, "you'll get him, I'm sure. I have no doubts that you're the best man for the job."

"Despite our differences?"

"Because of them." O'Dell leaned close. "Don't tell anyone I admitted this, but it's possible that biomodification *might* be useful in some circumstances, in the right hands. The Mole, however, is a prime example of its misuse. I'll be glad to see him fall."

"So you think he's biomodified?"

"I do now, yes. Something left over from the old times. There's no way an ordinary man could do what he does."

Roads was glad that O'Dell had not followed DeKurzak's line of reasoning. Even inside jobs left evidence of some kind. "What about the assassin?"

"It'll be interesting to see what happens after tonight. If the Mole is captured and the murders cease, then that'll solve all of your problems in one hit."

"You think the Mole and the assassin are one and the same?"

"Not as strongly as your man DeKurzak – but it's possible." O'Dell shrugged. "Only time will tell, won't it?"

Roads smiled to himself. "Time, or an awful amount of luck."

Word spread quickly of their arrival. David Goss, the RSD officer in charge of security, came down from the roof to welcome them in person. A giant with bulging muscles and close-cropped hair, he looked as though he might have been more at home in the military. Looks, however, were in his case deceptive. He was one of the most placid, patient men that Roads had ever met. His beaming smile was more than a match for O'Dell's.

Goss took them on a grand tour of the library, pointing out the additional surveillance systems installed that afternoon. Invisible laser trip-wires laced the corridors, floors had been laid with pressure-sensitive mats, every window and door had its own deadman switch, and there wasn't an inch of floorspace that a camera couldn't see. Infra-red detectors reacted to their body-heat, beeping as they passed.

"Better hope there aren't any mice," commented O'Dell.

"Everything is keyed to react to human stimuli," said Goss. "If the heat-signature is wrong or the mass too light, then the alarms won't ring." He stooped to run his hand along the floor. "And the trip-wires come no closer than ten centimetres to the ground. We shouldn't have too many false alarms."

The library's northern wall nestled against an administration complex, so the roof had been booby-trapped as well, along with a wrought-iron skylight that opened onto the main reading room where the data-storage facilities had been assembled. Every conceivable entrance had been covered, including the air-vents.

"You, Phil, will be in here." Goss opened a door on the first floor as they passed it, revealing a white-tiled room lined with cubicles: the ladies' toilets. An array of screens and monitors had been erected in one corner, at which technicians fussed and bothered.

Roads smiled. Incongruous though it seemed, it made admirable sense: close enough to the reading room to give him quick access, but not so close as to risk being stumbled across by accident. Even if the Mole suspected that Roads would be waiting for him, this was the last place he would look.

Roads glanced at O'Dell, who was also smiling.

"Yes?"

"I was just wondering what would happen if the Mole was a woman with a weak bladder."

Goss chuckled. "Then she'd get one hell of a surprise, that's for sure. Not that she'd make it this far."

"Right."

The tour concluded in the main reading room. The chamber was enormous, lined with shelves crammed with antique books. There were only two entrances to the room, one being the door through which they had come, the other high above. The marble ceiling was domed and rococo, terminating in the skylight.

The room had been chosen for its spaciousness, and its ready access to the landlines of the library. A score of long, leather-bound desks had been pushed aside to make way for the data-storage tanks in the centre of the room. Each tank was two and half metres high and as wide as two people, connected by thick fibre-optic cables to a central cluster of terminals. The whole array seemed sorely out of place in the stately chamber. It looked as though the university was conducting a refrigerator sale.

That private thought kept Roads amused until he spotted a familiar figure among the technicians.

DeKurzak straightened and dusted his hands. When he caught sight of Roads and O'Dell, he waved them over with a weary smile.

Goss made it halfway through introductions before Roads cut him short.

"That's okay, David. We all know each other."

"We sure do." Roads was surprised to hear a slight disapproving tone enter O'Dell's normally cheerful voice, and wondered what could have provoked such a reaction. Inter-departmental politics aside, DeKurzak and O'Dell should have had little ground on which to disagree.

"Everything's ready," DeKurzak said, apparently unaware of O'Dell's snub. "You're looking at the total datapool of Kennedy Polis."

"Everything?" asked O'Dell.

"You name it," affirmed Goss, "and it's here in this room. Right down to my shoe-size."

They moved closer to study the screen of the nearest terminal. As they did so, DeKurzak made certain he was between them and the keyboard – shielding the datapool like an over-protective parent – although the screen displayed nothing but a list of nondescript menus.

"When I arrived," O'Dell said, "I brought a data fiche containing historical records and statistics. Can I assume that this information is here as well?"

DeKurzak nodded. "It is. The original card is under lock and key at RSD headquarters."

"Good. Some of that information is sensitive, even today. I wouldn't like it to fall into the wrong hands."

"It won't." DeKurzak killed the display and turned to the others. "The city shuts down in half an hour, gentlemen. From that point on, it's up to us to keep it safe."

Goss grinned eagerly. "The sooner the better. My side of things will be ready by then."

Roads glanced at his watch. "The Mole has never made a move before eleven o'clock –"

"That we know of," said DeKurzak.

"Right, so I'll want to be in and settled by nine, just to be sure. Until then, I'd like to cover the building a couple of times, to get to know the layout."

"Sounds fair," Goss said. "I can give you one of the team, if you like."

"No, that's okay. A floor plan will be fine."

"Can do. I'll get it for you on the way out." Goss stepped away from the terminal to demonstrate the security provisions elsewhere in the room.

Before Roads could follow, DeKurzak motioned him aside.

"The Mayor wants to talk to you, Phil, when you're free," said the MSA officer.

"About anything in particular?" Roads fought to contain his reluctance. Mayor Packard was well-liked but, in Roads' opinion, something of an imbecile. In his five-year reign, they had spoken face-to-face three times and on each occasion exchanged nothing of any importance.

"About tonight, of course." DeKurzak's expression became mildly reproachful. "I think he'd appreciate some reassurance concerning the outcome of this venture."

"As would I."

"That's not what he wants to hear." DeKurzak shook his head. "There are people in the Mayoralty who question the wisdom of Operation Blindeye, and the Mayor is naturally concerned. It would be best not to joke about the risk you're taking on our behalf."

Roads met DeKurzak's stare, and held it. The inference was obvious: "you", not "we". If Blindeye failed, then a scapegoat would be required, and he'd obviously been nominated in absentia to fill that position.

"Fair enough, I guess," he said, trying to sound casual. "I'll call him when I can."

"Thank you." DeKurzak went to move away, but Roads grabbed his arm.

"Wait. You said some people disagree with what we're doing." The liaison officer nodded. "What about you, DeKurzak? Do *you* think we're doing the right thing?"

"If I'd thought of anything better, I would have tabled it by now." DeKurzak's eyes hardened. "I'd tell you to your face if I thought your actions inappropriate."

"Would you?"

"Believe me, Phil." DeKurzak pulled his arm free. "There's much more at stake here than your feelings."

The liaison officer went back to attending the datapool, and Roads turned to rejoin the others. Goss was showing O'Dell the security surrounding the main console.

"Lasers, infra-red detectors, pressure mats, you name it," said the big officer. "There's a dozen of each in this room alone. Not even Mister Mouse could get within three metres of this desk without letting half the city know."

Roads, thinking of the video Keith Morrow had given him, pursed his lips and said nothing.

CHAPTER EIGHT

10:35 p.m.

Roads glanced at his watch and resisted the urge to light a cigarette. The toilets were pitch-dark, apart from the inconstant glow of the monitors. The stench of disinfectant had become overpowering in the absence of other sensory input.

He had been in the toilet for an hour and a half. The five screens on the desk before him flickered between various views of the library. Besides a couple of inevitable false alarms, the night had been perfectly quiet. At his request, a separate terminal had been installed so he could work to pass the time, but that had paled quickly. There was nothing to do but wait.

After his guided tour with O'Dell, he had scoured the library from roof to basement, searching for any entrance that might have been overlooked. It had taken him two hours to concede that there was very little Goss had missed; even the chimneys had trip-wires installed. The exercise had proved worthwhile, however. By the time he had finished, he had known the building as thoroughly as he knew his own bedroom, and could have found his way around it with his eyes closed if he'd had to.

Throughout the evening's preparations, however, he'd found it hard to shake the feeling that he was being followed, especially when he went for a nerve-soothing run. Although Goss' team had secured the area for the night, the grounds were alive with subtle movements. He supposed that a few guards still patrolled the paths and lawns along which he ran. Nothing else explained the gut-level certainty that he was being watched again. It was odd, though, that no-one halted him to ask for ID.

He returned to the library feeling relatively refreshed and invigorated. A warm-down and a shower later, he was ready to ring the Mayor.

The conversation went exactly as he had anticipated it. Mayor Packard was in his early fifties, with the perfect mix of grey-haired respectability and charismatic good looks to guarantee a majority vote from the citizens of Kennedy Polis. City politics mirrored that of twentieth-century America in miniature: two major parties competed for both the Mayoralty and seats on the Council by drawing popular candidates from within their own ranks and pitting them against each other for preselection every four years. The conservatives advocated a need for pacifism, an egalitarian social system and complete isolation from the outside world, whereas the other – now synonymous with the Reassimilationists – wanted to reopen the city to the outside world.

In the twenty-nine years since the abdication of the Dissolution Mayor, who had ruled as a near dictator until sickness forced him to retire, every election had been won on an isolationist ticket. Mayor Packard, formerly head of the MSA, hadn't changed the formula even slightly when he had been re-elected the previous year – which only made his sudden reversal in the face of the RUSA envoy even more remarkable. Speculation had been rife of secret back-room deals, or threats, since the envoy's arrival; none, of course, had been confirmed by either the Mayor or his staff, and Roads preferred to believe that, for once, commonsense had reigned.

Once the formalities had been dispensed with, he assured Mayor Packard that he was confident of a successful conclusion to the evening, although that outcome might not be known until the early hours of the morning. Packard, in response, asked to be kept informed, no matter what the hour. He went on to reaffirm the serious situation in which the city found itself, and to reiterate the necessity that it present a 'clean bill of health' for Reassimilation.

"Let's show those bastards, eh, Roads? Let's show them we know how to defend our city."

Roads wasn't sure exactly what to make of that comment, but replied: "Of course, sir."

"We do know how to, don't we? I'd hate to think we didn't." A frown disturbed the perfect sweep of Packard's brow, albeit briefly. "If this plan of yours is successful, you can expect to receive a commendation."

Roads resisted the impulse to ask what he could expect if it failed. Instead, he apologised for having to cut the conversation short. Packard wished him luck on behalf of the rest of the city and broke the connection.

He'd had time for one last briefing with Goss, and then it was into the toilet to wait for the Mole. An hour and a half later and he was still wondering who Packard had meant by 'those bastards'.

Suddenly, a familiar voice whispered in his ear via a tiny earplug, startling him from his reverie:

"Howdy, boss."

"Hi, Barney." He glanced by reflex at his watch; it still said 10.35. "You're late."

"I was busy elsewhere. And, besides, my shift doesn't officially start for an hour yet."

"What happened to the fanatical devotion to duty?"

"Out the window, I'm afraid. When a handsome young captain asks you out, nothing gets in the way."

"Oh, so that's where you've been." He winced, hoping the camera in the toilet wouldn't pick up his expression. "And did you have a good night?"

"Simply . . . fabulous." Barney's imitation of her colleague, Shelley, was precise. No doubt there would be an interesting conversation between the two women the following day. Roads was positive he didn't want to overhear it.

"Some people will do almost anything to make me jealous," he said, hoping he had inserted the correct amount of humour in his voice.

"What's there to be jealous of? He's a married man, and I'm so much older than him."

"From the tone of your voice, I'd say that neither would be much of an obstacle, given the chance."

"What's the matter, Phil?" She chuckled. "You're not *really* jealous, are you?"

"Not at all. But this is hardly the time or place to discuss your sex life. Think of your reputation, for God's sake."

"*What* sex life? Besides, this is a private line."

"Lucky."

"By the way, DeKurzak asked me to remind you to use subvocals from now on."

"Is he still there?"

"Yes. So are David and Martin . . . Roger couldn't make it, unfortunately, so he misses out on all the perks we have up here, courtesy of the KCU staff room."

"Thanks." The makeshift command centre was in the heart of the building adjacent to the library, on the first floor. Roads glanced disparagingly at the gloomy confines of the ladies' toilets, and belatedly remembered the throat-mike. "Thanks a lot," he subvocalised.

"Oooh, you've gone all husky." She panted a throaty farewell. "I'll be watching you, remember."

"How could I forget? Call me when you can."

"Will do."

He settled back into the chair and closed his eyes. He wondered why he was so bothered by the thought of Barney having dinner with O'Dell. She and Roads were close, yes, and anyone intruding upon that closeness could be considered a threat – but he had no right to expect her not to see other men. He was her superior officer, for Christ's sake, not her lover, and there was the age difference to take into account as well.

But more than rank kept them apart; he was honest enough with himself to admit that. It was history – both his and the city's. A history they had never discussed completely.

If only her father had lived . . .

Casting the thought aside, he got to his feet and paced the length of the cubicles.

What had Packard said? "Let's show those bastards we know how to defend our city." Or something to that effect. An interesting choice of words, Roads thought. "Defence" usually referred to something from the outside; "bastards" implied plurality. If the Mayor had meant the Mole, as was suggested by the context, then he would have said "bastard", singular. But it would have been just as strange to refer to the assassin and possible accomplices instead, because the killer was doing exactly what Packard suggested: defending Kennedy from a perceived invasion.

Or was Mayor Packard suggesting that the Mole was an agent for another body altogether? It could have been nothing more than a slip of the tongue, but it was worth pursuing. The only external body that Roads knew of was the RUSA itself.

He cast his mind back six weeks, to the beginning of the Mole's campaign. Kennedy Polis had been in turmoil after the arrival of the RUSAMC envoy at the city walls. There had been an air of uncertainty in the Council, with the very real possibility that the envoy was going to be sent away, by force if necessary, and the offer of Reassimilation rejected. It had taken three weeks of solid debate to arrive at the decision to open negotiations with the RUSA, and the final vote had been close. Without Senior Councillor Norris' final summation, the Reassimilation Bill might have been repealed at the last moment. Roads could understand the RUSAMC sending a covert agent into the city back then, to ascertain the exact nature of the threat Kennedy represented. And yet . . .

Why had the Mole not been recalled? If the Reassimilation went ahead, the Reunited States would have unlimited access to Kennedy's datapool within a few days. Did they believe that the exchange would be incomplete – or that the Council, daunted by the assassin, would change its mind at the last minute?

And was that, then, why they had sent O'Dell to aid investigations – not to help catch the Mole, but to neutralise the killer?

Roads went back to the desk and checked the information he had been studying the previous night. The Kennedy mortuary records had been stolen two weeks prior to Blindeye. Either O'Dell had brought them up in conversation to deceive Roads, or the captain was unaware of his own government's covert activities. Or had the remark simply been a means of putting Roads off-guard, as he had first thought?

No matter which way he looked at it, it wouldn't fall into place.

He sighed. He was getting as paranoid as DeKurzak, substituting RUSAMC secret agents for a hypothetical

Old Guard in a situation where there couldn't possibly be either. The Mole had to be biomodified. The Re-united States, therefore, would hardly tolerate his existence, let alone employ him to further their ends.

He went back to the chair and put his feet up on the desk. The screens were mesmerising. After a while, he stopped counting the numbers of times they changed every minute and resigned himself to wait the whole night if he had to.

The Mole would appear when he was ready. There was nothing Roads could do to make him come sooner than that.

A voice jolted him to full alertness shortly after midnight. His left leg was stiff from maintaining one posture for so long, and he rubbed it absently while listening to the information Barney relayed.

"Boss? We've just had word from DP. There's been some sort of interference down at Emergency Services."

"The Mole?"

"An unauthorised request for data came through ten minutes ago. As no-one else is supposed to be using the system tonight, we feel safe assuming it to be our man."

"Fair enough," Roads said. "Although it's pretty stupid of him to let us know he tried like that."

"Unless he did it deliberately. It wouldn't be the first time."

Roads nodded, calculating times in his head. "Ten minutes. That gives him just enough time to get out of the building and across town. He could be here any moment."

"You got it." Her voice was breathless. "The show's about to begin."

"About fucking time." He stood, checked the microphone taped to his throat and his earplug, and stretched his legs. "Excuse me for a second while I take a piss."

"I promise not to listen."

When he returned, the silence of the library had thickened; he was more conscious of the lack of sound than he had been before. He found himself straining to listen for footsteps which didn't exist. If there was anyone in the building, the surveillance systems would have been triggered already.

Again, an image of the Mole flashed into his mind's eye. It was a sequence from the footage Morrow had given him: of the Mole walking through the laser beams undetected, of the Mole appearing to be invisible to infra-red cameras. He studied the endlessly changing screens, half expecting to see his dark half already inside the building.

"We've got something," said Goss.

The voice made Roads jump. "Where?"

"Outside, but . . . Hang on a second. It might be a false alarm."

One of the screens flickered and changed to an external view of the grounds. The image was predominantly grey and blue as a result of a light-intensification program. Something ran through a copse of trees – a shadow keeping low to the ground. The camera tracked it, zoomed in close.

It was the timber wolf.

"One of the lookouts spotted it," Goss said. "Sorry to give you all a start."

"How'd it get in?" Barney asked.

"Over the fence?" Roads suggested.

"Unlikely," said Goss. "The fence is two metres high."

"Not impossible," put in O'Dell, his drawl as lazily confident as ever. "Timber wolves have been known to jump higher. I've seen one leap over a man myself."

"Really? Where was that?"

"Back home. They bred like crazy after the War. You don't have them here?"

"Only one that I know of," said Goss. "And you're looking at it."

The wolf slid across the open expanse of a lawn like a streak of smoke-blackened silver. Their perspective shifted to that of another camera, allowing them to watch it in profile. Its muscles rippled beneath an evanescent coat; its eyes glinted emotionlessly in the pale moonlight.

"David, I thought you'd booby-trapped the fences?"

"We have, Phil. Maybe it dug a tunnel."

Roads shook his head, taking the suggestion seriously. The wolf's coat was clean and unmarked by dirt. "However it got in, it must've really wanted to."

"And it's headed right for us." He could hear the anticipation in Barney's voice.

"Forget it. It's a diversion." Roads glanced at the other screens. "David, tell your people to keep an eye out."

"Will do."

"A diversion?" asked Barney.

"To keep us distracted while he sneaks in somewhere else."

"So the Mole has a pet wolf?" asked DeKurzak.

"They *can* be trained," said O'Dell. "But you have to hand-rear them from birth."

"Really?" Roads found that interesting. It suggested that the Mole came from the northern regions of the continent – perhaps near Philadelphia, the RUSA capital.

"Here it comes." Goss tracked the wolf as it crossed the last open space before reaching the library. The animal circled the building once, then vanished into a clump of trees nearby. It did not reappear from the other side. "And there it goes. We've either lost it, or it's gone to ground. Sorry folks, but show-time's over."

The screen changed, became a map of the university grounds. Green dots marked untripped alarms surrounding the library. Roads studied it intently, waiting for a sign that the Mole had made his move. A minute dragged by, painfully slow; his heartbeat seemed loud enough to echo in the confines of the toilets.

"David? You got anything in the building?"

"No, just a couple of small movements."

"Where?"

"Basement and ground floor. Not worth worrying about. You know what these old buildings are like, settling after sunset."

"Are you sure?" The timing bothered him. "It could be –"

"Wait," breathed Barney. "I think we might have something."

Roads could hear Goss talking on another line in the background, but couldn't make out the words. The screens changed, and Goss came back.

"We've lost contact with two of the lookouts on the roof of the admin building. No alarms have been triggered on the library, though."

"That doesn't mean anything, judging from past experience."

"True. But let's hang on a moment longer. Don't want to jump the gun."

Roads fidgeted nervously as the screens surveyed the roof of the building. The view contained plenty of detail – ventilation outlets, antennae, even an old satellite dish – but was shrouded with shadow. Light-intensification could only improve the picture a little; without an infra-red scanner, there was no way to be certain exactly what he was seeing.

"Come on, you son of a bitch."

"What was that, Phil?"

"Nothing. Just talking to –"

On one of the screens, a shadow moved.

"Camera twenty-three, David – that's him!"

"Where, Phil? I can't see –"

"Zoom in on that duct, or whatever it is, by the grill – he's behind it. Watch carefully."

The picture slid in close, showing nothing for a second but moonlit metal. Then an arm appeared, little more than a blur with a suggestion of muscle. An instant later, it moved back out of view.

"Shit." Goss wound back the zoom, swung the camera to follow the motion. The shadow danced in and out of sight, leaping from darkness to darkness, visible only in a series of strobe-like glimpses. Its gait was awkward – sometimes crab-like, sometimes leaping, as though clearing invisible obstacles in its path.

Roads mentally pictured the security plan of the roof. "Jesus – he's stepping over the trip-wires!"

"How? They're invisible."

"I don't know, unless . . ." His stomach lurched. "Oh my God. He followed me here, watched you show me where they were. He's been here all the time!"

"But . . ." Goss' voice was incredulous. "What about the I-R sensors? Why isn't he setting them off?"

"Check them, David. I'll bet they're picking up heat outside the target bandwidth. If he's severely biomodi-fied, his body temperature could be –"

"Fuck. We should've thought of that." There was a rattle of keys as Goss fiddled with the security master-terminal, then a satisfied grunt.

"You've got him?"

"Yes."

"Where's he headed?"

"For the skylight, more or less."

"Right." Roads stood and unholstered his pistol. "I'm going in."

"Be careful, Phil." Barney's voice was sharp.

"Always. And you be ready if I need you."

"We will."

He carefully swung the door of the toilets inward, thankful that someone had thought to oil the hinges. Holding his breath tight in his chest, he craned his head around the jamb and peered along the hallway.

No-one. The corridor was pitch-black. Without switching on the torch, he padded slowly to the T-junction at the end of the corridor and stopped with his back up against the wall and the gun raised across his chest.

"Barney? You tracking me?"

"Sure am, boss."

"I want you to scan the way ahead. Make sure there's nothing waiting around the corner."

"Will do." There was a pause, then: "All clear."

He took the corner in a crouch all the same, ready for anything. Although he felt safe to assume that the Mole was on the roof and not actually in the building, he wasn't prepared to discount any possibility – even that of the Mole being in two places at once.

"The stairwell's clear too, Phil."

He opened the door and closed it gently behind him, then forced himself to take the stairs one at a time. The last thing he needed at that moment was to fall in the gloom and break a leg.

"Where is he now?"

"Still on the roof. He's stopped moving."

"Where?"

"Next to the skylight. Looks like he's waiting for something."

"The ground floor?"

"Clear."

The stairwell opened into a cul-de-sac stretching a short distance before ending in a T-junction. Roads tiptoed along it, gun in hand, and turned left. On his right, a row of locked doors marched into the distance; on his left, windows.

"Any change?"

"None."

Another corridor gaped ahead of him. The entrance to the reading room was third on his left. The door was closed. He shouldered the gun when he reached it and paused to take a breath.

"Reading room's clear," said Barney, and he stifled an exclamation of surprise.

"Jesus – don't do that!"

"Sorry. I just thought of something."

"What?"

"If the Mole was here all along, watching us and waiting, then who broke into Emergency Services?"

He hadn't thought of that. "Fuck. That means –"

His earplug rang with the sound of distant alarms, making him start violently. A computerised voice announced in the background:

"Data-retrieval systems activated! Data-retrieval systems activated!"

"Phil!" It was Goss, superimposed over a babble of voices.

"I can hear it. Is it remote, or – ?"

"No – it's local. Christ! He's in there – *he's in there*!"

Roads took a position facing the doors. "Can you see him? Where is he in the room?"

"We can't see him!" Goss' voice was shrill. "For God's sake, Phil, get in there before he gets away!"

Roads raised one leg and kicked in the door.

CHAPTER NINE

Monday, 17 September, 12:55 a.m.

Roads swept into the room and scanned the endless ranks of bookcases and cabinets. He took three steps to his left, holding the gun like a crucifix. He could see no-one. Taking care to keep an eye on the door, he slowly circled the tanks, checking every shadow for movement.

When he reached the point at which he had started, he stopped.

The room was empty.

"Which terminal, David?" he subvocalised silently through the throat-mike. "I can't see anyone in here."

"Number four. Third on your right."

"It's still running?"

"Shit, yes. The Mole has to be there somewhere, Phil."

"Can *you* see him yet?"

"We've got everything focused in there, but all the screens are empty, apart from you."

"Great." He stepped forward, still alert. "I'm going to try and shut down the terminal. Keep an eye on my back."

In the command centre, Barney watched anxiously as Roads crossed the floor of the reading room. Goss, O'Dell, DeKurzak and three technicians did likewise. The sound of held breath filled the silence around her.

"Come *on*, Phil," she muttered.

On a screen to one side, relatively unnoticed, the shadow on the roof still crouched beside the skylight, unmoving. It was visible only in profile, and then not clearly.

"Another decoy?" asked DeKurzak, indicating the image. His voice was loud in the hushed stillness.

"Probably." Goss did not look up from the screen showing Roads. "I'd say he's broken into the system and frozen the picture somehow."

"How?" asked Barney.

"The same way he gained access to the data-retrieval routines, I'd guess."

"Is it possible," put in O'Dell, "to do this from the outside?"

"No," said DeKurzak. "The modem lines are down."

"You sure?"

DeKurzak looked up sharply. "Are you questioning my competence?"

"Just asking." O'Dell shook his head and turned back to the screen.

Roads had finally reached the terminal. Barney watched nervously as he searched every corner for a sign of the Mole.

"Kill it, Phil," she whispered to herself. "Just kill it."

"The screens are clear," said Goss into the microphone. "But the image on the roof looks like another decoy, so he has to be down there somewhere."

"Any idea how he got in, David?" Roads' voice was faint.

"Through the skylight, I guess."

"Impossible. It's still closed."

"It is? Shit."

Barney watched as Roads took one last look around, then reached down with his free hand to grab the terminal's power cord.

"Here goes nothing . . . "

As his hand closed around the cable, Roads felt air brush his face. The movement was subtle, no more than an exhaled breath, but unexpected.

"Look out!"

In the same instant that Barney shouted, he dropped and rolled, bringing the gun up on –

– the Mole. His doppelganger stood not two metres away, staring expressionlessly at him from the middle of the room, with the nearest hiding place metres away.

"Where the fuck did he come from?"

The whispers in his ear were confused and sharp with panic. Strongest was that of Goss:

"From nowhere, Phil – he just appeared out of thin air!"

"He can't have."

"He did – I saw it with my own eyes!"

The Mole stepped forward, and Roads backed away, rising slowly from his crouch without moving the gun from its target.

"Don't move," he said, feeling like an idiot. "Put your hands behind your head and turn around."

The Mole kept coming until he was between Roads and the terminal. There was something about his face that kept Roads at bay – a terrible emptiness, a void of life that made him appear all the more dangerous. Like a reflection in a mirror about to shatter.

Roads shifted the gun to aim at the drive's power cable. The shot deafened him after the long silence, but the Mole didn't even flinch. The whirr of the drive ceased.

"I *said*, put your hands above your head and turn around."

The Mole didn't look at him, but did as he was told. Roads walked up behind him and cautiously reached out to pat for weapons.

"Be careful, Phil," said Goss. "He's smiling."

"He is? Well –"

He stopped in mid-sentence, puzzled, and stared at his hand. It lay on the Mole's side, apparently touching the fabric of a nylon coat. But it *felt* like cold stone.

"What the –?"

At his side, the terminal's VDU exploded.

Roads ducked down, a hand shielding his eyes as glass shards filled the air. The Mole pushed him off-balance and into the desk. He scrambled uselessly to regain his footing.

Ignoring the shouting in his ear, he rolled onto his back. The Mole loomed over him, arms outstretched. He fired twice, once above the left eye, once into the heart.

But the Mole kept coming, the bullets leaving no mark at all. Roads scrambled desperately away. The Mole pursued him, vicious canines sparkling moistly in the grey darkness, hands reaching out with fingers ending in inch-long claws.

Roads fired again, still to no avail. The Mole towered above him, poised to attack.

Suddenly, a noise from above startled them both. Roads looked up past the Mole's shoulder, at the skylight. It had swung back to hit the ceiling.

Roads kicked upward with both feet. The Mole staggered backward, becoming human again, and Roads stumbled to his feet, pointing the useless pistol at his dark half.

"Thank Christ," Roads muttered, not taking his eyes off the Mole. "But you took your goddamn time . . ."

The babbling voices coalesced, began to make sense.

"That's not us!" Barney was shouting. "It's not us!"

He risked another glance upward –

– into the eyes of a man he had never seen before in his life.

"Phil!"

Barney wanted to throw herself at the screen as Roads gaped up at the skylight. The entry alarm blared in her ears, Goss shouted instructions to the squad, the command centre filled with motion – but all she had eyes for was the screen in front of her.

The angle did not reveal what it was that Roads saw. His eyes widened, seemed to bulge slightly in the indistinct picture. She saw his gun-hand start to come up.

Before he could do anything, however, there was a flash of blinding, white light. The Mole vanished into it, disappearing as though he had never existed. Roads staggered backward with an arm over his eyes, his mouth open in an exclamation of pain and surprise.

Then an invisible force struck him on the chest and threw him across the room. He fell to the ground under an avalanche of books and didn't move.

Barney screamed her frustration at the screen.

Then the view unexpectedly shifted to the roof. The shadow – forgotten momentarily – had moved, triggering the security systems. Trading stealth for speed, it ran unbelievably fast away from the skylight toward the camera, crossing trip-wires as it came. Still too indistinct to be seen clearly, except as a silhouette, it ducked behind a wall and vanished from view.

Behind it, before the angle could change to another camera, the skylight exploded. Glass blew upward as though struck by an incomprehensible fist, followed by twisted pieces of metal flung free by the impact.

Barney stared in amazement, struggling to see what had caused the explosion. She had a glimpse of something indistinct turning in the air above the library's roof. Among the shards of the skylight, five shining points of light arrayed in a wide-spaced pentagon hung in the air, falling slowly like a ghostly snowflake. The array rotated, collapsing in upon itself as it fell. What it was, Barney couldn't guess: not fragments of glass, flung from the explosion of the skylight, or fireballs; the array's motion was independent of the rest of the rubble in the air, and far too ordered to be random . . .

Floodlights on the roof abruptly blazed into life, and the array vanished from sight.

Barney leapt to her feet and ran from the room, brushing past DeKurzak and O'Dell. Both stared at the screens with almost identical looks of astonishment on their faces.

INTERLUDE

1:15 a.m.

He ran, not caring where he was going at first as long as it was *away* . . .

He leapt from the roof of the library onto a nearby building, past the bodies of the guards he had knocked unconscious. Behind him, floodlights came on and something shattered, but he didn't stop to investigate. He kept to shelter where he could, relied on speed when he couldn't. The police issued from their nests like ants, but none of them saw him. If they did, he was gone before they could react.

Once he reached the wooded grounds, the going became easier. His long stride lengthened further, carrying him swiftly to the fence. Without worrying about triggering alarms this time, he climbed over it and sprinted for cover in the dark corners of the parklands.

The night enfolded him; the sharp adrenalin peak faded slightly. He allowed himself to slow his relentless pace for a moment. Not to rest, but to take stock and to decide where to go.

Only then did he realise that he was being followed.

He cursed his indecision and wove deeper into the undergrowth. If he hadn't followed Roads, hadn't felt compelled to watch instead of act, none of this would have happened. He should have approached the police officer, one way or another – he should have found out by more direct means whether or not it was him the police had been looking for two nights before. If he had known for sure, he could have taken action; he could have fled the city with Sanctuary while he had the chance. But instead he had watched them set their trap, waited for it to spring, and moved in to see what it was they had caught.

From his perch above the marble room, he had seen Roads confronting *himself*. The glimpse he'd had was enough to convince him that he wanted no part of it. He did not understand, and did not want to be given the opportunity to understand. It was beyond him.

Behind him, soft feet padded relentlessly, never gaining but never falling behind. He changed direction. The parklands petered out as he passed the innermost ring of the city's transportation network. He headed rapidly southward, the alleys and roads becoming narrower and darker as he entered a little-used quarter of the city. Brick buildings built after the War pressed in on all sides; his path wound at random through the gaps between them. As his desperation increased, his path become more tortuous. Even he would have been unable to retrace his steps.

But still the soft feet followed.

He had to do something.

He headed deeper into the darkness, toward the river and the maze of warehouses. The ways grew straighter and the distances between corners longer. At times he was able to glimpse the creature that followed him.

It looked like a wolf – the same wolf he had watched pacing the street outside Roads' house the previous night. Its cold, grey eyes were glazed, like marbles, but he could tell that it was watching him closely regardless.

Its gait was smooth and unhurried, as though it could overtake him whenever it wanted to. Why it didn't, he wasn't certain, but he knew he would rather die than lead it home, to Sanctuary, if that was what it wanted.

The harbour was full of dead-ends and intersections. He ran along the streets, seeking something suitable for what he had in mind, passing an endless succession of inviting doorways and jagged-tooth windows. He paused only once to grab a solid iron bar from a pile of refuse. Hefting it over his shoulder, he adjusted his balance to compensate for the extra weight and ran on.

A building of the sort he required eventually appeared: built before the War, an unstable mass of brick with a high, corrugated iron roof. He ducked inside and gripped the iron bar in both hands.

The warehouse was empty; endless rows of wooden posts no wider than one of his forearms supported the distant roof. He sprinted along its length, waiting for the wolf to enter the building behind him. When it did, he swung the iron bar with all his strength at every wooden post as he passed.

The posts were rotten with damp and age. They snapped easily – first one, then two, then half a dozen. He was halfway along the warehouse when the roof started to collapse, falling in a wave from the end at which he had entered. He snapped two more posts, then dropped the bar and ran.

He left the building just in time. Behind him, the roof collapsed with a sound like thunder. One of the walls fell with it. A cloud of dust rose into the sky, obscuring the street and the stars above.

He took shelter around a corner and waited.

The clatter of bricks and iron ceased as the wreckage settled. But he didn't allow himself to relax.

Something stirred under the rubble. A section of the roof shifted, and the dust swirled oddly as something emerged from beneath it.

It wasn't the wolf.

It was Roads. The *other* Roads.

And as he watched, caught between flight and fight, it took a step forward – and vanished. Again.

Something half-seen moved through the air towards him, casting no definite image in any spectrum.

He turned and fled as fast as he could. The game was over. He ran for his life.

The thing followed. It was like a mirage – flickering, inconstant and formless – and rapidly gaining.

He reached the pier with a bare second to spare. Legs pounding, he ran as far as he dared across the wood and concrete structure. If he left it an instant too late, it would be upon him.

Something swished at his neck – clutching for him, trying to drag him back –

He turned aside and leapt.

The water accepted his outstretched body with a heavy splash. He kicked powerfully, forced himself down and into the arms of the current. The river tugged him away from the pier, into deeper darkness.

He held his breath as long as he could before risking the surface. With just his mouth above the water, he sucked at air, then submerged again. He swam with strong, even strokes, putting as much open river between himself and the pier as he could.

When he finally stopped to look back, the pier was tiny in the distance. If his pursuer – whoever or whatever it was – was still watching, he could not see it.

Nevertheless, he trod the cold water for an hour before daring to head back to the shore, and to the threatening embrace of the city he had once called Peace.

CHAPTER TEN

10:00 a.m.

Roads regained consciousness to a feeling of utter disorientation. He lay on a narrow bed in a room that stank of disinfectant and metal. A headache stretched from the back of his neck to his forehead, unremitting and intolerant of even the slightest movement; his chest throbbed beneath the dulling effects of pain-killers. For a moment he thought he had been operated on, which took him back to his last hospital stay at the age of thirty-one. Then he realised that he wasn't attached to drips or monitors. He must have been injured instead, knocked unconscious – although he couldn't recall the last time *that* had happened at all . . .

He lay still for a minute before daring to open his eyes.

When he did, he discovered that he was in a ward of the RSD medical unit. The white ceiling stared at him like a rolled-back eyeball. A painting of a racehorse on one wall looked sorely out of place; there hadn't been a horse in Kennedy for as long as he could remember.

"Phil?"

He turned his head and immediately regretted it. Pain throbbed behind his right eye, nearly blinding him. A blonde blur sat in a chair beside the bed, watching him. "Shit . . . Barney, is that you?"

"Sure is, boss." She stood and came closer.

He tugged an arm out from beneath the covers and tried to look at his watch, but it was gone, a standard plastic bracelet with his name and an LCD display of his body temperature in its place. His hand and forearm were covered with tiny cuts and scratches. Much to his relief, none of them appeared to be bleeding.

"What time is it?"

"Ten past ten. You've been out about eight hours."

"Did I miss anything?"

"Plenty. But first, how are you feeling?"

"Like a building fell on me." He tried to sit, but the pain in his ribs was too excruciating. "What happened?"

"You don't remember?"

"I remember . . ." He thought for a moment. "Blindeye, yes, and the Mole. After that, it's a bit hazy."

"The Mole hit you." She frowned. "At least, we assume it was the Mole."

"Whoever it was sure packed a punch." He extended a hand and she helped him sit upright. When he started to slide his legs out of the bed, however, she stepped back in alarm.

"What do you think you're doing?"

"Getting up, or trying to. What does it look like?"

"You're hurt, Phil. You can't –"

"Bullshit. I can do whatever I want." He got his legs free of the covers, and reached out to steady himself as he levered his torso upward. Grey specks danced in front of his eyes; he did his best to ignore them. "See?"

"I'm getting a doctor."

He grabbed her arm and yanked her back, the effort making his ribs sing. "Don't, Barney. I haven't needed a doctor in forty years and don't plan on needing one now."

"Phil, I'm serious –"

"And so am I. Give me a pain-killer and get me home. I'll heal before you know it."

She looked doubtful. "I heard one of the doctors say you had a fractured skull and two broken ribs."

"What would they know? Did they take an X-ray?"

"I think so."

His gut turned to ice. "Did you see it?" The question blurted out before he had time to think.

"No, why?"

"It . . . doesn't matter." He took a deep breath to clear his head and flexed his feet, bracing himself for the big push. "Officer Daniels, as your senior in both rank and years, I *order* you to give me a hand."

She didn't relent. "Fuck you, Phil. I'm not having you die on me halfway down the hallway."

"Jesus Christ, Barney, I'm not –"

The door swung open and a white-uniformed nurse entered the room. With one glance she took in what was happening and, much to Roads' astonishment, smiled.

"Ah, you're up. Good." She moved closer and offered him a hand to get to his feet; puzzled, he accepted. "Director Chappel just called. She said to let you go whenever you felt like it."

"She did? Good old Margaret." Roads fought waves of pain that threatened to undermine his balance. "See, Barney? I told you I was better."

"What would the Mantis know?" She shook her head, washing her hands of the senior administration. "I give in."

The nurse handed Barney a bag containing Roads' clothes and personal effects, and pressed a carton of tablets into her hand. "Two every two hours, for the pain. Would you like a wheelchair, Officer Roads?"

"No, I'll be fine." He took a step and changed his mind. "Um, on second thoughts. Barney, could you –?"

She put an arm around him and helped support his weight as they slowly left the room. The end of the corridor looked kilometres away.

Barney chuckled darkly to herself as the nurse attended to her patients elsewhere.

"What?" he snapped.

"Did I tell you how glad I am to see you alive?"

"No. How glad *are* you?"

"At the moment, you old shit, not very."

The medical unit was in an annexe of RSD HQ, reached by two elevators and an endless maze of corridors from the main operations building.

Roads, although he felt his balance improve with every step, almost didn't make the distance to his office. The pain in his chest and head was incredible.

Barney berated him every step of the way, beginning with a list of all the things that could have been wrong with him and ending with a repeated complaint that he was goddamn heavy.

"This macho shit drives me crazy, Phil – from you of all people."

"It isn't macho shit. Honest."

"Then what is it?"

"Nothing. I just need to keep moving, that's all."

"Whatever; shit by any other name still stinks." She shifted his arm to a more comfortable position. "Do you know what concussion is? It's when your brain bounces around inside your skull, banging against bone and sloshing in its fluid like an ice-cube in a drink. It can result in a coma – even death. Did you know that, Phil?"

"Yes, Barney."

"Well, if you go into a coma, I'm just going to leave you here."

"Fine, but push me out of the way so no-one steps on me first. Okay?"

He grunted his way to the first elevator and let gravity do the work from there. His insides seemed to have successfully rearranged themselves by the time the carriage came to a halt.

The next leg of the journey to his office was slightly easier. He didn't have to rely as much on Barney's support, although her arm stayed where it had been, ostensibly to guide him in the right direction or to catch him if he stumbled.

"You smell nice, Barney."

"I very much doubt it."

"You're right." He sniffed. "You've been busy. Fill me in on what I missed."

She grudgingly described the events as she had seen them: Roads' confrontation with the Mole; the flash of light and the thief's disappearance; the sudden flight of the Shadow on the roof; the destruction of the skylight.

He winced. "Add that to the bill. What happened then?"

"We arrived to pick up the pieces." Goss' team had appeared on the scene in time to be showered by broken glass. No-one had entered or left the building from that point onward without passing a dozen armed security guards. Roads' unconscious body had been examined, placed on a stretcher and removed. Meanwhile, a trail of alarms and infringements had traced a path from the library to the university fence, where it had ended. RSD had made a thorough search of the area, but found nothing. The Shadow had escaped, as had the Mole.

"At least no data was stolen," he commented.

"Thank God for small mercies."

Barney had walked to the medical unit at four in the morning to check on Roads' condition, and managed to catch a couple of hours sleep in an unused bed not far up the hall. When she'd woken, she had discovered that the chain of command had deserted her; everyone involved in Blindeye had delegated their authority to underlings who were too cautious to make radical decisions in their superiors' absence. Chappel had locked herself in her office and was refusing to take calls. Occasionally she appeared on her own initiative to offer direction: Roads' release from the medical unit was obviously an example of one such time; to contribute to the ongoing transfer of data from KCU back to the city's separate datapools was another. Otherwise, in the wake of the previous night, RSD was temporarily on hold.

"Good," he said. "That gives me a little more time."

"For what?"

"I want to run the tapes of Blindeye through an image processor; there must be something we missed, something the cameras picked up that we weren't looking for."

"Such as?"

He remembered the Mole's face – changing, becoming wolf-like before his very eyes – but refused to believe what he had seen. The power of invisibility he also denied. There had to be another explanation.

Events had been set in motion over which he had no control. Depending on Margaret's efforts in the next few hours, he might still have a chance.

"To be honest," he said in response to Barney's question, "I have no idea."

The second elevator was crowded with RSD officers in uniform. He kept his eyes fixed straight ahead and tried to ignore the fact that he was dressed only in a hospital gown. Thankfully, the ride was short-lived and, from there, the walk to his office relatively easy.

He unlocked it, went inside, and collapsed into his

chair with a heartfelt groan. Before Barney could take a seat, he waved for the bag.

"I'm going to change and get some rest. In the meantime, I want you to start with the image processor. Begin from when the Mole appeared, and work backward. I'll call you in a little while."

"Sure," she muttered.

"You don't have to," he added. "If you'd rather sleep."

"No, that's fine." She straightened her posture with an effort. "It'll give me something to do, on top of worrying about you."

"Don't. I'll be right as rain before you know it."

"Somehow, against all logic, I believe you." She turned to leave.

"And, Barney?"

"What?"

"Thanks. I really appreciate your help."

"I know." Her smile was like the dawn after a long, cold night. "What would you do without me?"

When Barney had gone, Roads put his feet up on the desk and tried to relax. Pulling a bottle of water from one of the drawers, he washed down one of the painkillers. After a while, the pain ebbed, and he was able to approach its causes more objectively.

The doctors were partly right: he had cracked three ribs on his left side, and one on his right; they burned within his bruised chest like rods of red-hot metal. The fracture of his skull he wasn't sure about, though; it seemed fairly intact, if tender, to his questing fingertips. A fair proportion of his exposed skin – face, hands and arms – had been scratched by broken glass; more nicks in a body already far from perfect.

Switching on his terminal, he called up the city's bulletin-board network and began to browse. Blindeye, thanks no doubt to the efforts of DeKurzak, had been kept out of the headlines; apart from a brief paragraph on the break-in at the university, it wasn't mentioned at all. After the usual pro- and anti-Reassimilation rhetoric, the major topic of the day was another disturbance in the harbour suburbs, which led automatically to calls for a crackdown on street-crime. Talk of building new penal plants to replace those already full, or reintroducing expulsion for antisocial elements, rarely went any further than talk – and for that Roads was glad. The city had already devolved a long way from the complex organism it had once been; if it became any more authoritarian in approach, without genuine reason, then it risked breaking apart entirely.

An hour passed quickly, and Roads began to feel a craving for sugar. Next to the bottle of water was a bar of dark chocolate he had been saving, which he opened and ate in its entirety. Afterward, he felt better. His wounds were already healing; the pain was tolerable.

He dressed carefully, keeping his chest as unconstricted as he could. As he did so, he tried to predict the path of the X-rays through the various levels of Kennedy administration. If they had been taken upon his arrival, then a doctor must have seen them and forwarded copies to Chappel. He bet himself that they were sitting on her desk at that very moment – hence her call. He was tempted to contact her, but decided against it. She was too involved as it was. What happened next depended entirely upon who else had seen the X-rays, and how long Chappel could hold them at bay. The wheels of bureaucracy turned slowly in Kennedy, especially with a determined shoulder to the brake.

He sat behind the desk and disconnected the computer from the mainframe. There was a band-aid on the back of his neck which he removed in order to attach the electrodes. He leaned back into the seat and concentrated, trying to remember exactly what had happened in the split-instant before the Mole had struck him.

Both he and the Mole had looked up. Then a flash of light had blinded him and, according to Barney, had heralded the Mole's sudden disappearance. What he had seen in the instant before that flash, however, he could not remember.

When he opened his eyes, the picture on the screen brought it all back.

The face, framed from the neck up by the open skylight, was brightly lit. He must have taken the tag a split-second before the explosion of light had peaked. The first thing that caught his eye, then and now, was the vivid, cherry-red colour of the man's skin. Hairless, with a strong jaw and straight nose, the man stared open-mouthed out of the screen; his teeth were even and grey, not white at all; his tongue was oddly narrow. But his eyes were his most unusual feature: a non-reflective grey, like his teeth, with a darker pinprick pupil. They were completely inhuman.

He stared at the face of the Shadow for five minutes, but it was no use; he did not recognise it. Had he seen anyone remotely like that in his life, he was sure he would have remembered.

He printed a hard copy and removed the electrodes. Sighing, he went to stand at the window to think. The day was overcast, threatening rain. The wooded grounds of the university were hidden behind the crooked backs and shining, upthrust arms of the city. Kennedy Polis resembled a mixed gathering of people – half reaching for the stars, half trying to burrow back into the earth. The marriage of architectural styles was not a comfortable one, but appropriately symbolic, he thought. While Reassimilationists voted to open the city to the world around it, conservatives discussed plans to dig for landfills to plunder that might have been missed by the first wave of metal-seeking bacteria. Another desperate attempt to avoid the inevitable, but one it seemed many felt in sympathy with.

On the street below, a demonstration paraded slowly by, waving banners protesting the Reassimilation. The voice of the crowd was muffled by the double-paned window, but he didn't really need to hear the words. After years of struggling to keep Kennedy isolated from a dangerous and uncertain environment, he could understand that some people were willing to fight in order to preserve the status quo. Even though the Mayoralty had officially decided that the Reassimilation would go ahead, or at least supported an end to isolation in principle, some Senior Councillors had expressed doubts. This core of hard-line isolationists occasionally encouraged protests like the one Roads was witnessing, although they never actually went so far as to defy the Mayor outright, or even lend their name in open support of the protesters. None of them, in Roads' opinion, was the sort to kill their colleagues in order to change the Council's mind – but he had been surprised before by how desperately people fought to preserve even a non-viable status quo.

Still, he had trouble comprehending the motives of the anti-Reassimilation movement – and the killer in particular. It all seemed so simple to him. There was a point beyond which the fight for self-determinism became self-defeating. The only difficulty arose in defining where that point lay. In his opinion, the city had passed it six weeks ago, when the RUSA envoy had arrived. Reassimilation was an easy alternative to a painful, lingering death – the city's certain fate if it never opened its gates again.

The few doubts he had concerned the RUSA itself: its long-term goals, its aspirations. While it was all very well to open Kennedy in order to gain much-needed resources, it might not be so clever to thereby shackle the city's fate to that of an aggressive military machine. If the RUSA ever went to war, as aggressor or defender, Kennedy would presumably be required to fight alongside it. Whether that was likely or not, Roads had no way of knowing. He didn't even know if there *were* other nations on the North American continent, let alone ones that might be capable of fighting the RUSA.

Behind him, the door opened, interrupting his thoughts. Roads cursed himself for not locking it, and glanced into the window to see who it was.

"I'm sorry to bother you," said Antoni DeKurzak.

"What do you want?" asked Roads without turning around, already feeling defensive. He had little chance of avoiding the position of scapegoat awaiting him, but he would be damned if he went down without a fight.

The liaison officer raised a hand, as though to ward off an attack. "Margaret told me you were up and about. I thought I'd see how you were feeling before I went."

Roads turned and stared at him suspiciously, but could detect no sign of deception. For once DeKurzak seemed off-guard, even vulnerable.

"Thanks," he said, making an effort to soften his tone. "I've had better days, but I'll live. You?"

DeKurzak leaned against the door frame. "Likewise. I've got a meeting with the Mayor later. Not something I'm looking forward to, to be honest."

"Yeah. Sorry about that."

"That's okay, Phil. You gave Blindeye your best shot, and I'll be sure to point that out to the Mayor. It wasn't your fault, after all, that someone tipped the Mole off, or that he wasn't working alone."

Roads shrugged. He wasn't sure DeKurzak's analysis of the situation was correct, but was prepared to let the matter go for the time being. Full marks for enthusiasm, anyway. "Perhaps. I haven't had time to analyse what happened. Maybe when I have, we'll be able to say exactly what went wrong."

"I sincerely hope so." DeKurzak sighed heavily. "This assignment is much harder than I thought it would be. Maybe I should have turned it down and gone back to Records . . ."

"Don't be too hard on yourself," said Roads. "You're young and relatively inexperienced. That's nothing to be ashamed of."

"I guess not." DeKurzak shrugged. "But the fact remains: we *have* to catch the Mole." Suddenly animated, the liaison officer took two steps into the room. "I can't stress highly enough how important it is to close this case. Our relationship with the Reunited States, and therefore the future of the city, depends upon it. That may seem like an overstatement, but believe me, it's not. We're hardly in a strong bargaining position, at the moment, and we must fight for every advantage we can get."

The dark circles around DeKurzak's eyes stopped Roads from protesting that he wasn't stupid. Instead he said: "I understand what you're saying, and can assure you that we're doing everything possible."

"I know." DeKurzak turned his face aside, as though realising that he had stated his case too emotively. "We have to prove that we can manage our own affairs before they'll even consider leaving our present infrastructure intact. Blindeye's failure leaves us in a very vulnerable position, and the longer the Mole remains free –"

DeKurzak stopped with a sharp intake of breath. One hand rose to point at the screen on Roads' desk.

"What the hell is *that*?" DeKurzak asked.

Roads moved from the window. The Shadow's inhuman face stared out of the screen back at him.

"I took it last night," he said, wishing he had been more careful. "It's the man we saw on the roof."

"Do you know who it is?" DeKurzak's face had become suddenly pale.

"No. Do you?"

"No, of course not. If you hadn't told me otherwise I would have guessed it came from the archives – one of the aberrations from the old days." The liaison officer shuddered. "It's *disgusting*."

Roads studied DeKurzak, surprised at the vehemence of his reaction. The face of the Shadow was startling, yes, but not that horrifying, for all its differences from the norm. Then he remembered that DeKurzak had probably never seen such drastic biomodification before. From the viewpoint of someone born after the War, the Shadow did look demonic – a pure corruption of humanity, worse even than the berserkers, who had at least retained a passing resemblance to the rest of the human race.

DeKurzak blinked and wrenched his eyes away from the screen, back to Roads. "You'll let me know when you find out who it is, won't you? We can't have things like that in the city when General Stedman arrives."

"Of course not."

"Good."

DeKurzak left hurriedly, leaving the door open behind him. Roads closed it, not surprised by the liaison officer's parting comment. Given the RUSA's firm stand on biomods, the presence of such a "thing" would not look good at all for Kennedy Polis. Worse even than an uncaught thief.

Roads saved the picture, reconnected the computer and called Barney. Her face appeared in the screen, a picture of industry in miniature.

"You've been off-line," she chided. "I tried to call you several times."

"I was resting," he lied. "You've found something already?"

"Something weird. Do you want to come down here?"

"No. I'm not up to the exercise just yet."

"Okay. I'll bring coffee. Give me five minutes."

The line went dead, and he settled back to wait. Rather than dwell on the issues DeKurzak had raised – ones he himself had already considered – he drew up a list of the unknown quantities confronting him. How they fit into the equation was still beyond him, but at least he was beginning to know the right questions to ask. Five mysteries requiring, possibly, a single solution:

(1) The man in the hat and coat last seen fleeing from Old North Street. A coincidence, or significant?

(2) The items removed from 114 Old North Street: three of part-number EPA44210. What they were he still had no idea.

(3) The timber wolf. Until Blindeye, he had considered the animal to be irrelevant; since its appearance on the university grounds, he was no longer sure of that.

(4) The man on the roof of the KCU library, tentatively labelled 'the Shadow'. That he had followed Roads was alone sufficient grounds for suspicion. That plus the fact that he was clearly – radically – biomodified.

(5) The Mole himself. Roads' fingertips still tingled from the brief moment he had actually touched his

adversary. He remembered the cold most of all – possibly a side-effect of the method the Mole was using to make himself invisible. Whatever *that* was.

As was often the case with apparently unsolvable crimes, Roads suspected that one isolated piece of information was all he required to solve the mystery; it was just a matter of time before he found it. Time, or, as he had told O'Dell the previous day, unbelievably good fortune.

Blindeye, far from solving anything, had brought the matter to a head. An end was at last in sight, if not the end he had originally hoped for. Reassimilation would make certain of that.

Even without Reassimilation . . . He glanced at his watch. The fact that DeKurzak had not brought up the matter of the X-rays was a good sign, although not one he could rely on for long. He probably had less than twenty-four hours in which to solve the case or face the retribution of the city – a day at most before the call came, and that long only if he was lucky, or the Mayor was in a good mood.

I can't stress highly enough how important it is to close this case, DeKurzak had said. No mention at all of the killer. Whatever was going on in the Mayoralty – whatever made the Mayor so uneasy about keeping the city secure – seemed to revolve predominantly around the thief. But why? Why not the person or persons behind eighteen dead Councillors?

Roads had a horrible feeling that one day wasn't going to be long enough.

CHAPTER ELEVEN

1:30 p.m.

The RSD image processing algorithm was similar to that employed by a simple motion-detector. Of a given segment of video footage, one control frame was selected and used as a reference to check all subsequent frames for discrepancies. If an object moved into view, or if one that had been there previously changed position, the program noted the differences and informed the user. The only difference between the image processing program and the motion-detectors employed in Operation Blindeye was finesse; the IP program was considerably more discerning than its outmoded sibling.

"There," said Barney, pointing at the screen. It showed a section of a hallway on the library's ground floor. To Roads' eyes, it seemed completely unremarkable, and he told her so.

"That's what I thought, at first. You have to know what you're looking for before you see it." She rewound the recording and pointed again. "Watch the bottom left corner, where the skirting board meets the door frame."

The scene jerked back into life, and Roads watched obediently.

"Are you sure you've got the right stretch of tape?" he asked after a few seconds. "I still can't see anything but wall."

"Okay." She sighed. "We'll try again. This time, don't look for something concrete; keep your eye on the boundary between the skirting board and the wall itself."

"Gotcha. Don't look for something, but *any*thing – or possibly the other way around."

"Clear as mud. Ready?"

He nodded, and the recording began for the third time. He kept his eyes firmly fixed on the point she had indicated, but again saw nothing out of the ordinary.

"Either I've got rocks in my head, or –"

"Wait." She pointed at the screen. "There!"

He saw it: a slight dimpling of the picture, like a reflection in a warped mirror. The distinct edge of the skirting board deviated from horizontal for an instant, then snapped back into shape – as though a curved, glass lens, a hand's-width in diameter, had passed between it and the camera.

"Take it back." She did so. The effect was subtle; he could see no hard edges to define the area of distortion. "Could it be a glitch in the recording?"

"It's not."

"Sure?"

"Positive." She killed the view of the corridor and produced another image. He faced an entrance to a ventilation shaft; the duct opened onto a maintenance corridor in the library's rear and had no grill. The edge of the duct shifted in a similar fashion to the skirting board.

"I don't suppose you have any idea . . . ?"

She shook her head.

"I didn't think so." He rubbed a hand across his eyes. "Did you find anything else?"

She summoned a map of the library. "The dimple doesn't always show on the tape – you can't see it against a blank wall, for instance – but the IP program picks it up often enough to plot an approximate path through the building." She pointed, tracing a line from the basement toilets, up a stairwell, along a corridor, to the ventilation shaft and, finally, into the reading room. "*Voilà*."

"Whatever it is, it went right by us." He shook his head in disbelief. "Right under our noses, and we didn't even see it."

"That's not quite true. Do you remember just before the Shadow appeared on the roof, when David picked up a few 'small movements'? One of them was the door to the basement toilets. It moved slightly, as though a breeze had blown it open."

"But it wasn't a breeze."

"Evidently not. The tape shows the . . . *that* . . . going through the door quite clearly, once you know what to look for."

"Shit." He ran a hand through his hair. "But how did it get into the toilets in the first place? Are you going to tell me it was there all the time?"

"If the Shadow set off the alarm at Emergency Services, then it might have been – although that means someone must have known about Blindeye before we started setting up that morning."

"I don't want to think along those lines."

"Neither do I, but the only other entrance is via the sewers."

"And I think we can rule that out."

She let him ponder what she had found for a moment before calling up another image: Roads in the reading room, reaching out a hand to grab the power cable of the data fiche drive.

"I haven't shown you the best bit yet."

He groaned. "Go on."

"Okay. Look over your left shoulder when I run the tape."

He nodded, and she set it going at half speed. Predictably, the glitch glided into view from behind a bookshelf and drifted toward him. It grew larger, suggesting that it was getting closer, then became the Mole.

The transition was almost instantaneous. First the thief wasn't there, then he was. It looked like magic.

"A cloak of invisibility?" Roads suggested, only half believing it himself. "Some sort of gadget that can bend light around him, but not completely – hence the 'dimpling' effect?"

"Maybe. He'd get through the trip-wires that way."

"Easy."

"But you're forgetting infra-red –"

"No, it masks that too."

"– and his mass. The dimple passed over a number of pressure-sensitive pads without setting them off."

"He jumped over them."

"Don't be ridiculous, Phil."

"Have you got a better idea?"

"'Better' isn't the word I'd use." Her face was clouded as her hands moved over the keyboard, calling up an image of the Mole in mid-transformation. The thief's teeth looked longer than Roads remembered, and he hadn't noticed the subtle shift in posture. The Mole looked hunchbacked in the picture, crouched over a quailing Roads.

"Are you trying to tell me something?"

"I'm not sure, Phil." Next she produced an image of the five points of light she had seen emerging through the shattered skylight. That, in turn, reminded Roads of the recording Morrow had given him, of the Mole's image in infra-red: five points at throat, nipples and hips.

"A pentagram," said Barney, "often associated with werewolves, has five points."

"Don't be ridiculous. That's impossible."

"Less impossible than a cloak of invisibility?" She shrugged. "Weirder things have happened. Just *look* at him; have you seen someone do that before?"

"No, and I refuse to believe it. The Mole is not a werewolf."

"But what if he thinks he is?"

The small joke didn't raise a smile. "Besides, werewolves can't make themselves invisible."

"Can't they? Have you ever asked one? Maybe that explains why they've never been seen."

"Don't be a smartarse." He scowled furiously, even as he remembered his earlier "ghost" theory and his comment to Chappel that he was ready to believe anything. "There has to be another explanation."

"Right. Let me know when you find it," she said. "Look, I hate admitting this as much as you do, but I've got the creeps. The Mole can change his shape at will, can even become invisible whenever he wants to. We all saw him do it, but no-one can explain *how* he did it. If he's not a werewolf or whatever, then what the hell *is* he?"

"Better than us, that's all. His behaviour seems incredible, yes, but all we have to do is work out how he's doing it, what he's *using*, and it'll make sense. Trust me."

"That's what you said two days ago."

He was about to snap back a response when the intercom on his desk buzzed.

"Officer Roads?" The voice belonged to the secretary he shared with the other senior officers on the fifth-floor switchboard.

Roads tsked in annoyance. "What is it, Marion?"

"I know you said you didn't want to be interrupted, but there's somebody down at reception who simply won't go away."

"Who?"

"She won't say."

"What does she want?"

"To see you. All she'll tell me is that it's in connection with the incident on Old North Street."

Roads sighed and reached for another pain-killer. He didn't have time to waste on extraneous details – but he couldn't afford to turn away anyone who might have information relating to the case.

"Officer Roads?"

"Okay, Marion. Have her escorted up to my office."

"Yes, sir."

He swigged from the bottle of water and swallowed the tablet.

Barney shifted uncomfortably in her seat. "Do you want me to stick around?"

"If you like. We'll continue this conversation later." He switched off the screen, and the image of the bestial Mole vanished. "That's a promise."

The girl was Katiya, the one with the missing boyfriend. Roads let her in, dismissed the escort, and told her to take a seat. She sank into the chair, glancing nervously around the room.

"Coffee?" asked Roads. The woman nodded, and he buzzed for some via the intercom.

"Thanks for coming, Katiya," said Barney, smiling encouragingly.

"That's okay," she said. "If I can help in any way, it'll be worth it."

The coffees arrived. As Katiya took hers, the sleeve of her grey T-shirt rose a few centimetres and Roads caught a glimpse of her inner arm. It was pock-marked with tiny scars.

"I understand you have some information for us," he prompted.

The woman shifted in her seat. "I remembered something last night. It may not be relevant, but I thought you might like to know."

"What was that?"

"The house you were investigating – number 114? It used to receive deliveries after curfew."

Roads glanced at Barney. "What sort of deliveries?"

"I don't know, exactly. Every now and again, a truck would pull up outside. A couple of men would unload it and take stuff inside. Most of it was in crates, but occasionally I'd see something strange. They were unloading machines; not drugs or anything, just machines."

"What sort of machines?"

"I couldn't tell; it was always dark. They weren't weapons, if that's what you're thinking." Katiya hesitated for an instant, then added: "Some of the crates had been burnt in places, as though they'd been in a fire. I don't know whether that means anything or not."

"Maybe." Roads made a note on a pad. "How about the men? Would you be able to give us a description?"

Her response was instantaneous: "No. I never got a good look at them."

"And the truck? Did it have any markings?"

"Sorry. It was just a truck, like the ones they use down at the plants – but not one of them, if you know what I mean."

"I do." Roads *did* understand: it was dangerous to talk too openly in her neighbourhood. "Anything else?"

"No, that's all. Does it help?"

"It might." Even without a clear ID, she had given him something to consider: it now seemed likely that the stolen EPA44210s were parts of machines of some sort, as Morrow's description had implied. Whether that knowledge helped in the long run remained to be seen.

Katiya folded her hands tightly in her lap, the thumbs of each hand worrying at her knuckles. "Good," she said, clearly waiting for his next move.

Roads weighed his options. He could continue questioning her, probably without success, or he could find out whether she wanted anything in return.

"Well," he said, trying to sound casual. "Thanks for coming in. I'll see what I can do about getting you a lift home, if you like."

She leaned forward. "Not yet. I . . . I need to ask you a favour."

He retreated into the chair. "We don't pay for information, if that's what you want."

"No, I don't mean money." One hand rubbed absently at the scars under her arm, and Roads decided that they were old, symptoms of a past addiction.

"What, then?"

"I'd like to file a missing-person report."

"Your boyfriend hasn't come back?" Barney asked.

Katiya shook her head, scattering her long, dark hair. "No, and I'm starting to get worried. Really worried. He's never done this before."

Barney cast Roads a glance that clearly said: *I told you so*.

Roads switched on the terminal and called up the missing-person menu. Filing such reports was a simple process and wouldn't take more than five minutes.

"Okay." He glanced at her over the screen. "We need your name, first."

"Just Katiya."

He typed it in. "Occupation?"

"I, uh, work in a reclamation plant. Plastics."

"Address?"

"116 Old North Street. I don't have a phone, or a news terminal."

Roads noted the number. The woman had lied about living next door to the house the Mole had broken into. She must have gone elsewhere temporarily to evade the patrol he had sent to check that she'd left. "Your boyfriend's name?"

"Cati." She spelt it for him.

"Is that his real name?" The name sounded familiar, although Roads didn't know why. An automatic word-search through the latest population census revealed nothing.

She shrugged. "I think so. It was written on some of his clothes when I first met him, so I just assumed . . ."

"He never told you otherwise?"

"No." The faint smile reappeared. "But that's because he can't speak. He's mute."

Roads glanced at Barney, who raised an eyebrow. He jotted a note under the Description column.

"Can you think of any reason why he'd leave?"

"None. We're happy together, and I don't think he'd manage very well without me." She looked embarrassed. "We rely on each other an awful lot, and we don't have any friends."

Roads could sense her loneliness and felt sorry for her. To be so dependent on another person that life would crumble without them was a fate he had successfully avoided most of his life.

"I understand," he said. "I don't suppose you thought to bring a photo?"

"No. I don't have one."

"Okay. We'll patch together a verbal description, then. Where and when did you last see him, and what was he wearing?"

"Three nights ago. We went to bed together, but when I woke up the next morning, he was gone. I guess he'd be wearing what he always wears when he goes out. He has this floppy grey hat and a really old overcoat that I keep trying to throw out. And sunglasses, even if it's night . . ."

The expression on Roads' face brought her to a halt. Barney, too, was staring.

"What is it?" asked Katiya. "Have you seen him?"

"Wait," said Roads. "Three nights ago" was the night he and Barney had met Keith Morrow. He tapped at the keyboard for a moment, then turned the screen to face her. It showed the picture of the man Roads had chased from Old North Street: the huge figure, the hat and coat, and half a profile. "Is this him?"

Katiya's face fell. "He's mixed up in something, isn't he?"

Roads hastened to placate her, trying to keep the excitement welling in him under control. "We don't know for sure whether he's involved or not, Katiya, but we have to take a physical description. At the very worst . . . and I don't want to frighten you unnecessarily . . . we might need it to identify his body."

She took a deep breath and didn't meet his eyes. "He's big, and very strong. You know that already. What else would you like?"

"Does he have any distinctive marks?"

"A tattoo on his left thigh – not a picture, just numbers – and a scar on his back, across his shoulder blades. Apart from that, nothing, except for his skin itself."

Roads leaned forward. "His skin? What about his skin?"

"It's red. As though he's been scalded." She looked at him closely. "Why?"

"Nothing." He felt light-headed. "What colour is his hair?"

"He doesn't have any, anywhere. Not even eyelashes." She hesitated, and he could tell that there was more she wasn't going to tell him.

"What will you do if you find him?" she asked.

"That depends on the circumstances," he said by rote, trying to conceal his elation while he tapped the information into the computer. This was more than he could possibly have hoped for. "Unless we have good cause, he'll be free to go. As his partner, you'll be notified, of course – either way."

"Thank you." She glanced at Barney. "I hope I'm not being too much trouble."

"Not at all." Roads stood. "I owed you one anyway, for what you told me."

Barney showed her to the door, opened it.

"Wait." Roads gestured apologetically, as though he had just remembered something. "One last question, Katiya – something I should have asked you earlier."

She turned in the doorway. "Yes?"

"What colour are Cati's eyes?"

"Grey," she said. "And black."

He smiled widely. "Thanks. That's all I need to know."

She opened her mouth, as though about to speak, but turned away and disappeared up the hallway without looking back.

Barney closed the door and returned to her seat, where she leaned back with her legs crossed.

"So," she said. "Cati is the man from Old North Street. The description of his appearance matches almost perfectly."

"He's much more than that." Despite the aches and pains of his body, Roads had begun to feel good about the day at last. "His description matches that of the Shadow on the library roof."

Barney frowned. "How do you figure that?"

"Red skin, grey-black eyes and no hair." He could no longer suppress a grin of triumph. "That's the face I saw looking back at me through the skylight."

"Through the . . .? So *that's* what you saw. Why didn't you tell me?"

The lie came all too easily: "Because I wasn't certain my recollection was accurate."

"And you've let her go?" She leaned forward, half out of the chair. "He's her boyfriend, for God's sake! She must be worth holding for interrogation, if nothing else."

He held up a hand. "She doesn't know anything more than she told us. I'd bet money on it. She's just a frightened girl afraid that her boyfriend's in an awful lot of trouble."

"He might well be, Phil."

"But not for the reason you think."

She frowned. "I don't understand."

"Cati is biomodified."

Realisation dawned. "And she thinks we're after him because of that. Of course she would."

"He is both mute and physically intimidating. He looks worse than a berserker, and wouldn't stand a chance of defending himself before a Humanity court. He'd be expelled from the city for sure, or killed outright."

"So why did she come to *us*?"

"Because she wants to find him, first and foremost, and to discover how much we know. I don't think we've put her mind at rest on either score, but at least she's done something. It'll make her feel better, having tried."

Barney collapsed back into her seat. It was clear that she was unsatisfied with his reasoning, but he could give her nothing more.

"So what do we do now?" she asked.

"I want a stake-out on her building just in case Cati comes home. If we can haul him in, we might find out exactly what he was doing last night."

"Right. I'll organise it straight away."

"And then you can help me look through the datapools."

"For?"

"Anything." He went back to the screen of Katiya's Missing Persons report. "His name rings a bell, but I don't know why."

"A hunch?"

"Maybe. I don't think he's the Mole, but he's certainly involved. He'll lead us somewhere, I'm sure of it."

"You bloodhound, you. Half a sniff and your tail starts to wag." She smiled. "The resemblance between you and the Mole obviously goes deeper than I thought."

He pointed at the door, and she took the hint.

CHAPTER TWELVE

4:45 p.m.

He sent the report identifying Cati to Data Processing, where it would be put onto the daysheets for the attention of the next shift. He doubted the prompt would produce any results, but figured it was worth a try. Then he logged into Kennedy's central datapool and began to browse.

His first line of inquiry hit a brick wall within half an hour. The name 'Cati' had no reference anywhere in the files he pulled, except for one misspelled word in an old street directory. Next he scanned an alphabetical list of every name on record, but found nothing between Cathy and Catic.

If Cati was not officially listed among Kennedy's two million citizens, then trying to find him by inference would be like looking for one grain of sand in a salt-shaker by touch alone. Without a genetic sample to cross-reference through the population records, that avenue was closed.

Giving up on Cati for the time being, he moved to the Mole. Barney's 'weirder things have happened' theory didn't hold water as far as he was concerned, but he had to consider it regardless. He called up a file on were-wolves and skimmed through it to the end. Most of it was hearsay and legend, with a brief mention of the pop-culture that had grown around the myth during the mid-twentieth and early twenty-first centuries. The only thing he learned that he didn't already know was that there *had* been werewolf sightings reported to RSD since the War, but none more recent than two years earlier.

That left the cloak of invisibility, and another long shot.

He buzzed the switchboard.

"Marion? See if you can track down O'Dell. I don't know where he is, but I need to talk to him ASAP."

"Yes, sir." She returned a moment later: "He's tied up in a meeting. I can't break in."

"Okay. Leave an urgent message for him to call me as soon as he's free, will you?"

"Certainly."

He killed the intercom and glanced at his watch; time was running away from him. If the origins of both the Mole and Cati had eluded him temporarily, then he hoped that their motives would not.

Calling up a new notepad on the screen, he drew a series of circles linked by arrows in an attempt to organise his thoughts:

(1) CATI → ROADS → MOLE

Cati must have been following Roads during the preparation for Blindeye in order to know how to side-step the trip-wires on the roof of the library; Roads had been after the Mole for six weeks. The progression was smooth and simple, but not entirely self-explanatory. The Mole had also been trailing Roads – at least to the extent of breaking into his house every now and again – so that meant another arrow. And Roads, with the information given to him by Katiya, was now chasing Cati, giving:

(2) MOLE → ROADS → CATI
(1) CATI → ROADS → MOLE

The immediate temptation was to link each Cati/Mole pair with its own arrow, if only for the sake of symmetry. The simplicity, however, was deceptive. If the Mole and Cati were independent, then it was entirely possible that they were acting at odds with each other, with the question of motive unresolved. As far as he knew, Cati might be nothing more than an innocent bystander tangled in the web of the Mole's erratic exploits; or he was yet another player in the game of Catch the Mole. To suppose that both Cati and the Mole were after each other as well as Roads seemed ludicrous.

What made more sense was:

ROADS ↔ MOLE & CATI

It not only simplified the equation, but made his task a little less daunting. Supposing that Cati and the Mole were on the same team – maybe a team fraught with its own internal problems – meant that he only had one mystery to solve instead of several. If he could track down one correct solution, then the others would quickly follow.

His terminal flashed. It was Barney.

"The stake-out's organised."

"Good."

"What would you like me to do now?"

"That depends on how tired you are."

She shrugged. "I'll cope. If you think we're close to something, I'll work until I drop."

"I don't think it'll come to that, but thanks for the offer. I'm about to send you a file containing everything we know about the case, including some stuff I haven't told anyone about. Hunches, guesses, wild stabs in the dark – that sort of thing."

"Understood. And?"

"I want you to strip it bare, reduce it to as small a list of nouns as possible. Names, places, numbers, anything you think has an outside chance of being relevant."

"You want to run a search through a datapool?"

"Yes, but not just any datapool. I have something a little more dramatic in mind. A last-ditch effort."

"Do you want to tell me what we're looking for?"

"I would if I knew." He ran a hand across his ribs, fighting the urge to take another tablet. "Our problem is that we have too much unconnected information. We need to trim it back to a solid core of data from which we can extrapolate our way outward. As it is, I feel like I'm drowning – with werewolves, redskins and politicians pushing me under."

"I know what you mean." She brushed away a strand of blonde hair that had fallen across her eyes. "I'll get onto it as soon as you send the file."

"Thanks, Barney." Another icon flashed at him from the corner of the screen. "Gotta go. Call waiting."

He waved and killed the line. A second face appeared in place of hers.

"Hello, Phil," said Keith Morrow.

"Shit. Give me a second." Roads closed the office door and locked it, then regretted moving from the chair. "Ouch – sorry. What the hell are you doing, calling me here?"

Morrow tilted his head to one side, feigning hurt. "My, we're paranoid today, aren't we?"

"Not without good reason. I'm in trouble enough without my shady connections putting in an unexpected appearance."

"This line is secure. You can rest easy."

Roads tugged a cigarette from his pocket. "I hoped you'd say that. What can I do for you, or is this just a social call?"

Morrow leaned forward; a virtual light source cast deep shadows in his eye-sockets. "I've called to give you a warning, Phil. You may be in deeper trouble than you realise."

Roads drew a deep, smoky breath. "In what way?"

"You've stepped on someone's toes, Phil – heavily enough for them to want you dead."

"Who?"

"I can't tell you."

"Why?"

"I can't tell you that either."

"Then what *can* you tell me?"

"That there's a price on your head. A big one. It went on the market fifteen minutes ago."

Roads scratched absently at the stubble on his chin, trying to think who might want to kill him that wasn't able to do so themselves. Not the Mole, or Cati; he wasn't a match for either of them, and he was sure they knew it. It had to be someone else, someone who wanted to keep his or her hands relatively clean of Roads' death.

Someone he was obviously getting close to, without knowing it.

He smiled. "Thanks, Keith. That's the best news I've had all day."

"I'm glad you think so." The Head leaned back. "Can I assume, then, that the information I gave you the other night has been of use?"

"I think you can, yes. Is there anything you'd like to add?"

"Nothing that appears to be relevant. Someone vandalised one of the old buildings at the harbour last night, but I can't see how that would connect with your investigation. We get a lot of that sort of thing down our way. An occupational hazard, if you will."

Roads nodded, remembering the article he had read about the disturbance. The harbour – being a meeting place for all manner of criminals, from drug-addict to bounty-hunter – was often transformed into a battlefield for rival interests. Morrow's main role was as mediator, not instigator. The relative stability of Kennedy as a whole owed more than a little to the paths of communication the Head established and maintained in the underclass. This, Roads supposed, was why the Head would not reveal the identity of his would-be killer: thief's honour, or something similar.

A thought struck him: "What about Barney?"

"Your friend is safe. The contract is only for you."

"Good. Let me know if anything else turns up, won't you?"

"I will if I can." Morrow winked farewell. "Good luck."

"Thanks."

Roads extinguished the cigarette and reached for a pain-killer. It was all very well knowing he was close, but, without knowing what he was close to, it didn't really help. Was it DeKurzak's Old Guard, the Mayor's machinating RUSA, or someone else entirely? And how did they relate to the Mole/Cati dyad?

The matter of the contract itself did not greatly concern him; it would probably be a while before someone took the offer, and he could look after himself when the time came. He hoped. It was just not knowing who was behind it that bothered him.

He took Morrow's data fiche and added it to the official RSD file on the Mole, then sent the whole package to Barney. Barely had he completed that task when his terminal buzzed again.

This time it was Margaret Chappel. She looked frustrated and tired, as though she hadn't slept since the night before Blindeye – which, he supposed, she probably hadn't.

"How are you feeling, Phil?"

"Still a little sore." He tossed the tablet idly in one hand. The pain was returning, but nowhere near as severe as it had been earlier. "Looks like I'll live."

"Good. Any progress?"

He hesitated, then told her about Morrow's warning.

She shook her head, half-smiling. "And you take that as a positive sign?"

"It's the best I've had so far."

"Fair enough. Have you written a report?"

"Not yet, no."

"Then, without intending to seem callous, let me advise you not to waste your time. David's will be enough, if DeKurzak's corroborates it."

He let the advice sink in for a moment before replying: "That bad, huh?"

"Let's just say I'm doing the best I can to slow things down."

"How long do you think?"

"I may be able to stretch it until after Reassimilation, but I doubt it. It depends entirely on what sort of report DeKurzak submits."

"In that case, maybe it won't be so bad after all."

She looked surprised. "That's not what I expected you to say."

"I saw him this afternoon. He said he'd tell the Mayor it's not my fault Blindeye went so wrong."

"Well, well. That *is* interesting. I'll only believe it when I see it, though."

"I think you're underestimating him, Margaret. He's in a difficult position, stuck between the RSD and MSA, but he's genuinely trying to do his job – a job he didn't really want in the first place."

"Did he say that?" Chappel's eyebrows went up. "Don't let him fool you, Phil. He campaigned quite vigorously to get this assignment."

Roads mulled this over. "That's not the impression I got. Anyway, bad luck happens to everyone. Even me. No-one will deny that I'm one of the best officers in RSD."

"But what happens when he finds out *why* you're so good?"

"You and I both know that's irrelevant. I do my best, like anybody else."

"The Mayor might not see it that way."

"Then he's an idiot."

"And you're in trouble."

"I know." Roads tried to look nonchalant. "Listen, Margaret, I'm *already* in trouble. The Mayor wants my arse because Blindeye fucked up; somebody else wants my arse because I'm getting close to the Mole; if DeKurzak wants my arse too, then he'll just have to join the queue."

Chappel smiled. "You have a point."

"Yes, but what I don't have is time. I'll have to call you back later."

"Or I'll call you when word comes down from above."

"Fingers crossed I'll get in first."

He cut the line and reached into the drawer for the bottle of water. His palms were sweating profusely, and the urge for sugar was back.

"Marion? Can you do me a favour?"

"What would you like?"

"Two muesli bars and a sandwich from the cafeteria. I don't care what sort. And another cup of coffee, if there's any left."

"Coming right up."

"Thanks a million."

He called up another blank notepad and drew a second diagram, more complex than the previous one. The Mole was the focus of one side, Roads of the other. Beyond each of these were contributing parties: Cati and "???", the person or persons behind the contract for his life; RSD, the Mayoralty, the MSA and Keith Morrow.

He was just trying to decide where to put the RUSAMC when there was a knock at the door.

"Coming, Marion."

He cleared the screen and went to the door. His chest was less stiff than before, but still tender; he gave himself another three hours before a semblance of freedom returned.

He opened the door and performed a quick double-take, then waved his visitor inside.

"Hi, Martin. You're not the person I expected."

"I gathered." The RUSAMC captain – who, like everybody else in HQ that day, looked the worse for lack of sleep – put a heavily-loaded tray on the desk and distributed its contents: two mass-produced grain snacks, a sandwich and a cup of coffee for Roads, plus another sandwich and coffee for him. "Your secretary told me to bring you these, seeing I was on my way."

"Much appreciated." Roads opened one of the bars and took a bite. "You got my message?"

"I did, yes, but I was tied up in a teleconference with my superiors."

"Checking up on you, huh?"

"Not really. More the other way around." O'Dell frowned and changed the subject. "You're looking reasonably well, considering."

Roads gestured dismissively. "Just a couple of scratches."

"Oh? I heard you broke some ribs."

"You know how doctors exaggerate." He threw the spent wrapper into the bin. "I have some questions to ask you, Martin, and I'm a little short on time. If you don't mind, I'd like to get them over and done with."

"Shoot." O'Dell concealed his apprehension well. Roads wondered what the captain was expecting him to ask.

"First of all, exactly how far ahead of us is the Reunited States of America Military Corps?"

"Uh . . . Can I plead ignorance?"

"If that means you can't tell me because of some security bullshit, then that's fair enough. Just let me speculate for a moment, then you can tell me whether I'm wrong or not."

O'Dell looked uncertain. "Sure, go ahead. But I can't promise anything, understand."

"Of course." Roads folded his hands behind his head and leaned back in his chair. O'Dell had already demonstrated that the RUSAMC was more advanced than Kennedy Polis; the question was *how* advanced, exactly. "There's a rumour I remember hearing, shortly before the end of the War, and it keeps nagging at me now."

"What's that?"

"I was told that the entire War Room had packed up and moved to a shelter somewhere under the Appalachians to wait out the worst of the fighting. Certainly, no-one I know of ever heard of them after about 2050. I can't help wondering if there's some connection between that shelter and the Reunited States."

"Are you suggesting that we and the USA are one and the same? That the brass from the old days have emerged from the bunkers to reconquer the continent under a new flag?"

"I would have phrased it a little more subtly, but yes. That's what I'm wondering."

"It's a good theory, but you're wrong. Sorry. The brass never made it out."

Roads noted the carefully-worded sentence. "But somebody else eventually broke *in*, right?"

O'Dell smiled. "Maybe."

"'Maybe.'" Roads nodded. By the rules of this game, *maybe* inferred *yes*. "So the Reunited States Military Corps has access to all the military secrets up to and including the end of the War."

O'Dell said nothing, but his smile didn't waver.

"One more question, then: among the old plans and projects, was there a reference to a practical form of invisibility? Some sort of advanced camouflage unit, perhaps? Anything at all along those lines?"

The smile flickered, fell. "That one I can answer, Phil. There wasn't anything like that in the old files. Not even a hint."

"You're absolutely sure?"

"Positive. I've studied them myself. But you didn't hear me admit that, okay?"

"Of course, but . . . Oh, *damn*." He hit the desktop with the palm of one hand, then winced as the impact rattled his rib cage. "I was really hoping there might have been."

"I can guess why." O'Dell took a mouthful of coffee. "You're thinking that we might be involved with the Mole, or vice versa, right?"

"Partly, yes. The other possibility is that a faction from up your way managed to get hold of the plans. The technology, the timber wolf – it all points to a northern source."

"Not a bad thought. I might have had it too, if I was in your shoes – and it's not as if we don't have dissident

187

groups in the Reunited States. But you have to ask yourself why anybody would go to such lengths to invade Kennedy. This city may seem a big deal to those who live in it, but it's small fry in the context of the rest of the continent. Why should we bother reducing ourselves to stealing data from here when there are other places practically begging to let us in?"

"Because Kennedy is a symbol." Roads put his elbows on the desk and leaned forward. Again he received the impression that O'Dell was guiding him toward an answer. "It's all that remains of the old world."

"A world that almost killed itself."

"Yes, but a symbol nonetheless. We may have regressed as many years as we've survived, but we're still here. And that's what counts." He shrugged. "We'd make a good regional capital, if nothing else."

"And you will, if General Stedman has his way." O'Dell finished his coffee with a gulp. "But it takes more than sullen independence to attract the attention of a vibrant nation like ours."

"Point taken." Roads stood and went to lean on the window-sill. "We've not been a good neighbour over the years."

"True. The people around here – and there *are* people, some as close as fifty kilometres – generally keep their distance. I met some of them on the way through, heard the stories about the bad days: how four hundred thousand people starved on Kennedy's doorstep because the Mayor wouldn't open the Gate; how anyone trying to get in is caught and shot on sight; how repeated pleas for resources were ignored back in the 50s, resulting in the collapse of at least three struggling communities."

"All true, I'm afraid," Roads said. "The city could only produce enough to support so many people. If the

Mayor had let even more people in than he did, or spread the resources around, the city would have died as well. The decision wasn't simple, but the equation was."

O'Dell nodded. "I understand. But how about this: did you know that Kennedy kidnapped people to use in labour gangs when it built the Wall? Or that birth control is so tight that illegally-born children are killed and used, along with criminals and other misfits, to fertilise the farms? Or that secret MSA death squads regularly raid neighbouring communities to steal resources and rape women?"

Roads kept his expression neutral. "No."

"Exactly. But your neighbours think you've done it anyway, and more besides. That's what comes of not only being isolated and insular, but surviving as well; people begin to ask questions, and the answers aren't always what you'd like." O'Dell raised his hands, palms forward. "Hey, I'm as guilty of that as anyone. All my life I've been told stories about a city that survived the War intact: a city full of berserkers who eat human flesh. I used to lie awake at night for hours when I was a kid, terrified of being trapped in there, unable to escape, with all sorts of demonic creatures hunting me down. So, when I first learned that such a city *does* exist, and that it *does* possess technology from the old days that nobody else has any more, well, what else was I supposed to think?"

Roads did smile at that. "It must come as a relief to learn that we're not so well off these days."

"I wouldn't say that. Your reactor facility is something I'd love to get my hands on, for instance. And the bacteria cultures lost during the fighting that we're not allowed to breed any more." Noting Roads' sharp look, O'Dell added: "Peacefully, of course. None of it's worth invading over."

"Good." Roads returned to his seat, thinking over what O'Dell had told him. He too had heard rumours of atrocities in the bad days. Whether they were true or not would probably never be known, but he didn't have the confidence to deny them categorically. Such actions would have been typical of the time, when humanity's decline was at its lowest point. And even if Kennedy was guilty of such crimes, that didn't automatically make its neighbours saints.

O'Dell leaned forward to put his sandwich wrapper in the bin. "Well, that's lunch," he said. "Was there anything else you wanted to ask me?"

"Yes." Roads folded his hands across his lap and collected his thoughts. "For a favour, actually."

"Go ahead. Anything I can give you, you're welcome to it."

"All I want is information: everything you brought with you. Not just the old MIA records, but the rest as well." He looked at O'Dell closely. "You did bring more, didn't you?"

"Sure, but I may not be able to give you everything."

"Whatever you can spare, then. I'll take anything. In return, I'll give you a copy of my own private notes. You might find them useful."

"I'm sure I will." O'Dell looked tired for a moment, as though Roads had touched upon his own problems. "My superiors are anxious to study your progress."

"Really? Given what you've just told me, I'd have thought they'd be more interested in –"

He stopped in mid-sentence and stared off into space. "Phil?"

"– the *killer*." He blinked and returned to O'Dell. "Sorry, Martin. You know how it is: you get so involved in a case you forget what's going on around it. I just remembered something that might be important."

"The assassin? I thought he and the Mole were completely separate."

"Maybe." The price on his head suddenly seemed more than just a trifle to leave until later. "But I've got a funny feeling I might be seeing him in the future."

O'Dell looked puzzled. "I don't understand."

Roads glanced at his watch and then at the window; the sky was darkening. "Let's leave it there. I have work to do."

"And I have another call home to make." O'Dell stood, and Roads showed him to the door.

"The wife?"

"No, work again. But I'll get that information transferred to you first."

"Thanks, Martin. I appreciate your help."

"My pleasure. That's what I'm here for, after all."

As soon as O'Dell had left, Roads called up the notepad he had been working on and added two more circles: the killer and the RUSAMC, both in the no-man's-land between Roads and the Mole. If there was a connection between either one and any other party, then he needed more evidence to see it clearly.

Reaching for the intercom, he dialled Roger Wiggs' office number. Instead of the red-haired officer, he was put through to a junior assistant, who told him that Wiggs was tied up elsewhere in the building.

"He's certainly keeping busy," Roads commented, trying not to let frustration show in his voice. It had been several days since he and his offsider in homicide had last swapped data; he needed to know what Wiggs had found, if anything, before the killer came calling.

"It's that new guy," explained the assistant. "DeKurzak. He's had us profiling all the same old anti-Reassimilation spokespersons, plus anyone in RSD and the Council over sixty years of age."

"Looking for the Old Guard?"

"Like you wouldn't believe." The assistant sighed wearily. "I'll say one thing about him, though: if the Old Guard *does* exist, he's the one who'll find it."

"And if it *doesn't* exist?"

"Then maybe he'll find it anyway, if you know what I mean." Wiggs' assistant chuckled to herself. "When Roger gets in, I'll tell him you called. Any message?"

"No. Just tell him to be in touch."

"Will do. And good luck at your end, too."

"Thanks. We all need it."

Roads settled back to study his flow-chart for any new inspiration. There were possibilities in abundance everywhere he looked, but few certainties. The more he looked at the few shreds of evidence he possessed, the less likely it seemed that they would ever coalesce.

When he checked the mainframe half an hour later, a new icon had appeared, addressed to him: the RUSAMC data from O'Dell, still more to sift through. He sent his data in return, wondering why the RUSAMC captain had been so keen to get it – behind a suspiciously casual attitude – and why he had called his superiors back after already spending most of the day talking to them. What had Roads told him without realising?

Gulping down what he swore would be his last pain-killer, he opened O'Dell's file and began to skim through it.

CHAPTER THIRTEEN

8:15 p.m.

After barely an hour, Roads admitted defeat. The population of the Reunited States currently stood at fifteen million citizens, plus nearly double that again on a probationary basis, depending on the diplomatic status of the individual's home state. With so many people, and so much information generated as a result, any comprehensive datapool made that of Kennedy Polis seem minuscule in comparison.

Still, he had learned some things. O'Dell's statement that the RUSA had been in existence for fifty years was a white lie. The Reunited States had evolved twenty-one years ago from a smaller nation unified under the Philadelphia Accord that O'Dell had mentioned – a treaty that had, at its peak, covered an area not much larger than old Pennsylvania.

An abortive attempt during the Dissolution by the US Army to suppress a civilian rebellion in Philadelphia had served as the inspiration for the Accord. Roads could imagine why all too well.

The civilian rebellion that had taken control of the city must have known they were in trouble the moment teleoperated drones from the invading force flew overhead, transmitting tactical data back to officers still kilometres away. Well before the first and final call to surrender was broadcast by a second wave of drones, they would have resigned themselves to a bloody fight to the death. The rebellion – led by little more than an expanded police force, according to the files – had had no chance against the biomodified combat troops of the enemy.

The worst thing about it, in retrospect, was that in a sense there really *was* no enemy. That only made the decision to fight, once it had been made, all the more bitter. Knowing that you were about to be killed by your own country-folk didn't make dying any easier. If anything, it made it worse.

So when the invasion failed, that came as something of a miracle. Indeed, it seemed like a sign: if Philadelphia had been spared the fate of other recalcitrant cities, then it must have been for a reason. Certainly, the leaders of the rebellion used that as an excuse to justify the slaughter of the Army forces. And later still, when the Army was no more and the Dissolution was at its most terrible, that same excuse served to unite the region around the city. Shielded by a buffer of relative stability maintained by organisation and force, and backed up by an incident that quickly became legendary, Philadelphia remained intact through the middle of the twenty-first century – a feat only Kennedy Polis was able to emulate.

Neighbouring regions gradually joined the Philadelphia Accord. Although conditions within the united region were unstable for the most part – except at its heart, where industry had been revived and factories operated at close to their optimal productivity – local governments and people so long isolated joined the movement gladly. The only true weapon against chaos was order, and anything capable of delivering that order was welcomed with open arms.

When the member states voted overwhelmingly to replace the Philadelphia Accord with a new, national constitution based loosely on the old – and to change the name, prematurely perhaps, to the Reunited States of America – it therefore came as no surprise. And so civilisation began to rise again where savagery had reigned for over a decade: the ruins of New York, Boston and Pittsburgh were absorbed within twenty years; within thirty, it encompassed territories as far as Maine and Ontario to the north, Dakota to the west, and Carolina to the south.

The history of the Reunited States rarely mentioned other nations it had encountered – and, presumably, absorbed – during its expansion. The files were clearly biased in favour of a peaceful interpretation of the rise of the RUSA. But Roads did piece together some information on that score, reading inferences where hard data was not available.

The RUSA was fundamentally driven by machinery and might, so skirmishes had been frequent in the past. Expanding and holding territory was a priority, for conditions beyond the borders were constantly changing. Nomads, looters, small biomodified gangs – even a few surviving berserkers – had all at one time or another besieged the walls of the developing nation. And the RUSA Military Corps' response, unlike Kennedy's, was always to attack, not to hide.

Where other states had arisen in the vacuum left by the old USA, some traded willingly and peacefully with the RUSA while others became rivals. All were absorbed eventually, by one means or another. Only in two cases that Roads could find was serious resistance being maintained. The first, to the north-west, was a coastal alliance based around Washington and California with trade routes reaching as far inland as Wyoming. The second, to the south-west, was a New Mexican Alliance making steady inroads to the deep south. Even in the post-War conditions of the Dissolution, it seemed that the old rivalries – between north and south, and east and west – were still strong.

There was no indication anywhere in the files of how severe the conflicts had been, or if any was currently in progress. Obviously the data had been censored to protect the RUSAMC's military secrets. But Roads did notice one thing: that on a map of the old US, Kennedy lay almost exactly between the Reunited States of America and the New Mexican Alliance. Perhaps that was enough to explain why Stedman was so keen to Reassimilate it. As a military outpost, it would be in the perfect location. And the technological resources the city still possessed would be an added bonus.

At that point, however, he gave up. Everything he had learned was fascinating, but it had little bearing on the case at hand. Any clues that might exist would be found in the details, and the file was simply too huge for any single person to scan alone.

He therefore required help if he was to continue his current line of investigation. Besides, he wanted to move more than just his fingertips. The pain of sitting in one position was beginning to override the need to rest.

He went down to the fourth floor, but found it deserted and dark apart from a couple of night-shifters, cocooned behind partitions, huddling in the protective warmth of their yellow desk lamps. RSD HQ was in limbo, caught between one day and the next. Most of the active staff were out on the streets, waiting for something to happen.

Although General Stedman's imminent arrival had eclipsed RSD's regular routine, life went on regardless. The planned parade would attract a substantial proportion of the city's population the following day – including, perhaps, some who were more than simply curious. Both the Mole and the assassin were still out there, somewhere, and the coming Reassimilation wouldn't change that.

Barney's partition was dark except for the stand-by glow of her terminal. He wished she had told him she was heading home, if only so he could have wished her a good night.

He was about to leave when a faint noise attracted his attention to the floor behind the desk. He found her there, curled up on the carpet. Although he envied her ability to sleep in unlikely places, he understood that it was a talent born more of necessity than choice.

Asleep she looked surprisingly child-like for a woman on the far side of thirty. Her eyes were tightly shut, her fists clenched; the smooth skin of her brow puckered into a frown. Moving quietly across the room, he knelt beside her and brushed her cheek with his fingertips.

At his touch, her eyes startled open and she flinched away. Then, realising it was him, she flung herself forward and wrapped her arms around him.

"Oh, Phil." Her voice was husky, muffled by his shoulder. "Am I glad to see you."

His hands caressed the solid warmth of her back and shoulders. The urgency of her clasp did not fade. "A bad dream, huh?"

"I dreamt you were dead."

"Not me. I've got a few years left in me yet."

"But someone killed you!"

"Did they?" He hoped the dream wasn't prophetic. "I promise to take better care of myself, then."

She sniffed moistly and started to relax. Their embrace slowly loosened. "I'm sorry," she said, reaching into her pocket for a tissue. She rubbed her eyes, glanced around at the office. "What time is it?"

"After eight. Why didn't you go home?"

"I was waiting for you to finish."

"You didn't have to, Barney. You've done your fair share of work for today."

"I know, and yesterday too." She smiled fleetingly. "It's silly. All this werewolf business has me spooked. I wanted you to walk me home."

"I will, if it'll make you feel better," he said automatically. "But who's going to guard the guard?"

Her eyes were almost glowing in the dark as they stared into his. "Who says I want to be protected from him?"

Against his conscious will, he pulled her closer. Her arms slid around his shoulders and squeezed back. He could feel her fingers digging in, clutching at him, and he responded in kind, raising one hand to stroke her hair and neck, to tilt her head back. His body remembered what to do all too well – even if his mind rebelled . . .

He couldn't let this happen. He didn't want her to be hurt when she finally learned the truth. And if he let his own feelings out, then the truth would inevitably follow.

Hating himself, he turned what should have been a kiss into just another embrace between dear friends, and held her close.

"Barney," he whispered into her ear after the longest minute of his life. "You're hurting my ribs."

The pressure eased immediately. "Oh, Phil, I'm sorry. I completely forgot."

"That's okay."

Her eyes sparkled. "I promise to be more gentle in future."

"I know you will." He kissed her on the forehead; a brief peck, the most he would allow himself. "But I have something important to do, first."

The glow of the computer seemed dazzling as he climbed to his feet and took a seat behind the desk. He tapped at the keyboard for a second while she leaned over his shoulder, her breath warm in his ear.

"You finished the list?" he asked.

"Uh-huh. There." She pointed at a file with a fingertip. Her nails were short, but not chewed.

"Good." He took the file and sent it to the search program he had set up; the semi-intelligent algorithm, a survivor of the pre-War days, would perform the task of a dozen people, sifting through megabytes of data and looking for meaningful connections. Then he tugged over the icon for the RUSAMC data O'Dell had given him, explaining what it was to Barney as he did.

"You're going to run the search program through *that*?" she said, her eyebrows rising.

"And the entire Kennedy datapool as well."

"But that'll take –"

"About six hours." He turned to look at her, and their eyes met from barely a centimetre's distance.

"You really are desperate, aren't you?" she said.

"Absolutely. But if the search pulls just one thing I need to know, then it'll have been worthwhile." He instructed the program to call either of them at their home terminals when it had finished, then set it running.

He flicked off the screen, stood. "That's it. Let's get out of here."

"My place?" Her eyes stared directly into his, daring him to say no.

He hesitated. "If that's what you want."

"Are you kidding?" She slipped into her coat and flicked her fringe back. "It's about bloody time, I'd say."

The night was clear and calm, and warm despite the lack of clouds. The moon shone through the haze of the streetlights. They walked side-by-side without speaking, very conscious of each other's physical presence. Roads was glad at first that they had been unable to take a car from the RSD pool, and therefore had to walk – although that caused him to be reminded, with a twinge not unlike deja-vu, of a time almost seventy years earlier.

The last occasion on which he had shared any form of intimacy had been on a night similar to this – except that the streets of Sydney had been crowded and better-lit. The people brushing by him had been brightly-coloured and noisy, their bodies awash with technology: micromachines had invaded the cosmetic industry on every level, providing variable tattoos, clothes that changed colour or played moving images, and even instant hair; headsets, laser-firing contact lenses or implants kept information flowing at a heady pace; the infra-red beams that had replaced wires a decade ago laced the crowd like an invisible web – shining neon-bright to anyone with the right eyes to see. The night had been alive, literally, with movement and celebration on so many levels that the reality of War brewing even then seemed like an incredible fantasy.

Phil Roads had been twenty-five. Then – as it did now – a persistent itch between his shoulder-blades warned him that someone was watching him.

The journey passed all too quickly, even without taking the Rosette. On the pavement outside the entrance to Barney's apartment, Roads stopped and took her by the shoulders. She knew what he was about to say before the words had formed in his mind.

"You're not coming in, are you?"

He shook his head. "I can't. I still have work to do."

She sighed. "Look, Phil, be straight with me, okay?" He opened his mouth to cut her off, but she talked right over him, the words flowing in a sudden rush. "I can tell that you're unsure about this. I am too, if you want the truth. But I don't invite strange men into my house without a good reason, and I think I've reason enough after all the years we've worked together. If *you* don't think we should take our relationship any further, then just say so."

He stared at her, stunned into silence by her bluntness. He had avoided romantic involvement by choice for five years after that distant night in Sydney, then out of necessity for the rest of his life. The habit had become ingrained.

"No, it's not that," he said finally, not entirely certain himself it was true.

"Are you sure? Don't make me use the 'I'm a big girl; I can handle it' line."

"Cross my heart. You've just taken me by surprise, that's all."

"Really?" Her eyes searched his.

"Really." Lowering his voice until it was barely audible and speaking directly into her ear, he added: "If we weren't being followed, I'd be in like a shot."

She managed to stop herself looking over her shoulder. "Followed?" she echoed. "How can you tell?"

"A hunch; the same hunch I had before Blindeye, and look what happened then." He shrugged, prepared to admit that he still might be wrong. "I'll just duck back and see. If there is someone, I'll come back after I've shaken them. I promise."

"Are you sure you'll be okay?" she whispered back, her lips hardly moving. One hand touched his chest. "Do you want me to come with you?"

"No. It's harder to follow one than two. Besides, you need the rest." The crow's-feet around her eyes deepened, but he wouldn't change his mind. He didn't want Barney involved, if he could avoid it – not because she wasn't capable, but because it wasn't her problem. "Don't *worry*, Barney. I'll be back before you know it."

"I hope so." Before he could pull away, she kissed him firmly on the lips. With a tight smile, she added: "You fucking heroes . . ."

He watched her go into her house, waited until she had locked the door, then headed back the way they had come. The street was, as far as he could tell, completely empty – yet a sixth sense still told him that there was someone nearby. Until he was certain whether the sensation was illusory, or not, he wasn't prepared to take any chances.

He had ignored the itch at least once before when it had proved to be right, when it had warned of Cati's presence in the KCU grounds prior to Blindeye. He couldn't afford to take the chance that the itch was wrong this time.

Turning left off the main access road between B and C rings, he headed for his own home. No footsteps followed him; no shadows moved in the yellow half-light – ahead, behind or above him. The night was perfectly still. Only the occasional streetlight broke the darkness.

Without breaking step, he lit a cigarette with his left hand. Beneath his overcoat, through a hole in the pocket, his right hand unclipped the holster of his gun and lifted the weapon free. He gripped it tightly without allowing it to be seen. If Cati *was* following him again, he vowed not to be the easy tail he had been before.

Five minutes after leaving Barney's doorstep, he reached the corner leading to his building. Instead of turning into his street, however, he continued past. A hundred metres on lay a narrow alley that led to the entrance to an old restaurant, long abandoned. The ground floor was empty, apart from dust and spiders; an external fire exit linked the second floor to the rear of his building, hidden from the front. He had prepared the route some years ago as a means of making a hasty escape, but knew that it would work just as well the other way.

When he reached the alleyway, he stopped to light another cigarette and study the street. Still no sign. He counted to five, then dropped the cigarette at his feet.

Ducking into the alley, he brought the pistol out of his pocket. The first twenty metres, until he reached the shelter of the restaurant, were the most dangerous. Hemmed in by damp, brick walls, he was acutely conscious of his inability to dodge. The entrance to the alley bored like a giant eye into his retreating back.

When he reached the restaurant, he ran inside, velocity unchecked. The darkness was complete, but he didn't hesitate, hurrying up the stairs, along a mouldering corridor and into what had once been an office. A door on the far wall had a sign saying "Fire" in faded letters upon it.

There he stopped, breathing deeply and evenly.

And he listened.

From far away came the sound of a siren, the sigh of the wind, and a whisper that might have been someone shouting –

But no breathing, no brush of fabric on skin, no creaking boards.

Nothing. No-one was following him.

He allowed himself to relax slightly, and crossed to the door. To a casual glance, the lock appeared intact but a quick tug on the rusty metal had it open. The door sighed softly inward. Still cautious, he waited a moment before looking through it.

A metal walkway connected the restaurant's building with his. A flight of narrow steps led down to street-level. Six metres below, the floor of another alley was littered with old crates. Behind a pile of rubble –

He froze.

Behind the rubble were two men watching the entrance to the alley. From the angle of their heads, he could guess why they were there: anyone trying to sneak into his building either along the alley or across the walkway would be seen immediately.

He retreated back into the building, thanking his sixth sense for making him cautious – even though, in essence, it appeared to have been wrong about the details. He wasn't being followed at all; the assassins had been waiting for him to come home.

He had two choices: to make his escape, or to continue onward, somehow. If he fled, then the assassins would simply try again at another time, or even track him down to Barney's. He would have solved nothing. But if he kept going, he could get what he wanted from his home and possibly even learn who had put the price on his head as well.

Deciding quickly, he scrabbled through the detritus on the floor of the office until he found a piece of plastic building material about the length of his forearm. Hefting it, he returned to the doorway.

Opening the fire exit a second time – and praying that neither man would choose that moment to glance upward – he threw the stick as far as he could along the alley.

It clattered to the ground, horribly loud in the silence. The heads of the two men turned to face the sudden noise. One crept out of the shadows to investigate.

Roads ran swiftly across the metal walkway.

A voice whispered behind and below him, thick with static. The words were faint, barely intelligible:

"Everything okay back there?"

Roads carefully opened the fire exit of his building and eased through it.

"All clear," replied one of the men. "Just a fucking rat."

The radio fell silent.

Roads held his breath in the darkness of his building, trying to will his heart quiet. It had been a long time since he had done this sort of thing, but not long enough to have forgotten the excitement of physical danger and the breathless surge of adrenalin it prompted. He had to force himself to take it slowly, to remember that this wasn't as simple as Blindeye had been. There were two men in the alley behind him, plus, he assumed, an unknown number watching the front – and no security force assembled en masse to cover his back. He had to take every step as slowly as possible; one mistake could be fatal.

When he was ready, he stalled a second longer to remove his contact lenses. The difference was slight, but he needed every advantage he could get.

His rooms were one floor down. As he crossed to the stairwell, he noticed footprints in the dust. They didn't match his own, and appeared to have been left by bare feet. The last time he had checked his emergency exit had been three days earlier, and it had been clear.

He felt safe to assume that his mystery caller had arrived since Blindeye, or even more recently. Perhaps within the last few hours; perhaps he was still in the building.

Gripping the gun tightly, he descended the stairs one by one until he reached his floor. From there, he could just see the building's main entrance – but not Charlie. Roads cursed his luck. A call for attention was too risky. He would have to warn the elderly guard on the way out, if there was time.

The door to his apartment swung open when he touched it: unlocked. The hallway beyond was dark and silent, and smelled slightly of dust. Someone had definitely been inside within the last few hours.

He entered the first room in a running crouch, ready for anything.

The room was in turmoil; books lay on the desk with their spines broken; data fiches had been scattered on the floor alongside the frames of ripped paintings. The next room, his bedroom, was similar. The kitchen had also been ransacked.

But the apartment was empty. Whoever was responsible for the break-in had left some time ago.

The assassins, he wondered, or the man with bare feet? Or were they one and the same, as strange as that seemed?

Ignoring the mystery for the moment, he holstered the gun and went back into the bedroom. In the dusty darkness under the bed was a loose floorboard; he felt for it and lifted it free. From the shallow airspace below the floor he pulled a slim, leather case and put it on the bed.

A sports bag lay in the ruins of the cupboard. He put the case into it, followed by a change of clothes and a few other necessities.

Barely had he finished when he heard a door open downstairs. He ducked through the apartment with the bag in one hand and his gun in the other, and peered down the stairwell.

Charlie had opened the door to let someone in. The streetlight cast a dull glow across the man's back and head, but a shadow across his face. The elderly guard said something that sounded like, "Evening," and the man turned to nod in reply.

Moustache, receding brown hair, snub nose:

The Mole.

Roads crept up the stairwell and back to the second floor, thinking furiously as he went. The thief had impersonated Roads, and Charlie had let him in. That explained how the Mole had been able to gain access to his rooms so often in the past. But why had he come now? The only possible explanation was that the Mole had been following Roads – that his first instincts had been right after all.

At the fire exit, he paused and slipped the bag onto one shoulder. Opening the door an inch, he listened carefully for movement outside.

"Right," said the voice on the radio. "He's in. Get to your positions."

The two men in the alley below moved, their feet rustling through the rubbish. The fire escape creaked as they climbed it.

Roads sank quickly back into the room: the assassins – like Charlie – obviously thought the Mole was him, and that their wait was over.

The two men stopped just outside the fire exit, their breathing faint but clear. A minute passed. Roads could think of no other exit from the building apart from through a window. He felt his ribs; the pain was better, but he didn't trust them to withstand the impact of a twenty-foot fall.

The voice on the radio spoke again. "We're on. You two get inside and keep an eye on the back while the rest of us deal with the old fart."

Roads' stomach turned to ice. Caught as he was between the Mole and the assassins, he could do little to warn Charlie of what was about to happen.

The fire exit opened, and Roads hit the first man in the face with a clenched fist. The second man – a short caucasian with long, blond hair – gaped as his partner went down. Before Long-Hair could yell for help, Roads punched him in the throat and pushed him back through the exit.

A door slammed open two floors below; then came the sound of a brief scuffle, followed by a single gunshot. Roads winced.

The first man stirred, and Roads struck him on the side of the skull with the butt of his gun. Feeling through the man's coat pockets, he hunted for the radio. It wasn't there. Acutely conscious that an unknown number of men were prowling through the darkness on the floor below, he opened the fire exit.

Long-Hair was sitting up on the walkway, clutching his neck. Roads pushed him onto his back and rummaged through his pockets until he found the transmitter. With his foot on Long-Hair's chest, he leaned close and hissed:

"What's your friend's name?"

Long-Hair spat weakly in defiance, and Roads pushed the barrel of the gun against his nose until he felt the cartilage snap. The youth gasped in pain and tried to roll free. Roads turned him over, planted his foot into the small of his back and grabbed a fistful of hair.

"Tell me, you little fuck. I haven't got all night."

"Andy," gasped Long-Hair, his vocal chords ragged. "His name is Andy."

"Who pays you?"

"Fuck you –"

Roads pressed his heel harder, and Long-Hair gasped with pain.

"I said, *fuck* –"

Roads clubbed him unconscious and ran back to the restaurant. He couldn't afford to waste any more time.

Right on cue, the radio buzzed.

"He's not here, dammit. Have you two seen him?"

Roads raised the transmitter and attempted what he hoped was a credible impersonation of Long-Hair's voice.

"He just went past – looks like he's heading for the roof – !"

"Where are you now?"

"Following him – he took out Andy on the way –"

"Don't worry about Andy; we'll get him out of the building in time. Just keep after Roads. We're on our way."

The radio clicked off and Roads reached the exit to the restaurant. He padded silently through the old office and down the stairs until he reached the exit to the alley. There, he stopped.

Again he was faced with the possibility of an easy escape, and again he turned it down. He needed to know who the ringleader was and, if possible, who had hired him. Then there was Charlie's probable death to avenge. And, besides, he was curious:

The voice on the radio had assured Long-Hair that Andy would be removed from the building "in time". Something significant was about to happen.

He crept along the street from shadow to shadow until he reached his corner. When he was sure no-one was watching, he ducked across the intersection. A narrow lane wound its way between the buildings opposite his. He slipped into it, running on his toes to keep quiet. Every ten metres or so, a crack between buildings afforded him a glimpse of the street; he stopped when he reached the one that faced his building.

Five floors up, figures too small to be identified moved on the roof. Within moments, they had searched it thoroughly and realised Roads' ploy.

"You motherfucker," said the radio. Roads didn't give them the satisfaction of a reply, and the voice, assuming that he had made his escape, continued:

"Josh, he's gone. He got by Andy and Johns. He's probably blocks away by now."

"What do you want me to do?" asked another voice.

"Keep working. We'll be down in a minute."

"Will do, but I can't see the –"

The voice of Josh cut off in mid-sentence. Roads could see wild movement on the first floor, but was unable to distinguish what was going on.

There was a pause, then:

"Josh? What the fuck's going on down there?"

The men on the roof vanished. A minute later, someone screamed. Gunfire rattled. Muzzle-flashes flickered erratically on the first and ground floors as the assassins retreated from something Roads couldn't see.

Then three men suddenly issued from the building and headed for his hiding space, firing to cover their backs. The first was Danny Chong, the skinny bounty-hunter that Roads and Barney had seen at Morrow's bar.

Roads retreated back to the lane and ducked out of sight into a shallow alcove.

The three men entered the narrow passage. Whatever had attacked them in the building followed, judging by the sound of continued gunfire. Ricochets whined, followed by a sickening thud and a noise that sounded like someone trying to yell through a gag.

Chong was the only one to reach safety. He turned with a look of horror on his face and started to run along the lane.

As he went past the alcove, Roads tripped him. Chong went down hard and slid for a metre on his stomach. Screaming, he tried to crawl away on his hands and knees.

Roads followed, grabbed him by the scruff of his neck and pinned him against a wall. Chong fought with inhuman strength, empowered by fear. It took an arm-lock and all of Roads' weight to keep him still.

"I'm not going to kill you," Roads hissed, but it didn't make any difference. Chong writhed, bent his head back. His eyes were wide, almost completely glazed over.

Roads shook him. "What the fuck *happened* in there?"

In reply Chong produced a knife from his sleeve, twisted an arm free and stabbed Roads deep in the right shoulder.

Roads fell back, gasping with pain. The pistol slipped from his numbed grasp and discharged, throwing sparks from wall to wall as the slug ricocheted along the lane. Chong kicked him in the stomach, and he fell to his knees, then Chong turned and fled the way he had come, hesitating only to pick up the gun he had dropped. Roads staggered to his feet and ran after him.

When he reached the crack down which Chong had vanished, Roads stopped and stared in horror.

The concrete path before him was slick with gore. Two bodies lay tangled together against one wall as though torn apart by a wild animal. One severed arm reached for him in a mute plea for help.

His gorge rose, and he fought it desperately.

Then a bullet whined past his ear, and he ducked by reflex.

Chong was standing in the middle of the street, waving the gun in Roads' general direction. His face was a mask of absolute terror.

"What are you?" screamed the bounty-hunter, an hysterical edge raw in his voice. "What the fuck *are* you?"

Chong fired a second time and Roads pressed himself flat against the wall of the building. The assassin's aim was wild – the bullet went high and to his right – but it was only a matter of time before another found its mark. He was about to make a dash for it when something caught his eye.

Behind Chong, on the other side of the street, the solid line of his building *bent*, as though a heat-haze had passed in front of it.

Chong turned just as the dimple in the air reached him. It swirled with half-seen motion – like a soap-bubble warping in a breath of wind. Chong screamed and fired at it, then turned to flee.

Too late. The back of his head blossomed as something punched through his face. He flew backward through the air, a futile motor-reflex making his feet kick. He hit the road with a sodden thump.

Then, with a flash as bright as the noon-day sun, Roads' building erupted into flame. For a split-second, the plastic composite that normally kept bad weather at bay held the facade together. Then the composite disintegrated, and a fiery shockwave sent fragments of glass and brick hurtling across the street, into Roads' narrow shelter.

He dropped to the blood-stained concrete with his hands over his ears, screaming inaudibly through the noise. The shockwave buffeted him, scorched his skin. Shattered bricks rattled around him, making him flinch. One fragment struck a glancing blow to the back of his head as he turned to crawl for shelter.

The last thing he saw was a ghostly shape silhouetted against the fire: an eerily translucent cloud of grey, with five shining points arrayed in a rough pentagon at its centre.

Then it too burst into flame, like a new-born star, and he passed out.

PART TWO:
THOU SHALT NOT KILL

INTERLUDE

Tuesday, 18 September, 12:15 a.m.

The fire in Roads' building burned for two hours before the entire structure collapsed. With a roar of tumbling masonry, it fell outward and across the road, narrowly missing the Emergency Services vehicles assembled around the site. Peripheral fires lapped at the buildings to either side, but barely attained a foothold before powerful jets of water forced them back. None made it as far as the building directly across the road, where one red-skinned gargoyle larger than those around it crouched on the roof, watching.

In infra-red, the scene was a nightmare of colour. Orange and yellow heat blazed from the remains of the central fire, casting a furnace's breath along the street, reflecting off buildings, fences and the road. The generators of fire engines, ambulances, and police vehicles burned brightly in neon blue. Tiny green point-sources were people, scurrying to and fro like luminous ants, almost lost among the rest.

He switched to the visual spectrum and watched with detached interest as they cleaned away the bodies. He knew they would find more once the fire was out. Twelve people had entered the building after Roads, but only three had emerged.

Why they had died, why they had sought to kill Roads, and why the *thing* had killed them . . . did not concern him. He was beyond caring what happened to ordinary people, the ones who would find him wanting and hunt him down, if they only knew who he was.

Besides, the one called Lucifer had told him to hide – to *keep out of the way*. With what had happened to him in the harbour the previous night still fresh in his mind, he was happy to obey for once. It had been foolish to become involved in the first place – although he *was* involved, whether he liked it or not. He had become entangled in a series of events that threatened both his Peace and his life.

Searching Roads' apartment had been risky, but worthwhile in putting his mind at ease on one score. Curiously enough, the policeman did not appear to know who he was. Perhaps it was not too late, after all, to return to the life he had known – free from his controller, Roads and the *thing*.

Angry heat ebbed slowly from the street below. As the fire retreated, a swarm of police searched the area. A pair of ash-flecked officers combed the roof of his building, but did not find him. He lay curled in the womb-like spaces of a ventilation shaft, obeying orders.

Hide, his controller had said, so he did just that. There was a sense of security to be gained from the act of concealment, an illusion of safety, however short-lived. It was exactly what he had been doing for more years than he could number.

When the police officers were gone, he remained in his cocoon of metal. For the first time in two days, he truly slept.

CHAPTER FOURTEEN

2:45 a.m.

Barney paced the length of her study, unable to rest. Alternating between hope and despair, and with one word turning constantly through her mind, she stopped to make herself a cup of herbal tea, going through the familiar motions automatically, hoping against hope that a retreat into routine might ease her disquiet and allow her to sleep.

It didn't.

Outside, a sudden change brought rain to the city. It flurried at the kitchen window like a thousand tiny fists, beating to be let in.

The word was *metamale*.

Her hands were shaking.

The call from HQ had come two hours earlier, three hours after she had returned home from RSD. When the terminal had bleeped, she had rushed to answer it, only half-hearing sirens wailing in the distance as she did. The call hadn't been Roads, as she had half-expected, to apologise for his lateness. The reality had been far worse.

Emergency Services had been called to Roads' home in response to reports of an explosion shortly after nine o'clock. The building had been totally gutted, and had later collapsed. A number of bodies – four, at last count

– had been found near the scene; the genetic fingerprint of each had produced a match with the RSD datapool: Danny Chong, Ingrid Toffler, Jamie Bazz, and Mark Johns. All were known criminals wanted on old charges of murder; two of them – Chong and Bazz – were on the Most Wanted list. A preliminary search of the wreckage had found two more bodies, as yet unidentified. Of Roads himself, or of his body, there had been no sign.

Margaret Chappel had then called Barney personally, telling her to stay at home.

"There's nothing you can do, Barney. Emergency has it in hand; you'd only get in the way. I suggest you try to get some sleep instead."

"But I want to help," she protested. "I want to know what happened."

"You'll know as soon as we do, I promise. I'll make sure you're the first to be told."

"But –"

"Stay *there*, Barney. How else will we know where to call you?"

She almost cried then, and hated herself for holding it back. She needed to *do* something. If Roads was dead, then part of her would always blame herself for not going with him, until she found a suitable scapegoat.

"Who?" she asked, the lump in her chest half-strangling her. "Who would do this?"

Chappel shook her head, and told her about Morrow's warning.

"He *knew*?" Barney couldn't believe it. Roads had known that he was in real danger but had still gone after the assassins on his own. It was exactly the same brand of heroics that had robbed her of her father, years ago.

She found herself reliving the painful months following her father's death. The last berserker Kennedy Polis saw had systematically hunted down over a hundred and forty-five people before RSD had cornered it in an old downtown building, where it held a woman hostage. Nothing had driven it out, and the four volunteers who had offered to go in after it had been killed.

In an attempt to neutralise the threat, radio-triggered explosive charges had been laid around the foundations of the building. The berserker, aware of RSD's plan, had made an unexpected offer to negotiate. It would hand over the woman if it was allowed to leave the city. Three officers, one armed with the trigger for the explosives, had entered the building to negotiate. The officer with the trigger had been her father.

Barney had been seventeen and not yet a member of RSD, but Roads had been there. He had been in charge of one of the parties which searched through the rubble of the demolished building. The body of the hostage had been found the following day. The autopsy was inconclusive, but suggested that she had been dead for several hours before the explosives had gone off.

That had been enough for Roads to piece together a picture of what had happened to the negotiators. The berserker had wanted to go in style, not cornered like an animal. It might have waited until the negotiators had seen the body of the woman before attacking them, or it may well have attacked immediately. Either way, Barney's father had pressed the trigger, killing the berserker and himself in the process.

When Roads had told Barney of his theory, years later, she had disagreed. The berserker hadn't killed her father; machismo had. If he hadn't gone into the building in the first place, he would still have been alive.

And now, years later, she was in the same situation.

"Don't blame him, Barney," Chappel had said, "or yourself. If he wants to do things alone, he will. That's just the way he is. Nothing you or I could say would make him change his mind."

For the first time Barney noted the grief in the eyes of the Director of RSD: hidden behind the usual mask of efficiency, but inescapably there, and deep.

"You've known him longer than I have," she ventured, unable to put into words the question she wanted to ask.

"Yes." Chappel's expression softened. "But only just."

"And you were close, once."

"We still are." Chappel frowned at that. "But we weren't lovers, if that's what you're driving at."

Barney felt herself blush.

Not long after that conversation had come the reply from the RSD mainframe. The search program had finished. Barney had settled down to read the results, glad for something to make her feel useful.

Between the list and the combined Kennedy/RUSAMC datapool three matches had been made. The first frightened her, the second seemed irrelevant, the third . . .

She tried not to worry about Roads. He could look after himself. Only now did she know exactly how true that was.

That was when she had begun to pace.

In the kitchen, with the mug held tightly between both hands, she stared out from the confines of her claustrophobic, complicated world. She wanted to go outside and stand in the rain for a while, to literally drown her sorrows. Instead she turned out the kitchen light and watched the rain through the window.

She drank the tea without noticing it, remembering her father standing in that very spot, years ago, bemoaning the loss of smart cards. They had argued often when she was a teenager; so much that he had valued had seemed trivial to her, then. Who cared if e-money went the way of biochips and the World-Wide Web? Was technology really that important? The tragedy was that he had died before she could ever tell him how right he had been.

The tea wasn't helping. She was tired, worried despite herself – both about Roads and the Reassimilation, despite her intellectual acceptance of the latter's inevitability – and alone.

Putting the mug upside-down in the sink, she turned around just as someone ran past the window.

She gasped and jumped backward, almost tripping over her feet in surprise. The figure had only appeared for an instant – vaguely man-shaped, unrecognisable in the shadows. But it had been there, *in her yard*.

She ran to the study and grabbed her gun from the bottom drawer of her desk. Checking the windows in every room to ensure that they were locked, she tried to still her hammering heartbeat. If Roads' killers had come for her as well, she would put up a fight; she would not go down easily.

Back in the hallway, she listened to the hiss of the rain and pressed the pistol to her lips. Had she really seen light glinting in crystal eyes, or had *that* been her imagination?

Raoul's face came unbidden to mind, and her fear doubled.

Then a muffled thump at the door made her jump again. Something slid damply along the thin wood veneer, and the handle turned.

Unconsciously deepening her voice, she called: "Who is it?"

The reply, when it came, was as unexpected as any she could have imagined:

"Open up, Barney – it's me. Phil."

She was halfway to the door before she stopped, struck by a sudden doubt. "How do I know it's really you?"

"How . . . *what*?"

"I need to know you're not the Mole before I let you in."

He uttered a sound that might have been a laugh, then said: "Ask me a question that only the Phil Roads you know could answer."

What had she told him and no-one else? Nothing sprang to mind immediately. Her real first name was on file, as was her birth-date.

"Barney, it's raining out here, for Christ's sake." He sounded as though he was leaning against the door.

"Okay." She held the gun in both hands, steeling herself to fire if she had to. "Tell me what the search found."

"The search?" At the tone of his voice, she took a deep breath and raised the gun. "Do you mean the search through O'Dell's datapool?"

"Yes." She gritted her teeth to keep her response level. "Tell me what it found, and I'll let you in."

A silence followed, then Roads said: "It found *me*, Barney. Now, are you going to open the door or not?"

She let free the breath she had been holding and unlocked the door. When she opened it, he fell forward and slid to the floor before she could catch him.

Lying on his back in a growing pool of pink-stained water, he managed a weak smile.

"Philip G. Roads . . . reporting for duty," he said.

She didn't know whether to laugh or to cry, so she took his head in her hands and did both.

She helped him to the bathroom, trying all the while to avoid looking at his eyes. The one glimpse she'd had was more than enough to confirm her fears.

Roads' eyes were like perfectly transparent marbles filled with lenses: miniature glass onions, with layer upon layer of concentric skins that retreated or advanced as his gaze roved. When he looked at the light, half-seen processes occurred in each orb to focus and dim the glare; when he looked at her, they occurred again, but differently.

She was afraid that she would see the backs of his eye-sockets if she looked into them too closely, they were so amazingly clear. All she saw was darkness, however, like the heart of a zoom lens, and a faint hint of blue.

Roads was biomodified. He had broken the Humanity Laws. He was a criminal, and it was her duty to turn him in.

But he was still Phil Roads, and he needed her help. That more than anything convinced her to give him the chance to explain.

She turned on the shower, then peeled off his clothes layer by layer, exposing the wounds beneath. He shivered uncontrollably while she stripped him, but not from the cold.

"It's shock," he said, eyelids flickering closed. "Blood loss."

"I'm not surprised." The wound to his shoulder was viciously deep and had bled profusely. It would require stitches to heal cleanly. A variety of gashes and minor lacerations marred the skin of his face and hands; bruises scowled at her from the rest of his body. "What the hell happened to you?"

"They were waiting for me at my place, Chong and his buddies –"

"Waiting to kill you?"

"Yes. I was hoping to catch the assassin; instead, all I got was that bunch of goons."

"Don't be so quick to judge. They surprised you, didn't they?"

"No, I saw them before they saw me. I went in anyway."

"Typical."

"I had to get something." He opened his eyes and looked feverishly around. "The bag – I *was* carrying a bag, wasn't I?"

"It's inside, in the hall. Do you want me to get it?"

"No. Just so long as I haven't lost it."

She finished stripping him and tested the stream of water. Not too hot, and fairly clean; the rain of the last few days had flushed the city's reservoir of its recent brown colour. She stepped back and gestured.

"Get in."

"Why?"

"You're filthy, that's why."

He stepped naked into the cubicle, winced as the jet of hot water stung his wounds. The water ran down the drain in a swirl of deep red as it scoured away old, dried blood, then slowly lightened. He stuck his head under and rubbed at his face with his hands.

She stood outside with a towel, waiting for him to finish, studying him. He was even fitter than she had suspected; what he lacked in size he more than made up for in strength. His musculature was near-perfect: little excess body-fat, no lack of tone beneath it. From the neck down, at least, he might have been twenty-five, although his skin did have the minor blemishes of a man in his late forties.

But even so, she thought, he didn't look his age. Not his *true* age . . .

He shut off the taps and stepped out of the cubicle. The shivering had stopped. As he patted himself dry, she noticed that he was more than simply favouring his right arm. The knife-wound in his shoulder had obviously touched muscle – or, worse, a tendon.

"We're going to have to get you to a hospital."

He shook his head. His eyes glittered in the bright overhead light. "Not necessary. All I need is food."

"Why?"

"I'm starving, that's why."

"At a time like this?"

He held out his left hand. "You wouldn't know I'd shot my thumb off in the War, would you?"

She checked automatically, even though she knew the hand was whole, no fingers missing. "No. And if you told me you had, I wouldn't believe you."

"Well, I did. And here it is, thanks to the wonders of tissue regeneration and micromachine technology. That's what keeps me looking so young. But you need to feed the process with raw materials, like carbohydrates, and fuel it with glucose. Do you have any chocolate?"

"No, I –" She stared at him. "Are you telling me you *grew* it back?"

"It took me a week or two but, yes, I did."

"That's impossible – isn't it?"

"No, but I'm not sure I can explain it properly. Maybe later." He handed her the blood-stained towel. "Do you have anything I can wear until I stop bleeding, or would you prefer me naked?"

"I'll get you something." She found an old cotton sheet that had narrowly escaped recycling and wrapped it around him. Directing him to the kitchen, she sat him on a stool and tore strips off another sheet to use as makeshift bandages. While she tended his injuries, he ate a plateful of soya-steak leftovers.

"You haven't finished telling me what happened," she prompted. Between mouthfuls of food, he filled her in on the rest.

He had only blacked out for a few minutes after the explosion, and had woken to find himself lying under one of the bodies. Disoriented by the shock, he had staggered from the scene and fled the approaching sirens. He had become lost and wandered for an indefinite time before recovering his senses to find himself near Barney's; part of him must have been keeping track of where he was, and looking for shelter. Although convinced he hadn't been followed, he had been cautious enough to check Barney's building before knocking on the door.

"You scared the living shit out of me," she said, the annoyance in her voice half genuine.

"I'm sorry, but I had to be sure you weren't staked-out as well."

"I know, I know." She sat in a chair opposite him. "So, let's see if I've got this straight. The Mole killed the assassins, right?"

"Danny Chong, at least. I assume the others as well."

"Why?"

He shifted uncomfortably in the chair. "I think he was defending me."

"That doesn't make sense."

"I know."

"Did he survive the explosion?"

Roads thought about it briefly. "He might have."

"But you can't be certain?"

"No. I tried to tag the scene as it happened, but I didn't quite make it in time."

The reminder of his artificial eyes disturbed her. She had almost forgotten they were there. "That's how you took the picture of Cati, when you chased him from Old North Street?"

"Exactly. The old concealed-camera trick went out years ago."

"For you, maybe. Not for the rest of us mortals." She took away the plate and rinsed it, grateful for the chance to hide the flush she could feel creeping across her face. While at the sink, she poured them both a cup of coffee. "Let's go into the lounge."

He lay down on the sofa and rested while she set up her laptop on a coffee table in front of him. He was looking stronger than he had half an hour earlier; his skin had lost some of its deathly pallor.

"Just one more question," she said, sitting on the edge of the sofa with her back against his midriff. "Did you see Cati among the assassins?"

"No. Should I have?"

"I'd have bet money on it." She tapped at the keyboard.

"Why? What did the search find?"

"His name." She called up the file. "We didn't find it earlier because it's not really a name at all, or even a word. It's an abbreviation."

A single line of text appeared on the screen: "*Cybernetic Augmentation Technologies Inc.*"

Roads leaned forward. "Of course. I knew I'd heard the word before." In response to Barney's look of inquiry, he explained: "CATI was a military off-shoot. They handled special projects, mainly developmental technology and so on. I don't remember them producing anything noteworthy, though. Did they modify Cati?"

"They *built* him." The next page was a long list of complicated scientific jargon. "As far as I can tell, they force-bred him from tailored genetic material and brought him to physical maturity in under twelve months. The genetic tailoring amplified his size, strength, stamina and speed, reduced his brain size by five per cent, improved his senses of smell and touch, and raised his metabolic rate.

"Side-effects included abnormal skin-pigmentation, a slight lessening of intelligence, muteness and the inability to reproduce."

"He's sterile?"

"Worse than that. He's a metamale, Phil – a sexless drone based on the male form . . . but *not* male." Again she thought of wasps, and shuddered.

"Go on," Roads encouraged.

She took a deep breath. "After his body matured, they modified it further. They reinforced his bones with carbon-fibre struts, and installed tylosine and acetylcholine dispensers to reduce his stress and boost his stamina. They took out his eyes and inner ears and replaced them with implants, installed a short-range microwave transmitter/receiver under his brain-stem so he could communicate by radio, and damaged the language-recognition centres in his cortex so he would have difficulty responding to normal speech. Then they conditioned him, took away what free will he might have retained, and linked him to a microwave command grid. He has a control code to ensure his obedience. Without it, he won't even respond to orders, but with it he will do literally anything."

Barney vividly remembered the contents of the file, and the horror she had felt upon reading it. Even before the turn of the twenty-first century, neuropsychologists had been aware of the effects of transcranial magnetic stimulation (TMS): by applying rapid magnetic pulses through the cortex, it was possible to reset or influence brain cells, thereby making limbs twitch involuntarily or emotions appear from nowhere. But it wasn't until the CATI project that such stimulation had been used to actively direct cognitive flow: specifically, the so-called syncritical path that Keith Morrow's scientists had studied in order to build a copy of his personality.

If the human brain was comprised of many parts acting more or less in sympathy, and was essentially a chaotic system, then by nudging one of those many parts in just the right way, it was possible to change the future outcome of the brain's overall activity with a fair degree of accuracy.

The process didn't allow direct mind control, but it was still persuasive. And it was this that made Barney feel ill. The technique could have been employed to unscramble damaged psyches; instead it had been used to damage those already working perfectly, to alter the standing waves of children whose minds had yet to find their own, natural equilibria.

TMS was, essentially, a mild dose of electro-convulsive therapy, and if applied over long periods could be just as dangerous. Symptoms of overuse included memory damage, hallucinations, altered states of consciousness and brain seizures. By repeatedly applying pressure to the parts of the cortex used to guide Cati's consciousness – to make it *obey* – there was a risk of fatigue stress on that part of his mind; flexure cycles, where force was applied in one direction then another, could cause his mind to snap at a crucial moment, depending on how "elastic" his mind was, or how strongly he resisted his orders.

In other words, the more Cati fought the magnets in his head, the more dangerous the magnets became to his sanity – and therefore the more dangerous *he* became to those around him.

Barney had needed time to think it through, and she paused to give Roads the same. It didn't take him half as long, perhaps because he was more used to the concept of biomodification than she was.

"Physically superior, perfectly obedient, unintelligent without being stupid . . ." Roads half-laughed, bitterly. "He sounds like the perfect combat soldier."

"It's not funny, Phil. He's incredibly dangerous. Given the correct code he'll obey *any* order."

"Yes, I can see that. And, if the code existed, I would be worried. But he must have been a last-minute development, right before the end of the War; he might even have been a prototype, an experimental model. The code would have been lost along with everything else, wouldn't it?" Noticing her expression, he grimaced. "You're going to tell me it wasn't, aren't you?"

"CATI built sixty like him, all clones, all identical. With them, they formed C-Brigade. The existence of C-Brigade was a closely-guarded secret, which is why you never heard about it even though it was in operation for at least three years. In theory, it was designed for ground assaults, as a vanguard for 'normal' troops. In practice, it was used mainly on uprisings and for covert strikes.

"Then, in 2046, a group of high-ranking generals rebelled. They programmed a handful of CATIs to kill the President and her Chiefs of Staff. The rebellion itself failed, but the assassination was a complete success. This prompted the VP's emergency government to order the recall and destruction of C-Brigade."

"And . . . ?"

"The records suggest that all were killed."

"But one of them survived."

"It looks like it. Or saved on purpose." She couldn't keep an edge from her voice. The possibility that someone – some*thing* – like Cati was roaming the streets unchecked made her feel both frightened and angry. "And now someone's found the control code. Someone with access to the old RSD files."

"Wait – you're going too fast. Why RSD? Wasn't this information pulled from O'Dell's datapool?"

"Most of it was – the top-secret parts – but not all." She flicked to a new page. "I found this in the Mayoralty archives. It's all that remains of a file concerning the operation of the old CATI network. The rest was lost in the solar storm of "66."

The page was an excerpt from an instruction manual, with Cybernetic Augmentation Technology Inc's logo in the top right-hand corner. She waited while Roads skimmed through the text until he reached the part that had caught her eye:

"For a list of control codes, including [CYPHER] and [PROTOCOL], see Appendix 7–2 . . ."

"When I checked the data from the States," she said, "their version was abbreviated. Only Kennedy had the file with the appendix."

"You think there was a complete copy of the file somewhere else in Kennedy?"

"I'm sure of it. It's the sort of thing RSD would have stored away in its own datapool."

"But it's not there?"

"Erased. I checked the access dates for that section. Someone took it six weeks ago."

Roads brushed his singed moustache with the back of a finger. "Someone with access to RSD archives and the authority to erase historical data."

"Obviously."

He leaned back and stared at the ceiling. The ramifications of the discovery were only slowly sinking in. "He'd make the perfect assassin."

"My thought exactly. That's why I bet myself Cati would be among the people who attacked you."

"I didn't see him there. I don't think I'd be here now if he had been." Roads rubbed at the bridge of his nose and closed his eyes. "And if he wasn't there, then he and the Mole must be working separately – unless whoever I'm getting close to didn't want to use Cati, for some reason. Maybe he thought the assassination would fail, and didn't want to waste both valuable assets on one operation . . ."

"Maybe." She turned back to the screen. "But there's one thing I haven't told you."

"More bad news?"

"I'm afraid so. The CATI company was founded by a Dr Marcus Schonberg in 2024, two years after his previous company, Boston CyberKinetic, folded."

"So?"

"BCK was the company that designed the berserkers. Cati is a later and improved version of the same model."

"Christ." Roads' glassy eyes zoomed in on her face. "Without the control code, we'll never catch him."

"I know." Again the memory of Kennedy's last berserker sprang to mind. She had never forgotten Roads' description of the berserker's naked blood-lust, its apparent invincibility. And Cati was a *superior model*. "He scares the crap out of me, Phil. Promise me you won't go after him alone."

"If you want an invite, I'll have to ask first –"

"Don't joke about it. I'm serious."

"Okay." His face looked haggard in the dim light of the screen. "It's Roger's case, and therefore Roger's problem. I'll just stand back and watch, if that makes you feel better."

"Thanks. I'm not sure I believe you, but it's better than nothing."

His hand emerged from beneath the sheet and stroked her back. "Did you find anything else?"

"Only one thing worth looking at now: a reference to 'EPA44210'."

He blinked. "You did? Where?"

"In O'Dell's file, on an invoice of goods that General Stedman will be bringing to town tomorrow."

"What are they?"

"Batteries; very powerful, very compact batteries."

"Manufactured by the Reunited States . . ." Roads looked puzzled. "Why would they be in one of Morrow's hideaways?"

"More importantly, why would the Mole want them?"

"Well, that's easy enough to explain. His cloak of invisibility, or whatever it is, must require heaps of power. Any mobile source will do, I suppose, but the EPAs would be better than anything we've got." He looked thoughtful for a moment. "And it also explains why he waited so long before taking them: he didn't move on Old North Street until his power supply was running out." His hand moved up her back, to her neck. "At least that's one mystery explained."

"One of many, unfortunately." Barney grabbed his hand and squeezed it. "I'm tired. Let's hit the sack."

"Are you sure? Don't you have anything you want to ask me first?"

"Plenty, but we can talk about it in bed."

"'We'?"

"Of course. I've only got one mattress." Her eyes grew warm. "And you don't really think I'd let you out of my sight again, do you?"

He shook his head. "At least let me see what else you found, first."

She sighed. Suddenly she didn't want his explanation. It made things too complicated, too fraught with contradictions. He was Phil Roads, not some sort of berserker to be feared or reviled, like Cati.

"Please, Barney."

"All right." Turning reluctantly back to the terminal, she retrieved the last of the three word-matches.

It was an old army record: facial and profile photos compressed from 3-D, plus a few biographical notes, a brief list of commendations and a genetic fingerprint.

The name on the top was: Major Philip Geoffrey Roads, Third Mobile Battalion.

The last two lines in the file read:

>>Missing In Action, presumed dead.<<
>>Dishonourable Discharge effected posthumously.<<

"Hello soldier," said Roads softly, eyes fixed on his frozen image.

"Another long story, right?"

"Very long. But you need to hear it. I want you to understand –"

"Okay." She turned off the terminal and helped him to his feet. "But make it quick. We don't have all night."

At shortly past four in the morning, Barney woke from an unusually peaceful sleep to find Roads beside her, clad only in the sheet. Unused to sharing her bed with anyone, she lay still for a while, listening to him breathing; his every sound, no matter how faint, was amplified by the darkness until it almost seemed to echo.

When she finally tired of the situation, pleasantly novel though it was, she rolled to fit her body to his and put an arm across his chest.

He was instantly awake, grunting a half-intelligible inquiry.

"You brute," she whispered into his ear.

"Me, Barney? What have I done now?"

"Nothing. I fell asleep and you didn't wake me up."

"That's right; you were tired. So?"

"Did you finish the story?"

"More or less. The best bits, anyway."

"Oh." She tried to remember, but was still too sleep-fogged to recall more than the odd detail: something about Philadelphia, and blood. She was uncertain exactly how much of it was real, and how much the product of her dream. Or whether she really wanted to think about it just then.

Raising her hand in front of his face, she asked him: "How many fingers am I holding up?"

He made no sound as his eyes shifted automatically, found the correct spectrum. "Two."

"Now?"

"Four."

Mischievously: "Now?"

"Ah . . . Does that count as a finger?"

"Not really, I suppose."

"None, then. Can I go back to sleep now?"

"Definitely not, but I'll let you close your eyes."

"I'd rather not."

"If you don't, I'll be forced to turn on the lights."

Giving in, he rolled to embrace her. Her hand stayed exactly where it was, for a while longer.

CHAPTER FIFTEEN

8:00 a.m.

A call came at eight that morning. Barney took it while Roads listened in from the neighbouring room, where the terminal's lens would not pick up his image. Even though he was unable to see the screen, he instantly recognised the voice.

It was Margaret Chappel. Barney was in charge of a crowd-control squad during the parade later that day, and although the two of them discussed it briefly, Roads could tell it wasn't the real reason for Chappel's call. Sure enough, she soon turned the subject to the ruin of his building, and the operation that was still searching through it.

A total of fourteen bodies had been found: three out the front, nine inside, two at the back. Roads was still missing, which wasn't news to him or Barney – or, it seemed, to Chappel herself.

"If Phil's there with you," she said, "I need to talk to him urgently." When Barney hesitated, she continued: "I can assure you that this conversation is strictly off the record; it isn't being monitored or recorded, and there's no-one in my office but me. I'm calling as a friend, like last night, not as head of RSD. Just tell him to call me as soon as possible, if you see him."

"I'm not sure –"

"It's okay, Barney." He stepped into the room and came forward to face the terminal. "I have to appear eventually, I suppose. Hello, Margaret."

"Phil, your little vanishing act had even me worried."

"Really? I never knew you cared."

"If I didn't, I wouldn't be calling now." Her face hardened. "What happened?"

He quickly brought her up to date on everything that had occurred between his leaving Barney's house the previous night and the explosion.

"So *the Mole* killed them . . ." She frowned. "That's a different story to the one going around HQ."

"Which is?"

She shook her head, dismissing the question. "There's a meeting in my office in two hours. I suggest you be here."

"How bad is it?"

"Let's just say it would have been worse if you'd died last night."

"I see." He understood perfectly; there was only one thing better than a scapegoat, and that was a *dead* scapegoat. "I'll be there. Thanks for the warning."

Chappel raised a hand. "One thing more before I go."

"Yes?"

"I strongly advise that you wear your contact lenses. Barney has obviously taken the news well, but I can't guarantee that the others will."

"Point taken. See you in two."

Chappel killed the line, and Roads turned back to Barney.

She was staring at him oddly. "She knew?"

"From day one. Her father was expelled from the city under the Humanity Laws when she was a child, and she's never forgotten. She helped me get a job when I arrived in '58."

"Anyone else?"

"Martin O'Dell guessed. He ran a comparison between old Missing In Action files and the most recent Kennedy census; my name came up on both lists. And Keith Morrow knows, of course."

"Why didn't you tell *me* long ago? You should've trusted me."

"I know, but . . ." He turned away. Even now, he retreated from telling her the real reason. The instinct for secrecy that had kept him safe through the last four decades was hard to break. "Look, tell me how you felt when you first found out."

"Shocked, mainly, and a little as if you'd betrayed me."

"It didn't bother you?"

She looked uncomfortable. "Well, yes, but I'm getting used to it."

"Are you sure?" He turned back to her, but she didn't meet his eyes. "Would you have felt that way about your own father?" he asked. "He was like me, an ex-army officer drafted into security after the War. We shared the same secret."

Barney opened her mouth to say something, then closed it again. Her eyes moistened.

"I never knew," she eventually said.

"No. He made me promise not to tell you until after he died and his body had been cremated. But then, when I had the chance, I couldn't do it. You'd learned the lessons in school too well: that biomods were evil and anyone who had them was a perversion. If I'd told you then, you wouldn't have wanted to know."

Barney shook her head. "You're right. I wouldn't have believed it. Not of Dad."

"And I couldn't tell you about myself, either, without telling you about him. You were a teenager when he died. I'd known you since you were a small child. I never guessed we'd be in this situation, where my failure to tell you might threaten . . ." he shrugged ". . . whatever it is between us."

"But you stuck around," Barney said softly. "You took care of me. You've always *been* there, Phil, unchanging and reliable whenever I needed help. And I rely on you so much. How could I not have trusted you?"

"I know, I know." Roads nodded. "And I *do* feel like I've betrayed you –"

"Don't be stupid. I would have suspected years ago, had you been anyone else. The only reason I didn't is because I wouldn't let myself." She put a hand on his arm. Her face was still serious, but at least her eyes met his again. "It's not your fault your body ages at a slower pace than mine. God knows, you'll probably outlive me by decades –"

He smoothed her forehead with a fingertip, trying to erase the frown. "Don't think that far ahead, Barney. You've got plenty of other stuff to worry about. Right now, I need a shower and a change of bandages. And then I'll show you my box of tricks."

"That sounds ominous," she said with the slight beginnings of a smile. "Is it?"

He smiled back. "That depends whose side you're on."

The injury to his shoulder was healing nicely, although full movement had not yet returned to the arm. The wound was filling with a mass of pinkish cellular material that would later migrate and specialise to become dermal, muscular and nervous tissue, guided by shepherd machines as small as red corpuscles. Within a week, he guessed, his shoulder would be as good as new.

His ribs were still tender, however. Bones were more difficult to mend than flesh, even for his modified system.

After Barney had cleaned away the dried blood that had leaked overnight, and rebound the joint, Roads dressed in the clothes he had rescued from his house. Sitting down at the kitchen table, he wiped away the years of dust ingrained on the leather case, then opened it.

Inside, among an assortment of old tools, was a spare set of contact lenses which he rinsed and inserted. They fitted snugly, unfurling on contact to cover most of each eye's surface. Simple machines in their own right, the false retinae reacted to light, contracting and dilating as a normal eye would, and came complete with imitation blood-vessels.

"You'd never guess," said Barney in admiration. "I certainly didn't."

"These were standard-issue for undercover work, for 'sensitive' situations. Even back then, some people were uncomfortable with biomodification, and didn't like to be reminded."

"I can understand that, to a certain extent."

"You didn't have to deal with them." Roads remembered the neo-Luddites clearly. In the late 2030s, the Puritans had preached a modern sanctity of the flesh: no implants, no gene therapy, no metabolic alteration. They had claimed that it interfered with God's plans.

On the reverse side of the coin were those who had been denied the new technology, yet craved it bitterly. One such group had hunted biomodified troops during the Dissolution and drained them of their blood. By drinking the bodily fluids of their victims, they had hoped to acquire the micromachine elements standard in all retrofitted combat soldiers.

"Progress always leaves someone behind," Roads said. "Cars, computers, biomodification – they're all the same in that sense."

"And the Reassimilation, too."

"Exactly. There's nothing to be gained by fighting the future." He replaced the items he had removed and handed her a tiny hemisphere no larger than a grain of rice. "So put this in your ear."

She eyed it warily. "What is it, first?"

"A short-range transmitter/receiver. It'll allow us to communicate directly, without a radio or a phone."

She raised it nervously.

"Don't worry. You might feel a slight sting as it anchors itself, maybe a tiny movement, but it won't do any harm."

She pushed the tiny device into her auditory canal, then wriggled as it tickled its way toward her eardrum.

"How's that?" he asked, without moving his mouth, and she jumped. "Can you hear me clearly?"

"I . . . As though you're whispering in my ear. Weird."

"To reply, all you do is subvocalise my full name and talk. The bead will pick up the vibrations through your skull and cheekbone."

She tried it, counting slowly from one to ten. Her voice in his ear was gravelly but perfectly clear.

"Good," he said. "I wondered if it was still working. It's been a long time since I last used it."

"How *does* it work? At your end, I mean."

"One of the most common implants in the old days was the cyberlink; sort of an advanced cellular phone or modem without the visible hardware. Mine is a little more sophisticated, but operates on the same principle. My optic and auditory nerves can receive data, via an antenna wired along my spinal cord, from about five kilometres."

"What about power? Don't you have to recharge every now and again? Or do you just change batteries?"

"Most of the power comes from here." He pointed at his gut. "The human body produces its own electric potential. Mine has been boosted, that's all. As long as I don't overdo it, I'll be fine."

She grimaced theatrically.

"What?"

"Sorry. I was just imagining what would happen if you had a short circuit."

"Well –"

"I don't think I want to know. And don't expect me to share a bath with you."

He smiled back. "I won't."

They went into the lounge, where the laptop was still resting on the coffee table by the sofa. Switching it on, he took a data fiche from his case and fed it into the drive. The program took a moment to configure itself to the unfamiliar system, then announced its readiness with a simple command screen.

The logo in the top right-hand corner said: 'PolNet.'

"Now what?" asked Barney.

Roads shook his head and tapped a few commands into the keyboard, opening the modem line to RSD's mainframe and calling up access to its communication towers. When everything was ready, he leaned back into the sofa and closed his eyes.

This was much harder than simply opening a cyber-link to Barney. There were pathways to be explored that he hadn't touched for thirty years – pathways that might have changed or devolved, perhaps even atrophied completely, with forty years disuse – both within him and within the city.

After a moment, he sighed with relief. A list of commands scrolled down the screen.

"That's it," he said aloud.

"That's what?"

"I'm on-line." He opened his eyes. Superimposed at the corners of his vision were glowing green and red menus surrounding a stylised command screen. "My internal processor is broadcasting to RSD communications at several million bits per second. This means I can interface with the RSD mainframe through the program in your terminal. The complete PolNet command network is gone, but the abbreviated backup here will do for now. I can access files, take calls, run programs – all without even closing my eyes. Much easier than the old manual interface I keep in my office at HQ."

He experimented with a few commands. The skills were still fresh in his memory. In fact, it was almost too easy.

His two lives, until that moment, had been quite separate, linked only by the implants in his eyes and ears. Accessing the system was like putting on clothes he had worn in another lifetime; he felt as though part of him had been resurrected. But he was no longer the same person he had been. The young Phil Roads had died in the Dissolution forty years ago, and comfortingly familiar clothes could not change that.

He sent an image in 2-D to the RSD mainframe, then had Barney's terminal display the picture. The process was perfectly clear, but fairly slow. The image grew from the top of the screen down, line by line, in the time it would have taken to download it directly. It showed her staring back at him, eyes wide.

"Very funny." She leaned closer and brushed at his temples. "It's hard to imagine all this gear in your head."

He guided her hand to the rear of his skull. "Actually, it's here."

"Wherever, it's still unbelievable."

"Not really. Better than anything we have today, but based on the same principles. If not for the berserkers, the anti-technology riots and the Humanity Laws, Kennedy might still have retained a crude biomod capacity." He shrugged. "But I doubt it. The technology is too advanced for the reclamation factories. You can't build nanomachines and biochips out of left-over data fiches and broken computers."

"Which is why we have to Reassimilate," she said. "Before we end up in the steam age again."

"To put it bluntly, yes. You could already see it happening when I arrived here, ten years after the end of the War. Datapools were less sophisticated; there had been no technological progress at all, and the number of personal computers was on the decrease. Kennedy's done well to last this long, but it has to open up eventually. In five years, we won't be able to repair the RSD mainframe any more. There'll be nothing left to scavenge."

Barney folded her arms around herself. "I keep telling myself these things, but it still doesn't seem real."

Roads glanced at her, noticing her uncertainty for the first time. "The world is a scary place," he said softly.

She nodded. "It's like growing up, I guess. You want to be an adult, but don't want to leave childhood behind. I feel the same way when I think about Stedman. And you, with all your toys. I feel . . . *disempowered*, if that's a word."

"I'm not sure it is," Roads said, reaching to touch her shoulder, "but it should be."

She shrugged, and squeezed his hand. "Don't worry. It's just a mood. Have you got anything else to show me?"

With a flick of a mental wrist, Roads banished all but a basic "ready" icon, in the shape of a stylised police badge, and a clock. The menus he had once known as well as the backs of his hands vanished into the timeless spaces of computer memory, awaiting his command. Just knowing they were there made him feel more confident.

"Actually, it's 9:15," he said. "We really should get going. Better done quickly, and all that."

She brushed her hair back and stood. As he locked the case in a cupboard, she turned to him.

"You have a clock built in as well?"

"Of course. Do you want to know the time in Sydney?"

"No. But why, then, do you wear a watch?"

"To make myself normal. I can't avoid my ears or eyes as often as I'd like to – they're just there – but the rest is optional. If I have to use them, I will, just like I did when I first saw Cati, but the less I think about them, the better. To blend into Kennedy I have to hide the truth even from myself, in a sense. So no more PolNet, and no more magic clock."

She smiled and shook her head. "You'll never be normal."

"Maybe not." He patted the back of her hand. "But that doesn't stop me trying."

CHAPTER SIXTEEN

10:00 a.m.

The day of the Reassimilation promised many things, as though the weather itself was ambivalent: dark clouds vied with irregular flashes of blue for control of the heavens, while occasional, startling glimpses of the sun turned the city to gold below.

With atmospheric carbon dioxide levels still high, despite industrial emissions being only a fraction of what they were before the War, weather was unseasonal as a rule. Lacking global or even regional data, Kennedy forecasters could only guess what each day might bring. Community efforts – incorporating everything from cloud-watching to casting runes – contributed to this process. When sudden shifts in temperature could halve a staple crop's produce almost overnight, everyone wanted to have their say.

Barney and Roads arrived at HQ on the dot of ten, breathless from the brisk walk. She went immediately to her desk to prepare for the day while he continued upward to the top floor, ignoring the occasional startled glance in his direction. The only person he met on the way who seemed at all keen to talk was Roger Wiggs, who accompanied him for the last few floors.

"Someone told me you were dead," said Wiggs, brushing his hair in the lift's mirror. "Obviously they were wrong."

"Obviously." The existence of the rumour explained why people had been staring at him. He wondered briefly who had started it. "You in on the meeting?"

"Unfortunately." Wiggs put the comb back in his pocket. "Any idea what it's about?"

"Not really, but I've got a bad feeling."

"Me too. DeKurzak has had me going over the files for two days now and hasn't said shit. That worries me."

"At least you haven't got Blindeye on your back."

"True. But we still don't have anything to go on. We're just as lost as we were a month ago."

Roads said nothing, although he itched to take his fellow officer aside and brief him on Cati. There simply wasn't time to do so before the meeting.

The lift came to a halt and the doors hissed open. Michael, Chappel's secretary, met them and guided them through to the office without a word. Raised voices, heard behind the door, ceased in mid-sentence when Michael knocked.

"Come in."

Chappel was seated behind the desk, facing DeKurzak and O'Dell. A powerful tension filled the air. As Roads and Wiggs entered, the RUSAMC captain looked up with obvious relief and rose to his feet.

"Speak of the devil," he said to Roads.

"Nothing bad, I hope."

O'Dell hesitated. "No, of course not. The foyer guard just buzzed to say you were on your way up. It's good to see you're still with us."

Roads inclined his head in gratitude. DeKurzak pointedly ignored him. As he took the seat on O'Dell's right, he noticed with a sinking feeling what the liaison officer was holding in his lap.

The X-rays.

When Wiggs had settled into the one remaining chair next to Roads, DeKurzak finally spoke.

"Perhaps we can begin now, seeing we're all here." His voice was flat and expressionless, and his face closed, but beneath the surface clearly seethed the argument that had been interrupted. He spoke directly at Chappel, ignoring the others. "I have an appointment at eleven to finalise the security arrangements for General Stedman's arrival, and I must not be late."

She met his stare. "I know. I have to be there, too." To Roads and Wiggs she explained: "General Stedman's arrival has been brought forward to three o'clock."

"Really?" said Roads. "The timing's been to the split-second for a week now. Why the last-minute change?"

O'Dell looked embarrassed. "Apparently the convoy made better time than we anticipated."

Roads smiled graciously, allowing the explanation to pass without believing a word of it. He found it more likely that the General – and therefore the RUSAMC – had chosen to test the readiness of the city.

DeKurzak cleared his throat pointedly. Chappel shuffled printed files on her desk.

"All right. As Antoni and Martin know, I received a memo from the Mayor this morning, which, among other things, makes a couple of recommendations I feel we should discuss."

"Discuss?" DeKurzak scowled in annoyance. "What's there to discuss? They seem perfectly clear to me."

"What does?" asked Wiggs, nervousness showing on his brow, glistening.

"We'll get to that."

"Tell them, Margaret." DeKurzak gestured at the letter on her desk. "Or I will."

She glared at him. "Need I remind you, Antoni, that these are simply *recommendations*? I have the final say in RSD affairs – not the Mayor, and certainly not the MSA."

He waved a hand dismissively. "It doesn't matter who makes the decision, as long as it's the correct one."

"And I remain unconvinced that this is correct." She glanced at Roads and Wiggs, then down at her desk. "Nevertheless, it seems I have no choice." Her eyes rose again to meet Roads'. "In his letter, the Mayor recommends that, effective immediately, all investigations into the Mole and the assassin be handed to the MSA/RUSAMC cooperative, where they will be jointly handled by Antoni DeKurzak and Captain Martin O'Dell."

"The sonofabitch," said Wiggs, shaking his head. "All we need is a little more time."

"'*Time*'?" DeKurzak stood, on the attack. The sheaf of X-rays punctuated important points as his hands moved. "Reassimilation is today. Not next week, or next year – *today*. You've had more than five weeks to produce results. Do you expect us to sit back and wait until the killer hands himself in?"

"We're doing our best –"

"Which is obviously not good enough. The moment has come to let someone who knows what he's doing take charge of the investigation."

"Like you, I suppose?"

"Martin and I have already agreed upon how we shall divide responsibilities," said DeKurzak stiffly. "And I will be assuming control of your investigation, yes."

"Great, just great." Wiggs looked at Roads for support. "Come on, Phil. I can't believe you're just sitting there taking this shit."

"I'm waiting." Roads folded his hands in his lap, trying to radiate an aura of patience he wasn't feeling. "There's more to come."

"Indeed there is," said DeKurzak without looking at him, returning to his seat. "Read the rest, Margaret."

Chappel unfolded the letter. "Mayor Packard also recommends that you, Phil, be placed under house arrest pending an inquiry into the nature of what he calls your 'surreptitious and not infrequent relationship with various criminal elements within the city'. He goes on to suggest that your allegiance may not be wholly with the city in this case, and that your judgement may therefore be compromised."

"That's bullshit. I'm as straight as they come."

DeKurzak turned on him. "Then how do you justify your secret dealings with Keith Morrow?"

"He supplies me with information –"

"Which you fail to include in your reports. Concealing information regarding a known and wanted criminal is alone tantamount to corruption."

"Depending on the circumstances."

"RSD regulations disagree with you."

"Everyone on the force has a grass. It's the way things work –"

"Granted, and we might be prepared to overlook it this once – but for these." DeKurzak waved the X-rays. Clearly visible on the transparent picture were Roads' various biomods.

"I can explain –"

"Can you? You illegally entered the city, forged your date of birth on RSD records, falsified a medical examination and lied to protect your secret on a number of other occasions. In this light, any explanation you have must be regarded with extreme suspicion." DeKurzak threw the X-rays to Wiggs, who had indicated that he would like to see. "I can't believe we entrusted a position of such responsibility to a man with . . . with *machines* in his head." DeKurzak's face was red, made suddenly old by his anger. "And don't bother protesting that you're a good cop. It's no wonder you're so good given your unnatural advantage over the rest of us. How did it feel to rob the marksmanship title from someone more worthy, Roads? Did you feel superior? Was it guilt that made you retire from the competition, or had you set your sights on a higher goal – ?"

"Antoni," Chappel tried to interrupt, but DeKurzak rolled on over her.

"No, Margaret. These are questions we should all be asking. Let's see if he can answer them to anyone's satisfaction."

Roads' face flushed with barely-checked anger. "I never once used my abilities in any other capacity than as dictated by my profession. I am not a cheat, and I do not feel superior to anyone born in a time less-advantaged than mine –"

"But we have only your word for that, don't we? The word of someone who has already proved to be a liar."

"I believe him," put in O'Dell.

"And what would you know?"

"More than you, obviously –"

"That's enough," Chappel interrupted, scowling at them all across the expanse of her desk. "This is not a trial and I am not a judge but, by Christ, I'll throw the next person who speaks out of line into the can for a week. We're here to discuss the cases first, and Phil second. You've had your say, Antoni, so be quiet."

DeKurzak's lips drained of blood as he retreated into his seat and crossed his arms. Roads tried to read the tangled knot of emotions displayed before him. What, he wondered, was DeKurzak afraid of?

Only one answer made sense, and that was *failure*. The cases were still open; neither the Mole nor the killer had been caught. That would have an adverse effect on

DeKurzak's record – unless, of course, he could pass as much of the blame onto Roads as possible.

Not just righteous indignation, then, Roads decided, but treachery as well.

"Roger?" asked Chappel. "Do you have anything you'd like to say?"

The red-head declined the opportunity to take sides. "I'm staying out of it, Margaret. Sorry, Phil."

"That's okay. I understand."

"And, as for the case," Wiggs added to DeKurzak, "I'll be glad to get back on day shift. The fucker's all yours, buddy."

Chappel intervened before the liaison officer could speak. "Martin?"

"I agree with Phil's theory that the Mole might be a Northerner – in which case I'm the obvious choice to head the case." He shrugged at Roads. "But I don't think we can blame Phil for being the way he is, or for trying to hide it. The knee-jerk reaction is even stronger here than back home." He cast a scathing glance sideways at DeKurzak. "What I'd like to do is to point out a fact in Phil's favour that the X-rays don't show."

Chappel nodded. "Go on."

"I am obviously too young to remember either the War or the Dissolution, but I have access to military records that document their history, at least in part. One episode concerns the final days of the Third Mobile Battalion. Briefly, the battalion was ordered to Philadelphia in 2047 to spearhead the suppression of a civilian rebellion. Orders were to kill on sight, not to detain, until such time as the leaders of the rebellion were neutralised. A bloodbath, basically, is what the military wanted, to teach the city a lesson."

Roads closed his eyes with a wince, but didn't speak. He remembered it more vividly than that. Being reminded of it by the RUSA files the previous day had been bad enough. In this context, it was horrific.

"The battalion's third in command," O'Dell continued, "a major on exchange from the Australian Armed Forces, led a mutiny against his commanding officers. He refused along with over a third of the battalion to comply with orders of that nature. Under other circumstances, he might have been commended for his actions. During the mutiny, however, while defences were down, the civilian rebellion attacked and the battalion was wiped out. Although the force behind the battalion tried, it was unable to gain control of the city without the Third Mobile. The major who led the mutiny – Philip Roads – disappeared, and was subsequently presumed dead."

"You can substantiate this?" DeKurzak broke in.

"It's all in the files. Files to which, I should point out, Phil had no access. They could not have been falsified."

"And your point?"

"That his actions displayed strength of character and moral conviction. He may have betrayed his command, but only to further a greater good." O'Dell smiled ironically, and added: "Philadelphia, as you must know, is now the capital of the Reunited States of America."

DeKurzak made a mocking noise, but Chappel waved him silent.

"Phil?"

Roads stirred himself from the memories O'Dell had awoken. "I have only one thing to say, and I'll keep it quick. I doubt there's anybody in this room who would deny that I'm one of Kennedy's most qualified officers –"

"So you've said," DeKurzak sneered. "But that only makes your inability to apprehend the Mole doubly suspicious."

"No. He's simply better than I am – and I'd like to wish Martin the best of luck. He's going to need it."

O'Dell looked uncomfortable, but said nothing.

"What I will say is this: I may not have caught the Mole, but I know who the killer is."

The reaction was instantaneous. Chappel and O'Dell looked startled; DeKurzak was caught speechless, open-mouthed.

"You *what*?" Wiggs gasped, turning a mottled shade of purple.

"The killer is a type of berserker," Roads said, "one we've never seen before. A later model, if you like, and twice as dangerous." Before he lost the upper hand, he explained everything known about Cati: the history of his development, the general nature of his extreme biomodification and the significance of the control code. "Cati was built to do only two things: to kill and to obey. With no morals, no opinions and no conscience to get in the way, he is the perfect assassin for anyone in a position to command him."

Wiggs' high colour gradually ebbed, but he remained flushed in the cheeks. "They really had such things?"

"Yes. You'll find an incomplete description in the States datapool. I suggest you dig it out and look for the control frequency. If we can trace the source of the transmissions, we might be able to find out who's controlling him: the person or persons who want to stop the Reassimilation."

"He can't be working on his own?"

"No. He's designed to follow orders, not to be independent. Cut the chain of command, and he'll be neutralised. Disarmed."

"Okay." Chappel turned to O'Dell. "Can you find that data for us, Martin?"

"Of course. It won't take long."

"I wouldn't bother, if I were you," said DeKurzak.

"What? Why not?" The young captain turned in puzzlement to the MSA liaison officer.

"Because there's no point." DeKurzak chuckled softly. "Nice try, Roads, but it won't work."

Roads felt his face turn red. "I'm sorry?"

"You can't make yourself look better by conjuring up some demon from the past."

"I'm telling you the truth. The file is there. You can check it yourself."

"Of course it is. Are we to assume that this is something else you chose to omit from your reports?"

"No, I only realised this morning –"

"How convenient. Something that has eluded homicide for six weeks just comes to you in a flash. Next you'll be telling us that this . . . *freak* . . . was responsible for the deaths last night."

"No. As far as I know, he wasn't even there."

"So you admit it? You killed them in cold blood?"

"Me?" This time Roads was taken off guard. If that's what the rumours were saying, then he was in deeper trouble than he realised. "It was the Mole."

DeKurzak laughed openly, shaking his head as though in pity.

O'Dell had turned grey. "What makes you suspect the Mole?"

"I saw him, that's what." Roads look at Chappel. "You don't really think it was me, do you?"

"What we think doesn't come into it," interrupted DeKurzak. "A board of inquiry will be called to decide whether you used an excess of force."

"This is crazy."

"Is it? Any crazier than the theory you've proposed?" DeKurzak also turned to Chappel. "A mythical, mentally disadvantaged combat soldier who has hidden unnoticed in Kennedy for an unknown number of years suddenly discovers politics and begins killing again to make a point –"

"It's not *him*. It's whoever's *controlling* him –"

"Let me finish, Roads. We all agree that the killer has access to information not available to the general public, so it has to come from someone reasonably high up in the government. Why not you, Roads? You're biomodified; you'd know exactly who to kill; you have contacts in the underworld; and you're in a prime position to misdirect investigations away from you. All we have against this theory is your word plus a ridiculous attempt to shift the blame elsewhere."

Roads managed to break in. "Why would I possibly want to do this?"

"I can think of a number of reasons. There may be another government interested in Kennedy, apart from the Reunited States; you may be plotting with them to foil the Reassimilation. You might even be behind the Mole as well, stealing information for the benefit of your superiors. Or you could simply be looking after yourself; keeping the Reunited States away in order to ensure your own personal power. Perhaps you're just a born Judas; you did, after all, betray your own commanding officers before coming here –"

"That's it." Roads fought a sudden urge to grab the liaison officer by the throat. "I've had enough of this shit. Make your decision, Margaret, before I kill him."

"Are you threatening me?" DeKurzak stood, fists clenched.

"Sit *down*, Antoni." She glanced at her watch. "We're almost out of time. We'll have to continue this discussion after Reassimilation."

DeKurzak didn't back down. "If you're suggesting that we leave Roads in charge until then –"

"I'm not. I'm transferring the cases, as the Mayor advised. Assuming you and Martin can work together, it'll be your baby from now on."

"Good." DeKurzak looked partially satisfied; slowly, he moved away.

"And what about me?" Roads held his breath.

"Consider yourself relieved of all duties until we can look more closely at the situation. You can keep the ID, but the gun will have to stay here." Her regret was obvious, but the cold feeling rising in Roads' gut wouldn't let him sympathise with her. "It's the best I can do, Phil. I'm sorry."

DeKurzak wasn't pleased either. "I hardly feel enough has been done to –"

"Shut up, DeKurzak." Roads stood and faced the liaison officer. "You've got what you wanted."

"What I want is what's best for this city, which is to Reassimilate as smoothly as possible. If seeing you brought to justice will help that process, then that's what has to happen. And if you don't see it that way, then that's your problem."

Roads ignored him. O'Dell looked like he had something he wanted to say, but obviously thought better of it. Wiggs stared at his shoes, keeping carefully neutral. Only Margaret braved the moment with a slight shake of her head that told him there was nothing more she could do.

He understood instantly what she meant: not even the Director of RSD could block an inquiry once evidence of biomodification became widespread. Just delaying the response must have cost her plenty. If she fought too hard to defend him now, suspicion would be cast upon her as well. And any last chance RSD had of weathering the storm might vanish as a result.

Roads left the room breathing heavily through his

nose. Only when the door was safely slammed behind him, did he dare vent his frustration by hitting a wall.

"*Fuck* it."

Michael hid behind the reception desk as he stormed past to the elevator, nursing his fist.

On the way down, he opened the cyberlink to Barney.

"Meet me in my office, pronto."

"What's the matter? Didn't it go well?" The concern in her voice was obvious, even through the subvocal transmission. "What happened, Phil?"

"They took me off the case – *that's* what happened. And if DeKurzak gets his way I'll be up before a Humanity Court this time next week. The sonofabitch shafted me."

"Christ. I'll be there as soon as I can."

He ignored Marion's cheerful hello when he reached his floor and headed straight for his office. Opening the bottom drawer of his desk, he emptied out the net of contact electrodes and put it in his pocket. When he turned to the terminal to transfer his files onto data fiche, he noticed that it had already been activated.

The screen displayed an excerpt from the Mayor's letter, a single paragraph with one sentence highlighted:

"Acting on reports submitted by both Antoni DeKurzak and Captain O'Dell, I have no choice but to recommend that Senior Officer Roads be suspended from duty until such time as his circumstances can be adequately re-evaluated."

Roads stared at the screen.

. . . and Captain O'Dell . . .

He collapsed into the chair and rubbed at his brow. The message was obviously from Chappel; she was the only one with both the authority to override his terminal and access to the Mayor's memo. The question was whether she had intended it as a warning to be discovered prior to the event or as an explanation afterward. Either way, she'd truly had no choice. In the face of *two* negative reports, not just DeKurzak's, any action apart from suspending him would definitely have put her in the firing line with him. Kennedy law imposed the same penalties on both the biomodified and the people who harboured them.

Barney stormed in, her lips pursed with anger. "That fucking little low-life. What's he playing at?"

Roads looked up. "Hi, Barney. Thanks for coming."

"What choice did I have? We have to do something about this, before it's too late."

"There's nothing we *can* do. I'm out, and Martin's in. It's as simple as that."

"But what about DeKurzak? He's going to get all the credit for finding Cati!"

"Maybe. I don't know. As far as he's concerned, Cati's just a myth."

"What? But it makes *sense* –"

"He thinks I'm involved, that I'm trying to cover up."

"Of all the . . ." Barney gesticulated her frustration, lost for words.

Roads understood the way she was feeling. "DeKurzak wants three things: one, to discredit me to make himself look better; two, to set me up to take the fall for either the Mole or the killer, or both; and three, to weaken RSD's hold on law enforcement in Kennedy. The last in particular. I wouldn't be surprised if that's been his mission for the MSA all along: to infiltrate us, and thereby catch us with our pants down." He switched off the terminal with a flick of his finger. "He was out to get me before I even walked in the door, despite what he said yesterday. And I can't fight him. Not when he has everything on his side."

"But you can't just give up either."

"I'm not going to. The Reunited States' convoy arrives in four hours. If Cati strikes again, it'll be tonight for sure, before the treaty's signed. And he'll be after big game, this time – bigger than the Mayoralty."

"The General?" Her eyes grew wide as she realised what he meant. "Cati's going to assassinate *General Stedman*?"

"With Stedman out of the way, the balance might swing in favour of the conservatives."

"Oh my God. I hadn't thought –"

A knock at the open door cut her off. Both of them turned to face Martin O'Dell.

"I didn't mean to interrupt," he said. The RUSAMC captain hovered in the doorway, looking distinctly uncomfortable. "I just came by to say I'm sorry. I had no choice."

Roads pretended to be busy clearing his desk. Barney looked from one to the other, clearly sensing the tension between them.

"If it makes any difference," continued O'Dell undeterred, "I only wanted the case, not the inquiry into your conduct. I'd like you to know that if worse comes to worst you're welcome in Philadelphia. You don't have to stay here. Quite apart from your past involvement, we can always use good people, and there's certainly more opportunity back home to –"

"Thanks, Martin. You can spare me the campaign speech."

O'Dell looked pained. "I'm only trying to do my job, okay?"

"I know." Roads looked up. "But what the hell *is* your job, exactly? You're a soldier, not a cop."

"I'm both." O'Dell hesitated in the doorway. "I have my orders. Remember that, if nothing else."

"How can I forget?"

The RUSAMC captain left. Roads sighed and put his hands on the desk, tired of petty politics getting in the way of the things he had to do.

Barney came to him and put her arms around his shoulders. "You can go back to my place, if you want to."

"No. I haven't got time." He squeezed her hand, grateful for her sympathy even as he rejected it. "I need two favours."

"Anything."

"Are you sure?" Roads looked her in the eye. "I can't go to Margaret for this – or anything – while RSD is at risk. But I don't want to drag *you* down instead."

"If I was worried about that, would I be here now?" Barney returned his stare. "Tell me what you want, and I'll see what I can do."

"A bike, first of all, if you can get hold of one; and a schedule for the next twenty-four hours. Security plans of Mayor's House would be good, but I don't want to push my luck."

She leaned away. "You're going after Cati, aren't you?"

"I have to. If we're right and he is the killer, then someone has to stop him."

"Unarmed?" Her eyes were filled with concern. "Don't, Phil, please. I can talk DeKurzak into it."

"He won't have the time to listen to you until tomorrow – and by then it'll be too late."

"But Margaret –"

"It has to be me. I'm sorry."

She put her head on his shoulder. "You stupid sonofabitch."

"Senile, actually. I'll be ninety-five next month."

Barney pulled a face. "Don't put it that way. It sounds so –"

"Old? That's exactly how I feel when I look at O'Dell and DeKurzak."

"No. *Serious*." Her hands tightened. "But remind me to throw you a party, if you're still around."

"Thanks," he said. "I think I'll need it."

CHAPTER SEVENTEEN

12:30 p.m.

The threat of rain had passed by the time Roads managed to escape HQ on a bicycle Barney had borrowed from the RSD pool. The streets and sidewalks of the inner suburbs were busy with people.

General Stedman's convoy was still some hours away, but the reclamation and reprocessing factories had already shut down. Regardless of political persuasion – for, against, or even indifferent – everyone in Kennedy Polis seemed to be taking advantage of the first public holiday in over a year. Parties had begun in parks, Rosette stations, and little-used intersections. Bands played on roof gardens, sending snatches of melody aloft on the wind. The smell of freshly-cooked food drifted at random through the streets.

There was always a sense of guilty pleasure in taking time off, however. The struggle to maintain viability had been so long and desperate during the Dissolution that an egalitarian lifestyle and obsessive work ethic had become indelible parts of the city's culture. *Not working* had connotations far worse than simple laziness: it hurt everyone in the long-run.

A measure of anti-Reassimilation sentiment found its source in this guilt – as though a slight lapse in concentration on internal issues would result in the collapse of the fragile bubble that was Kennedy. Roads could understand that, and even felt a measure of it himself: old habits, forged when survival seemed most unlikely, were always the hardest to break. The fight for the city was won on many levels, not just by keeping possible threats Outside.

A splash of red, white and blue caught Roads' eye, distracting him temporarily from his thoughts. One daring person had unearthed an old flag and raised it above a converted post office. The Stars and Stripes, for so long forbidden, was an unusual sight, and an evocative one.

As he furiously pedalled along the streets, Roads wondered whether the flag was a gesture of celebration or of warning. Was the arrival of the RUSAMC a threat or an opportunity? Only time would tell.

Of only one thing was he completely certain: that Cati's controller would strike again. Anyone so anti-Reassimilation as to kill in the past would not stop once Stedman was in the city. And what more tempting target could there possibly be? Certainly far more relevant than Councillors or aides who had supported the bill before it became reality.

He steered the bike past a pile of recently fallen masonry that had spilled onto the road, and called up the PolNet systems. The menus reappeared super-imposed upon the street ahead, like neon hallucinations more real than reality itself. He searched through them, found the access number he was after, and dialled.

Morrow's bodiless head appeared in the depths of his vision, always a fixed distance ahead of him.

"No image," said the Head, "and a simulated voice. This can only mean one thing."

"That's right." Roads smiled despite himself. "I've succumbed to temptation."

"Good for you, Phil. It was only a matter of time. Welcome back to the electronic fold, my boy, where you belong."

"Not by choice, I'm afraid."

"Shame." Morrow sniffed. "Please bear in mind that I'm here when you need me. If you take the fall, I'll be there to catch you. DeKurzak doesn't frighten me in the slightest."

"How much do you know about that?"

"Probably more than you."

"I hope so. I was set up and I want to know why."

"Start asking questions, then, and I'll tell what I can."

"Right, the assassination first. Who hired Danny Chong, and why?"

"Pass." Morrow's face displayed sincere regret.

"Okay. Where did Chong get the explosives, then? I haven't seen anything that powerful in twenty years."

"From me, of course. You should have known."

"I guessed, but needed to know for sure. That makes them imports. From the same place as the EPA44210s? The Reunited States?"

"Perhaps. Do change the subject, dear boy."

Roads pedalled steadily onward, glad that one guess had proved correct. "Back to DeKurzak. What can you tell me about him?"

"He's an orphan, like your assistant. Both his parents were killed by a berserker in '57."

"Interesting, Keith, but hardly relevant."

"Perhaps not. He's certainly driven by something, and regarded as a golden boy by his allies. He worked his way up the MSA in record time while Packard was head. If he continues at this rate, he'll be running the entire city within a couple of decades."

"Is that fast enough, do you think?"

"Not for him, certainly. For me, I could wait forever."

"What do you know about his analysis of Blindeye, and the Mole?"

"Only what he's told the Mayor in his report. He wants you strung up as an example, just in case any more of the Old Guard think of trying anything silly." Morrow tut-tutted. "The boy is paranoid, but quite sincere, it would seem. And he makes a convincing case. The Mayor seems quite won over by his enthusiasm, even though the Mayor himself would be a possible suspect."

"I know. O'Dell, too? Does he agree with DeKurzak?"

"Doubtful. His report carefully avoids the matter, as though he is trying not to commit himself. His only recommendation is that he should take over the Mole case in place of you, and his reasoning there is inconclusive."

"Did he mention my biomods?"

"No."

Roads paused while he took a corner, pondering DeKurzak's actions. The recent change in the MSA was at the core of them, he was sure. As the necessity to maintain external vigilance had gradually ebbed, so too had the number of people required to patrol the Wall. The active staff numbers of the MSA had therefore atrophied, with personnel drifting into other areas such as security and administration. Still, a position in the MSA automatically commanded respect and admiration, out of respect for the organisation's past. To be part of the MSA meant that one was actively involved in the defence of the city, unlike RSD, which defended the city from itself.

Reassimilation, however, would nullify the reason for the existence of the MSA, and increase the need for internal policing. DeKurzak's actions made more sense when this was taken into account: by breaking up RSD and absorbing the pieces, he could give the MSA an entirely new portfolio, and thus a reason to exist.

O'Dell's motives, however, were far from clear.

The streets became less crowded the further Roads went from the city centre. Patriot Bridge appeared briefly from behind a building, then vanished again. He consulted a street map in the RSD datapool and realised that he was closer to his destination than he had thought.

"One more question, Keith. I'm trying to track down an old CATI soldier. It looks like one made it to Kennedy during the Dissolution and is now being used by whoever wants to derail the Reassimilation. Do you know anything about him, or where he might be hiding?"

"'It', you mean." Morrow's face remained stonily blank. "I took the liberty of browsing through the files of your lovely assistant last night, and learned of your discovery that way. It seems obvious to me that the Mole is entirely unconnected with this CATI operative. You should return to your original search immediately. You'll be wasting your time, otherwise."

Roads detected more than a faint warning in the Head's tone of voice, but ignored it. "I don't think so. There's a connection here somewhere. All I have to do is find it."

"Perhaps. But you are treading a dangerous path that might, eventually, lead nowhere."

"That's a chance I'll just have to take."

"Very well." Morrow sighed. "Was there anything else?"

"Just one more favour. A big one, this time. I need a security pass to Mayor's House for tonight. I don't think I'll be able to get in otherwise, and I can't afford to miss any of the action."

Morrow pondered the request. "It'll be tricky, but I can do it. I'll call you later with a rendezvous."

"Thanks, Keith." That Morrow could deliver wasn't in doubt. Being an artificial intelligence, he had immediate access to more cognitive resources than any human. Had it not been for the War, he might have been running the entire country, not just a few shady operations in an isolated city.

Roads turned another corner, and realised that he had made it at last. He glided slowly to a halt and balanced on two wheels and one leg in the middle of the street.

"I have to go."

"Already? Must our conversations always be so brief?"

"I'm afraid so. You're a 'criminal element', remember?"

Morrow didn't smile. "Ah, yes. I do keep forgetting."

Old North Street was empty as far as his eyes could see. One hundred and fourteen was still sealed with RSD Major Crime tape, and looked deserted. He had no doubt that, if he ventured down into the concealed cellar, he would find that empty as well.

Opening the cyberlink to Barney, he softly called her name. Her reply was instantaneous.

"Shit! Sorry, Phil. You startled me. Where are you?"

"Old North Street. Any news from the lookout?"

"None since I last called."

"Good." He leaned the bike against the wall of number 113, inside which the stake-out was hidden. There was no response from within the building, but he knew the bike would be watched along with the building across the road. "How're things at your end?"

"Slow. I'm down by the Wall, and the crowds are fairly quiet. The heat's making everyone docile, I guess."

"That won't last. Any protests?"

"One group tried to string an anti-Reassimilation banner across the road, but we got rid of them easily enough. There've been a couple of scuffles, nothing too exciting. Some of the lads are hoping for a minor revolution in our vicinity, to relieve the boredom, but I don't think that's likely."

Roads lit a cigarette. "Anything from the bosses yet?"

"The Mantis made a speech not long ago, to explain that we will be co-operating closely with the MSA and the States in future. No specifics, and she's been quiet since then. There's a bit of gossip going around, some of it concerning you, but I'm keeping on top of it."

"That's my girl. You'll let me know when the fun starts, won't you?"

"The parade? Sure. I finish my shift at seven, if you want to meet me somewhere then."

"Maybe. We'll see how I go."

"Call me."

"I will."

He cut the line. While he finished his cigarette, he ran through everything that Morrow had told him.

The Head was obviously smuggling RUSA products into the city – hence the crates arriving at 114 Old North Street in the dead of the night and Morrow's possession of the batteries – although exactly how he had obtained them was still a mystery. That ruled out one possibility: that the explosives Danny Chong had used to blow up his house had been supplied by the people who had ordered his assassination – i.e. the RUSAMC itself, or a faction within it.

So the RUSAMC hadn't tried to kill him. That was some relief, but it still left him short of an actual suspect.

He had had a half-formed idea that the assassination attempt might have been a set-up: that Chong and co.

had been deliberately killed in order to incriminate him. That made the Mole, as Chong's killer, the source of the contract. But he doubted it; it was too complex a plan, relying on too many variables. Why would the Mole go to so much trouble when it would be easier to kill Roads himself and be done with it?

No. The Mole had nothing to do with Chong's mission. His assumption of the previous day had been wrong, therefore: he was close to catching *Cati*, not the Mole. That meant Cati's controller had been behind the attempt to assassinate Roads. He or she – or even *they* – must have used Chong to throw him off the scent, on the off-chance that the attempt to kill him would fail.

DeKurzak still professed a belief in a member of the Old Guard being behind the killings, and had tied up much of homicide looking for evidence to support his case. O'Dell did not seem to have allied himself with DeKurzak in this instance, however, and that difference of opinion was worth noting. Not that it helped Roads terribly much. Whether Cati was investigated or not, Roads felt safe assuming that he was close to solving, if not actually dealing with, that half of the problem. All that remained was the thief.

Suddenly, a new thought occurred to him: in six weeks of random thievery, the Mole had killed no-one. Then, during Blindeye, he had struck Roads a blow that might have killed an ordinary man. The following night he had killed fourteen people. What had changed in the thief's situation to warrant such violence? Or had the situation changed at all?

On the one hand, the Mole had tried to kill him. Then, after weeks of eluding him, spying on him, doing everything he could to confound the man he had impersonated – he had actually saved his life. Why the inconsistency?

An answer came instantly, more from intuition than thought: just as Morrow wanted him to catch the Mole, so too did the Mole want Roads to catch Cati.

But that didn't make sense. Two nights ago, he had known nothing about the killer, apart from a photo or two; hardly enough to make him suspect anything specific. Not until the search through the datapool had found the old CATI file did he guess the truth, and even then he had kept it quiet for several hours. Whoever had decided that Roads knew the truth had made a very large assumption – or had access to his data.

The cigarette had died some time ago. Throwing the butt illegally into a gutter, he crossed the road and mounted the steps of 116 Old North Street. He straightened his clothing in the reflection cast by a shadowed window; despite the fact that he rarely wore full uniform, plain-clothes felt awkward. He still had his ID, however – the subtle distinction between "holidays" and suspension having allowed him to keep that, if not his gun.

Two other things DeKurzak's attack had left him with were time and freedom to pursue the case fully. He knew he would need both if he was to succeed.

General Stedman would be in Kennedy Polis within a handful of hours, and Cati would try to kill him. Roads felt safe assuming this, although he lacked the evidence to prove it. The only way to stop the killer was to neutralise the person controlling him, so that's exactly what Roads planned to do.

The Mole would have to wait, if he only would.

Katiya answered on the second knock. The door to the second-floor apartment swung open with a rattle of locks and chains, and her eye appeared in the crack. When she saw who it was, she opened the door wider and let him in.

She looked as though she had just woken from a deep sleep. Her hair was tangled; her eyes were bagged. She wore a cotton nightshirt that barely reached the tops of her knees. A silver pendant shaped like a miniature ingot hung from a chain about her neck – the only item of jewellery Roads had seen her wear.

She guided him into the lounge and collapsed onto an old sofa, rubbing her eyes. The room was threadbare: the sofa and one companion chair, a small table; no ornaments, no carpet. Damp had stained the ceiling black in places and made the paint peel from the walls. The air smelled of closed spaces, of claustrophobia.

"I'm sorry to disturb you," he said, standing awkwardly in the middle of the room.

"I don't mind." She curled her legs beneath her, resting her head on the sofa's massive armrest. Child-like, she watched him. She seemed less nervous on her own ground.

He sat down in the other chair. "I only came to talk."

"Have you found Cati?"

"No. Has he contacted you?"

"No." She shook her head, eyes liquid. Silence claimed them again. He waited for her to speak – for he sensed that she wanted to – but she didn't. After a minute or two, he broke the silence again:

"I'm sorry. Can I have a cup of water?"

She went to another room without a word, and returned with a small glass. Roads placed it on the arm of the chair without drinking from it. She watched with interest as he removed his contact lenses and dropped them into the water. They drifted to the bottom of the glass like curious jellyfish, and stared vacantly back at her.

"I know all about the way Cati is," he said, raising his naked eyes. "But that's not why I'm here."

271

She nodded, understanding the gesture for what it was: an exchange of secrets, and therefore of trust.

He continued: "I simply want to know more about him – where he came from, how you met, what he does, and so on. I need to *understand* him before I can help him."

She nodded again, and her eyes wandered. They drifted aimlessly across the walls, the floorboards, ceiling – everywhere but at him – as she retreated into her memories. When she spoke, her voice was soft.

"I first met him ten years ago, by accident. I was . . . working . . . for a man called Jules. Had been since I turned thirteen. He kept me in money, as long as I did my bit. He looked after me, in his way."

Roads remembered the scars under her armpits. She had probably been a prostitute, enslaved by addiction to her pimp. Some sort of tailored drug, perhaps, brewed in the dark quarters of the city; maybe even one that had heightened her sexual response, inducing a volition in the act which would have made the degradation acceptable at the time – but even more abhorrent, later.

"Jules was a sadist, high on a power trip," she went on. "Occasionally he'd get paranoid and freak out for a day. We – I wasn't the only one working for him – we knew when to avoid him if things looked like they were going bad. Still, he'd sometimes catch us off-guard. He'd beat the shit out of anyone handy until they confessed to whatever it was that had him in a spin. He'd make it up later – with real doctors, real sympathy – but we all knew he'd killed a girl once, and kept out of his way as much as we could.

"Late one night, I was almost home when he caught me by surprise. I hadn't even made it through the front door when he was suddenly *there*, waving a knife, threatening to kill me. I tried to run, but he was too fast.

He hit me and I fell down. He kicked me a couple of times, just to hear me scream, and went to cut my throat with the knife.

"Then this guy appeared out of nowhere: it was Cati, although I didn't know him then. He grabbed Jules and threw him to one side like a rag doll, then came back to see if I was okay. I was more afraid of Cati than Jules, and tried to crawl away. His eyes were like nothing I'd ever seen before. But he wouldn't let me go. Jules went for him with the knife – I guess he'd only been stunned – and Cati knocked him out. Didn't kill him, just put him down with one punch. I'd seen Jules fight three men and win when he went crazy, but Cati was so much stronger . . . he knew exactly where to hit . . ."

She hesitated for a second to clear her throat. Roads waited patiently, guessing that she was unused to talking at such lengths, especially about the life that she had kept secret for so long.

"I was hurt," she went on. "Jules had broken a rib where he'd kicked me, and must have cut me at some stage without me noticing. Cati took me to his hideout in a wrecked Rosette cab and fixed me up – wouldn't let me go, wouldn't answer any of my questions. Just looked after me until I was better."

Her eyes clouded over, and Roads knew what she was remembering. How long had Cati held her? Long enough for her ribs to knit, at least, and for withdrawal symptoms to begin; long enough, perhaps, for them to pass. Depending on the particular drug she had been addicted to, her physical distress may well have been acute.

Until she was *better*, she had said. In more ways than one.

"I don't know how long he looked after me; maybe a week or more. In all that time he didn't say a word. I soon worked out that he was mute, that he couldn't speak. When I was able to, I tried to write questions on paper, but he couldn't read either. He could only understand a little speech, and make himself understood in return with his hands. When I was well, he made it clear that I was free to go.

"But I didn't want to. He didn't frighten me any more. He had healed me, freed me, saved my life. I think I loved him even then, although all I understood was sex. I wanted to thank him that way, to know him better, but he wouldn't. He wouldn't touch me.

"I cried when he showed me why. I thought that it had been . . . taken away from him. That he had been castrated. It wasn't fair, for either of us.

"But I stayed anyway. He didn't really want me to go, and I eventually got used to the idea. He looked after me, and I looked after him. I was the only person in the world that hadn't run away from him and didn't want to turn him in. I was the only one who had loved him in all his life."

She cried then, letting free the emotion that had been accumulating during the days alone. He watched her silently, building a mental picture of their relationship. She needed someone non-threatening and strong, he someone who could accept what he was. Without communication, without even a sexual bridge, it was hard to imagine any relationship succeeding; yet theirs obviously had, cemented by needs that transcended the everyday.

And was it so strange? She had never had a normal relationship. If one could accept the idea of sex without love, why was love without sex so unimaginable?

"We lived in the hideout for a month until Jules tracked us down and tried to get me back," Katiya went on, wiping her eyes with the back of a hand. "We moved elsewhere to avoid a scene. Cati doesn't like to hurt people. Jules kept coming for over a year, until one of his rivals killed him in a fight. Only then could we really settle down." She looked around her, reliving her life in the apartment. When her eyes returned to him, they were sad, but composed.

"He's been gone over three days now," she said. "The only reason why he wouldn't come back would be because it's dangerous for me somehow; he's like that, very protective. But if he's in trouble, then it's not something he caused. He's the most gentle man I've ever met, almost a child. He wouldn't hurt anyone . . . would he?"

Roads thought carefully before saying anything: "He may not have wanted to, but I think he has."

She wiped her hands on her nightshirt and met his stare. "I'm sorry. I'll answer any questions you want to ask. Anything to help bring him back. Life without him just wouldn't be worth living."

"When we first met," Roads began, "you said that Cati occasionally left during the night."

"Only recently. In the last month or so."

"Could you tell me exactly when?"

She nodded and went to get something from another room. When she returned, she flicked through the pages of a small, bound diary and called out dates.

Roads committed them to memory. At least two of the dates matched with his recollection of Roger Wiggs' file.

On these two nights that Cati had disappeared, a supporter of the Reassimilation Bill had been killed elsewhere in Kennedy.

It wasn't proof, but it *was* enough to convince him. With a sinking feeling, he continued his interrogation of Katiya:

How did Cati occupy his time? What did he do?

Nothing. Before she had met him, he had lived by stealing food at night – usually after curfew, when the chance of detection was small. During one such raid, he had come across Katiya. She didn't like stealing, and neither did he, so she had ultimately found conventional employment. He stayed home during her shifts; they kept each other company at other times.

How?

Just by being together. Sometimes she'd talk to him, irrespective of how much he actually understood. Other times she'd teach him how to cook, or to use his strength productively. Recently, they had discovered Tai Chi in an old book; Cati had a natural affinity for the ancient discipline.

Did he ever seem to drift off, as though he was listening to voices she could not hear?

No.

Was she aware of the existence of the control-code?

No. She didn't know what he was talking about.

Had he ever acted irrationally? Harmed her in any way?

No. The only time she had seen him use physical force was against Jules.

Did Cati know anything about the Reassimilation? Had he expressed an opinion regarding it?

No. She didn't think he truly understood what was going on. He saw the world on an interpersonal level, and had difficulty with the more abstract concepts of governments and governmental departments.

Did she know when he had first come to Kennedy, or how?

No. She assumed that he had crept past the automatic machine-gun emplacements somehow. They were supposed to be impenetrable – and Roads assured her that this was more or less the case – but she didn't put anything past Cati's superhuman abilities.

Had Cati told her anything at all about his past?

No. He was unable to speak.

"But I guessed a little," she added, "from the way he is. I heard stories about people like him when I was younger, before I skipped school and hitched with Jules. He must have been in the army at one stage, or something. To be honest, I try not to think about it, just accept him the way he is."

"So he can only communicate with you by hand signals and gestures?"

"Yes. Except for when he has something really important to tell or show me."

"And what does he do then?"

"He'll draw me pictures."

"Can I see them?"

She hesitated for a second, then went to get them. She returned with a cardboard box two-thirds full of sheets of paper torn from notebooks. On every one was a hand-drawn picture, usually in black and white.

The drawings were crude – minimalist in a child-like way – but competent. Cati conveyed information, not detail. People were outlines possessing few features. Only Katiya herself was drawn with care, as though she was the one real person in the world. Kennedy was portrayed as a series of empty boxes with blank spaces between them.

All in all, the pictures concerned events that Cati had seen and did not understand, or things that were important to him. There were a lot of pages to glance through, although less than might have been expected for ten years' work. Roads browsed through them all, hoping there might be something useful among the mass of detail:

Katiya in their home on Old North Street; the bent span of Patriot Bridge; two men arguing, one holding a gun; a woman with a small child in a pram; two dogs mating; an object that he did not at first recognise, then realised was the necklace around Katiya's neck.

"He gave me that when we first moved here," she said, noticing the picture in his hands. Without embarrassment, she added: "He doesn't understand the idea of bond contracts, so this is the closest I'll get to a wedding ring. I never take it off."

Roads continued browsing. The further he went through the box, the more yellow the pictures became. The last fifty were especially brittle, and obviously drawn as a series – telling a story of sorts, perhaps. There were images from Cati's life before Kennedy: the War, the Dissolution, other dark-skinned men that could only have been his fellow CATIs, things that Katiya would not have understood without knowing more about his background. Detail was especially sparse in this sequence, and Roads remembered with a shock that Cati must have been no more than five years old at the time these events took place.

Five years old, and already a killer. Roads found it hard to imagine what Cati's thought processes must have been like. Human? Mechanical? Or alien – different in an entirely new way? Certainly the things that he had been compelled to record in his pictures were atypical of the everyday person's concerns: no friends, no scenery, no joy. Just facts, one after the other, as interminable and impersonal as the pages of a calendar.

And yet, strangely, Cati was human enough to feel love.

Then Roads reached the final picture in the box. Not the first picture drawn, for it was clear the box had been rearranged over the years. Expecting it to be just another in the series, he turned it over . . .

And froze.

Katiya noticed the abrupt change in his expression. "What is it?"

Roads held it up to the light so she could see. "Do you know who this is?"

"No. Someone Cati met, I guess. Is he important?"

"I think so." He turned the picture around to study it again. The sudden sinking feeling in his stomach was matched only by annoyance at not suspecting sooner.

It was a portrait of a man – someone Cati had obviously known well, for it was drawn with surprising detail. The man's features were irregular, twisted; his head and face were completely bald. Most telling of all, however: the man was portrayed only from the neck up.

And in the picture, Keith Morrow was smiling.

CHAPTER EIGHTEEN

2:45 p.m.

"Keep them *out*!"

The cry rang out across the crowd like a profanity at a wedding. Barney studiously ignored it as she patrolled the perimeter of her allocated area – nodding at fellow officers, smiling at children, making her presence felt in a dozen small ways. The best way, she knew, to prevent sticky situations was simply to *be* there. Not only would it have been impossible to silence every dissenting voice, but it might even have been counter-productive. Many a gathering had inflamed into riot as a result of over-zealous policing.

She only hoped that *being there* would be enough.

The crowd had begun showing signs of restlessness half an hour earlier, as three o'clock drew near. Bunched against the Gate, it spilled along the main road into the city like water behind a dam. All in all, perhaps twenty thousand people had turned up to watch the arrival of the RUSAMC. The straight, grey line of the eastern arterial freeway split the mass of heads in two, aimed like an arrow for the centre of the Rosette. The road was lined with RSD officers, plus several squads of MSA troops, conspicuous in their black uniforms.

Although the occasional anti-Reassimilation cry did nothing to ease the tension, the greatest threat came from small-time agitators eager to create a stir. Groups of teenagers dotted the crowd, jostling people nearby purely for something to do. Easily bored, yet easily impressed by novelty in a city where nothing had changed for decades, they waited just as nervously as the others around them. Occasionally this nervousness betrayed itself in short-lived squabbles that needed to be dealt with quickly before they developed into anything more serious.

She kept one hand at her side at all times, within easy reach of her radio. If there *were* serious troublemakers out there, she would be ready. She also kept a close eye out for anyone in an overcoat, sunglasses and hat, half-dreading a glimpse of bright red skin burning under the sunlight. If Cati did appear, she had no idea what she could possibly do to stop him. Neither she nor her squad was armed with anything more deadly than a baton.

At two fifty-five, a muffled cheer went up from the people closest to the Wall. The cheer echoed through the crowd, returned stronger than before from those further up the road, then died. A false alarm, Barney assumed, noting that the people watching from rooftops nearby – and therefore able to see over the Wall – had failed to take up the cry.

Yet, regardless, her pulse quickened. She was as human as the rest, just as unsure about what the Reunited States might do to the city in which she had lived her entire life. Stedman's arrival would bring Reassimilation one step closer. Once he was here, there would be no turning back.

And once the RUSAMC was in the city, Roads' time would be almost up. He had already lost the cases – regardless of his stubborn pursuit of Cati. Given the Reunited States' firm stand on biomodifications, a Humanity Trial would not be far behind.

She wondered how she would have felt if her father had been in his shoes. No less confused, certainly. Everything she had taken for granted had been turned upside down in less than twenty-four hours.

Taking a deep breath, and trying not to think about the future, Barney settled back on her heels to wait.

At exactly three o'clock, a stronger cry went up as the Wall's automatic defence systems were deactivated. Warning lights that had flashed upon its summit for as long as she could remember suddenly died along the arc before her. The background hum of generators gradually ebbed and died.

Without consciously realising it, Barney inched forward to find a better vantage-point. As she did so, she became aware of a new sensation. Like a subsonic, the faint rumbling eluded her actual hearing, making its presence felt in the bones of her skull instead. Puzzled, she glanced around her, catching the eye of one of her squad.

"That's something I haven't heard for years," he said, sticking a finger in his ear.

"What is it?"

"Heavy machinery, acoustically-dampened." The officer took off his cap and brushed back his grey hair. "And lots of it."

Barney turned back to the Gate, wishing she was with the MSA guards on top of the Wall. The sound set her teeth on edge. More than anything she wanted to see – and feared – what was waiting Outside to be let in.

Then, silently beneath the rumble and the buzz of voices, the Gate swung open, sliding on runners still smooth after years of disuse. The gap widened metre by metre until it reached its full twenty-metre extension. And when the way was clear, the vanguard of the RUSAMC convoy entered the city.

The crowd fell back as one in the face of what appeared before it. First came four pairs of anti-tank missile launchers. Massive, six-wheeled machines painted a dark olive, they crept forward like insects at a slow walking pace, completely automated. The stings of their missiles pointed to the horizon over the heads of the crowd; a variety of optical sensors mounted on their curved flanks impassively regarded the sea of people, scanning for possible targets.

Next came personnel carriers, each carrying fifty foot-soldiers. The RUSAMC troops stood firmly to attention, saluting the crowd. Their uniforms were standard khaki, as they had been a century ago; only a few slight changes, that no doubt meant a great deal, differentiated the soldiers of this army from those of the one that had preceded it.

There followed an impressive variety of combat craft: ground-effect skimmers mounted with machine-guns; jeeps loaded with anti-aircraft shells; tanks armed with pulse-lasers and sonics; ground-to-air hybrids that looked part-jeep, part-helicopter; and many others outside Barney's experience. Troops rode in the vehicles or marched alongside them, as disciplined as the machinery they accompanied.

Barney watched in awe as the procession rumbled by. The Reunited States of America Military Corps had arrived in style – she couldn't argue with that. She had expected an army of refurbished left-overs from the old regime, not this bewildering display of newly-minted weaponry. Kennedy Polis wouldn't last a day against the might of such an invading force.

Of course, she reminded himself, this was exactly the point General Stedman was trying to make.

Barney noted with surprise that General Stedman himself hadn't appeared. She would have expected the figurehead of a peaceful invasion to ride in an open vehicle at the fore. Perhaps, she thought, his absence implied a lack of confidence, or trust. Either way, it was a slightly ominous sign.

Gradually, the initial display of brute force mellowed into one more sophisticated. Unarmed troops marched in file, flanked by security androids. Spindly snipers barely as tall as an average person dodged and weaved among the troops, nimble and well-coordinated on two legs, their red "eyes" flickering and darting. Surveillance robots dodged between marching feet like skinny, six-legged rabbits, startling adults and delighting children by occasionally ducking into their midst.

Robots. Barney hadn't expected such advanced technology even in her wildest dreams – although with biomodification outlawed, there was a tactical niche to be filled. If people couldn't be given the capabilities of machines, a machine with the manoeuvrability of a human was the logical alternative.

But not even the old USA could have built AIs with the required sophistication small enough to fit into the cranial cavity of one of the "rodents". Each robot would be linked to some sort of central processor, she guessed – a separate vehicle. She kept a careful eye out for such a control van, keen to grasp even the slightest weakness to this overpoweringly superior force. It would be large, probably covered in antennae and, by its very nature, vulnerable. If someone were to destroy the centre, the robotic proportion of the RUSAMC would be effectively wiped out.

It was a comforting hope that the force arrayed before her might have some weakness, no matter how small.

The procession of troops ended suddenly. The tramp of boots faded, leaving another peculiar sound in its wake: a faint buzzing, the rasp of a distant chainsaw. The crowd muttered to itself, curious to see what was coming.

When it finally arrived, Barney's air of cautious amazement shattered, leaving her unsure *what* to think.

Three vehicles glided through the Gate. All three were windowless and painted a dull black; a circular coat of arms in blue and gold was their only decoration. The first two were no larger than tanks and might have been automated. The third was as large as a moderate building – a chain of linked structures similar to a desert caravan. There were no antennae to be seen, but Barney guessed nonetheless that this was the control van. It seemed completely undefended.

Most incredible of all was the fact that none of the vehicles appeared to have any means of propulsion. Black spines pointed downward and at odd angles from the belly of each craft; strange energies stirred the dust on the road beneath. The nasal buzzing grew louder as they approached.

All three vehicles floated one metre above the earth.

The crowd fell silent.

As Barney watched, a hatch on the top of the foremost "caravan" opened and a familiar face rose into view: General Stedman, the leader of the RUSAMC envoy, at last. He was an imposing figure, even from a distance: at least two metres high and solidly built, he possessed a full head of grey hair and light-brown, weathered skin; his face was stern behind its smile. Barney sensed indefatigability radiating from the man.

The General nodded in greeting at the crowd around him and raised a hand to wave. Half the crowd cheered; more than a few remained speechless. Only a small proportion dared to boo.

One of these latter, taking the unenviable role of David in the face of such an invincible Goliath, actually threw a rock. The stone, larger than Barney's fist, arced through the air toward the control van.

"Kick them *out*!"

Stedman's eyes followed the stone, unconcerned.

Had it continued unchecked, it would have missed the General by a metre or so and struck the hull of the van. Instead, it was suddenly deflected downward into the ground by an invisible force, and shattered harmlessly into fragments.

The crowd stirred. A squad of RSD officers moved in to apprehend the rock-thrower. Stedman, untouchable behind the invisible defences of the control van, smiled more widely and began to wave.

Only then, as the caravan drifted past, did Barney remember her promise to call Roads.

"Phil?" she subvocalised. "Are you watching this?"

A moment passed before he replied, his voice muffled but clear through the cyberlink: "No. I've been busy. What's happening?"

Not sure whether he would believe her, she described the arrival of the RUSAMC at the city gates. When she reached the floating vehicles that had just passed, she realised she lacked the words to summarise it accurately.

"Field-effects," supplied Roads. "Force feedback, levitation, boundary-blurring, whatever. You can use them to do anything from float a house to make its walls invisible – even build it out of energy alone, if you like. The technology was talked about during the War, although I never saw it in action."

"And that's what they're using?" Barney shook her head. "If you'd told me, I wouldn't have believed you. I never dreamed such things existed."

"They might not have, until now. Stedman or his predecessors must've dug the plans out of the old bunkers."

"Thank God. I was half-expecting you to say: 'Sure, they were everywhere when I was a kid. Every home had one.'"

"No. Not at all. We –"

"Hang on." A group of people were trying to rush the cordon to follow the procession up the road. Barney joined the squad to force them back, noting the uncertainty in the eyes of the citizens of Kennedy, the occasional fearful stare – even in those who weren't protesting. She didn't blame them.

The unruly group didn't put up much of a fight. When the cordon was secure again, the crowd began to disperse. A couple approached the Gate to peer Outside. Barney pursued them to request that they fall back, and to take a quick look herself. All she saw was the rutted remains of the highway and a green plain rolling off into the distance.

"Sorry." Barney returned her attention to the cyberlink. "After all this waiting, I almost expected to be disappointed. I simply had no idea –"

"None of us did," Roads said.

"And – Christ! I thought I was going to die when he stuck his head out of the control van, or whatever it was."

"Who?"

"Stedman. I just knew something bad was going to happen. I could feel it in the crowd. I kept thinking of Cati, and of what a big target El Generalissimo had made of himself." She snorted, then explained the ease with which the rock had been deflected. "What a bloody joke. You might as well give up now."

"I think I see your point. If Cati can kill Stedman, then what chance do *we* have of catching him? And if Cati tries and fails, then the States are quite capable of dealing with him themselves. Right?"

"Spot on. Better to quit while you're ahead, Phil."

"Nice try, but sorry. Machines are just machines. They have to be powered somehow. Field-effects – and robots, for that matter – will be thirsty; Stedman will have to turn them off eventually. Anyway, he's going to have to leave the control van to meet the Mayor. What about when he's inside Mayor's House?"

Barney sighed. "You won't give up, will you?"

"No." Roads faded for a moment, then returned as strong as ever. "DeKurzak was right in one sense: Stedman is *here*. We're out of time. Tonight's our last chance to regain any ground at all."

Barney heard the determination in his voice. Everything he said was true, but she didn't have to like it.

"What time do you knock off, again?" he asked.

"Seven, if the crowd has cleared by then. I'll take an hour or two break, then head into Mayor's House."

"You're going to be there tonight?"

"Wouldn't miss it for the world, regardless of what happens. And neither would Roger Wiggs. He'll be there as well."

"I sympathise. If nothing happens, we should all be grateful. We have to get together before then. There are a couple of things we need to discuss in person, not over the cyberlink."

"Such as?"

"Ah . . . developments. Let's leave it at that for now."

"Okay. Call me later, while I'm on break."

"Will do."

Barney waited for more, but the cyberlink was silent. She walked to the edge of the freeway. A fair few people remained, clustered in groups. They seemed slightly stunned, still trying to absorb what they had seen.

The officer who'd recognised the sound of acoustically-shielded machinery came to stand next to her.

"Quite a day," he said, not meeting her eye, watching the crowd instead. "I wonder what would've happened if we hadn't opened the Gate?"

"Don't," she said, as much to herself as to him. "Don't even think about it."

Roads edged the bike through the crowd, following the procession as it wormed its way toward the city centre. The RUSAMC kept the pace fairly slow, giving everyone in Kennedy a chance to absorb what they were seeing, and he had no difficulty surpassing the slow crawl.

When he caught up with the control van and its two companion vehicles, he stopped to watch.

Field-effects. The rumours he had heard about such things had been vague and noncommittal; although he had been curious, he had never received confirmation that they actually existed. He hardly needed to any more. The vehicles in front of him were enough.

Picking up speed again, he dodged through the crowd. He wanted to tell Barney about what he had discovered in Old North Street. A detailed picture of Morrow's face among the others Cati had drawn highlighted a relationship between the two that went deeper than a casual meeting. The obvious explanation was that Morrow was Cati's controller.

But it would have to wait until they were together. He couldn't be certain that Morrow hadn't tapped the old PolNet circuits.

Instead, he studied the soldiers. They looked as young as Roads had been when he'd joined the Army – even younger in some cases. A handful returned the curious stares of the crowd, but most simply faced forward, keeping their eyes carefully above the horizon, like robots.

Or like Cati would've done, Roads thought, if ordered to. That was the ultimate aim of every army: to possess soldiers both skilled and completely trustworthy. Biomodification wasn't the only means to achieve that end, although it was all too easy to imagine it happening again. Unlimited access to the Old World's military science almost cried out for misuse. While the RUSA had vowed never to emulate its predecessor's downfall, cautious scepticism was only natural.

Roads knew that few people deliberately chose the path to self-destruction. It was a gradual, almost unnoticeable course. With biomodification in particular, the progression was simple: everyone wanted to be stronger, faster, fitter, better – but there had to be a point at which one drew the line. For all he knew, the decline in standards might already have begun, with O'Dell's pragmatic acceptance of Roads' implants. Perhaps it *could* only end with the likes of Cati and the Mole.

Children in Kennedy – and Outside, Roads assumed – had been told the berserker stories for long enough to have made biomodification synonymous with evil. The phobias were so well established that he doubted that the old technology would arise in that form. Yet it was still possible, and he wondered whether that was part of why DeKurzak was so worried. Did he believe that, by allowing Roads to escape unpunished, some sort of floodgate would open, filling Kennedy with monsters and cybernetic villains?

To combat monsters the city needed superheroes, of course, but Roads didn't feel much like Superman. He understood from experience where that feeling led, and what true powerlessness was like. The reactivation of PolNet had revived the memories with a vividness that stung.

The one time he had allowed himself overconfidence – perhaps even a sense of superiority – had been fourteen years before the War. He had drunk too much celebrating both a promotion and the subsequent installation of the first of his implants. When he had been challenged by a gang of Puritans in a public street, instead of walking away or summoning assistance, he had accepted the challenge – and won. With heightened senses and a super-charged adrenal system, he had defeated the gang single-handedly at odds of five to one.

Then, two nights later, on New Year's Eve 2026, he had been walking the same street with his partner, Carol. Apparently by accident, a large man had bumped into him and shoved him into an alleyway. Before he could resist, hands had pinned his arms and a bag had gone over his head. The last thing he remembered was a blow to the back of his neck – until he woke up in hospital a victim of violent assault.

But that hadn't been the worst of it. Two days later, he had been called to the forensic labs to identify his partner's body. Carol had been raped by every member of the gang over a period of six hours, then dumped in a cul-de-sac near Sydney Metro Police HQ where she had bled to death. The policeman who had turned back the sheet had had eyes like jewels – eyes like *his* – glinting silver in the cold, white light.

Genetic traces – skin, semen and hair – had enabled the police to track down the young gang responsible, and they had been duly punished by a court of law. But Roads had never forgotten the lesson behind the act itself.

No matter how strong he felt, and no matter what his advantage over an opponent, he was still weak in some way. His love for Carol had allowed his opponents revenge on that occasion; it would be something else next time, something he had not anticipated.

So he had sought strength from within, through discipline – just as Kennedy had, many years later. He had quit the police force and joined the army, rising swiftly through the ranks until a transfer to the United States had been offered to him. He had trained in a biomodified squad for two years before earning a second course of surgery. He had gained new eyes and new ears; his entire body had been taken apart and rebuilt by a team of biogeneticists over a period of six months. He had spent a further half year learning his new capabilities – and, at the end of it, had still felt weak.

It took him most of a decade to realise that true strength came from a *denial* of strength, and an acceptance of weakness. Everything he saw during the War confirmed this: the Armed Forces – including the CIA and the FBI – had been too powerful for too many years, and ignorant of their own inherent flaws. Every last spasm of the United States had been a flexing of dying muscle; during the Dissolution, the corpse of the nation had torn itself apart – slowly, but inevitably – along with the rest of the world, as a result of its unwillingness to believe that it was no longer in control.

General Stedman's desire to revive that old corpse did not in itself seem unhealthy, but Roads could not help but wonder.

Roads wound his way past a knot of schoolkids arguing with an MSA officer. They wanted to catch one of the rodent robots, but the guard had forbidden them from stepping into the convoy's path. Their shrill entreaties fell behind him and became indistinguishable from the noise of the crowd and the steady rumble of machinery.

An icon winked in his field of vision: someone was trying to get through to him on the old PolNet lines. He opened a communications port automatically, then wished he hadn't.

Keith Morrow's face smiled at him, superimposed over the crowd. "Phil. I have your pass."

Roads hesitated slightly, unsure how to respond. "Uh, thanks, Keith. How do I collect it?"

"Go to the memorial on the corner of First and Rankin. Someone will be waiting for you there."

The ghostly Head vanished and Roads hurried forward. Although he had expected the call, it still came as something of a surprise. Morrow obviously didn't know that Roads had learned of the connection between Cati and the Head and the suspicions that aroused.

Business would have to proceed as usual, at least until Roads was certain enough of his latest theory to risk a confrontation. He had no choice; the deadline was too close to turn down the chance of getting into Mayor's House.

The memorial was on the convoy's route. The crowd around it would hide anything. If he was walking into a trap, he might not know until it had been sprung.

He turned into a side street and wound his way through the less-crowded streets away from the procession. When he reached the road leading to the memorial, he followed it back toward the crowd.

From behind, the memorial seemed deserted. A granite statue of ex-US President and chairman of the NAMCP, Robert Mulcahey, who had approved the building of Kennedy Polis in 2010, stood ten metres high on a raised marble dais. Steps led to the base of the chair upon which the old President sat. The crowd had taken over the steps, seeking a better viewpoint.

Roads circled the memorial warily, keeping an eye out for any suspicious signs. The procession had only just reached the area; the crowd was busy waving at the marching soldiers. No-one seemed to notice him where he stood waiting.

A whistle from above and to his right attracted his attention. Someone was standing on the statue itself, on the ex-President's lap; someone tall, with skin that looked dark against the granite, and round sunglasses.

It was Raoul. The black man waved for Roads to come closer. He did so carefully, weaving through the spectators crowding the steps of the memorial. When he was near enough, Raoul threw down a rope.

Roads mentally tossed a coin. Leaning the bike against the base of the monument, he grabbed the rope and climbed up to join Raoul on his unusual perch.

"Welcome," said the Head's messenger, pulling the rope back up. "Take a seat."

"You have the pass?"

"Yes. What's your hurry?"

Roads forced himself to be patient. "No hurry."

"So let's watch the show."

Raoul sat with his legs crossed on the President's knees. Roads followed suit, keeping a respectable distance between them. A brisk wind blew past them, much stronger than it had been at ground level.

Below, the might of the RUSAMC rolled by. Row after row of troops tramped along the road toward Kennedy's centre.

"I wonder where they'll all sleep," said Roads.

"Anywhere they like, I'd say," Raoul responded. "Actually, only a handful will be staying. The rest will be out of the city before long."

"What makes you say that?"

"Well, they're only here to impress us, right? To show us how strong they are. Once the point has been made, they'll go back Outside to their camp."

"You seem pretty certain of that."

"It's what I'd do. Besides, I've seen their orders."

"You have?"

"More or less." Raoul winked. "De Head know everythin', mon."

"So it seems. His problem is that he keeps most of it to himself."

"Not if you're close." White teeth flashed from the black face. "You could have been close, if you'd wanted to."

Roads turned back to the convoy. "Perhaps."

"Perhaps nothing. The Head likes you. He doesn't want to see you get into trouble."

"What sort of trouble would that be, exactly?"

"That's up to you, my friend. If you look for it, it'll find you."

"Are you threatening me?"

"Quite the opposite. The Head asked me to give you a warning. He won't hurt you, but there's plenty who might."

Roads absorbed this in silence. That was the second time the Head had hinted at forces massed against him. A genuine warning? Or a threat, despite the messenger's protestations of innocence?

Seeing Raoul again brought back memories of their first meeting, in the cellar on Old North Street. The sight of another person with biomodifications in Kennedy had taken Roads completely off-guard. Fear that Raoul might recognise him – might even have been under his command and remembered what he had done – had left him frozen, unable to think. He had believed himself alone for so long that to learn otherwise had shocked him to the very core of his being. Only later had he realised that he should have suspected earlier.

Morrow was a junkyard man, quite literally, but he collected more than just machines; he collected people as well. Roads had needed his help to survive in the past, and it made sense that others had come along since then

– and not all of them would share Roads' law-abiding nature. Biomodifications before the War had proliferated outside the armed forces as technology had become cheaper. Raoul could have been anything from a tech-freak to a hired killer. Morrow had lost a valuable ally when Roads had joined RSD, and would regard Raoul's abilities just as highly. No wonder that he had been in charge of the Old North Street operation, or that Morrow had sent him to deal with Roads in person.

But why now? *Did* Morrow suspect that Roads had learned of a connection between him and Cati? Was Raoul – like the RUSA – a threat, or an opportunity to be exploited?

"Tell me something, Raoul. What do *you* think of the Reassimilation?"

"Me? I think it's a bad deal."

"In what way?"

"Well, just look at them." Raoul gestured at the troops below. "They come here offering us equality and a place in their government and all that shit, but that's not what they're *really* here for. They're a military state, and they want what all military states want: *power*. Over us, and the rest of the continent. We're just a small step along the road they're travelling, another hurdle to be crossed."

"You think they're going to take us over?"

"They won't need to. Not that we could resist if they tried. I mean, all these years we've been thinking that Outside was full of savages, and look what rolls in. I haven't seen stuff like this for years. Ever! Field-effects, for chrissake? No, they won't need to invade us; we'll just roll over and play dead."

The control caravan wasn't in view, but it was obvious that Raoul had already heard about it. No doubt from Morrow, via his own implants and the underworld equivalent of PolNet.

"They're going to kill us by economics," Raoul said.

"Economics?"

"It's simple." The black man took off his glasses and wiped his crystal eyes. "When we join the Reunited States, we'll become part of a vital industrial nation. We'll have to compete on equal terms with everyone else, which means we'll have to produce in order to survive. But what exactly do we produce here? Recycled shit, that's all. We'll be buried alive."

"We'll adjust –"

"Sure, eventually, but not before we're in debt. And once in debt we'll *always* be in debt. They'll make sure of it."

"So you think we shouldn't Reassimilate?"

Raoul shook his head. "That's the problem. We have to; in a manner of speaking, we already *have*, by letting them come this far. I just don't like to see it happening this way, that's all."

The summary reflected Roads' own feelings on the matter. Again he wondered what Raoul's occupation had been before the War. Not the same as his – Morrow had suggested as much when Roads had asked – but not simple thuggery either. His opinions were too considered.

"What about Keith?" Roads asked. "How does the Head feel about it?"

"Oh, he's cautiously ecstatic, as you can imagine. All the new gadgets to play with, all the new markets to invade. He'll be in computer heaven once the lines are open."

"Yes. That's what I thought." Roads pointed at the control van, which had just floated into view. "But what if he's outclassed? What if their computer technology beats his?"

"It won't. He's easily the most sophisticated artificial intelligence on the planet. Being stuck in Kennedy for forty years hasn't kept him from growing."

"The States won't approve of him. They hate biomodification as much as Kennedy does."

"He knows that. But he's not biomodified; he's bio-*transcended*, as he puts it. A whole new class entirely."

"But in their eyes –"

"Yes, yes. Let's just say he'll keep his head low and leave it at that. He's got more to gain from an alliance with the States than any of us."

Roads nodded. That much seemed to be true, even though it didn't jell with what he'd learned. Why would Morrow send Cati to kill anyone in favour of the Reassimilation he wanted to happen?

"And here's the man himself," said Raoul sharply. "The invader from the north . . ."

The control van had reached level with the statue. General Stedman was visible from its upper entrance, waving every now and again. Whether word had spread or this section of the crowd was more genial than that by the Gate, there were no disturbances. Roads said nothing as the RUSAMC leader rumbled by on his un-likely vehicle, for all the world like Santa in a Christmas pageant.

As though consciously echoing the metaphor, a long line of supply trucks followed the control caravan, all loaded down with food and equipment: the first shipment of outside goods to Kennedy Polis. Roads thought about Raoul's gloomy prediction. The first shipment was free, but who would pay for the second?

He watched as the last of the trucks rolled by. The final vehicle was a ground-effect jeep. Two metres above it, a banner snapped and flicked in a nonexistent wind. There was no pole.

A hologram, obviously, but it looked convincing enough. The blue and black RUSAMC emblem was as crisp as reality, with every detail sharply delineated. Roads had seen the design several times before, but had never studied it in detail. He did so now, using his implants to enhance the image.

The motto was unclear, and seemed to be in French not Latin, suggesting possible Canadian ties. An animal crouched among symbolic heraldry, clutching a knife in its mouth. Something about the animal rang a bell, and he zoomed closer still. The image at the heart of the RUSAMC's coat of arms appeared crystal clear in his field of vision. Roads remembered a grey shape loping across a dark lawn, lean muscles rippling in moonlight.

The animal on the RUSAMC coat of arms was a timber wolf . . .

"Here's your pass," said Raoul, handing him a sliver of black plastic. "It'll get you through a side way: Exit Fourteen. Once you're in, it's up to you what you do."

Roads accepted the pass and slipped it into a pocket. "Thanks. Tell Keith I owe him."

"That you do." Raoul rose to his feet and dusted his pants. "Just be careful, man. Someone wants your arse."

"I know. Everyone keeps telling me."

The black man slid down the shins of the statue and vanished into the crowd.

INTERLUDE

4:00 p.m.

The air in the ventilation shaft had become scaldingly hot, but he did not notice. Midway between sleep and wakefulness, he waited patiently for something to happen. What, exactly, he wasn't sure. Until his orders changed, he was incapable of moving.

Outside his metal womb, he could hear birds, the whistle of the wind and a crowd of people gathering. The mingled voices reminded him of his life before Sanctuary: whenever crowds had gathered, it had always been to drive him away, or to kill him. Anger was part of this crowd's faint tone, but he could hear laughter among the arguments, and children, and singing.

The people seemed to be waiting, just like him.

Time passed quickly. As the city focused its attention on a place a kilometre or so from him, he allowed himself to relax. No-one would be looking for him. He would be safe for a while – safe to rest, safe to sleep.

He closed his eyes and curled tighter around himself.

The dream, when it began, was unexpected – even welcome, in that it was familiar. It was one he'd had on several occasions before:

He was dodging into a gutted building with bullets cracking like whiplashes at his naked back. As he stumbled up the stairs, he warded off the blows of an old woman wielding a broomstick. Although his hands were large enough to snap her like a twig, he did not.

It had begun with a confrontation, as it always did. Perhaps he had walked into a village and been driven out ahead of the witch-hunt. Or he had been discovered in the wasteland by a band of fellow-wanderers and forced to retreat. He might even have been startled from hasty dream-sleep in some ruined shelter by a hand on his shoulder or a knife thrust in his face. His assailants were always strangers, and their brutality robbed them of any individuality they might have possessed. They mobbed him, tore at him, hunted him like an animal – when all he wanted to do was leave them alone, let them get on with their lives as they had before his arrival.

But it was too late: the truth of his nature had come to light, and a near-primal anger had erupted, a tide of hatred directed solely at him, against which he was unable to defend himself. All he could do – all he was *permitted* to do – was flee for his life.

The unreasoning wave of violence carried him on its crest for what felt like hours, until he despaired of ever awakening – until it seemed that it was his destiny to be persecuted, to run just ahead of the pack, never dying and never killing, forever.

Yet, although the dream began as a nightmare, it did not normally end that way. As he fled, unable to fight the ones he was supposed to protect, he heard a woman calling to him. Her voice was soft and gentle, almost inaudible above the baying of the pack, but insistent. She called him by his real name – the name he and his brothers had once shared. She told him to come to her, to be with her, to love her and to protect her.

No matter how much he ached to return her call, he could not. His throat was as silent in the dream as it was in waking life. His only course of action was to follow the voice to its source, to a city in the middle of a wilderness, surrounded by gnarled forests of hatred.

The woman's name was Sanctuary; the city's name was Peace. And this was reality, beyond the dream. He had simply become so used to the nightmare in his years before Sanctuary that part of him still thought it would never end.

But this time the dream didn't end the way it usually did, with him in that city of Peace and the woman called Sanctuary at his side.

This time he found himself standing on a building in the heart of the city. A crowd had gathered beneath him, filling the streets as far as he could see: a veritable sea of people, all standing still and silent, all staring upward, watching him. The mute intensity of their regard made him nervous.

Just as he realised that Sanctuary's voice had stopped calling for him, the crowd began to change. One by one, as though a wave had rippled across them, the people shimmered and vanished, leaving only a faint heat-flicker where they had been. The wave of invisibility spread rapidly through the silent masses, until the streets themselves seemed to liquefy and melt, and the city floated like a herd of icebergs in a sea of bent light.

The people were still watching him. He could feel their combined stare like pointed fingers on his skin, testing, probing, dissecting, *judging*.

Exposed and therefore vulnerable, he quailed and tried to hide. He ducked behind a ventilation duct, but that too dissolved into nothing, leaving him as naked as before. Panic welled in his chest as he ran from side to side, leaving a path of evaporated shelters in his wake. And still the crowd watched, the weight of eyes becoming heavier by the second.

When the top of the building was smooth and featureless he fell to his hands and knees in despair. There was nowhere left to run: the long chase was over, and he had finally lost everything.

Then the building itself vanished, sending him falling into a roiling gulf that pulled at him, yawned to accept his spinning body –

"I am Lucifer."

He awoke with a panicky start, the echoes of the voice still ringing in his mind.

"I am Lucifer!"

He screamed silently into the void, pounding the sides of the ventilation shaft with his feet and fists, exorcising the fear and hopelessness of the dream by attacking the space within which he cowered.

The city hated him, everybody wanted to kill him, and his controller would not let him forget. Perhaps *reality* was the dream, and the nightmare had been biding its time all along.

What had he done to deserve this?

"I AM LUCIFER!" repeated the voice, more firmly still, as though sensing his anguish, his unwillingness to obey. He wanted to shout his defiance, to rebel against the authority that made him do wrong, made people afraid of him.

But he could not voice his protest. He was as mute now as he had been in the dream. And the wrongness of disobeying far outweighed the crimes he was forced to commit.

Regaining a measure of self control, he forced his heartbeat to slow and his panic to subside.

Closing his eyes, he whispered acceptance of his fate outward into the distance.

And the voice that called itself Lucifer told him exactly what he had to do.

CHAPTER NINETEEN

7:55 p.m.

Mayor's House lay half a kilometre north of Kennedy City University. At the summit of a low rise, its white marble and plaster facade reflected the light of spotlights much as that of the long-destroyed White House had – and was just as well maintained, despite the Dissolution. The building was extensive, four storeys high, and contained most of the official chambers required by the Council. A ring of lawn approximately twenty metres across surrounded it, with a thick wall of trees shielding it from the city. The grounds were in turn protected by a three-metre-high mesh fence with security emplacements every fifty metres. Two wide gates formed the entrance and exit of a gravel driveway leading to the building's massive, pillared foyer. Apart from one or two official cars, the drive was normally empty; now, however, it served as a parking lot for the fifteen largest vehicles of the RUSAMC convoy, including the control van.

Roads, watching from the shelter of the trees, noted the clockwork precision of the RUSAMC troops as they patrolled the area. Most wore night-specs and carried automatic weapons; every security pass, including his own, was checked before admission to the grounds was granted. Through the gloom, he could make out the occasional scampering robot shadowing the patrols and checking in spaces that the troops could not enter. Perhaps one hundred men and women had taken over the lawn, plus the local RSD squads beyond the fence: two hundred and fifty or more, he estimated, all to protect one man.

General Stedman had left the control caravan shortly before sunset and entered Mayor's House on foot with a small contingent of bodyguards and officers. The control van, with its humming field-engines inactive, had settled on sturdy, retractable legs onto the gravel drive and hadn't moved since. Apart from that, and the ceaseless patrolling of troops and robots, the evening had been uneventful.

Roads glanced at his watch: 8:00 p.m. The crowd of sightseers around Mayor's House had dispersed some time ago. He envied their ignorance. What happened in the next twenty-four hours could decide the fate of Kennedy Polis, once and for all.

He turned at the sound of approaching feet. A woman in the uniform of an RSD officer ducked underneath a branch to join him at his unofficial post.

"Sorry I'm late," Barney said, slightly out of breath. "I walked back in. No free lifts available."

"That's okay. Did you bring it?"

She slipped a rucksack from her shoulder. "As requested."

"Thanks." He rummaged through the bag and removed her laptop.

"The batteries are fully-charged," she said, putting a hand on his arm. "Are you okay? You didn't want to talk earlier –"

"I couldn't." Roads squatted down and put the computer on his knees. A flickering glow painted patterns on his face as he switched it on. "Give me a second and I'll fill you in."

The PolNet program booted automatically. Working in the dark, using his amplified sight to see the manual keyboard, he tapped his way into the network's rock directory.

"Anything happening out here?" Barney nodded restlessly towards the parked convoy.

"Nothing much. Stedman hasn't reappeared, and neither has the Mayor. If I can get into the security program we might be able to find out what they're talking about." Roads shrugged. "Otherwise I'll have to go in person."

"Morrow produced the goods, then?"

"I hope so. I mean, I have a pass – but God only knows whether it'll get me into the building or not."

Barney crouched down beside him. "You don't trust him?"

"Not any more." While he fiddled with the program, Roads briefly outlined what he had found at Katiya's that afternoon: Keith Morrow's face in Cati's catalogue of non-verbal memories.

Barney stared at him. "You mean the Head – ?"

"Why not? He has access to all the city's databases, so stealing the CATI file wouldn't be a problem. He understands the old biotechnology better than I do. He can also hijack official transmitters to broadcast the code, if he needs to." Roads turned to face her. "I'm beginning to think he's the only person in Kennedy who *could* be Cati's controller."

"So what's the problem, then? Why are you here instead of down at the harbour?"

"Because it feels wrong . . . somehow. I don't know why. What's his motive, Barney? What does he stand to gain by keeping the States out of Kennedy?"

"Market share?" she suggested.

"Perhaps. But that's still not enough."

"Okay, then," said Barney. "Maybe he's afraid the States will catch up with him. He *is* outlaw tech, after all. If he thinks they're getting close, he might try something like this in self-defence."

"And end up making things worse for himself?" Roads shook his head. "It doesn't seem likely – too dramatic by far. More likely he'd try to infiltrate their databases and distort the evidence. He – or anyone, for that matter – would need a more pressing reason to keep the Reunited States out of the city."

The laptop chirped, and both looked down at it. A silver icon encrusted with spikes had appeared on the screen.

"Good. We've reached House security." Roads tapped at the keyboard again, using PolNet overrides to bypass the required password. Once he had entered the system, he browsed through menus and subprograms, looking for one in particular. Although Mayor's House lacked the tight security net RSD had installed in the library at the university, it did have a closed-circuit monitoring network linked to the central security program. Within moments, Roads had gained access to all the data and had routed it through the screen and his implants.

He and Barney settled back to watch, neither immune to the importance of what they were seeing.

The historic first meeting between General Stedman and the Mayor of Kennedy had begun in one of the building's largest conference halls, normally used only for special sittings of the Council. While not open to the general public, the room was filled with people representing both factions: senior officers from the Reunited States on one side, city dignitaries on the other. MSA bodyguards – ubiquitous since the assassinations had begun – hovered around every entrance. Scanning the crowd, Roads recognised Margaret Chappel and the head of the MSA, Adam Xenophou. Not far away was Antoni DeKurzak, watching proceedings from the end of a row, his tall frame allowing him a clear view over the heads in front of him. Martin O'Dell sat at the front of the hall, the superior position earned by his work in the city thus far. Stedman and Packard, with their respective deputies, sat together at a large oak table facing the small crowd. The General was dressed in full uniform, his white hair neatly combed back over his proud forehead and his attention focused firmly forward. The Mayor wore a formal suit and gown of office, and had just started his speech.

Roads turned up the volume on the computer for Barney's benefit while he eavesdropped via his implants:

". . . through the trials of the Dissolution," Mayor Packard was saying, "Kennedy Polis has stood alone, not immune to the tragedy that befell the rest of the country but strong enough to keep it at bay. After four decades of social engineering – including legislated birth control, strict rationing and recycling, and adherence to the Humanity Laws – the democratic principle has remained firm in our minds. Indeed, in the microcosm that is Kennedy Polis, we have preserved intact a fragment of what has been lost, guarding it jealously for this generation and for future generations to come.

"Yet we are not too proud to admit that the time has arrived for us to open our doors, to bring to an end the egalitarian way of life that has protected us these long years. The growth of the Reunited States of America has been both remarkable and admirable, and fuelled by desires similar to our own. In joining together we will become partners in a new endeavour: not merely to rebuild what went before, but to create a new society that has learnt from the errors of the past, one that is wiser and stronger for the tribulations its creators have endured . . ."

Barney chuckled softly as the speech continued. "He's laying it on a bit thick, isn't he?"

"That's his job." Roads indicated the screen. "And the brass seem to like it."

"Well, they would, wouldn't they? The MSA loves pomp and circumstance, so I guess Stedman's gang would too." Barney shrugged, her smile fading. "Some of what he says makes sense, though. We *have* been hanging onto the past. That's why it's so hard to believe the Reassimilation's finally here. After all the waiting and all the talk, we don't have any choice but to let go."

"Not necessarily." Roads studied her image in infrared while the scene in the meeting hall continued in a window on the screen. "As Roger Wiggs said the other day: 'It's never too late in politics.'"

"Meaning?"

"Meaning that nothing's certain. Stedman's offer has been tabled, but Packard can still reject it, or Stedman can renege on it. Until the deal is up and running, I wouldn't place any bets."

"You mean Cati, don't you? If he kills Stedman –"

"Not just Cati." Roads sighed. "The more I see and the more I think about it, the more positive I am that the States are responsible for the Mole. They want something from Kennedy that they're not telling us about."

Barney stared at him for a long moment. "The Mole's a spy? Is that what you're getting at?"

"I don't know. Maybe that's what he is, maybe not. But I can't ignore the wolf element any longer." Roads ticked facts off with his fingers. "The timber wolf first appeared around the same time Stedman's envoy arrived; then it turned up on the university lawns the night of Blindeye; and you yourself thought that the

Mole was some kind of werewolf. Add that to the fact that timber wolves are common up north – to the point where the States have a picture of one on their coat of arms – and you'll see where I'm headed."

Barney looked uncertain. "It's a bit tenuous, Phil."

"I know, but it's there. There *has* to be a connection."

"Maybe not the one you think, though. Why would one of Stedman's spies be protecting you, for starters? And why would he continue stealing data when –"

Roads grunted. "I thought of that, too. Rationally, it looks ridiculous, yet intuitively it doesn't. As much as I like – and, to a certain extent, trust – Martin O'Dell, I can't shake the feeling that he knows something about this. Something he's not telling me."

"Or isn't *allowed* to tell you."

"Probably." Roads sighed again, then rose to stretch his legs. "And the worst of it is, there's nothing I can do about it. Martin has the case, now. If he *is* involved, he'll find a way to cover it up."

"Then the best thing to do is to forget about it, don't you think?"

"Hardly. The Mole is a killer, too. I can't stand by and let someone get away with murder."

"So what do we *do*?" Barney asked.

"We keep going. We're halfway there, you know. Before, we didn't know what Cati was. Now we do, and all we have to do is find out who's controlling him. The Mole is the other way around: there's a chance we know who sent him into the city. Find out who he is and why he's here, and we'll be home free."

"Put that way, it almost sounds easy."

"Right."

They stood in silence, Barney watching the scene inside Mayor's House, Roads, with his hands in his pockets, staring at the convoy. From behind them came the occasional buzz of hand-held radios and the steady plod of RSD officers patrolling the fence.

"Well," Barney said, "there's not much I can do out here. I'm going inside where it's comfortable. You?"

"No. I'll stay here for a while. The view's just as good. And besides, I don't want to run into anyone I know – DeKurzak, for instance."

"Just don't do anything stupid. I'm here if you need me; all you have to do is call and I'll come after you."

"Thanks, but I think you'll be more use on the inside. I'll check through the security system for loopholes; if I find something, I'll let you know. And if my pass is a dud when I do try to get in, at least we'll be able to talk it through." He lowered his eyes to meet hers. "Still, I really appreciate the offer . . . And your patience. It's not easy for me, having to rely on someone else like this."

"Pffft." She gestured dismissively. "I'd do the same for anyone in your shoes."

"That's not what I meant."

"I know." Her eyes twinkled in the darkness. "When it's pay-back time, I'll let you know."

"You do that." He returned her fleeting kiss and used his implants to follow her as she walked away.

Barney ducked under the trees and across the lawn, heading for the main entrance of Mayor's House. She hated leaving Roads behind, but there was very little he could do inside that he couldn't do where he was. His unlimited access to the security system guaranteed that.

Although that in itself was worrying: if he could get in so easily, why not someone else? Cati's controller, for instance – *especially* if he was Keith Morrow . . .

When she reached the main door, an RSD officer stopped her. She showed him her pass, and he waved her through.

The plush reception area had been refitted with metal detectors and another security checkpoint. There she handed in her service revolver and, after verifying her pass through a phase correlator, pinned an ID badge to her uniform. Several stone-faced RUSAMC soldiers watched the procedure closely from nearby; only one responded when she smiled at them.

"Have I missed much?" she asked, exploiting the opportunity to talk with the newcomers.

"The meeting started half an hour ago," the soldier said with an accent similar to O'Dell's. "Do you know the way?"

She waved aside the implied offer. "That's okay. I'm not here for the speeches. Moonlighting on the security side of things instead."

The soldier nodded, then looked away.

"Roger Wiggs is already here," said the RSD officer behind the security checkpoint. "He asked me to send you straight up."

"Good. Thanks, Jim." Barney headed for the lifts. The doors hissed open, and she stepped inside. Rising with a jerk, the carriage took her to the second floor, where she disembarked. Another RSD officer – looking out of place among the almost obscenely luxurious fittings of Mayor's House – checked her pass a third time, comparing it with the ID badge.

"All quiet?" she asked.

"Dull, if you want the honest truth."

"Let's hope it stays that way." Barney glanced along the corridor. "The command centre is in the northern wing?"

"The Reagan Suite, fourth on the left."

"Thanks." Barney's feet made no sound at all on the thick carpet as she went on her way. Indeed, apart from the soft whisper of air-conditioning, the entire building was silent. She found it hard to believe that the most important event in the city's history was taking place just a dozen metres from her.

Or was it? The initial meeting, she knew, was little more than a publicity stunt, a symbolic gesture. No doubt the real negotiations would take place later, behind doors closed even to this evening's elite audience.

If Cati didn't act first . . .

When she reached the entrance to the Reagan Suite, she made certain her ID badge was clearly visible to the camera overhead and waited impatiently for someone to let her in. After ten seconds, the doors opened, filling the corridor with the welcome sounds of people hard at work: modems chattering, computer terminals whirring, voices darting back and forth across bowed heads. Below it all droned the steady tones of General Stedman. The Mayor's speech had obviously finished while she was in transit.

Barney stepped into the Reagan Suite and the doors locked automatically behind her. The room held fifteen people – including David Goss, who had followed his work on Blindeye with the assignment at Mayor's House – and at least twice that many terminals. A wall of monitors along one side gave her a choice of views of the conference hall. She stopped at one at random to watch the General in action, and reaffirmed her first impressions of the man: a born leader, long used to command. What the General's manner of public speaking lacked in style, it more than made up for in sheer implacability. Even Barney, after just a few minutes, felt herself being tugged along by his relentless, steady drawl.

Looking around to break the spell, she caught sight of Roger Wiggs in one corner. The red-headed officer sat on the edge of a desk, watching the proceedings below with ill-disguised boredom.

She hesitated before greeting him. A thought had suddenly struck her: DeKurzak had accused Roads of using his position to interfere in the search for the Mole. Clearly that was not the case, but the idea was sound. Couldn't Wiggs, by the same reasoning, be Cati's controller? He had been in a perfect position to deflect any investigation that might uncover Cati's existence and his role in the murders.

Barely had she thought the idea than she dismissed it. Wiggs hadn't the computer skills to raid archived files in the RSD datapool. He had enough trouble browsing through bulletin boards. Besides, he'd professed ambivalence regarding the Reassimilation on enough occasions to convince her that he wasn't obsessively against it.

As though sensing her thoughts, he glanced up. She waved, and he motioned for her to come closer.

"Hi, Roger," she said, joining him at the desk.

"Barney. I've been waiting for you to turn up."

"Well, sorry I'm late." Barney noted his solemn expression and wondered at its cause. "And sorry, too, about the case. Phil told me what really happened in the meeting this morning."

"That's what I want to talk to you about." Wiggs' eyes narrowed slightly. "Did he tell you about his theory? About what the killer might be?"

"More the other way around, actually," she said. "I told him last night, after we ran a search through the city datapools."

"Good." Wiggs leaned forward. "Then please tell me you kept a record of everything you found."

"Of course we did." Barney studied his face; it was pale, even for him. "Why? It should be in the datapools where we found it."

"I wish it was." One of the security staff brushed past by them. Wiggs took Barney's arm, led her to a corner.

"The case is DeKurzak's baby, now. He's had us going over profiles of senior council members and high-ranking officers – like Phil – for the last few days, looking for evidence of this fucking Old Guard of his." Wiggs indicated with a simple gesture what he thought of that idea. "I'm not supposed to be working on my own initiative, but Phil's theory – your theory, whoever's – had me curious. It could be checked, and it seemed a shame not to at least go that far. So I did everything Phil suggested we do. I hunted for the old CATI records, tried to track down the control frequency, even called up a friend in archives to take another look, to make sure I didn't do anything wrong." Wiggs lowered his voice. "I didn't. The information isn't there – and, for all I can tell, never was at all."

"But –"

Wiggs held up a hand to silence her protest. "I know, I know. I'm not sure what I'm hoping you'll tell me – that Phil made the whole thing up, or that someone's removed the evidence. Either way, I don't like it. And I can't just let it go, Barney. This might be the only sensible lead we've had for weeks. To let it slip through our fingers now –"

"I understand." Barney turned away to avoid Wiggs' searching gaze. The data was gone; therefore someone had erased it from the RSD datapool. It seemed obvious to her that Cati's controller was trying to cover his tracks – although to anyone else the absence of evidence wasn't evidence at all. It was simply incriminating.

"Give me a second, Roger," she said, "and I'll find that frequency for you. Is there a free terminal I can use?"

Wiggs inquired with Goss. The big officer found Barney a vacant station in one corner. With one hand on the keyboard and the other at her ear, she subvocalised Roads' full name.

"Hello, Phil? Are you there?"

"Yes," came Roads' voice over the cyberlink. "What's the problem?"

"Cati's controller is definitely onto us."

"What makes you say that?"

Barney outlined what Wiggs had told her, and added: "If he knew about the data we lifted, then he must have had access to Margaret Chappel's files. That's where the investigation stopped."

"Exactly." Roads was silent, thinking. Then: "You said 'he'. It could be a 'she', you know."

"Are you talking about Margaret herself? I thought she was on *your* side."

"She is, but . . . No, that makes even less sense."

"I agree. No use being paranoid." Barney tapped at the keyboard, recalling her thoughts about Wiggs. "Anyway, the file on Cati should still be in my laptop. Can you send it to me?"

"Easy. Where are you?"

She fiddled with the terminal's operating system. "*CNTRL14/mhsec.rsd.kp.namcp.*"

"Okay. I'll transfer it straight away," Roads said. "While I've got you: I just finished a sweep of the monitoring program."

"And?"

"There are a couple of dead zones: one on the first floor, another in the basement. The system hasn't raised an alarm in either case because cameras cover exits from each area, but still . . . They should be checked, at least."

"I'll do it myself when I've finished here."

"Good. I'll give you the whereabouts while I send you the file."

"Thanks, Phil." Barney jotted down the exact locations of the unmonitored areas and tucked the scrap of paper into a pocket. Moments later, the screen in front of her came to life.

"Roger?"

Wiggs leaned over her shoulder. "You've got it?"

"The lot." Barney stood, motioned him into the seat. "I'd take a hard copy, if I were you. Can't be too careful around here, it seems."

"Right." Noticing her eagerness to move on, he inquired: "You're not sticking around?"

"No. I've got something to do. But I'll come back later to see how you got on."

"Thanks. If you see Phil, say hi and tell him I'll do my best."

Behind them, the doors to the command centre swung open and a handful of people entered. Two plain-clothed RSD officers came first, followed by Martin O'Dell and Antoni DeKurzak. Barney glanced at the monitors, belatedly realising the meeting had finished.

"Excuse me, Roger." She headed across the room, clutching the piece of paper in her pocket. If something was going to happen tonight – and she, like Roads, didn't dare doubt that it would – then they were running out of time. Stedman was loose inside the building, no longer watched by dozens of people in the conference hall. The risk of attack had just risen significantly, and she needed to check the dead zones before it was too late.

DeKurzak caught her eye as she hurried for the door. "Officer Daniels," he said.

Barney forced a smile, but didn't stop to chat. After what the liaison officer had done to Roads, she'd be just as happy never to see him again.

DeKurzak raised an arm to stop her. "Leaving so soon?"

"There's work to do, sir," she said tersely. "I need to inspect dead zones on the first floor and basement."

"Alone?" DeKurzak raised his eyebrows in concern. "This is highly irregular – especially given your close relationship with Philip Roads. Let me assign someone to accompany you. Officer Dobran – ?"

"That's okay." O'Dell's placid drawl intruded between them. "I'll keep an eye on her. The exercise will do me good, after sitting down for so long."

DeKurzak glanced between them, almost suspiciously, then nodded. "Very well. You will, of course, report any irregularities to Officer Goss or myself –"

"We will." O'Dell saluted dryly. "Come on, Barney. Let's go."

When they reached the corridor outside the suite, Barney let go of the breath she had been holding.

"Thanks, Martin."

"Any time." He motioned for her to lead the way. "I'd avoid him for the rest of the night, too, if you can. He's a little uptight about security, for obvious reasons."

She looked at him. "You agree with Phil, then? That something *might* happen?"

"Of course. We're not stupid. This is the killer's last chance to make a real impression on the Reassimilation process, and it's our job to make sure he doesn't." Martin grinned lazily. "Which he won't. Although . . . Are there really dead zones in here, or was that just an excuse to take a look around?"

"They're real."

"Someone's been sloppy, then." O'Dell shook his head, then added: "No offence meant to David Goss in the RSD command centre, of course. Which shall we look at first?"

"The first floor, if you like. But you don't have to, you know."

"I know. My excuse was real, too. All this talking gets to me. It's good to be *doing* something, for a change."

"I agree – although I'm more than half-hoping we'll be wasting our time . . ."

Roads watched through his implants as Barney and O'Dell left the command centre. Jealousy played no part in the frown that creased his forehead; rather, he was concerned that O'Dell's involvement in whatever was going on might compromise his reactions to any critical situation.

Still, he told himself, Barney knew what she was doing. If he couldn't trust her, then who *could* he trust?

Turning back to the laptop, he resumed working on the program he had installed in the security system of Mayor's House. Unlike the earlier image processing algorithm Barney had used to locate the 'glitch' in the Blindeye recordings, this was designed to keep track of one single image. No matter where General Stedman went within the building, the program would keep tabs on him. That way, if anything went wrong while Roads was distracted, he would be able to view the scene immediately rather than hunt through all the different cameras to find the optimum angle.

At that moment, the General was sharing a toast in Mayor Packard's ample study with a handful of city leading lights – Margaret Chappel one of them, nodding politely in response to conversation. Roads watched for a while, but soon became bored. The General wasn't a heavy drinker, it seemed; the snifter in his hand remained entirely untouched until he eventually put it down on a nearby table.

Roads activated the tracking program and, feeling superfluous, stood. There was very little he could do but wait. Unless Barney and O'Dell found something in the dead zones, the rest of the night lay in the hands of Cati's controller.

Yet crouching in the shadows like a thief was beginning to wear at his patience. His shoulder and ribs still ached, and the numerous bruises across his body were beginning to nag. Leaving the laptop hidden in a split tree trunk, he went for a quick walk around the grounds to stretch his limbs.

Apart from light reflecting from the front of Mayor's House, the lawn and surrounding tree-line were almost entirely unlit. The clouds had thickened with sunset, obscuring the stars. The rising moon was barely visible. Behind the building, where the Councillors and other permanent staff had their offices and quarters, the night was particularly black.

With his feet scuffing over age-torn tarmac, he jogged across the open space to the regular carpark.

Before he reached cover, two RSD officers stepped out of the gloom. Clad in black uniforms and night-specs, they looked inhuman, robotic.

"Pass, sir," said one, holding out her hand. The other held an automatic weapon at the ready.

Roads produced the forged card and handed it over. The officer – instructed to inspect ID regardless of who was holding it – studied the pass closely then returned it to him. Twice, now, Morrow's handiwork had survived official scrutiny; if the Head did intend to betray him, then it would clearly take a more subtle form than having him arrested by RSD.

"Thank you, sir." The guards waved him on, and stepped back into the shadows to reassume their position.

"Wait." Roads walked with them. "How have things been out here?"

The second officer answered. "Quiet."

"No unusual disturbances? Noises from overhead, that sort of thing?"

"None, sir." The officer swung the rifle onto his shoulder. "Not so much as a bird."

"Good." Roads exhaled heavily through his nose: not quite relief, far too premature for that. "Don't feel foolish about reporting anything unusual."

"Of course not, sir."

Before they decided that he himself fell into that category, Roads turned and headed off into the darkness.

Keeping closely to the shadows, he circled the rest of the way around the building without mishap, coming no closer than twenty metres to the RUSAMC envoy. A scurrying robot passed him briefly, swivelling its electronic eyes upward to look at him, but hurried away again without a sound. Obviously his image didn't constitute a threat as far as the Reunited States Military Corps was concerned. That was something, he supposed.

Returning to where he had started, he unfolded the laptop from its hiding place and assumed his former position. The brief journey had confirmed that security was reasonably tight, and that his pass still seemed to be valid. It hadn't, however, helped shake the apprehension steadily building in his gut, the feeling that something was going to happen at any moment.

If General Stedman shared that feeling – and Martin O'Dell *had* indicated that the RUSAMC also suspected that the killer would try to strike sometime soon – then he displayed none of it in public. For all the concern on his face, he might have been attending a friendly drink at a local club.

Did they have such clubs in the States? Roads wondered whether he would ever be given the chance to find out. Even if Reassimilation went ahead, his own fate remained far from certain.

Shortly before ten-fifteen, Roads glanced away as the General excused himself to go to the toilet. An instant later, a small alarm chimed on the laptop and the picture suddenly froze. Roads examined the screen. The picture had split down the middle into two halves, both filled with grey noise. Tapping at the keyboard failed to rectify the problem; the screen remained obstinately frozen. The program had crashed in mid-frame.

Puzzled, he reset the laptop and ran the program again – with the same result. The program refused to run.

He tried his implants. General Stedman appeared through them as clear as a bell, standing in the Mayor's chambers again. Whatever had crashed the program, therefore, had nothing to do with the data coming from Mayor's House. The problem had to be elsewhere.

He reset the laptop a third time and probed the operating system. The first thing he checked for was evidence of deliberate interference, thinking that his intrusion might have been detected – by the RSD security team, the RUSAMC or even Cati's controller. But he found nothing to suggest that any of these was the case. His implants were fine. His surreptitious observation of Mayor's House only came to a halt when he tried to run the image processor program – and then only on General Stedman's image.

Something to do with the program itself, then? Perhaps, he thought. It had run perfectly until ten-fifteen. At that time, some aspect of the feed from Mayor's House must have changed to make it crash. But what?

Roads settled back onto his haunches to examine the program in more detail, while at the same time using his implants to keep an eye on the General. Whatever had happened, it was almost certainly unimportant. A slight shift in baud rate, perhaps, or an unexpected switch to another secure machine-code.

But it wasn't that simple. Both the program and the feed seemed sound. He tried resetting the laptop yet again, and received the same output: two regions of flickering snow divided by a black bar down the middle of the screen.

Staring at it, Roads was struck by a possible explanation. The black bar hadn't been there before. It had to be significant. Maybe . . .

He returned to the program itself, reeled through modules and subroutines until he found the one he wanted, and made a single, tiny change. Then he rebooted the computer.

This time the program ran perfectly – although its output made no sense at all.

On the way to the basement, Barney and O'Dell shared the elevator with another RUSAMC officer, a thick-set brunette with close-cropped hair.

"To be frank, I'm glad it's over." She directed her words at O'Dell. "After the last few days, I'll be more than happy to get a decent night's sleep."

"You have quarters?" Barney asked.

The woman nodded, looking at her for the first time. "I'll be leaving for base camp in an hour."

More out of politeness than any real curiosity, Barney pursued the conversation: "How many are staying behind?"

"As few as possible. Maybe a couple of dozen."

"That's all?" Barney glanced from O'Dell to the woman. The number seemed unreasonably small. "But what about security?"

"Don't worry about the General," O'Dell said. "He'll be okay."

"But I thought you said –"

"Yes, we think the killer might try tonight. But if he does, he'll fail. I guarantee it."

Barney wished she had his confidence, and said so. "What's all *this* for, then?"

"To make you feel useful." The twinkle in O'Dell's eye told her that he was only half serious. Barney bit back an irritated retort with difficulty.

The doors opened on the ground floor, and the woman indicated that she was getting out.

"Have a good night," said the woman to O'Dell. "I'll see you in a couple of days."

"That you will."

When the doors had shut and they were alone again, Barney immediately confronted O'Dell.

"Let's try that again, Martin: why are you here with me? And don't give me any bullshit this time. I hate being patronised as much as anyone."

"Sorry. I suppose that's fair." O'Dell's smile faded. "It's nothing much. One, the exercise; two, to get away from the brass; and three, good old curiosity. If the killer *does* get in, I want to know how he did it. The only chink in the security of this building appears to be the dead zones. Unlikely though that seems, it's worth checking out. You never know, we might even catch him in the act."

"Earning us both medals?"

"Or broken necks." Perversely, that made O'Dell's smile return. "Either way, we'll have done something constructive."

Barney nodded, accepting the explanation even though the chance of them achieving anything seemed remote: the dead zone on the first floor had consisted of an empty corner in an otherwise secure room; no chance of an illicit entry there. The second zone in the basement would just as likely be similar.

The lift shuddered to a halt. Barney held the door open while O'Dell exited the cab. The basement consisted of a series of storerooms and wine cellars connected by a single corridor running along its entire length. From the distance came the smooth chugging of a compressor, pumping fresh air throughout the building. Ancient fluorescent lights behind wire grills every three metres illuminated the hallway.

"No guards down here?" asked O'Dell, noting the absence of life.

"No need," said Barney. "The lift's the only way in, and it's guarded from the lobby. And besides . . ." She indicated the cameras at each end of the corridor.

"Which way, then?" O'Dell asked.

Barney pointed to their left. "Second to last storeroom on the right."

"Okay. Let's get it over with."

Together they walked along the hallway to the door. It was shut, but not locked. Barney turned the handle and swung it open.

The storeroom was unoccupied, with rough plaster walls and a concrete floor. A metal rack full of boxes lined one wall, opposite which had been stacked three large crates. Dust filmed every horizontal surface despite the gentle breeze issuing from an air vent high on one wall.

"Cosy," said O'Dell, crossing the room to examine the dead camera. "This seems fine," he said. "Must be an electrical fault."

"I'll have a technician look at it tomorrow." Barney made a mental note to tell Goss when they returned to the command centre.

O'Dell seemed in no hurry to leave, however. He browsed through the contents of the rack, turning over items and putting them back. "Spare parts," he mused.

"Your reclamation facilities are quite impressive, you know."

"They have to be, to keep us going," Barney said, fighting an impatience to return to the upper floors. "Without them, the city would have ground to a halt years ago."

"Yes. We're far behind you in that respect." O'Dell glanced at her, then returned to his inspection of the room. "That's one lesson we've never had to learn."

"Half your luck." Barney noted his words with interest. "You don't sound surprised that we might have something to teach you."

"Should I be?"

"No, of course not – but that's not the impression I get from a lot of your people. Sometimes I feel as though you're letting us into the States purely out of charity."

O'Dell squatted on his haunches by a stack of crates. "Don't let those impressions tarnish our intentions, Barney. I'm sure they're real, but they're not representative. We have differences of opinions, just like you do."

"Under Stedman?"

"Of course. Under Christ himself we'd still have dissent. That's what democracy is all about." O'Dell ran a hand across the middle crate of the stack of three he was leaning against, and nodded at recent wheel-marks and footprints on the dusty floor. "These look like some of ours," he said, pointedly changing the subject. "God only knows what they're doing down here, though."

"I can check with R&R, if you like."

"No, that's not necessary. As likely as not the Mayor decided to keep them for himself. Must contain something interesting, I guess." He rapped his knuckles on the wood.

"Either way," said Barney, "there's nothing for us here."

"Wait," said O'Dell. He knocked on the box again, lower this time. A third time, then a fourth, and Barney heard the pitch of each rap change.

She was about to ask what he was doing when he knocked on the bottom crate. His knuckles provoked a hollow thud.

He glanced up at Barney. "This one sounds empty. Give me a hand."

Together they lifted off the top two crates and exposed the lid of the one on the bottom. The seal seemed intact until Barney worried at the edge of the lid. With a slight groan, the top lifted smoothly off.

"Well I'll be damned," said O'Dell.

The crate *was* empty – and obviously placed at the bottom of the stack to hide that fact.

"What are you thinking?" asked O'Dell.

"I'm wondering why anyone would bother to store an empty crate down here."

Barney stepped back to examine the dust on the floor. The mess of footprints surrounding the crates was difficult to interpret. One faint trail, however, led from the stack to the wall opposite the door. The prints weren't of shoes, but what seemed to be bare feet.

O'Dell rose, dusting his hands on his uniform pants. "How does this sound?" he said. "Someone arranges to have the crates diverted in transit, replaces the contents of this one, and has them delivered here. The dead zone allows whoever's inside to get out, rearrange the crates to cover their method of entry, and . . ."

"And what? They can't leave the room without being seen." Barney's eyes followed the footprints to the far wall, then rose upward. The air vent stared back at her. A tremor – half excitement, half fear – stirred in her stomach.

O'Dell followed her gaze. "The ducts?"

"It's the only possible way." Barney crossed the room in two steps, reached up to tug at the grill. It came away cleanly, with no shower of dust – obviously moved recently. Peering inside, she saw a dark metal tube barely a metre across and forty centimetres high.

O'Dell looked uncertain. "I don't know. Could someone squeeze through there?"

"If they had to, they could." She leaned the grill against the wall and stepped away. "If they were more flexible than most people."

"Biomodified," O'Dell finished the thought.

As though he had confirmed her guess rather than simply agreed with her, her uncertainty suddenly vanished. "Cati could be anywhere in here!"

"Maybe." O'Dell raised a hand to pacify her. "We don't know for certain it was him, or if anything has happened at all."

"But it's worth checking, surely?"

"Of course. Hang on a second, and I'll let someone know." O'Dell stepped out of the storeroom, and put a finger to his ear. Speaking rapidly under his breath, he outlined the situation by intercom to one of his fellow officers.

Barney prowled the room while she waited. Swinging a box off the rack and into position below the vent, she climbed onto it and peered along the duct. Without a light, she couldn't see very far, barely enough to ascertain that the first two metres were empty.

"They're querying the delivery with the command centre," O'Dell said, stepping back into the room. "That shouldn't take long."

"I hope not." Barney stepped down from the box.

"When . . . hang on." Again O'Dell's hand went to his ear. This time Barney made out the flesh-coloured throat-mike taped above the hollow of his neck.

"Okay," he said when the brief conversation had finished. "It looks like a false alarm. The crate was emptied when it was delivered this evening; apparently the Mayor wanted to inspect some of the goods personally, before the speeches. The duct was cleaned yesterday morning as part of an overall air-conditioning service. The dead zone must be a coincidence."

She absorbed this in silence. "Who told them that?"

"Someone in security."

"I guess they'd know better than we do." Barney glanced down at the footprints in the dust: now more than ever they resembled marks left by bare feet. "Still, I don't like it. It seems entirely too plausible for my liking."

"I agree. So I suggest we get upstairs to keep a closer eye on things." O'Dell waved her through the door ahead of him.

"Seconded," she said. "It gives me the creeps down here."

As they waited for the elevator to descend to the basement, Roads' voice intruded loudly into the silence of the cellar.

"Barney? Are you there?"

She jumped. "God, I hate it when you do that."

"Sorry. Listen, I think I've found something important."

"You have?" The cage doors opened, and they stepped inside. With a jerk, they began to ascend. "Don't tell me it's in the air-conditioning system, please. We already thought of that."

"No. It's on the second floor, now." Roads spoke quickly, urgently: "I ran an IP through the security system to keep tabs on the General. Just after the meeting in the Mayor's office, the program crashed. When I tried to find out why, I worked out that the IP wasn't equipped to handle multiple recognitions: it could only track a single image, and failed the moment it came across two or more. If Stedman looked into a mirror, for instance."

"Why should that make a difference?"

"I didn't guess at first, not until the program was up and running again. And even then, I had to check manually before I could believe it."

"Believe *what*? That Stedman has been brushing his hair for the last hour?"

"No." Roads hesitated for a moment, as though he himself didn't accept what he had found. "At 10:15 the IP program picked up two images. Both were in the ground floor toilet, as thought Stedman *had* looked into a mirror. But then one of them left and the other stayed behind. While the first retired to one of the staterooms to freshen up, the other snuck out a side entrance with a couple of guards and returned to the control van outside. Since then, the IP program has run perfectly.

"*That's* why Martin isn't worried about Cati: there are two General Stedmans, and one of them is a fake."

CHAPTER TWENTY

9:25 p.m.

Before Roads could finish what he was saying, the elevator doors opened on the second floor and the sound of animated voices cut him off.

Barney gaped at the crowd of uniformed people swarming past. Her first thought was that Cati had struck the command centre – that she and O'Dell had mistakenly arrived at the right place too late. But then she realised that the noise was more indicative of disorganisation than urgency. Confusion, not panic.

This conclusion was supported by O'Dell's annoyed curse. "Talk about bad timing," he said. "We'll never get through this lot."

"I'm sorry, Phil," she subvocalised over Roads' voice. "I'll have to call you back. There's something going on up here." She counted heads quickly as the crowd bustled past: roughly twenty clustered around a central point; half of them RUSAMC officers, the rest RSD and MSA; all of them rubbing shoulders awkwardly, not yet used to working so close to each other. As she counted, the group bundled to a halt just past the elevator.

"At least they're heading in the right direction," she said. "More or less."

Barney stepped out of the elevator and into the crowd, bumping into a RUSAMC private as she did so.

The young man scowled, then immediately adopted a more friendly approach when he noticed O'Dell behind her.

"Sorry, ma'am," he said. "Didn't see you there."

"Forget it," she responded. "What's the hold-up? We need to get through."

The private nodded ahead, at the heart of the group. Barney could just make out the white-haired head of General Stedman listening to something one of his guides said in his ear. His voice carried through the buzz of the entourage, but not clearly enough to make out his words. Judging by the direction of his gaze, he seemed to be studying a painting on the wall in front of him.

"A guided tour," explained O'Dell. "Unscheduled from your end, but planned from ours, if you know what I mean."

Barney thought she did. Another test of the city's flexibility – and its patience.

"We could be here forever," she hissed. "There has to be another way around –"

"No, wait. He's moving." O'Dell put a calming hand on her shoulder. "We'll get there, don't worry."

The crowd shuffled forward again. Barney, fuming to herself, noticed O'Dell gesture to one of his colleagues, who instantly moved to join him. The two RUSAMC officers exchanged a brief, whispered conversation, then separated. O'Dell returned to Barney's side with something like his usual smile across his lips.

"Everything's under control," he said. "The General's just taking his time."

"Unfortunately for us." And for security, she added to herself. In the confines of the building's corridors, a planned march was difficult, an unplanned one doubly so.

But there was no use pointing this out to her companion. O'Dell would only reiterate his stubborn belief that

Stedman was safe – perhaps because the Stedman before her was nothing but a stand-in. And maybe that was the real reason behind the unscheduled tour: not to test the Mayor's patience, but to flush Cati from wherever he was hiding.

Yes, it made sense – although Barney wouldn't have had the stand-in's job for all the money in the world.

The huddle around Stedman moved slowly along the corridor. Only when it reached another painting and Stedman paused for a closer look did she realise that Mayor Packard himself was accompanying the General. As the mingled bodyguards attempted to settle into secure cordons around their respective leaders, she wondered what would happen to bystanders if Cati attacked during the tour. The General might well be safe – but what about those with him?

Her nervousness returning, she craned her neck for a better view of the hallway. The focus of Stedman's attention was a portrait of the city's first mayor in watercolours, framed by recycled wood. The flattened semi-circle of bodyguards reached from one side of the hallway to the other and for several metres along it. Delicate light-fittings hung from the walls every three metres, casting an unobtrusive yellow glow across the scene. Ten metres further up the hallway was the entrance to the Reagan Suite.

So near, thought Barney. Yet it might as well have been on the other side of the city . . .

As her eyes wandered, she noticed something she had missed earlier: an air-conditioning vent in the wall directly above the painting. Similar vents lined the walls every five metres, roughly the same size as the one in the basement.

She stiffened. The Mayor quietly explained the significance of the woman in the painting, but Barney heard none of it. Instead she studied every inch of the grill, the screws holding it fast to the wall, the gaps between each slat, the darkness within – searching for anything out of the ordinary.

But she saw nothing.

Paranoid, she told herself. What had she expected? Pointed fingertips protruding through the grill? Fetid breath misting the air? Sulphur smoke issuing from the perverted flesh of the very devil himself?

No. Security had told them that the dead zone in the basement was a false lead. Yet she couldn't let go of the idea. But how could Cati possibly know where the General would choose to stop, and when the opportunity to attack would arise?

Forcing herself to relax, she shuffled forward a step as the General indicated that he would like to move on.

And at that moment, when the mingled cordons were at their most disorganised, the vent exploded.

Roads caught it perfectly through his implants.

The grill flew out of the wall with enough force to tear its screws completely from the plaster. Warped out of shape by the force of the blow that had struck it, it shot across the hallway and into the light fixture opposite. The globes shattered, and shadow shrouded the area below the opening in the wall where the grill had once been.

Into the shadow – and the confusion – a red-skinned figure slid smoothly out of the hole in the wall. Roads stared at it in impotent horror: it was the same face he had glimpsed the night of Blindeye, the same eyes, the same hairless scalp, the same powerful body with whip-lash reflexes and incomprehensible reserves of strength.

Cati gained his footing in one fluid movement and reached forward with a single giant hand to grasp General Stedman about the neck.

As Cati's fingers closed, the first shot was fired. More out of luck than any genuine aim, the bullet struck Cati in the shoulder. Blood spattered bystanders, but the biomodified giant hardly flinched. With a vicious flexing of muscles, his fingers closed, twisted, pulled . . .

And came away empty.

Bare tenths of a second had elapsed, long enough for weapons to be unholstered but not sufficient time for orders to take effect. The mess of officers and soldiers milled in confusion, unsure exactly what had happened. Roads saw Barney lunge forward, and Martin O'Dell, hand still on her shoulder, attempt to pull her back.

The second shot missed. Cati struck again, this time pivoting on one leg to kick General Stedman in the heart. On an ordinary man, the blow would have smashed through bone and flesh, but General Stedman simply recoiled intact, as though Cati's foot had struck solid stone.

Roads' fists clenched as Cati backed off and reconsidered the situation.

Finally the bodyguards remembered their orders and sprang into action. RSD officers armed with pistols dragged Mayor Packard away from General Stedman and buried him under their bodies, while others aimed their weapons at Cati. The latter group found themselves in direct conflict with the RUSAMC soldiers, who physically placed themselves between the Mayor's bodyguards and the two men in the middle of the circle.

Barney struggled helplessly in O'Dell's grip, screaming her frustration into the chaos around her. O'Dell held her back with his jaw clenched.

In the centre of the circle, alone but for each other, stood General Stedman and his assassin.

Deep black eyes regarded the turmoil around him as Cati tensed for a third attempt. Blood streamed down his right arm and dripped onto the carpet – a rich, electric red, much brighter than normal blood; hyper-oxygenated to feed the energy demands of such a massive frame. He took one wary step to his left, as though considering his options.

Attack or flee? Obey orders or put survival first? Roads knew which would win in the end. He wasn't surprised when Cati suddenly sprang to enfold the General in a killing embrace.

Before the two men met, General Stedman vanished.

Cati twisted in mid-air and landed facing the way he had come. Shock spread across his inhuman features as his wide eyes searched the air, tried to find either the General or an explanation for his sudden disappearance.

Roads did the same, with difficulty. The signal from Mayor's House flickered peculiarly through his implants. It was as though a bubble of glass had passed between the camera and the scene below – exactly the same phenomenon Roads had witnessed moments before Danny Chong died.

Then five such bubbles converged on a point opposite Cati, stabilised in a rough pentagon, and shimmered strangely.

General Stedman reappeared an instant later, as solid as ever – but only for a second. Barely had he re-appeared when he began to change. His skin colour darkened; his form filled out, became taller. His clothes melted into his body like wax, and he became someone else entirely:

Another CATI.

The two giants stared at each other, black eyes reflecting to infinity, surrounded by confusion as the officers around them milled in panic. Further up the hallway, the door to the command centre opened.

Stedman/Cati smiled and opened his arms.

Then the original Cati cocked his head, as though listening to something, and the lights went out entirely.

Roads received a momentary impression of movement through the camera's microphones, followed by the sound of a single gun-shot. Then the feed from Mayor's House ceased. His link with PolNet failed at the same moment.

He returned abruptly to the real world – stuck outside the house, surrounded by rustling trees and darkness. Distant shouts echoed from the RUSAMC camp as soldiers stirred. RSD officers in the now-gloomy foyer swarmed around the doors.

Without stopping to hide the laptop, Roads leapt to his feet and started to run. Branches whipped at him as he threaded through the trees and around the building to exit fourteen. The same officers who had stopped him earlier, alerted by confused messages coming from within the building, had taken position by the door.

He raised the pass as he approached, but they stopped him anyway.

"I'm sorry, sir," said one. "No-one in or out."

"But I have to get *in* there!" Roads pleaded.

"Until the situation is contained –" began the other, but was stopped by the sound of breaking glass.

Roads turned away from the door and ran back around the building. The floodlights that had once illuminated the grounds had been extinguished along with the security system, but his implants easily supplemented the lack of visual light.

Running across the lawn was one large figure, extremely bright in infra-red.

Without even stopping to think about what he was doing, Roads sprinted after it. The glowing figure darted through the ring of trees in the direction of the nearest fence. The RSD patrol that should have been waiting for it had been halted further along the fence, confused by the sudden radio silence. The shape climbed over unobstructed and loped onto the street.

Roads followed a second later, cursing the lapse in security. Shinning over the fence with a grunt, he continued the chase across the street and into the dark city centre. The glowing figure led him along a main road and around a corner. The distance between them gradually widened, despite Roads' best efforts. By the time he turned the corner, the figure had disappeared.

Then, two storeys up, on the southern side of the street, he saw a broad, red-skinned figure with the same infra-red pattern as the one he had been chasing. Massive shoulders flexed as it lifted itself up and onto the rooftop. Barely had Roads caught sight of it than it was gone.

"Shit!" He stumbled to a halt, breathing heavily through his mouth. Glancing around him, he oriented himself. He could think of only once place Cati might be heading, and that was a long shot.

Running again, he took the nearest corner left, and stared along the street. If he wasn't too late . . .

One hundred metres down, barely within range of his implants under such poor light, a figure leapt from roof to roof across the road, and vanished again.

Heading roughly south-west.

Roads ran back the way he had come and found Mayor's House in complete confusion. No-one checked his pass as he ran through the rear gates and jogged to the carpark. Only when he started the engine of an unlocked car did someone come to see what was going on. And even then, the officers who had spoken to him twice already that night let him go.

Panic made Barney's heartbeat race as the lights went out: in darkness, stripped of all the trappings of civilisation, she felt like a child again, waiting for the berserkers to come.

Surrounded by shouting people all trying to make themselves heard over the racket, she finally twisted free of O'Dell's hand and lunged forward through the milling bodies. Ahead of her, someone screamed – a woman. A single shot, fired in panic, made her ears ring.

Barney cursed the darkness. Who could have known they'd need night-specs *inside* the building?

The sound of shattering glass came to her from the end of the hallway. She wrestled free of the crowd to pursue the noise. As she passed the entrance to the Reagan Suite, she collided heavily with a person running in the opposite direction. Whoever it was didn't stop. Recovering her footing, she continued on her way past the command centre and around the corner.

A single broken window opened into the night air at the end of the hallway. Leaning through the frame, she glanced down.

Cati was gone. All she saw – and then only briefly – was a long, sleek shape slipping rapidly through the trees skirting the lawn around Mayor's House.

The timber wolf.

Then a hand touched her on the back and she spun, ready to strike.

"It's me," said O'Dell, backing away a step. Muted moonlight painted his face in silver. "You okay?"

"No, I'm *not* okay," Barney snapped. "What the fuck did you think you were doing back there?"

"Stopping you from getting too close, of course." He tilted his head to one side. "You saw what happened. Do you think you could have helped?"

"No, but –" She wanted to throttle him, to lash out. Instead she pushed angrily past him. "You'd better have a good explanation for this, Martin."

"Oh, we have, Barney," O'Dell called after her. "Better than anything you could have imagined!"

She ran back around the corner and into the growing crowd. Most of the people from the command centre – including David Goss and Roger Wiggs – had arrived, bringing torches with them. The scene was lit by strobes of light that illuminated patches for an instant – the hole in the wall, the twisted remains of the grill, spots of blood slowly darkening on the carpet, startled faces everywhere – then moved rapidly on.

The Mayor had struggled to his feet and was being led amid muffled protests to an emergency stairwell.

"What the hell's wrong with the lights?" Barney asked Goss.

"Power's gone," he said, his voice low and dangerous. His enormous frame loomed heavily in the gloom. "Someone's killed the entire network – along with security, RSD communications and –"

"How?" she interrupted.

"By using the proper codes. And we can't switch any of it back on until we find out what they were."

"You don't know the codes? Who does?"

"About half a dozen people, I'd guess."

"That narrows down the suspects, at least."

"If we could find Margaret, we'd be up and running before you knew it. She programmed the codes herself." Goss' eyes roamed the chaos. His thoughts were obvious: how to find the Director of RSD when it was hard enough talking face-to-face.

A RUSAMC soldier stepped forward. "Word from below. The building is sealed."

"Too late," said Barney. "Cati's gone. He left via the window back there."

"He – *it* – went past me," said the woman who had screamed after the lights went out. She rubbed her

340

shoulder as she spoke. "It pushed me out of the way, and kept going."

The RUSAMC officer glanced from Barney to the woman. "Then we'll need some sort of search party."

"He could be halfway across the city by now," Barney said. "You're better off trying to get the power back on."

The officer hesitated, obviously reluctant to take no action at all. "Who's in charge here?"

Goss glanced around him again, looking for authority and finding none. "I guess I am, for the moment. Tell Jim Farquhar on the desk to round up as many people as he can. We have to seal and quarter the grounds. I'll be down as soon as I can to sort things out here."

"Yes, sir," said the officer, and relayed the orders through his throat mike.

Barney turned away, feeling worse than useless. No-one had been hurt, but that didn't assuage her bitterness. If she had followed her instincts, she might have prevented the attack. Instead, she had let Phil down.

Belatedly remembering the cyberlink, she called silently for Roads. "Phil? I hope you saw all of that, because you'll never believe me if you didn't."

She waited a moment, then repeated: "Phil? Phil, are you there?"

No answer. PolNet must have crashed along with RSD and the house security. She hoped he had made it into the building. God only knew, she needed his help to make sense of everything that had happened.

Cati had obviously been in the vents, as she had first thought. But security had told them not to worry about the dead zone in the basement. Security had therefore been wrong – or deliberately misleading. And the more she thought about it, the more the latter seemed probable.

She and Roads had already ascertained that Cati's controller had to be someone high up in RSD – or exceptionally skilled with the city's datapool – in order to gain access to archived data. Furthermore, that same someone must have arranged for the crates to be brought into the building, eavesdropped on RUSAMC information to tell Cati where to wait for the General's appearance, and then used the override codes to kill the power when escape was called for. If security had lied to prevent Cati from being detected, then that meant . . .

Cati's controller had been in the command centre during the attack.

The crowd had thinned slightly, but the sense of chaos remained. Barney threaded her way through to Roger Wiggs, who stood near where the air-conditioning vent had fallen.

"I still can't believe it," he said when he saw her. "Right under our noses –"

"Neither can I," she agreed, although she didn't have time for sympathy. "Listen, about half an hour ago, a call came from one of Stedman's cronies to ask about the air-conditioning in the basement. Do you remember who took that call – or at least who answered the question?"

Wiggs frowned. "I don't remember. We were busy."

"Think – it's important!"

"I don't know, okay?" Wiggs glared at her, and turned away.

"Shit." Barney went to find Goss, but caught sight of the imitation General Stedman instead. Restored to its original shape, the latter stood motionless, frozen like a statue to one side of the hallway. Occasional pools of light darted across its immobile features.

One of the RUSAMC officers had her hand buried up to the wrist in its side. Barney backed away as its face began to change again, becoming blank, neutral – a vacant template of a man. Then the image dissolved into a short-lived pillar of snow, and five balls hung in its place, floating unsupported in the air. Each was silver, roughly a hand-span across and buzzed softly.

"Oh my God," she said, all thoughts of Cati's controller suddenly evaporating. Again she called for Roads, and again she received only silence in reply.

"Neat, isn't it?" said O'Dell, suddenly at her side.

Barney spun to face him. "You sonofabitch," she gasped. "You knew all along!"

"No. Not until Blindeye."

"But you still didn't tell us?" Anger made the words choke in her throat.

"I couldn't. What use is a defence like this when everyone knows about it?" O'Dell waved at where the statue of Stedman had once stood. "They will now, of course – but it worked once, and that's the main thing. Cati's controller won't try again. I think we've demonstrated the pointlessness of resisting us any longer, don't you?"

Barney shook her head, speechless. O'Dell's grin mocked her ignorance, her lack of sophistication – mocked all of Kennedy Polis with her. For one timeless moment she hated him more than she had hated anyone in her entire life.

Then:

"Has anyone seen Antoni or Margaret?" asked Goss, shouldering his way through the crowd toward them. "They have the codes. We need either of them to restore some sort of order to the system."

"I saw DeKurzak heading downstairs earlier," said O'Dell. "He said he was going to check the foyer. I'll have someone try to track him down, if you like."

"Fuck DeKurzak," Barney whispered, feeling her grip on the situation slipping entirely. "Where the hell is *Phil*?"

CHAPTER TWENTY-ONE

11:05 p.m.

Roads took the freeway at sixty-five kilometres per hour – the fastest he could squeeze from the RSD vehicle's small electric engine. He had no clear idea of what he would do if he came face-to-face with Cati. He needed backup, a weapon, some sort of advantage. Yet, with PolNet down, he had no way to talk to anyone. Even the radio standard to all RSD vehicles was silent. The communications network had obviously been silenced from within. Until it was brought back on-line, the city was effectively dumb.

And he was on his own.

Instead of cursing fate, however, he used the time to consider the five small 'glitches' at the heart of the substitute Stedman.

That it was a technological product, not magical or biological, was obvious. The degree of sophistication it displayed was more advanced than anything Roads had ever seen – both before and after the War – but that didn't make it impossible. The RUSA had openly demonstrated a working knowledge of field-effects, which alone would account for the 'levitation' of the balls, the apparent solidity of the image and possibly even its knack of becoming invisible. The image itself was probably nothing more than an extremely high-resolution hologram, similar to that employed by both the Head and the RUSAMC's flag-bearing jeep. Compact batteries could power the whole arrangement, perhaps even EPA44210s like the ones Morrow had hidden in his stockpile on Old North Street.

Roads mentally sketched the design of the machine: at least two balls to generate the hologram; perhaps another two for the field-effects; and one to collect sensory data of its immediate environment. The last might also contain transmitters and receivers to relay data and instructions.

That left no balls remaining for its 'brain', but Roads didn't for a moment contemplate that the RUSA scientists had managed to squeeze an entire AI into the spheres. He guessed that the artificial Stedman had received its instructions from the control van; the General and his assistants had probably directed the thing remotely, never leaving it to its own devices. Certainly it would have been easier to relay Stedman's voice in real time rather than generate it artificially; that way, the stand-in's responses would appear genuine on every level.

The device was ingenious. Expensive, obviously, and clearly a breakthrough in miniaturisation alone. Roads would have had nothing but admiration for it, had it not been for one thing: there was more than one in the city.

The similarity between the Mole and the Stedman-substitute was too close to be coincidence. The Mole had imitated Roads with uncanny accuracy, could become practically invisible and change its shape, and had demonstrated the familiar five-point arrangement on at least two occasions. The theft of the EPA44210s was explained by its need for power; the strange delay between locating them in Morrow's inventories and actually stealing them, likewise: the Mole wouldn't take the batteries until it was actually running low. And the lack of an obvious command centre didn't necessarily refute his theory, for the "brain" could be hidden anywhere in the city and communicate with the "body" by means of a little-used radio frequency.

When the fields were collapsed, the ball arrangement made it far more manoeuvrable than any human. This led to the conclusion that the Mole had indeed gained entrance to the KCU library via the sewers. Pursuing that thought, Roads called up a scale plan of the KCU grounds from his onboard memory. The nearest drain to the library opened in the small clump of trees where the timber wolf had vanished on the night of Blindeye. That made the wolf a mobile shape the Mole could assume when a less human appearance was more appropriate, and the intermediate stage, the werewolf form that had startled Roads in the library, a possible self-defence mechanism, designed to frighten people away rather than draw them into a confrontation.

So the Mole *was*, in a sense, a werewolf. And it belonged to the RUSAMC.

But what was it *for*?

Several possibilities sprang to mind – covert surveillance being the most obvious – but Roads could come to no firm conclusions without more data. All he could do was speculate about the Mole's motives – and those of the RUSA. He found himself in the unfortunate situation of now knowing *what* the Mole was and *who* had built it, but not knowing *why* it did what it did.

And until he knew the *why*, exactly, he was unable to decide what he should do in response.

He turned off the southern arterial freeway and headed into the older suburbs. Fifteen minutes had passed since the attack on General Stedman. Even allowing for Cati's superhuman pace and his own relatively slow progress, Roads felt safe that he would arrive in time.

Old North Street was darker than the rest of the city: no parties here, no lingering merriment. The whirring of the car's electric engine echoed from forbidding stone facades as he pulled to a halt outside 116. The familiar building stared mutely back at him.

Climbing out of the car, he jogged across the road and up the stairs. The building was silent, ominously so. Even with his artificial cochleae at their maximum sensitivity, he could hear no-one. Only the sighing of the breeze disturbed the stillness.

He nudged the door and it swung easily open. The lock had been broken. Moving swiftly, he crossed the narrow hallway to the stairwell. The only footprints on the dusty steps were his and Katiya's – yet he couldn't shake the feeling that somebody else had been here, and recently. All of his modified senses itched. His right hand ached for a pistol, anything.

At the entrance to the apartment Katiya and Cati shared, he stopped. The door was slightly ajar. Taking a deep breath, he pushed it open.

The room was dark. Furniture lay in ruins, torn to splinters. The sofa had been hurled against the wall. Roads could see a blotch of fading warmth where someone had recently sat, and a deeper patch in another corner. Stepping gingerly over the rubble, he bent to examine the latter, and found a pool of blood.

Moving rapidly from room to room, he found destruction everywhere. Someone had turned the apartment into a junk-heap. Every item in the small cupboards had been tossed to the floor; clothes lay torn beneath broken boxes. In the hallway, Roads almost slipped on a pile of scattered paper: Cati's wordless 'diary', strewn at random.

In the bedroom, the mattress had been torn in half. Foam and ripped sheets covered every flat surface, most thickly in the corners. Scrabbling through one such pile, he finally came across something warm: a bare, human arm.

Grabbing it with both hands, he pulled Katiya's body out of the wreckage and examined her. A deep bruise blackened her right temple. Roads bent lower over her face to check her eyes. She was alive, but concussed. The blood trickling from her left ear was still wet.

He grimaced, both with distaste and the ramifications of that observation. Katiya must have been knocked out only minutes ago. There was a fair chance that the responsible party was still nearby.

"Katiya?" he whispered. "Can you hear me?"

The woman didn't respond at first, and he tried again, a little louder: "Katiya!"

She stirred, scrabbled weakly at the air. He sat her up and swung her into the moonlight coming through the window.

"Can you hear me?"

She opened her eyes and stared wildly, her gaze blank and unfocused.

"It's okay, you're safe." He brushed her hair back from her face, trying to soothe her by touch. "Can you tell me what happened?"

When her eyes finally met his, her entire body stiffened and she opened her mouth to scream.

He smothered the cry with one hand while making desperate shushing sounds. "Hey – it's okay, it's okay. Whoever did this, they've gone!"

"No!" she hissed through his fingers, writhing under his touch. With one hand flat on his chest, she pushed herself away and crawled back into the corner. "Leave me alone! Go away!"

"Katiya, it's me. Officer Roads from RSD, remember?" He tried to smile reassuringly, and held out his hands, empty. "I'm trying to *help* you."

"Liar!" Her eyes regarded him from the corner. One was pinching shut as the bruise on her temple spread. "And I already told you: I don't know where Cati is!"

"But I do. He's on his way here."

"He is?" Katiya regarded him suspiciously.

"He was heading this way last time I saw him. He's wounded and in a lot of trouble. He needs your help."

Her eyes flashed. "When he sees what you've done, he's not going to be happy."

"What *I've* done . . . ?" Roads stared around him, realisation suddenly dawning.

The Mole had beaten him there.

Before he could protest his innocence, the window burst inward. Shards of glass showered through the room, and Roads flinched away, bringing up one arm to protect his eyes. The heavy crunch of feet on the fragments coincided with Katiya's gasp:

"Cati!"

Roads rolled away to the far side of the room. Through the glittering starlight he saw the killer silhouetted against the broken window. He was even larger in real life than Roads had guessed, topping his modest height by at least forty centimetres. Despite his wounded arm, roughly bandaged with scraps of cloth, and his otherwise naked body, Cati looked like every soldier's nightmare brought to life: a demon made flesh, unstoppable and indefatigable. Just the sight of him made Roads feel defenceless.

Katiya still crouched in the corner, only slowly coming to her feet. As Cati looked around at the ruined bedroom and his wide, grey-black eyes took in the damage, his expression changed to one of intense fury.

"Cati, listen," Roads began, "she's safe, we're all safe – *don't* – !"

The killer crossed the room in a single, leaping step, his arms outstretched. Roads lunged aside and tried to scramble away. Before he had travelled a metre, two mighty hands grabbed his neck and belt and lifted him off the floor. With an incredible surge of strength, Cati threw him bodily through the bedroom doorway.

Roads struck the ground, skidded across the hallway and thudded heavily into a wall. His newly-healed ribs sang; his skull rang like a bell. He might have blacked out then, had it not been for the sight of Cati approaching.

Roads rolled aside, managing to gain his footing at the entrance to the lounge room. He ducked a whistling blow aimed for his neck, struck Cati in the stomach, and ducked again as the killer drove both fists down, aiming for his spine. A kick to Cati's left knee had no effect except to send Roads himself off-balance. Before he could recover, a glancing blow to his right cheek sent him spinning back to the floor.

Cati loomed over him. One massive, bare foot descended to stamp on Roads' face, but he slid away in time, blinking blood from his eyes. His hands found a plank of wood that had once been part of the lounge. He swung it at the killer's head. Cati used one hand to knock it aside, giving Roads a brief opening. A solid kick to the chest made the killer stumble back a step. Then Cati's guard was up again, and Roads backed away.

The trickle of blood from Roads' cheek met his lips, and he tasted copper. Fighting the urge to gag, he circled the room, looking for another weapon before the killer resumed his attack. Or for a chance to escape . . .

Cati noted his glance at the doorway, and lunged. Roads sidestepped, grabbed Cati's massive forearm and twisted with all his strength. On an ordinary man the move would have dislocated a shoulder, but all it did to Cati was make him stumble. Flexing his biceps, he tossed Roads aside, sending him into the ruins of the sofa. Roads slid a metre down the wall before recovering. A fist smashed into the plaster beside his head. He twisted away and pushed backward with both feet.

Even with all his weight behind the thrust, he only just managed to overbalance the killer. They fell to the floor among the fragments of furniture. For the first time, Roads heard Cati grunt with surprise. It wasn't much, but it was encouraging.

Then – so suddenly he cried aloud – his head exploded with light and sound. The reactivated icons and screens of PolNet filled his mind, blinding him to reality for a bare instant. Data scrolled down his vision; remote inputs booted up his implanted processor, checked its status and opened the channels he had tried to access on the way to Old North Street. And on top of all of that, Barney's voice urgently called his name.

Cati's fingers found his throat while he was distracted. The killer lifted, began to squeeze. Roads dangled like a rag doll. The muscles in his throat and the strengthened bone of his spinal column prevented Cati from actually snapping his neck, but there was little he could do to stop the closure of his windpipe. He pulled at the clenched fists with all of his fading strength and shifted them less than a centimetre. His modified autonomic systems slowed his heart and diverted as much blood as possible to his brain, yet still he could feel consciousness gradually ebbing.

Gritting his teeth, he stared into the killer's alien eyes. The babble of voices intensified as darkness filled his vision and the fire in his lungs began to go out.

Then the hands suddenly eased, allowing him a brief gasp of air. He struggled, kicking more by reflex than

351

anything else. His body still fought desperately for life, despite its slim chance of survival. Whether any of his blows struck home, he couldn't tell. His eyes hadn't recovered from the lack of oxygen in his blood, and his limbs were little more than vague nerve-endings a long, long way away.

Then he was in the air, flying across the room in slow motion. His eyes cleared enough for him to see the wall coming for him. There was little he could do to stop it. The pain was like a bomb going off in his head as he hit.

He slumped face-forward onto the bare floorboards, retching for breath. Outrage burned everywhere in his battered body, and the taste of blood was stronger than ever: like failure, sharp and bitter. But he had to move. His life depended on it.

With an effort so draining that he thought it might burst his heart, he managed to roll over and look up.

Frustration cut deep the lines of Cati's face; despair lay in the bottomless black pools of his eyes. But he wasn't coming for Roads. He stood exactly where he had been moments ago, frozen in place as though by some terrible internal struggle.

As Roads watched, the killer shook his head once, raised his clenched fists to the ceiling. His mouth formed an O, and he screamed silently. Every muscle in his body quivered in rebellion.

Barely had Roads registered this impression than Cati sagged. Every muscle went limp, and the killer looked down at the floor. Any thoughts Roads might have entertained of taking advantage of Cati's distraction vanished. The killer already looked beaten, doomed.

Then Cati moved. So quickly that Roads could barely follow, the killer ran from the lounge and into the bedroom. The crunch of footsteps traced his path to the window and beyond.

Roads twitched, wanting desperately to set off in pursuit: Cati was slipping through his fingers for the second time that night, and unlike before he had no idea where the killer might be going. But there was nothing he could do in time; he could hardly even keep his head up to listen.

A gentle thump from the roof above followed, then a thud on the building across the lane. Footsteps led into the distance, gradually fading even to Roads' sensitive ears. Finally, only Katiya's voice remained, calling the killer back, sobbing helplessly for him to return.

Cati was gone. Apart from the voices calling both inside and outside Roads' head, the night was silent again . . .

"Phil? Will you *talk* to me, for God's sake?"

"Take it easy, Barney." Martin O'Dell leaned over the seat she occupied. "He's probably busy, and you're annoying the hell out of him."

"For ten minutes? He can't be *that* busy."

O'Dell shrugged and moved away. In the dim light glowing from the screens and control panels of the RUSAMC control van, his face looked different. More serious; in a strange way, more at home.

Barney wasn't sure she liked the change, even if he was helping her. For the first time, *she* felt like an Outsider.

"Phil, this is an emergency. I need to talk to you *now*!"

Nothing.

She closed her eyes and rested her head in her hands. The last sighting of Roads had occurred almost three-quarters of an hour ago, when he had stolen a patrol car from the back of Mayor's House. Nothing had been seen or heard of him since. She was beginning to suspect the worst.

Behind her, O'Dell oversaw the rest of the operation. RUSAMC technicians had isolated the frequency of Roads' cyberlink, and were using the control van's transmitters to boost Barney's signal. Also, the information from the old CATI files retrieved from her laptop had enabled them to search for any illicit transmissions through the radio-silence still blanketing the city's official airwaves. They had already detected one such transmission, and were working hard to decode it.

Barney sighed. If the cipher proved to be impenetrable they were wasting valuable time.

Outside the control van, chaos reigned. Visible through a monitor was the ring of MSA officers surrounding Mayor's House, each armed with a rifle and under strict orders to keep everyone out – RSD and RUSAMC included. Search parties had found no sign of Cati, and the city's communication network was still effectively down, despite the mysterious substitute that had appeared to take PolNet's place. Communication was limited to the few intercoms the RUSAMC had loaned to the RSD squads during their retreat from the area.

Yet she refused to give up. The long-run was more important than the short: neither Cati nor the Mole had been captured; both had disappeared along with Roads. She needed him to help them resume the search, before the Mole or Cati went to ground again.

She kept trying, sending her voice echoing across the city, boosted by the RUSAMC transmitters.

Finally, after another five minutes of calling, a weak signal returned:

"Barney, be quiet. I'm here." Roads' voice issued from the speakers in the console in front of her as well as in her ear. He sounded terrible, even over the cyberlink, but Barney was too relieved to notice at first.

"Phil!" Her cry brought O'Dell instantly from the far side of the control van. "Is that really you?"

"Don't start that again. I'm not up to it."

"We've been looking for you everywhere. Where the hell have you *been*?"

"Hunting," he said, "and being hunted. I saw Cati escape from Mayor's House and guessed he was heading back to Old North Street. The Mole must have guessed as well, or followed me part of the way, because it beat me here. By the time I arrived, the place was a mess and the Mole had gone. Then Cati arrived, thought I'd done it, and –" He stopped.

"And?" she prompted uneasily.

"Let's just say I'll live, and leave it at that. I've no idea where he is now. Katiya's still here. She's been knocked around too, but she'll be okay."

"Cati hit her?"

"No, the Mole did. Why, though, I'm not sure."

"Maybe to enrage Cati," said O'Dell, leaning across the console to talk into a microphone.

"Is that you, Martin?" Roads asked, surprised to hear the extra voice through the cyberlink.

"Yes."

"I guess you'd know better than any of us what the Mole really wants. It's your toy, after all."

"Perhaps." O'Dell glanced at Barney. "But we'll talk about that later. For now, we're in the control van listening in on the old military frequencies. There was an unauthorised transmission about fifteen minutes ago that we think came from Cati's controller –"

"It did," Roads interrupted. "If not, I wouldn't be talking to you now. Have you translated it?"

"Not yet. We're doing our best. Do you have any ideas?"

"No. As I told Barney, I'd only heard of the CATI

project by name – no details. You've tried all the standard encryption keys?"

"Everything in the old files. None of them match."

"Then it must be something unique to the project, and could take hours to crack. Although . . ." Roads thought for a moment. "PolNet's back on the air. Does that mean RSD is up and running again?"

"No," Barney answered. "PolNet just started working again. No-one knows why. We thought *you* might have had something to do with it."

"Me? No – in fact, it damn near killed me. But I have an idea who *is* behind it." Again Roads hesitated. "And I think I know him well enough to guess that he's listening in right now. If he'll hear us out, I'd like to ask him for help again. And to be given the chance to apologise."

Barney opened her mouth to ask Roads what the hell he was talking about, but a new voice over the cyberlink cut her off:

"Apologise?" The voice spoke from the console's speakers with an amused – and familiar – air. "My dear boy, what on earth is there to apologise for?"

"For thinking that you were Cati's controller, of course."

Laughter filled the line. "Really? If you believed that even for a second, then you don't know me as well as you think."

"No?" responded Roads. "You're here now, aren't you?"

"Too true . . ." The chuckle tailed off into silence.

Barney stared at the console. "Phil, is that who I think it is?"

"Probably. You tell her, Keith."

"Keith Morrow at your service again, my dear."

Barney wasn't quite sure what to say. She and O'Dell exchanged quick, disbelieving glances.

The RUSAMC captain cleared his throat. "I'd always imagined our first meeting to be on somewhat less cordial grounds," he said.

Again the Head chuckled. "I'll bet you did, Captain O'Dell. And don't bother trying to trace this transmission."

"Why would we do that?"

"You know very well why," returned the Head. "For someone so cruelly maligned by both RSD and the Reunited States, I have certainly gone out of my way to help you all in the last week. I hope you appreciate that."

"We do, Keith," said Roads. "We do. And if your face hadn't appeared in Cati's diary, I wouldn't have suspected you at all. It took me far too long to work out the real reason behind that."

"Wait – let me get this straight." Barney rubbed a hand across her forehead, trying to retie the threads of the conversation. "*You* resurrected PolNet?"

"Of course," replied the Head. "Do you think Phil is the only person in Kennedy with a working copy? Or that my motives are necessarily malign?" The Head tsked impatiently.

"Did you pick up the CATI command?" Roads asked.

"If you mean the most recent, from nineteen minutes ago, then yes."

"Can you decipher it for us?"

"Decipher, yes; I already have. For you, though, I don't know. Should I?"

"That's entirely up to you. Just remember, we only want the controller. Cati's as innocent as I am, despite all he's been made to do. He had no choice in the matter, and shouldn't be punished."

Barney opened her mouth to protest, but O'Dell touched her on the shoulder and shook his head.

"My thoughts exactly," said Morrow. "The controller ordered Cati to rendezvous with him at Patriot Bridge in forty-five minutes. Twenty-six minutes from now."

"Did he say why?" Roads asked.

"No."

"Then that probably means he suspects we're listening, and doesn't want to broadcast too much."

"I'd say so. All previous transmissions were quite explicit."

"You mean – ?" she began, but again the hand on her arm silenced her.

"What about the control code?" asked O'Dell before she could push him away.

"No," said Morrow. "One person has it already, which is bad enough."

"But having it would save us a lot of trouble. We could just order him to –"

"My point exactly." Morrow's voice was regretful but firm. "Humans don't know when to stop. How you ever reached the point where you were able to create an intelligence as sublime as mine is quite beyond me, to be frank."

"We've had this conversation before, Keith," interrupted Roads. "And now isn't the time. You've given us what we need and, for that, I'm grateful. The rest can wait until later. Did you catch all of that, Barney?"

"Clear as a bell."

"Okay, tell Margaret to send reinforcements ASAP. Keith said 'he' every time he mentioned the controller, so she's in the clear. But be careful who else you talk to. We don't want to scare Cati's controller away."

"Understood, but –" She paused. "It may not be as easy as that."

"What do you mean?"

"There've been some problems at this end. The MSA has assumed control of Mayor's House, sealed it tight. All RSD personnel not inside have been ordered off the grounds, along with Stedman's troops. Martin and I barely made it to the control van before it got ugly."

"How ugly, exactly?"

"The Mayor issued a statement half an hour ago announcing an assassination attempt on *him*, not General Stedman. Margaret has been arrested on charges of conspiracy, along with David Goss. A warrant for you has been issued as well."

Roads grunted. "The Mayor said this? Are you sure?"

"Positive: he's in there, running things. It's not a coup, if that's what you're thinking."

"A gross over-reaction, then."

"It seems that way. DeKurzak's obviously been giving him ideas."

"Have you tried talking to him?"

"No chance. Until the phone network is running again, we don't really have a way to contact them."

"There are signals coming out of the building along one of the landlines," put in O'Dell, "but they're also coded. Given their frequency, we're assuming them to be official, some sort of emergency system we can't tap into."

"And how's your boss taking this, Martin?"

"In his stride, for now," the RUSAMC captain replied. "He understands how the assassination attempt looks, and how you feel about the Mole. But it's still a stand-off. There are Reunited States personnel inside the building, too, and we haven't heard from them for almost an hour."

"Shit," Roads said. "This could mean the end of the Reassimilation."

"Or worse," Barney added. "But there's not much we can do until the Mayor decides to talk."

"No, not really." Barney heard the frustration in his voice as clearly as she felt her own. "Our only option is to keep after Cati," he went on. "I'll head straight to the bridge. It shouldn't take too long by car."

"If you leave now," said O'Dell, studying a map of the city on a screen. "We'll do what we can from this end – maybe rustle up reinforcements from somewhere. Whatever we do, you'll beat us there by at least fifteen minutes. You won't have backup for that long. Do you think you can handle him?"

"Do I have a choice?" asked Roads. Barney thought she heard an echo of a sigh through the cyberlink. "Anyway, I need to get moving if I'm going to make it in time. I'll call when I'm on the way. You can fill me in on the Mole then, Martin."

"Will do," said O'Dell. "I think it's time you all knew the truth."

"Agreed. See you at the bridge," said Roads, and killed the line.

Roads let his head fall back onto the floor. The pain had ebbed slightly during the conversation as endorphins rushed through his body, but he still felt terrible. He rubbed the tight skin of his cheek, felt the roughness of dried blood, and willed himself to move. He didn't have time for self-pity.

The apartment had fallen strangely silent while he talked with O'Dell and Barney; the background weeping had stopped. Opening his eyes, he looked upward.

Katiya was standing over him with a knife in one hand. She stared fixedly at him with her one good eye narrowed. The other had closed entirely, pinched shut by the vivid bruise on her temple.

"I was listening to you," she said softly. "You were talking to yourself, you said that Cati was innocent, and . . ." Her hands were trembling. "And you're bleeding."

"Yes." He leaned on the nearest wall for balance and struggled to his feet. She backed away automatically. "What does that tell you?"

"That you're not the same one who was here earlier."

"That's right." He straightened his clothing and brushed off the dust.

Katiya lowered the knife to her side, where it dangled uncertainly.

Roads wished there was something he could do to ease the woman's obvious pain, but time was too short. "I can't stay here. Will you be okay?"

"Where are you going?"

"To find Cati."

"You know where he is?"

"Yes. Or at least where he'll be very soon."

"Then I want to come with you."

"It'll probably be dangerous –"

"I know." She glanced down at her shaking hands, then back at him. Her eyes blazed in the darkness. "But what else can I do? He *needs* me. He doesn't want to hurt people. Maybe . . . maybe I can even help him free himself –"

"Okay, okay," he relented. "But I'm leaving *now*. If you're coming, we have to hurry."

"Yes." She nodded. "Yes, I understand." She looked around the room, at the devastation of her home, and straightened her shoulders.

As soon as they were on the way, Roads reopened the cyberlink and whispered across the city:

"Okay, Martin," he said. "Tell me everything."

CHAPTER TWENTY-TWO

11:55 p.m.

"The device you call the Mole is known under another name in the Reunited States," said O'Dell, "and even then only by a few. We call it Project Cherubim – after the word's original meaning: a creature that is half-human, half-animal and full of eyes."

"So it *is* a spy," said Barney. "But –"

"Let me finish." O'Dell's tone was brisk, almost terse – as though delivering a lecture to hostile students. "I'm probably going to get my ass kicked for talking about this, so at least give me the chance to get it right.

"By experimenting with field-effects and making a few improvements on the old designs, and by using camouflage techniques we developed ourselves – not stolen from the bunker files, as you thought, Phil – we've built a robot capable of changing shape at will. Holograms give it appearance, while the fields make it solid when it needs to be. Given enough data, it can assume the appearance of anyone it chooses – right down to the smallest visual detail. It can even simulate body heat and voice patterns, which enables it to pass identity tests that many other methods of impersonation do not.

"This makes it perfect for internal security, as you now know, but it can also be used for espionage. It can imitate and replace anyone in a rival government sufficiently well to fool all but their closest companions."

"It's not perfect, then?" Roads asked.

"The less frequently it comes into contact with people the better, obviously, for not even we can design a machine that will completely recreate a person. The perfect subject is someone who lives alone, and whose job allows them to be fairly independent."

"Someone like me, in other words."

"Exactly." O'Dell's voice displayed discomfort. "You were chosen from a group of ten candidates as having the best lifestyle for the Mole to imitate. Usually the target would be someone fairly high up in a local defence force or government, but not *too* high; the original has to be disposed of, of course, and we don't want to be accused of disrupting the target government if found out. Our information suggested that you lived alone and were high enough in RSD to give you access to sensitive information. You were an ideal target for Project Cherubim."

"Wait a minute," said Barney. "Isn't disrupting the government the idea? Send it in, get it to become the local mayor or whatever, have it initiate a take-over from within and –?"

"No," O'Dell said. "That's not the idea at all."

"But it *can* be used that way. And if it *can* be, then it *will* be one day. Isn't that the way the military mind works?"

"Not everyone's." O'Dell sighed. "But I take your point. You have to understand that without the old bunker files the Reunited States' expansion would have been much slower than it was. On a small scale, the weapons and tools in the archives provided an in-valuable means of combating biomodified enclaves. The rogue packs had an edge over us norms that we could counteract only by superior weaponry. We've had no choice but to develop new weapons.

"But we required something more sophisticated when dealing with larger communities – biomodified or not. Some of the collectives, west and south of here, are as large as the original states. Outright war is expensive, not to mention bad for public relations. We are attempting to avoid the mistakes of the past, after all, and that makes negotiation our most important tool of all.

"Yet at the heart of all negotiation lies information, and information is often best gathered by espionage. We needed a way to infiltrate rival states without arousing their suspicions, and preferably without risking our own people. The best way to do this was by exploiting internal corruption, but that can take time too. And General Stedman wants to reassimilate the continent peacefully before what remains devolves too far – or other nations dig their heels in and force us to fight."

"The Mole is a kind of middle ground?" asked Roads.

"Exactly. The pacifists like it because it reduces loss of life; in the long run, it might even encourage peace. The expansionists, on the other hand, admire its efficiency, its ability to keep campaign costs down."

"So you sent one into Kennedy. Can I ask why?"

"For several reasons. The obvious one is to assist Reassimilation. Things aren't as perfect on the Outside as you've heard, and official military policy is delicately balanced at the moment. There's been a lot of resistance to our expansion in recent years, so much that some of General Stedman's colleagues are calling for a big push: one single offensive that will crush everything in its path. If that happens, we will be betraying everything we've stood for – so it's all the more important that the

Reassimilation of Kennedy goes ahead smoothly. If it doesn't, then the warmongers will have even more leverage."

The image of the Reunited States Military Corps sweeping across the face of North America like some fiery angel of the Apocalypse filled Roads' mind for an instant before he could banish it.

"So the Mole followed me," he said, "broke into my house, studied me in enough detail to allow it to *become* me. But why go to so much trouble for so long? You didn't put the Mole into position until the envoy arrived; even then you must have had a fair idea that the Reassimilation Bill would be accepted. Why continue with the operation when you knew you'd have complete access to the Kennedy datapool in just a few weeks?"

"Because the information we needed wasn't *in* the official datapool," replied O'Dell simply.

"It wasn't? Neither the MSA nor the Mayoralty have any obvious secrets, as far as I know."

"That's right. They don't."

"Then –" Roads broke off as a thought suddenly struck him. "Wait," he said. "I think I'm beginning to understand now."

"The thefts," O'Dell said.

"Yes. The EPA44210s, and the explosives."

"And much more besides."

It was Barney's turn to be confused. "Will someone please tell me what you two are talking about?"

O'Dell sighed. "To put it succinctly, one of General Stedman's purposes in coming to Kennedy Polis was to hunt down a criminal and bring him to justice. That criminal wasn't the Mole – although he was a thief – and he wasn't Cati, either. He was a smuggler in a small town who made the fatal mistake of underestimating his opposition."

"You mean –" the tone of Barney's voice effectively conveyed her disbelief "– the *Head*?"

"Who else?" Roads said. "The EPA44210s stolen from Old North Street had to have come from somewhere, and their disappearance would have been noted."

"Noted, and responded to," added O'Dell. "The thefts began over five years ago. A major trade route between Philadelphia and our southern frontiers passes near here, and I guess it proved fairly easy to arrange a few 'accidents' along the way, with help from allies on the Outside. At first we thought Kennedy itself was behind it – until we actually contacted the city and realised how entrenched its isolation was. You didn't even know we existed. Later information relayed by Project Cherubim suggested that an independent person or organisation was responsible."

"I can't believe it," said Barney. "You came all this way to deal with Morrow?"

"Why not? Most of the supplies were intended for a campaign in South Texas. He was hurting us, hurting the expansion; we had to do something. And he was hurting you too, don't forget."

"How?"

"By letting things in that should have stayed outside. Like Cati."

"Eh?"

"Morrow's a high-tech pack-rat, Barney," O'Dell said. "He never would have been able to resist something like that for his collection.

"Of *course*." Barney groaned bitterly down the cyberlink. "*That's* why his face appeared in Cati's diary. The bastard."

"My sentiments exactly," said O'Dell. "Which only makes me wonder why he's helping us now."

If Morrow was listening, he made no comment.

"So the Mole did what it was supposed to do," Roads said, bringing the subject back to its intended focus. "It followed me everywhere I went in order to learn my behaviour, then raided datapools using my face as a cover. But I'm still here. Why didn't it substitute itself for me at the first opportunity?"

"Because this is only a trial run," explained O'Dell. "Cherubim had never been used in an uncontrolled environment before."

"We're guinea pigs?" asked Barney.

"Yes. Kennedy was chosen as the testing-ground because it was isolated, and any mishaps could be quashed more easily. Add to that the fact that we needed to know for certain who was behind the thefts before we entered the city, but didn't want to make any overtly hostile moves until – or unless – we absolutely had to. The Mole's substitution imperative was therefore disabled: it was instructed, in other words, not to harm you or to allow you to come to harm, although it would continue to perform all other tasks unimpeded."

"Is that possible?" Roads interrupted. "I mean, its fundamental purpose is to imitate someone. By removing the condition required for it to do that, surely that violates its core programming?"

"And why didn't you call it off when you knew the truth about the thefts?" interrupted Barney.

"I couldn't." O'Dell answered Barney's question first, obviously a little overwhelmed by the interrogation. "By the time I guessed what we were dealing with, it was too late."

"Bullshit."

"I'm not lying, Barney. I knew we had a source in Kennedy, but didn't suspect what it was until Blindeye, when I first saw the Mole in action. And even then I didn't know for certain until I finally squeezed a confession out of my superiors."

"At which point," Roads leapt ahead, "they ordered you to take the case from me, to avoid a diplomatic incident?"

"Partly. They also ordered me to do everything I could to *find* the damn thing . . ."

There was a long, contemplative silence until Roads said: "Are you telling me you've *lost* it?"

"More or less. It seems that even from the beginning things weren't going well. First, it failed to deliver a convincing version of your speech. Second, it transmitted data but didn't respond reliably to instructions beamed into the city. Then, when it was finally cornered during Blindeye, it stopped transmitting altogether. No-one's sure exactly why, but the technicians we brought with us think it might have been because of Cati."

"How?"

"Well, part of its mission as a Military Corps tool is to detect and eliminate biomodified agents. As soon as it saw Cati, it reported the discovery to its human controllers. Some damn fool ordered it to dispose of the threat, thinking that Cati was a berserker and a possible threat to the General. They should have known better. The Mole ceased transmitting immediately, and now refuses to respond to all priority codes, including self-destruct."

"I don't get it," said Barney. "Why would telling the Mole to kill Cati make it refuse to respond to orders?"

"As Phil suggested earlier: its original program included the urge to kill the person it was impersonating. In an ordinary computer, that wouldn't be a problem – but the Mole is anything *but* an ordinary computer. Its processing core is modelled on the human brain, with numerous independent cognitive modules acting chaotically as units yet combining to give one coherent response. That makes it more flexible than a machine, but also less robust. Complete reprogramming takes time and, due to the elasticity of consciousness, can give rise to greater chaos than before. The usual method is not to get rid of what's already there, but to map a new equilibrium over it: to take a given state and nudge it in a slightly different direction. This is very tricky, requiring chaotic tendencies to be ordered first, and then ordered again; the risks of destabilising the system are very high.

"So, when our programmers started mucking around with the Mole's basic tenets, by subverting the original 'kill' direction with a 'don't-kill', they deliberately disturbed the balance slightly. The Mole was allowed to steal data and mimic to a certain extent, but couldn't dispose of Phil even if it wanted to. The new equilibrium it found was unstable, however, and caused it to behave erratically in some areas.

"Then, when it was ordered to hunt down and destroy Cati, matters only became worse. The 'don't-kill' was supplanted by another 'kill' and the system had to find yet another equilibrium. Unfortunately, this new path was even more unstable. As you saw, Phil, when the assassins ambushed you outside your apartment, it was behaving in a highly violent manner in order to protect you – which it was still trying to do, even though we had ordered it to kill Cati. Now it appears to have found a new compromise: it wants Cati to kill you for it."

"It still wants to impersonate me?"

"That's what I think. This evening, when it attacked Katiya, it was trying to arouse Cati's anger. If Cati had killed you, then it could have taken your place without violating its overrides. After which I imagine it would have wiped the slate clean by killing Cati itself."

"I can't believe the Mole is really that intelligent," protested Barney. "I mean, it's only a machine –"

"It's far more than that, Barney. It has to be. Quite apart from the way it thinks, the Mole has a Cyc-type commonsense knowledge base that we designed especially to help it know what it's sensing. The computers you're used to wouldn't be able to tell the difference between a cat and an atomic missile, but the Mole can. Two years of development brought it to the point where it was able to complete its tasks independently of its controllers – and although the bugs obviously haven't been ironed out completely, I think you'll agree that its performance is pretty impressive. To comprehend and interact with an environment as varied and ambiguous as a city requires more processing power than that contained in all of Kennedy itself, and –"

"Sorry, Martin," Roads butted in. "We're almost out of time. After we've neutralised Cati's controller, how do we bring the Mole to heel again?"

"To be honest, I don't know," O'Dell admitted. "Maybe seeing Cati in our hands will bring it back to a state in which we can control it. Failing that, we can attempt to trace its processing core. It'll be hidden somewhere in the city, smuggled in by the Mole itself and placed well out of sight. The signals between the mobile units and the core will be hard to locate, though; the artificial intelligence will have relays everywhere, casting false transmissions in every direction. It might take us weeks to track it down –"

"By then it'll be too late," said Roads. "We have to deal with this before it gets even more out of hand. If we can't bring Cati to heel, we could be in the middle of a war before the night's out. The last thing we need is the Mole on top of that." Again Roads' voice faded for an instant, then returned: "Are you two on your way?"

"Fifteen minutes, minimum," said Barney. "Things are still messy at Mayor's House. No word from the Mayor or DeKurzak, although shots have been fired inside. I couldn't get sense out of anyone until I found Roger. He was out of the building, and able to put a squad together from a few people loyal to Margaret. We're coming as fast as we can, so don't feel abandoned."

"And I'm not far behind," said O'Dell.

"You're not together?"

"No. Barney's in a squad-van, using the cyberlink bead you gave her to keep in touch. I'm in one of our transports with a dozen personnel, connected by radio to the control van. We'll be there in about twenty minutes, if we don't get lost along the way."

"The rendezvous is scheduled for two minutes." Roads thought for a moment. "I'll go in ahead of you and see if I can keep the controller busy until you get here. At the very least, I should be able to find out who he is. When I do, I'll let you know. Until then, keep the line clear. Use the PolNet channels Keith has given us to talk to each other, and don't drag your heels. When Cati arrives, if he hasn't already, I'm going to need all the help I can get."

"Understood," O'Dell said.

"We're on our way, Phil," said Barney, her voice gravelly. "Just don't die or anything before we get there, okay?"

"I'll try not to," said Roads, and brought the conversation to an end.

He slowed to a halt a dozen metres short of a gash in the road, and parked the car in the shelter of a ruined wall. Peering through the window he saw no sign of life, apart from the occasional night-bird or bat wheeling above the water.

The suburbs near Patriot Bridge had been abandoned for ten years. Once it had housed refugees, as had the warehouses in Keith Morrow's jurisdiction; later it had been rebuilt to accommodate the unemployed. Once the population had stabilised, however, most of the area's inhabitants had moved inward, away from the cold damp drifting off the river and closer to the Rosette. Most of the buildings, temporary structures at best, had slumped upon themselves or collapsed entirely. The southern arterial freeway wound for a full kilometre through an uninhabited wasteland of rotten *E. coli* plastic building materials and concrete before finally coming to a halt at the base of the bridge itself. There, the tarmac ribbon had been severed with explosives early in the Dissolution, just as the span across the river had been blasted by mines to prevent easy access from the far side of the river.

"This is it?" asked Katiya from the passenger seat, her arms crossed across her chest. She had hardly moved throughout the short trip, locked in her personal misery.

"I'm afraid so," said Roads. "If you'd prefer to wait in the car –"

"No. I want to come."

Roads sighed. "Then keep well back. I'll go first to make sure it's safe. Don't join me until I call you, okay?"

She shrugged, then nodded.

"Good." Roads opened the door, swung his legs out. "Wait five minutes before following, and for God's sake, keep quiet."

Climbing out of the car proved a painful exercise. Every muscle complained and his head throbbed. A cool breeze brought the smell of a blocked sewer across the wasteland of empty buildings. The erratic, high-pitched squeaking of bats was the only sound. Ahead and up, the rusted spans of the bridge hung clearly visible against the night sky.

Hugging his coat tightly about him, Roads started off along the road. The bridge had once housed a hundred or more squatters, unofficial entrants to the city unable to set foot on Kennedy's banks but stubbornly refusing to return to the far side and the ruins it contained. Roads' night vision enabled him to pick out the remains of a handful of old habitats in the tangle of metal. Little more than scraps of cloth fluttering in the breeze, they looked like flags: a constant reminder of the dispossessed who had once lived there. The squatters had been evicted at gun-point or killed outright in the first decade after the War, when the bridge had been mined.

But the bridge had been made to last, and its pylons remained more or less intact. Some sections of the road were still in one piece, and the walkway along one side seemed mostly complete. He imagined it would be possible, with luck, to cross the river unimpeded.

Forgoing the direct route onto the bridge, along the shattered freeway, Roads followed an access road to the base of one of the massive pylons. A rusty ladder took him to the underside of the bridge. After testing his weight on the ancient structure, he climbed rapidly upward. With every step, his unease grew. Gambling his life on a handful or two of corroded metal wasn't his idea of a good time – and it was likely to get worse the further along the bridge he went.

At the top was an unsteady walkway which led to a flight of stairs. The stairs dog-legged up to the western walkway, the one that seemed most complete from the ground. More slowly this time, wincing every time the stairs groaned in complaint, he made his way onto the road-level of the bridge.

There, as his head broached the concrete surface, he stopped and checked his internal clock. He was overdue for the rendezvous by three minutes. If Cati and his controller were nearby, then there was a fair chance they had heard him arrive. Holding his breath, he crawled over the final step and rolled behind the nearest cover: a rubbish bin dented on one side.

The breeze was stronger from his higher vantage point. He could hear nothing over it but the occasional creak from the bridge's infrastructure. He moved in a crouch to the walkway, glancing along its length as he did. The metal platform ran parallel to the road with rails at waist height on either side. Subtle warps not visible from the ground had twisted it like a snake, making it difficult to see very far – which ultimately worked to his advantage. Breathing shallowly but evenly, he began to move south along the bridge, away from the city and into the darkness.

Barely had he travelled a dozen metres when something clanged behind him. His heart froze. The sound had come from the stairs. Katiya, he presumed, following hard on his heels – and making plenty of noise despite his warning not to. He waited ten seconds for any reaction to the sound, heard none, then continued forward.

He passed no-one along the way, and the starlight was too dim to make out footprints; the bridge might have been empty for all he could tell. Part of him wondered if he had been tricked; Morrow's information might have been wrong, or deliberately false. Had the Head wanted Roads out of the way, he could hardly have chosen a better place to send him.

He paused to catch his breath halfway across the bridge. Stretching the aching muscles in his neck and shoulders, he tried to blot out the pain. The small of his back itched mercilessly – although whether from paranoia or a genuine warning he couldn't tell.

"Phil?" O'Dell's voice startled him through the cyberlink. "We've worked out how to tap PolNet's visual transmissions. Can you give me a feed from one of your implants?"

"Good idea, Martin." Roads called up the appropriate menus. "How's that?"

"Clear as a bell. We'll record it, just in case."

"Here's hoping." Roads stood, flexed the muscles of his legs. "Any news from Mayor's House?"

"Nothing, except a few more shots on the inside. It's impossible to tell what's happening from out here."

"Keep me posted if anything changes."

"I will."

Roads recommenced his awkward crouching run, heading silently along the walkway.

Silently, that is, until his left foot encountered empty air where there should have been metal.

He lunged forward desperately. If the gap in the walkway was wider than the reach of his outstretched arms, he had no way of arresting his fall. As he dropped, he had a quick glimpse of dark water rolling far below, and his heart lurched when he realised just how far above the water he was.

He fell spreadeagled across rusty iron a split-second later, landing with a thud solid enough to send that section of the walkway rocking. His feet dangled in midair, but his knees quickly found purchase. The gap had been less than a metre across.

Scrambling to his feet he stood up and looked around. Everything was dark; even to his modified eyes, it was hard to make out anything at all.

Then he froze.

Twenty metres ahead of him, surprised into motion by the sudden sound, three hot blotches stood out against the cold backdrop of the bridge. One was large and wide, almost certainly Cati. The other two were smaller and unrecognisable, but almost certainly men.

Two men?

Roads ran forward, uncaring now how much noise he made, mindful only of the surface beneath his feet. Although his fall had given his presence away, he probably hadn't been seen. If the controller wasn't biomodified – which seemed safe to assume, since he used Cati to do his dirty work – then Roads' indistinct form would make a difficult target through the shadows. He kept his head down anyway, just in case.

A moment later, he was glad he had. A bullet cracked close by, sending sparks flying from the rail to his right. He weaved and ducked lower. As though startled by the gunshot, one of the smaller shadows ducked away to its left and vanished into the indistinct background of metal. The large shape of Cati remained immobile.

The third shadow was the one which had fired the shot. In infra-red, the man stepped backward along the bridge with both hands held before him, the white-hot eye of the pistol scanning in Roads' direction. This time Roads caught the muzzle-flash as a second bullet whizzed past his head. Clearly the person taking aim was either biomodified or wearing night-goggles.

Roads rolled out of sight behind the guard-rail, hands searching for something to throw.

Among the flakes of rust he found a relatively solid chunk of twisted metal narrow enough to fit in his palm: better than nothing.

When he peered over the rail seconds later, however, the figure with the gun had disappeared as well.

"*Shit.*" Only Cati remained where the three had been, frozen in place much as he had been for an instant while attacking Stedman at Mayor's House. Awaiting orders? Roads wondered again.

He could feel the killer's dark eyes watching him through the darkness, but sensed no immediate threat.

The other two men he wasn't so sure about. They were clearly under cover, or else he would be able to see them. By the same reasoning, they wouldn't be able see him either. Unless . . .

Cati could see in infra-red. The killer could tell the controller where Roads was hiding.

He ducked out of sight behind the guard-rail and crabbed along the bridge to his right. Barely had he travelled two metres when a noise made him look up. There was a fleeting movement in the shadows – a confused flurry, as though someone had stirred the night with a man-sized spoon – then a nebulous shape loomed out of the confusion and lunged for his chest.

He leapt backward before the blow could land. Both hands came up and clutched at the distortion in the air. His fingers met a stiff artificial fabric, ribbed with plastic. He gripped and twisted, and was gratified to hear a hiss of pain. A knife clattered onto the rusted walkway at his feet. His left knee came up and met flesh, and the arm he was holding tried to pull away.

Roads fought the misleading data gathered by his eyes – which told him he was fighting a liquid shadow, not a man – and groped with one hand for a better grip. It found a neck, and teeth. Roads kicked again, heard something crack, and felt the man go limp.

Without loosening his grip, Roads let the body sag to the walkway. Then he felt along its back and shoulders until he found a seam, tugged at it until it tore. Instantly the shadowy cloak fell away, revealing a man lying face-down on the road, dressed in a black and grey body-suit with the distinctive markings of the RUSAMC on its sleeves.

"My God," said O'Dell, his voice brutally loud in the darkness on the bridge.

"One of yours?" Roads subvocalised back.

"One of our nightsuits, anyway. Similar to the Mole's camouflage, but designed specifically for night combat."

Roads studied the suit more closely. From a distance, it might have looked like an ordinary uniform, but close-up the difference was obvious. Bulges at the hips were batteries, he supposed, with wires embedded in the suit's fabric providing the distorting field-effect.

Roads rolled the man over and removed the night-goggles covering his face. His features were unfamiliar: pale skin, lank brown hair, late-forties. Blood trickled from the man's nose where Roads' wild kick had struck: definitely unconscious.

"The suit was stolen, you think?" he asked O'Dell. "Keith again?"

"No," sighed the RUSAMC captain. "He's one of us."

"Then what the hell's he doing out here?"

"I've no idea. And that's the truth."

Roads bent to check the unconscious man for weapons. "Tell me about him, then. He must be here for a reason."

"He's not a career soldier," O'Dell said, "but an engineer. He was drafted a couple of years ago to give technical advice on Kennedy and Project Cherubim. There's a good chance he won't be armed."

"There goes that thought." Indeed, Roads' hands had found nothing under the nightsuit. "Okay. Hang on and I'll see who else I can find."

Roads clambered to his feet and looked around. Cati stood several metres away, exactly where he had been before. His black eyes tracked until he caught sight of Roads, then stopped. The controller must still be watching, although there was no sign of anyone apart from Cati. Banking on the fact that the remaining man would have to step into view in order to fire – and that he could move fast enough to avoid being shot – he bent down and lifted the unconscious man by the collar of the nightsuit. A hostage was better than nothing.

"His name, Martin?"

"Lieutenant-Colonel Sam Betheras."

Roads cleared his throat, making certain the unconscious man was clearly in Cati's line of sight.

"I have Betheras," he called. "Put your weapon down, and step into view with your hands above your head."

He waited for an answer. Cati didn't move. The only sound was the whispering of the wind through the infrastructure of the bridge.

"Can you hear me?" he called. "I have Betheras! We know what you're planning!"

Again nothing.

Roads shifted his grip on the RUSAMC officer's neck and stepped over the guard-rail. Cati watched him as he did so, dark eyes following his every movement. The killer's immobility bothered Roads. The controller had a weapon, so why wasn't he using it? All he had to do was instruct Cati to kill Roads, and that would be the end of it. Bluff called, Roads would lose.

Unless the controller *wasn't* watching any more. He might have fled while Roads and Betheras were scuffling, and abandoned Cati, leaving him to follow orders that hadn't yet been countermanded.

But that was unlikely, for if the controller had fled, he would have run headlong into Katiya by now.

A shrill scream abruptly split the night air.

Roads turned automatically to face the source of the sound. Cati echoed the movement, swivelling his massive torso. The sound came from the direction of the Kennedy shore, not far away.

The scream ended suddenly, leaving a flat echo in its wake. The walkway boomed as something struck it, followed by the sound of scrabbling at metal.

Roads cursed himself. Katiya had slipped in the same gap he had – or run into the controller. Either way, she was obviously in trouble.

Cati took a step forward, to rush to his lover's aid.

Then a gunshot aimed over Roads' head split the night, followed by a voice from behind him:

"Don't move. Both of you!"

Roads stiffened, letting Betheras fall to the ground. Cati flinched in mid-step, took another pace forward. Barely had he made it two metres when the voice muttered something under its breath and repeated:

"Don't move! Do as I say, damn you – you know you don't have any choice!"

Cati froze again, his dark eyes staring helplessly into the blackness.

The back of Roads' neck tingled as the controller's attention returned to him.

"Don't try anything stupid Roads." The man's voice was familiar. "I'm armed, and I won't hesitate to shoot. You've caused me enough trouble. Do you understand?"

Roads nodded.

"Good. Move next to Cati – slowly. Bring Betheras with you. Don't rush it, and keep your hands where I can see them. That's close enough. Put him down. Now, tell the woman to come forward or I'll shoot you dead."

"Katiya?" Roads called, keeping his hands up. "If you can hear me, keep coming. Be careful, though. There's someone here with Cati, and he has a gun. I think we'd better do as he says."

Footsteps rattled the walkway and Katiya nervously emerged from the shadows. As she came closer, Roads made out patches of rust on her clothes and grazes from when she had fallen; otherwise she was unharmed.

She began to say something, but the voice cut her off, instructing her to join Cati and Roads in the middle of the roadway. They stood motionless together, waiting to see what would happen next. Katiya's eyes were fixed on Cati, studying his face, his wounds, the blank rigidity of his posture.

If Katiya believed her presence would help Cati break the power of his control codes, then Roads hoped she was right. That possibility certainly existed, if Cati's mind was flexed just the right way, just often enough . . .

Fatigue stress, he recalled from the CATI file. Take a metal rod and bend it one way, then the other; repeat until it snaps. That was exactly what might happen to Cati if he was pushed too hard for too long.

Whether that would be a good thing or not depended on how Cati snapped, and when.

Footfalls sounded from a point behind Roads, breaking his train of thought. The controller had finally emerged from his hiding place.

"Phil, you have to get a look at him," whispered O'Dell into Roads' ear.

"Be patient," he said. "I'll do what I can."

The controller came to a halt behind Roads and Katiya. "Well," said the voice. "Here we all are. How cosy."

Roads shrugged. "Not really."

"No. Hardly a satisfactory outcome for any of us." The controller moved closer. "I should kill you both now, you realise?"

"I'm wondering why you haven't already," Roads said.

"Because I don't need to." The controller stood so close that Roads could almost see his body-heat reflecting off Cati's broad, hairless chest. "Not yet. Not until I find out how much you know."

"I told you," Roads said. "We know everything about you and Betheras."

"Then why haven't you addressed me by name? And why are you two alone? If you'd known before you came here, you would have told someone else, and the bridge would be crawling with people. The fact that it isn't suggests that either you *don't* know, or for some reason you've told no-one. Which is it?"

Roads shook his head slowly. Cati's controller was clearly unaware that Barney and O'Dell were already on the way. That slightly improved his chances of surviving the next few minutes.

"The rest of RSD is back at Mayor's House, dealing with the situation there," he said, hoping to convey the impression that he had decided to be honest. "I managed to trace the last call you made to Cati, and decoded it with Katiya's help." He indicated the woman with an inclination of his head, the lie coming easily. Anything to keep Katiya's true connection with Cati a secret. "Nobody would listen. There wasn't even time to convince Barney to come with me. It all happened so quickly."

"Yes. General Stedman's little trick took even me by surprise." Reluctant admiration made the voice pause, but only briefly. "What about Betheras? How did you know his name?"

That stopped Roads for an instant, until O'Dell said via the cyberlink: "He was a member of the original envoy. You recognised him as a technical consultant, one of the three at the first meeting with the Mayor."

Roads echoed the information, and was gratified to feel some of the controller's tension ease. He had supplied the correct answer.

A low groan issued from the RUSAMC officer, as though the reference to him had pulled him back to consciousness. He stirred sluggishly at Roads' feet like someone emerging from a bad dream.

"Good," said the controller, seeing Betheras' movement. His voice hardened. "It's not too late, then. Help him up, Roads. Remember: don't make any sudden movements, or it'll be the last thing you ever do."

Roads did as he was told, and finally came face to face with Cati's controller.

INTERLUDE

Wednesday, 19 September, 12:35 a.m.

Sanctuary!

She was so close he could have reached out to touch her, had he been permitted to. A wide scrape marred her cheek, and her swollen temple forced one eye into a lopsided squint. The rectangular pendant around her neck glinted in the cold starlight: the only hard point of her whole being. She looked so small, so vulnerable. She shouldn't be here!

Caught between two worlds – those of his despised past and his fragile present – Cati could only watch as the woman he loved joined him and Roads in the centre of the roadway.

Voices echoed around him – Roads' and the controller's, mainly – but none were directed at him. Most of the words were therefore blurs without meaning, unstructured sound lacking form or purpose. Unless one of them used the control code, his attention was focused solely on Sanctuary. Every time she spoke, his whole body shook, yearning to be set free -- to flee with her back to safety, back to Peace, and away from the shadow-man, who so closely at times resembled the *thing*.

"A person is a person," Sanctuary said, "no matter what they're made of. You can't say that someone doesn't feel – or have rights – simply because they're not like *you*."

The words struck the very core of his dilemma. He was imprisoned by his own exotic nature; even he knew that. He didn't know why or how he had been programmed to obey, but he could feel the imperative deep in the heart of him. Iron-hard, inflexible, it held him still while every cell strained for release.

"You're crazy," she continued, defending him when he had no defence of his own to mount. "And . . . *evil* for doing what you've done to us."

The controller moved around to confront the three of them again, mouthing incomprehensible words as he did. Roads watched warily, but the pistol in the controller's hand never strayed. The shadow-man, bleeding from a broken nose, still worried at the straps and buckles of the garment being fitted across his back. The discussion became more heated, heavier with the threat of violence. It was only a matter of time before one of them broke.

But it wasn't going to be him. He had too much self control, voluntary or not, to allow disobedience. No matter how much he wanted to. He felt exposed and vulnerable, just as he had in the dream the previous night.

"That's not fair!" protested Sanctuary. "You have no right to use him like that!"

The controller laughed. His voice mocked her in reply. Then Roads spoke, and the controller turned the pistol on him, eyes shining with anger. Raised voices ricocheted from the stanchions and girders of the bridge surrounding them. All he wanted to do was to reach out as the controller brushed past him, grasp the thin neck between his fingers, and *squeeze* as he had been trained to do – *squeeze* until the life ebbed out of the one that hurt him so much . . .

As though the controller sensed the mutiny in his thoughts, his hand flashed out and slapped him across the face. He blinked, but made no other response. The controller seemed to find that amusing. Sanctuary stared at him with a horrified expression on her face.

"You have no right to do this!" she gasped. "Why can't you just leave us *alone*?"

This time the controller didn't laugh. The man took several paces back and looked around, noticing for the first time the sound of sirens that had been growing gradually louder during the preceding minutes. Small lights moved on the city shore as vehicles pulled to a halt.

There was a scuffle. Roads grappled with the shadow-man; a shot was fired. But he paid little attention to anything other than Sanctuary, who had taken shelter behind him; even if the controller's orders actively forbade him from helping her, at least he could stay still.

Then the voice of Lucifer spoke directly into his mind once again:

"They've found us, Cati. I'm going to have to leave now in order to avoid them, and I don't want any evidence left behind. When RSD arrives, put up a fight and make sure they see you, then throw yourself off the bridge. We don't have time for games any more."

The controller waited until he sent confirmation via the inaudible voice reserved solely for such direct communication.

"Good," said the controller. "Before you do that, though, there's one other task you have to perform. Roads is a traitor, a threat to the security of the United States of America, and this is his accomplice. I want you to kill them both – Roads first and then the girl. Do it now, before either of them tries anything. Understood?"

Horrified to the core of his very being, he could only nod *yes*, and obey . . .

CHAPTER TWENTY-THREE

12:35 a.m.

"Remember," said DeKurzak, "don't make any sudden movements, or it'll be the last thing you ever do."

Roads helped Betheras sit upright, then stepped back when the RUSAMC officer waved him irritably away. DeKurzak stood with one hand holding the gun on Roads and Katiya; the other remained hidden in his coat pocket. He looked nervous, as though the appearance of Roads had startled him more than his voice revealed.

"The sonofabitch," whispered O'Dell in Roads' ear. "I thought he was in Mayor's House!"

"That's obviously what you were supposed to think," replied Roads, fighting a terrible sense of tiredness. "This is starting to make sense, at last."

"Now we know who took our query about the boxes in security control," said Barney.

Roads nodded. So much was falling into place: DeKurzak's protectiveness of the Kennedy datapool on the day of Blindeye; his furious over-working of Roger Wiggs in the hunt for the killer; his shock at seeing Cati's face on Roads' office monitor; and his about-face once he realised how close Roads was getting.

"What's the matter, Roads?" asked DeKurzak, moving to confront his captives. "You don't look terribly surprised to see me here."

"Should I be?" Roads asked. "Nobody else was in a better position to do what you did. You had access to the city's archive files, and knew enough about data processing to erase entire sections without them being missed. You knew who to kill in the Mayoralty because you were involved in the Reassimilation debate. You helped coordinate Stedman's arrival as a representative of the MSA, so you knew how to smuggle Cati into position. And once you managed to worm your way into the RSD investigation of the murders, you were perfectly placed to keep us looking in the wrong direction.

"If I didn't guess before," he said, "it was only because I underestimated your ambition. I thought you were after RSD, not all of Kennedy."

Betheras groaned again, and climbed unsteadily to his feet, clutching his broken nose. His voice was rough, a low growl:

"What's going on, DeKurzak?"

"It's not as bad as it looks," DeKurzak said. "Roads decoded the last command I sent to Cati and followed us here; that's all. It doesn't change anything. It might even make things easier, in the long run."

Betheras grunted. Under the nightsuit, the RUSAMC officer's frame was stocky, less imposing than it had seemed before. No wonder, Roads thought, he had been so easy to overpower.

The RUSAMC officer turned to look around him, seeking something.

"An engineer, you said," Roads subvocalised to Martin O'Dell, "on Project Cherubim – the Mole, in other words. Are you thinking what I'm thinking?"

"I'm trying not to," replied the RUSAMC captain.

Betheras spotted what he was looking for, and headed off along the bridge to collect it. He returned a moment later with a sealed black bag that he put between himself and DeKurzak.

"So now what?" he asked. "Do we go ahead?"

"Of course." DeKurzak waved the gun, indicating that Roads and Katiya were to step away from Cati. "Our plans are unchanged."

"What about these two?" Betheras cocked his head in their direction.

"I don't know yet. They may come in useful, depending on how things develop. Particularly Roads."

"If you think I'm going to help you –" Roads began.

"Whether you like it or not, you will." DeKurzak's fingers tightened on the pistol. "At the very least, all we really need is your body, so don't push your luck."

"You still want to frame me as the Mole?" Roads feigned incredulity. "Is that it? You'll shoot me yourself – instead of getting Chong to do the job for you – and call yourself a hero?"

"That's one option. There are others worth considering." DeKurzac smiled. "You can join me, or become a victim. The first option relies upon how far I believe I can trust you. The second is simply a matter of timing: how best to discredit you, and which crimes to 'solve' by the application of your death."

Roads did his best to look sceptical. "You make it sound so simple."

"I'd be offering them a quick solution, and they'd take it. Who wouldn't, in their shoes?"

Beside them, Betheras had opened the bag and laid out a number of items on the tarmac. He glanced up at Cati as he worked, clearly nervous of the giant's biomods and size.

"And what do you hope to gain out of all of this?" Roads asked DeKurzak. "To be King of Kennedy Polis as it falls to pieces around you?"

"Not yet. It'll be some time before I'm ready to move against the Mayor."

"The city's going to die no matter what you do, or who's in charge. Nothing will keep it going longer than a decade without input from the Outside you're so afraid of."

"Who said anything about being afraid?" DeKurzak snapped. "I've nothing against the Reunited States or anybody else. We can have all the resources we want without sacrificing the city to their pathetic cause."

"You really don't get it, do you?" Roads shook his head. "As you yourself said: we don't have any choice. Kennedy is just a small pool surrounded by a rising sea. Cut it off from that sea, and it will die. It'll smother on the inside."

"But that doesn't mean it has to be *engulfed* – that we must give up and let it happen. Whether or not it makes any difference in the long run, it's our choice to remain isolated for now."

"*Your* choice. Not mine."

"But you're not one of us, are you? Maybe if you were, you would feel differently." DeKurzak raised one hand to scratch his cheek. "You were so close to the truth. Of course old-timers like you wouldn't fight to keep Kennedy intact. You're all so pathetically grateful just to be alive. Kennedy needs someone like me – vital, and prepared to act – to keep it from being taken over. To give its citizens a *reason* to live."

"By assassinating them." Roads grimaced. "That's a bit extreme, isn't it?"

"Necessarily so. This is a *war*, Roads – undeclared, but undeniable. You have to expect some casualties."

"That's easy for you to say," Roads sneered. "Sitting back in comfort while your docile killer hunts and kills your enemies for you."

"Don't be stupid, Roads." DeKurzak's eyes flashed. "It's more than just political murder."

"As if that wasn't bad enough."

"Oh, come on, Roads! Stop playing the dumb RSD officer."

Cati's muscles flexed beside them, making Betheras flinch away. The odd assortment of items he had produced from the bag unfolded to become a massive combat harness large enough to fit Cati's frame. The RUSAMC officer had barely begun slipping it into place when the killer's small movement had given him second thoughts.

Roads sighed. "Okay, okay," he said. "You're trying to make people afraid. Is that it?"

DeKurzak relaxed slightly, as though Roads' understanding of his actions automatically vindicated them. "Of course. A frightened populace is easier to control. People are more likely to accept draconian restrictions if a threat is perceived to be real."

"Like the berserkers."

"Precisely. My generation saw the damage they inflicted upon innocent people. The fear of biomodified agents was high, and we agreed to almost anything to keep them out. But now, that threat has waned. The fear is ebbing. We need a new enemy to keep the latest generation from getting restless."

"Cati."

"Why not?" DeKurzak shrugged. "We honestly thought we'd seen the last of your kind. You and Cati are evidence of how cunning and insidious you can be. Luckily for us, you've reappeared at the right time."

"A person is a person," Katiya said, defying DeKurzak quietly, unexpectedly, "no matter what they're made of. You can't say that someone doesn't feel – or have rights – simply because they're not like *you*."

"You're wrong." DeKurzak shifted the pistol to point at the woman. "You of all people should agree with what we're trying to do. You and the children, everyone threatened by the revival of creatures like this."

"Come off it," Roads snorted, hoping to divert attention back to him. "You don't really believe that crap, do you?"

"Does it matter?" DeKurzak swung the pistol back. "It's what people will listen to that counts."

"But they're not fools. They know we're not the only people who have Humanity Laws preventing this from happening again –"

"That's irrelevant, and you know it. There was supposed to be an international law in the 2020s forbidding human experimentation, but who paid heed to that when the berserkers were built? Biotechnology is tempting, and the thought of such power will pervert even the greatest of people. Not necessarily someone in the government, maybe an independent operator instead – but it *will* happen. If the capability exists, then it's bound to be exploited."

"Just as you exploited Cati?" Roads broke in, gesturing at the giant killer standing motionless behind him.

"Cati is a tool," DeKurzak said, "a thing, an ugly reminder of the old ways. He exists to be used. If I hadn't used him, then someone else would have."

"But he's not an object," Roads retorted. "He's human like any one of us, under the differences."

"He's *dangerous*," DeKurzak responded.

"Only when used in a dangerous way – which makes you a hypocrite."

"Perhaps it would, yes, if I'd made him myself. But I didn't. And what could be more appropriate than using him against the ones who threaten to revive his kind? An elegant solution, don't you think?"

"You're crazy," burst out Katiya. "And . . . *evil* for doing what you've done to us."

"Not at all," DeKurzak replied. "Just doing my job as I see it." He sidestepped to his right, coming around Roads until he stood opposite Katiya. "Kennedy survived the fall of civilisation because it closed itself off from everyone around it. In order to survive, it must maintain that policy a little longer. Yes, I stand to gain by forcing it to do so, but I really only have the city's best wishes at heart."

Roads glanced at Betheras, who had finished strapping the harness into place around Cati's chest and shoulders. What the RUSAMC officer thought of DeKurzak's argument, if he was even listening, didn't show on his face.

"You're a fool if you think you can get away with this, DeKurzak," Roads said.

"Why?" The liaison officer rounded on Roads. "There's a warrant current with your name on it. As an officer of the Mayoralty, I'm arresting you."

"You know what I mean."

"Not at all. I'm in charge of the hunt for the killer. If I can't pin the blame on you, then there are a thousand other ways I can lead the States off-course."

"Someone will catch up with you, sooner or later. Or Cati will be captured, or killed. Where will *that* leave you? No better off than when you started."

"Exactly." DeKurzak took the question seriously, although Roads had intended it only as a gibe. "I've already decided that Cati's usefulness to me is at an end. The time has come to stop edging around the problem and strike right at the heart of it."

"Let me guess," Roads broke in. "Something big: not one target, but many? I'm sure Cati will prove to be as effective at mass-murder as he is at assassination. It'll take days to bring him down, and any evidence of your involvement will be erased along with him."

"Very good." DeKurzak nodded appreciatively.

"That's not fair!" exploded Katiya. "You have no right to use him like that!"

"No?" DeKurzak laughed, unimpressed by the outburst. "*He* hasn't complained."

"Only because he can't," said Roads.

"Of course. He was built to obey. Without orders, what is he? Nothing! Just an old machine abandoned to rot – that's all." DeKurzak walked around Betheras, and raised a hand to slap Cati across the face. Cati hardly blinked in response, his face as unreadable as ever.

"I have the code," DeKurzak said. "And that gives me the right."

"You have no right to do this!" Katiya gasped, her face twisted with grief. "Why can't you just leave us *alone*?"

"Not an option, I'm afraid." DeKurzak put a hand to his ear. "Now quiet, please. Something's happened." He cocked his head, listening to a voice only he could hear. Betheras likewise stopped his work on Cati; not to listen, but to watch DeKurzak.

"Martin?" Roads subvocalised. "What the hell's going on?"

The voice of O'Dell returned almost immediately: "The Mayor refused to release our people, so General Stedman ordered the control van back into the grounds of Mayor's House. There have been no aggressive moves against it as yet, but the threat is present all the same. What's left of RSD, under Roger Wiggs, has formed a cordon protecting the control van. Our troops are on stand-by to move in if needed."

"Shit." Roads could imagine the scene all too clearly; the tension that had existed for years between the MSA and RSD had finally reached flashpoint, with the RUSAMC acting as a catalyst. Civil war was a very real possibility, with the RUSAMC on hand to pick up the pieces. "Can't they hang on a little longer?"

"That depends on what the Mayor does. If he lets our troops go, then nothing will happen. If he doesn't, though, or tries to attack, it's bound to get nasty."

Roads clenched his jaw muscles. "How far away are you?"

"Very close. Barney will be there in a minute or two."

"Is she listening?"

"Yes, boss," came her voice through the cyberlink bead.

"Good. When I tell you to, turn on your sirens: lights, horns, the works. Give it everything you've got. Until then, keep quiet."

"Understood. We'll wait for your call."

Roads turned his attention back to DeKurzak, who looked as tense as Roads felt.

"How long until you've finished, Sam?" the MSA officer asked Betheras.

"Not long."

DeKurzak scowled. "Well, hurry it up. We need him back at Mayor's House ASAP. Things are coming to a head quicker than we thought."

Roads stared more closely at the harness strapped to Cati's shoulders. It consisted of numerous pouches and pads designed to carry tools and protect vulnerable parts of the body. On Cati, it looked grotesque. A crude version of Betheras' nightsuit lined Cati's legs and arms, probably designed more to confuse enemies than to deceive them. Around his bald head, Betheras had strapped a combat communicator with an eye-feed tugged back over the ear – obviously to imply that he was in communication with superiors elsewhere. The effect of the communicator was to make plainly obvious what Cati already *was*: a combat soldier controlled by others, not a random berserker.

"That's standard-issue equipment," put in O'Dell, studying Roads' close-up zoom by remote. "*Our* equipment."

"I thought it would be," replied Roads, his heart sinking. His apartment had been blown up using RUSAMC explosives; Cati was dressed in a RUSAMC battle-harness. The new enemy DeKurzak needed wasn't just biomodified agents: it was the Reunited States of America Military Corps.

"He's setting us up!" O'Dell's outrage was clear through the cyberlink. "After all the work he put in to 'smooth the way' –"

"Exactly," interrupted Roads, remembering how keen DeKurzak had been for Roads to catch the Mole. "The backlash will be even stronger, if he can convince people that you're behind Cati *and* the Mole."

"What, and start a war?"

"Only if you won't leave. Most people would be happy just to see you gone. If you're Outside, they don't care what you do."

"Until we came back in force."

"Would Stedman really do that?"

O'Dell was silent for a moment. "I hope not, of course – but if the interventionists have their way –"

"You need Kennedy that badly?"

"Of course. It's only a matter of time before someone takes it. If not us, then the New Mexican Alliance."

"Or good old rot," muttered Roads, although O'Dell's words had prompted a disturbing new thought: of a map of the North American continent with the Reunited States and the New Mexican Alliance to the north and south, and Kennedy midway between them . . .

Betheras had fastened the last of the straps around Cati's stomach. By tapping studs on the control-belt one by one, he tested the camouflage system. Strange ripples of ambiguous colour rolled along Cati's limbs, startling the giant.

"You're playing a dangerous game, DeKurzak," Roads said aloud.

"With the lives of powerful friends in the balance, not my own," the MSA officer shot back. "Even if everything does go terribly wrong, I hope to come out of this relatively clean. It's a win–win situation, as far as I'm concerned."

"Perhaps . . ." Roads pretended to consider his next words: "But what about me? You hinted that I can help you. In return for what?"

"Your life and a free ticket out of here. Exile, if you like, in exchange for information."

"What sort of information?"

DeKurzak stepped closer, almost within arm's reach. "We need to know the whereabouts of Keith Morrow."

Roads didn't have to feign surprise. "Why?"

"Why do you think? Sam Betheras tells me he's the only one in Kennedy who actually *impacted on* General Stedman. With him on our side, we could not only force the States out of the city, but make sure they never get back in . . ."

Before Roads could answer, Betheras deactivated the combat harness, stepped back and wiped his hands on his thighs. "Okay, he's ready. It's crude but it should do the job."

"Good." DeKurzak straightened his posture. "Time we were moving – and for a decision, Roads. What's it to be? Your help or your body?"

Roads opened his mouth, then shut it.

"Barney," he subvocalised, "*now*!"

Instantly, the sound of sirens disturbed the stillness of the night, cutting across the surface of the river and to their position on the bridge. The liaison officer backed away, startled, and looked toward the shore.

A string of RSD and RUSAMC vehicles had pulled to a halt at the end of the freeway. Even without magnification, their headlights were clearly visible.

"What the –?" whispered DeKurzak, backing away to view the sight from the walkway. Betheras stared at the lights with mute shock. Neither man was paying full attention to their captives.

Roads ducked under the line of DeKurzak's pistol and behind Cati. Before DeKurzak could react, he dragged Katiya after him, into the shadow of Cati's bulk, then emerged to grab Betheras about the neck.

The RUSAMC officer hissed and tried to pull away, but Roads tightened his grip.

DeKurzak watched furiously, unable to find a clear line of fire.

"Put down the gun, DeKurzak," Roads warned. "They know everything."

"No. I refuse to believe that. I interrupted PolNet myself; there's no way you could have told them."

"Then why are they here?"

"Chance." DeKurzak raised the barrel of the gun. "Maybe they're after *you*, not me."

Betheras stiffened as DeKurzak aimed the pistol. "No, wait –" he gasped.

Roads pushed the RUSAMC officer towards DeKurzak. They collided, and the pistol cracked loudly. Katiya screamed. Betheras crumpled to the ground. DeKurzak backed away, brushing blood from his clothes. Before Roads could reach cover the gun was on him again.

He froze, cursing his luck. He hadn't expected DeKurzak to shoot Betheras. And from the fleeting look of shock on his face, DeKurzak hadn't expected it, either.

"I don't want any evidence left behind," DeKurzak was saying into the microphone of a small radio transmitter he had pulled out of his pocket. "When RSD arrives, put up a fight and make sure they see you, then throw yourself off the bridge. We don't have time for games any more."

Beside them, Cati nodded.

"Good," the MSA officer continued. "Before you do that, though, there's one other task you have to perform. Roads is a traitor, a threat to the security of the United States of America, and this is his accomplice. I want you to kill them both – Roads first and then the girl. Do it now, before either of them tries anything. Understood?"

Katiya stared despairingly at Cati as he nodded. His enormous frame stirred into life and he took a step forward.

"I'm in trouble," Roads said into the cyberlink. "Barney, Martin – how far away are you?"

"Not far. The area is secure. A couple of minutes."

"*Shit*." Too long. He ducked away to his right, trying to put as much distance as possible between him and the assassin. Cati's movements were slow, almost sluggish, but he knew how quickly that could change if the killer's resistance crumbled. DeKurzak's well-timed order had saved him before; now, he would have no such rescue. Despite Katiya's attempts to hold him back, the giant frame turned to face him.

"We'll be cut off from your feed for the next few minutes, while we're moving on foot," said O'Dell. "You'll have to tell us what's going on via the cyberlink alone, if you can."

Roads didn't break his concentration to reply. He backed away until he reached the walkway on the west side of the bridge. His searching fingers found a length of rusty iron behind him – part of the guide-rail skirting the road. Flexing every enhanced muscle in his shoulders and back, he wrenched it free.

With a diffident shrug of his right arm, Cati tossed Katiya aside. Pausing only to rip the RUSAMC battle-harness from his shoulders and to throw the headset away, he assumed an open-armed stance, ready to attack.

"Interesting," said DeKurzak, watching Cati's actions with a crooked smile, "if a little primal. I'd stay and watch the rest, but for RSD's untimely arrival. I'll have to get back into the city by the far bank in time to head off the Mayor. Don't want him going off half-cocked until the final scores are in – although I have no doubts how it will look: you, your friend and an officer of the Reunited States Army, an unholy alliance in life *and* death."

"Don't be too sure about that, DeKurzak," Roads muttered, setting his implants to record. He had only one chance left to test if his hunch about DeKurzak's true motive was correct. "The game's not over yet."

"No? I stand by what I said: they can't possibly know what I've done."

"And what would *that* be, exactly? Helped the Mayor sell out the city just to keep his precious power base?" Roads paused for effect, then added: "Or been part of Betheras' little scheme to sell Kennedy to the New Mexican Alliance?"

DeKurzak paled and raised the pistol. For a moment, Roads thought he was about to shoot. Then, without replying, the liaison officer turned and hurried towards the safety of the far side of the river.

Roads likewise readied himself for a sudden dash. Twenty metres in the same direction DeKurzak was heading, a maintenance gantry led into the canopy of girders and cable above. If he could get past Cati and to DeKurzak, then there was a chance he could use the MSA officer as a body-shield and stay alive long enough for Barney to reach them.

Barely had DeKurzak gone fifteen steps, however, when something flashed down from the bridge's superstructure and alighted upon his shoulders.

DeKurzak's surprised cry brought a sudden halt to Cati's slow approach. Roads glanced up just in time to see the shape on DeKurzak's shoulders shift as it folded its transparent wings, absorbed them into its body, and changed shape.

DeKurzak stumbled, flailed in vain to shift the thing on his back. He raised the pistol to ward it off, but the gun was snatched away and hurled into the night. Five rotating balls of light darted around the liaison officer's head for an instant as incomprehensible forces *twisted*. The beginning of a scream was cut off at his neck, severed in a spray of blood that reached two metres into the air. DeKurzak's legs spasmed once then went limp. For an instant, only whirlpooling field-effects kept his body upright.

Then the five silver balls ceased their furious dance, and DeKurzak's headless corpse fell limp to the road. Blood formed a pool of hot darkness spreading across the roadway.

The balls floated toward the three stunned observers, assuming a familiar five-pointed arrangement as they did so. Half-visible planes of force softened, curved, assumed colour and definition. A faint mist of blood hissed away from its "skin" as the transformation reached its final stages.

Roads gaped open-mouthed, horrified, as his mirror-image stared silently back at him. There was no way of telling if it recognised him, or cared that he recognised *it*. Its eyes were empty, and its face was dead.

A shiver of ice crept down Roads' spine at the true realisation that within the facade of humanity was nothing but air, and five silver balls. Knowing the principles behind Project Cherubim was nothing compared to seeing it in action. He was facing a modern ghost, a phantom made of caged energy.

A phantom that could kill, he reminded himself. It had done so in front of him twice now.

Roads hefted the rusty bar in his right hand. Katiya had turned away at the sight of DeKurzak's death and retched noisily. Cati stood between them and the Mole, apparently frozen by indecision. The Mole itself – standing with its "hands" deep inside the "pockets" of its "coat" – still didn't move.

"Barney," Roads subvocalised through the cyberlink. "I don't know where you are, but be careful. Something's going on. Something weird."

"What?" Barney's voice was thick between rapid breaths.

"The Mole's arrived," he explained. "It just killed DeKurzak, and now it's not doing anything at all."

"The *Mole*?" O'Dell's voice came over the line, openly surprised. "What the hell – ?"

"Where's Cati?" broke in Barney.

"Right here. He's not doing anything either. He's just staring at the Mole and me and . . ." Roads broke off as realisation suddenly dawned. "Oh Christ, the Mole must have followed me here from Old North Street. It either killed DeKurzak because he ordered Cati to kill me, or simply because he was Cati's controller and therefore breaking the Humanity Laws. Now it's confused Cati by showing him two of me when there should only be one." Roads shook his head: the killer didn't know which of him to attack. "Cati doesn't want to obey the orders anyway, so he's not fighting too hard to work it out."

Stalemate.

"But DeKurzak's dead," protested Barney. "Surely that makes Cati's orders invalid?"

"Why should it? Orders are orders. Depending on how Cati views the world, the actual person who issues them might be irrelevant. Only the control code followed by the words themselves matter."

Roads stopped as Cati moved. The massive head turned from side to side, looking from Roads to the Mole and back again. The killer's broad, eerie face displayed no animation whatsoever.

Katiya joined Roads' corner of the frozen tableau. "Cati? Can you hear me?" she said. "*Please*, Cati – you don't have to do this!"

Cati's black, impenetrable eyes regarded her solemnly. Then his hands began to move, chopping at the air in short, sharp strokes. When he stopped and glanced away again, the woman bit back a sob of frustration.

"What did he say?" Roads asked the woman.

She shook her head. "He won't listen to me," she said. "But he knows what he's doing is wrong. He just doesn't have any choice . . ."

"Hold on a little longer, Phil," Barney said via the cyberlink. "We're on our way."

Roads gripped the metal bar tightly and counted the seconds. The sound of distant feet pounding along the walkway insinuated itself into the distance. So close, but still too far away. If he could hear it, then the Mole could as well. And if O'Dell was right about the heart of the AI's confusion –

Before he could complete the thought, the Mole broke the stalemate.

A lightning flash high in the infra-red spectrum split the night in two. Blinded, Roads staggered backward, raising a hand to shield his eyes. He clearly heard Katiya's puzzled gasp but could not see what had prompted it.

Squinting, Roads tried to see through the haze in his eyes. Tiny artificial irises slowly adjusted until he could dimly make out his immediate surroundings: Katiya, Cati, also dazzled by the bright flash, and . . .

"Where's it gone?" the woman asked him.

Roads realised next. Either his eyes were less sensitive than Cati's or the flash had been directed more in the killer's direction.

The Mole had disappeared.

Cati looked first at Roads, then where the Mole had been standing a second ago. Seeing only empty air, the killer glanced around him, but the Mole was nowhere nearby. Finally, his eyes returned to Roads – and stayed there.

By the time Cati reached the obvious conclusion, Roads was already running.

CHAPTER TWENTY-FOUR

1:05 a.m.

The road surface was uneven and, when he reached DeKurzak's remains, slippery as well. As he negotiated the puddle of blood, he saw the bloody transmitter still in DeKurzak's lifeless fingers. Without breaking step, he picked it up and slid it into his coat pocket.

Then the sound of pursuit came from behind him. Cati's few seconds of confusion had enabled him to reach the base of the maintenance gantry unscathed. A flight of narrow, steeply-inclined steps led upward into shadow. There was no way he could tell where they went, or how far, but he had no other option. On the flat, open surface of the road, Cati would rapidly overtake him.

He climbed as fast as his aching body would allow, taking three steps at a time. The killer's heavy footfalls made the whole gantry shake. Flakes of rust rained around him as he fled higher. The shrill, unintelligible shouts of Katiya floated after them.

He reached a junction. A walkway leading to the far side of the bridge stretched to his right. Another flight of steps beckoned higher to his left. He continued upward, passing girders, stanchions and cable housings – but nothing to suggest what the gantry had originally been for, years ago. Maintenance, yes, but of what, exactly? Could it possibly serve him to any advantage?

He reached another possible change of course. This time a walkway led out of sight behind a massive girder. He ducked along it and pressed his back against the weathered metal. Cati's booming steps approached rapidly, and stopped at the top of the stairs.

Roads could almost hear the puzzlement radiating from Cati's unseen figure. Which way? Up, or along the walkway?

When Cati finally moved, it was toward his hiding place. Roads gritted his teeth and raised the metal bar in readiness to strike.

The killer stopped just before the girder, obviously wary of a trap. Roads waited impatiently, feeling sweat trickle down the back of his neck.

Movement from above broke the tableau. Something fell onto the walkway by the stairwell, making it shake. Cati grunted with surprise, and took a single heavy step back. A loud thud followed.

Roads risked a quick glimpse around the corner. The Mole was locked in a fierce embrace with the killer, stubbornly resisting Cati's attempts to break its back.

Protecting Roads . . .

He stole off along the walkway while Cati was distracted. It led nowhere, ending in a cul-de-sac surrounded by thick, long-dead power cables. Looking around him, he saw the stairwell not far away. Only a few metres' gap separated him from safety. Swinging up into the cables, he began to climb across the gap. Far below, he could see the flashing of torches as Barney and O'Dell ran along the western walkway to where Katiya and DeKurzak's body waited. They were still too far away to be of any real help.

He dropped down into the stairwell as gently as he could, but not gently enough. The battle below changed tempo the instant his boots touched metal. Hurried footsteps from below suggested that the Mole had broken free and was leading Cati away.

No, not away, Roads realised as the stairwell began vibrating around him again. Leading Cati upward, directly for him.

Why? he wondered. The Mole had disposed of DeKurzak easily enough. What prevented it from doing the same to Cati?

There was only one possible theory, and he didn't like it.

He began to climb again, fighting a growing sense of futility. The diversion *had* gained him valuable seconds, though, in which he could attempt a second ambush or simply find somewhere to hide.

He reached another junction. This time the walkway led in a straight line across the bridge. No chance of hiding there, although the complex tangle of supports and cables seemed even denser than before. He assumed he was nearing the top of the bridge. Above him, even through the closely-meshed metal web, Roads could see stars.

The stairs ended at that point and became a series of ladders. Roads climbed as fast as he could, ignoring twinges in his ribs and shoulders. His whole body ached, but he couldn't let the pain slow him down. Not far below him, Cati reached the ladders and also began to climb.

Roads risked a quick glance. Cati was alone. The Mole had disappeared again.

"Barney! Where are you?"

"We've just found DeKurzak. Where the hell are *you*?"

"There's a gantry further down that leads into the superstructure. If you look up, you might just be able to see me."

"What on earth – ?"

"Cati's not far behind me."

"Oh, understood." Barney paused for a few seconds, presumably to relay the information, then returned: "Is Katiya with you?"

"No. She's not down there?"

"No."

"Phil, this is Martin." O'Dell's voice came clearly over the cyberlink. "Barney's on her way to the gantry, but I'm staying behind. I've brought the laptop with me to access PolNet again. From now on, I can tell her what's happening without her disturbing you."

"Thanks." Roads was grateful for that, at least. Not that the feed from his eyes currently made inspiring viewing – ladders and more ladders, each leading further up into the scaffolding.

But not forever. Barely thirty seconds after O'Dell reopened the link, the ladders came to an end. Roads clambered upward onto a ten-metre-wide metal platform at the very summit of the bridge. He looked around, saw bird-droppings and nests, and the dim lights of the city to his right. The ragged remains of an old tent-like structure flapped from one edge. The wind was colder, whipping at his clothes like insubstantial hands trying to drag him from his perch. The maintenance platform had no guard-rails.

Curving down and to either side were the massive, carbon-fibre suspension cables of the bridge, each wider than his thigh. He considered making his escape along one of them, but decided against it. Even with the killer's greater mass taken into account, Cati's agility far exceeded his own; he'd have to proceed at a near run just to keep ahead. His sense of balance wasn't up to the task.

It was time to make a stand. Taking a position at the head of the ladder, with the rusty bar gripped in both hands, he waited for Cati to arrive. Height was his one advantage, and this his only chance.

Then a noise from behind him made him turn. Cati's massive head appeared on the other side of the platform, followed by his arms and shoulders. Roads backed away from the ladder's summit, realising that he had been tricked. Cati had obviously anticipated the ambush and taken the last few metres by another route. For someone who had proved his climbing ability on the roofs of Kennedy Polis, the detour wouldn't have been too difficult.

Yet . . . Roads frowned, momentarily puzzled. The sound of someone climbing the second-to-last ladder came clearly from below. If that wasn't Cati, then it could only have been Katiya – or the Mole.

But as Cati swung himself up onto the platform, another Cati appeared at the top of the ladder.

Backing away from both of them, unsure which was the illusion, he cursed O'Dell and his damned machine.

When the second Cati had climbed completely out of the ladderwell, the first suddenly vanished, sending five small dimples scattering into the darkness.

Roads and the real Cati squared off and circled each other warily. Roads kept the iron bar poised between them, ready for the slightest move. Cati seemed content to wait for the moment, however, balanced between caution and the need to obey orders.

Caution . . . or reluctance? Roads didn't want to hurt Cati, but could the reverse really be true?

When the attack came, it almost took Roads by surprise. Cati stepped back onto one leg and lashed out with his other foot to knock the bar aside. Roads ducked as the giant's right hand chopped at his neck. He drove his shoulder upward into Cati's stomach and heard a slight grunt.

Then Cati's elbow hammered down into his back, and he rolled aside, riding the blow. A fist followed, connected glancingly with his shoulder and sent him spinning. Both blows had been slower than he had expected, perhaps indicative of Cati's unwillingness to obey the orders of his controller – but they were still powerful.

Another kick pushed Roads toward the edge of the platform, and he scrambled for grip on the shreds of cloth. Cati followed, reaching down to grab Roads' outflung arm and tear it free.

Then an invisible force knocked the killer aside, giving Roads barely enough time to regain his footing. Cati staggered, enveloped by the Mole's whirling field-effects, confounded by something he could hardly get a grip on, let alone fight.

While he was busy, Roads scrambled hastily to his feet and ran for the ladder.

Before he could reach it, however, the Mole disengaged from Cati. Roads felt a tentacle of force wrap itself around his waist, tug him irresistibly back to meet Cati, then let go.

The biomodified killer's face displayed open confusion as they faced each other again, back where they had started.

Roads circled to his left, to where the iron bar had fallen. Cati moved to cut him off, but too late. Roads snatched the bar in one hand before Cati arrived, and swung it upward to strike the killer in the stomach. Knocked off balance, Cati staggered backward. Driving home the minor advantage, Roads delivered a double kick to the killer's stomach and knee.

Instead of falling as he was supposed to, Cati jack-knifed down and forward, reaching out and across as he did so to sweep Roads off his feet. The metal bar glanced off Cati's hairless skull as Roads fell, making the killer wince but doing little to ease his grip.

Caught in an ungainly tangle, they struck the platform together. With blood beginning to trickle down his face, Cati wrapped an arm around Roads' throat and squeezed.

The platform immediately below them, weakened by the weight pounding at it, abruptly gave way. The buckled metal plate groaned, tipped, then dropped with a loud crash into the superstructure of the bridge.

Roads experienced a moment of terrifying giddiness as both he and Cati scrambled for a hand-hold, the fight temporarily forgotten.

Cati grasped a stanchion with one hand as it went past, arresting his fall with a jerk. Roads' fingers slipped on bird-droppings and lost their grip. The iron bar dropped with a clatter into the blackness below. He too fell unchecked – until something wrapped itself around his hand and yanked him upward.

He rose rapidly through the air, was wrenched sideways, then landed awkwardly on an intact section of the platform. Winded, he clambered onto his hands and knees.

A swirl of energy darted away and disappeared into the background.

"Martin," he gasped into the cyberlink. "Are you catching this?"

"Yes," came back the voice of the RUSAMC captain. "I'm not sure I believe it, but –"

"It's trying to protect me, but at the same time protecting *Cati* because it wants him to kill me?"

"That's what I thought might be happening. It can't kill you itself, so it has to use someone else. But it can't stand by and let you be killed, which is why it keeps saving you at the last moment. But it can't let you escape, either – or Cati." O'Dell whistled. "The conflict must be incredible; it's a wonder the AI is still functioning at all."

"Yeah, wonderful. And it's only a matter of time before Cati takes us both by surprise and gets past the Mole's guard. Then I'll be dead, and Cati won't last much longer. Once he outlives his usefulness, the Mole will be able to return to the last orders you gave it, which were to dispose of him." Roads grunted as Cati's hands appeared at the lip of the hole, dragging his enormous body back into the night air. The bandage had fallen off his injured arm, and blood flowed freely again. "There has to be something we can do."

"I'm sorry, Phil. I'm out of ideas."

Cati climbed slowly to his feet. Blood trickled in a hot, steady stream from his temple and down his chest. A ragged gash down his right thigh testified to the narrowness of his escape when the platform gave away. Skirting the wide hole between them, he came with arms outstretched while Roads, unarmed, kept well out of reach.

INTERLUDE

1:20 a.m.

Warning pains trembled in the muscles of his left thigh and right arm, but he ignored them. More serious was the sensation of weakness spreading outward from his gut. The energy-expenditure of his body was enormous; he needed solid food and water soon, or his performance would begin to deteriorate. His breathing was already twice its normal rate, echoing his heartbeat – but oxygen alone wasn't enough.

The damage to his tissues could wait. There would be plenty of time to repair and recuperate once his orders were fulfilled.

His orders –

Roads is a traitor

– compelled him to attack, even though his mind screamed caution. The traitor had demonstrated evasive abilities he had never seen before: sometimes duplicating himself or vanishing entirely. The traitor could deflect his blows as though made of a material stronger than steel, yet at other times injured more easily than he did. Inconsistencies like this were dangerous. He was being toyed with, used.

The traitor circled to his left, hunting for a weapon. Before it could complete the curve, he shifted position, cutting it off. The traitor feinted, and he responded with a stabbing kick to the rib cage. Ordinarily, he would have followed the move with a hail of blows, but he didn't on this occasion. Something held him back, something that he had no cause to be considering when his orders were at stake. He focused his mind on the task at hand –

a threat to the security of the United States

– and struck again. This time, the blow missed completely, and he was appalled by his clumsiness. What was happening to him? Why was he so slow, so uncoordinated?

The traitor took advantage of his disorientation and lashed out at his throat. He knocked the fist aside, ducked under another blow. Reaching over his head, he grabbed the swinging arm and twisted the traitor off his feet. Something indefinable, only half-visible, swirled at the corner of his eye as the traitor crashed heavily to the platform, but this time it made no threatening moves.

He was gratified to hear the distinct *crack* of snapping bone when the traitor landed. Regaining his footing, he skirted the hole in the platform to find a better position from which to attack. Not long now. The traitor was seriously wounded. One opportunity to press home the advantage was all he needed to finish him off, after which he could turn his attention to the rest of his orders.

The unidentifiable distortion threatened to take shape as he approached the traitor he had been ordered to kill. He ignored it. The fallen . . . *man*, he forced himself to think, although it defied his programming . . . tried to crawl away, scrambling crab-like for a safety that didn't exist. He followed it, every muscle in his body tensed for the final blow.

Behind him, the sound of feet climbing the ladder suddenly ceased. Suspecting that the traitor's allies had finally arrived from below, he raised his fists and prepared to leap.

But all he saw was a lone woman – the second traitor – struggling upright to face him, her mouth open and saying something he couldn't understand.

Sanctuary?

Then the distortion moved, stretched out a limb to prod him forward. He stumbled toward the first traitor, his mind screaming rebellion but his orders –

kill them both

– forcing the rest of him to obey.

The traitor had ceased trying to escape. He approached within an arm's-length and looked down at his intended victim. One blow would be enough – one kick downward too fast too dodge, and the traitor would be no more. It was almost too easy, at the end. And yet –

Roads first and then the girl

– so difficult.

He shifted his balance, ready to strike.

Then the second traitor was between him and the first, beating at his chest, crying at him. He flinched, raised his hands to ward off the attack, but only succeeded in making her protests louder. The conflict in his mind made it difficult to think. The woman's voice cut deeply into him; he could hear her pain, her suffering, even though her words eluded him. He didn't want to hurt her, but the incessant echoes of his orders almost drowned her out completely. He winced, raised his hands to his ears, desperate for a respite, for release from his torment.

The traitor was on his feet again, beyond the woman. His orders howled at him to move before the traitor could escape –

a threat to the security of the United States

– and suddenly he couldn't hear the woman at all.

Something in his mind had given way under the pressure. He finally knew what he had to do to relieve the tension. The pain peaked in resonance with the controller's final orders –

kill them both

– as he reached with both hands for the woman's throat.

CHAPTER TWENTY-FIVE

1:25 a.m.

Roads, hampered by his broken left arm, could do nothing to help Katiya. Cati's hands wrenched, and the woman flinched as though struck. There was a tiny snap, almost inaudible over Katiya's gasp of fear, and Cati's hands fell away.

Then the killer shoved the woman aside. The object in his hands flashed at Roads, glinting in the starlight as it flew toward him. More by reflex than conscious intent, Roads clutched with his one good hand and snatched it out of the air.

Trapped in his fingers was a necklace, from which hung Katiya's pendant. He could feel the edges of the solid, rectangular block of silver as he opened his hand and stared at it in confusion.

Cati moved silently away, his deep eyes watching him, begging him to do something. But what? Of what conceivable use was the pendant – the only present, Katiya had said, that Cati had ever given her? What he needed more than anything else was a *weapon* . . .

Then he turned the necklace over. Engraved in the silver was an identity code and three short words:

I AM LUCIFER

"Officer Roads!"

He looked up in time to see Cati draw back a clenched fist, and ducked clumsily aside. He lost his footing on the platform and fell onto his broken arm. The darkness lit up as pain flashed through him. Hissing through clenched teeth, he forced himself to concentrate. With Cati's dog-tag clutched tight between his fingers, he thrust his good hand deep into his pocket.

Cati loomed over him. One giant hand reached down for his face, blotting out the stars as it came.

For the first time in his life, the thought of blood didn't make him hesitate as he brought DeKurzak's portable transmitter to his lips.

"I am Lucifer," he gasped. "Cati – listen to me! *I am Lucifer! You don't have to kill us!*"

The hand froze, but didn't withdraw. Uncertainty flashed across Cati's face.

Roads slithered aside. Katiya helped him regain his footing, glancing between him and her lover.

"Phil!" O'Dell's voice burst into Roads' implants. "Phil, your feed is breaking up. Can you hear me?"

"Yes," he transmitted back. "What's going on?"

"We lost visual for a second, then audio as well, and now we've picked up another transmission on the CATI frequency –"

"Yes, I know," Roads interrupted. As he stepped away from the killer, Cati's upper torso turned to follow him. The wide-spaced eyes with their pinprick pupils didn't once look away. "Just wait a second, Martin. I'm onto something here."

"But –" The line went dead with a crackle.

"He's querying the order," said Keith Morrow, the artificial voice gliding smoothly into the silence.

"He's what?" Roads asked. "I thought I put it clearly enough. Don't tell me I need a specialised language as well –?"

"No, but you have to phrase the order correctly. You must reassure him that 'Roads' is no longer a threat to the United States of America and that he can be allowed to live. You have to follow the protocol built into him."

Cati's depthless eyes watched Roads as he moved across the platform. The killer's fist had fallen to his side, but it remained at the ready. Roads raised the communicator to his lips again.

"Cati, listen to me. Listen to me carefully," he said. "Your previous orders have been superseded: Phil Roads is no longer a threat, and neither is the woman with him. You are not required to kill them. Do you understand? They can live." He paused, then added: "Please indicate your understanding immediately."

Cati nodded, and straightened to a more relaxed posture.

Roads took a deep breath.

At that moment, the Mole reappeared, ran across the platform and collided bodily with Cati, knocking him to the metal surface. Katiya screamed and went to his aid, but the Mole dashed her aside.

The artificial image flexed and twisted as force-fields warped; fingers stretched, became talons like pointed daggers, impossibly sharp at the tip. Cati rolled away as they stabbed down at him. One slashed his abdomen, but the others missed and buried themselves deep in the metal of the platform. The Mole twisted again, following Cati as he tried to escape. Its gait was no longer possible to mistake as human – like something out of a bad dream, impossibly silent and deadly – and far too quick for even Cati to avoid for long.

Then a voice shouted at both of them: "Freeze!"

Roads, Katiya and Cati turned as one to face the voice coming from the ladderwell. Only the Mole ignored it. While Cati was distracted, it stabbed forward again with five rigid talons aimed directly for the killer's undefended throat.

The gunshot blew it backward across the platform, warping active field-effects at chest-height so it seemed to collapse inward upon itself.

Barney aimed again as its shape readjusted and came forward. This time the bullet did not encounter anything solid, and passed through the illusion unimpeded. A third time Barney fired, and kept firing until her clip was empty – aiming at throat, hips and nipples . . .

She hit something with her last shot.

Sparks flew from a point somewhere within the hologram's right chest, and the Mole froze in mid-step.

With a fierce crackle, the image dissolved into static, then winked out completely. All that remained were the five silver balls at its heart, hanging motionless in mid-air and humming furiously with pent-up energies.

As though in sympathy, everything else became still: Roads lying on his back with the bloody transmitter still clutched in his hand, Katiya on the far side of the platform where the Mole had pushed her, Barney in a sharp-shooter's stance next to ladderwell – and Cati, solemnly watching them all.

Then, before anyone could react, Cati turned and ran for the edge of the platform.

"Cati!" Katiya screamed.

But Cati took two bounding steps and dived gracefully into space, his huge frame hanging motionless for an instant, then curving as it fell.

By the time Katiya reached the edge, Cati was gone.

From far away, almost lost beneath the moaning of the wind, Roads heard a splash.

Katiya turned away and buried her face in her hands.

Barney brought the gun down, wiped sweat from her forehead.

Roads sagged onto his one good elbow and winced at the pain in his back. "Behold the cavalry," he muttered.

"In the nick of time, right?" Reaching into a pocket, Barney replaced her pistol's clip without looking away from the Mole.

"Silver bullets?"

"Lead, actually. I pinched them from Martin."

"Speaking of which . . ." Roads subvocalised: "Can you hear us now?"

"Clear as a bell," replied the RUSAMC officer. "Whatever caused the problem must have fixed itself."

Roads mentally thanked Keith Morrow, and remained silent.

The sound of further movement came from the ladderwell. Barney stepped quickly aside to allow a line of RSD officers onto the platform. They held their weapons nervously, looking for something to aim at.

"That," said Barney, pointing. "If it so much as moves, give it all you've got."

Only when she was certain the Mole was covered did she turn away. Crossing the platform to where Roads lay, she reached down to help him to his feet.

"How're you doing, old man?"

"Feeling my age, for once." Roads forced a smile through the pain of his injuries. "You missed most of the action."

"Well, I'm here now." She cast him a mock-scathing look. "The least you could do is show some gratitude."

"What do you want? You turn up late and scare Cati away, and you expect me to carry you on my shoulders through the streets?"

"A 'thanks for trying' would be something."

"Fair point." Roads put his good hand on her arm. As empty as he felt on the inside, she didn't deserve to take the brunt of his disappointment. "I'm sorry. You weren't to blame for Cati. DeKurzak ordered him to jump off the bridge after he had killed me and Katiya."

"He did? Why bother when we were already on the way?"

"To hide the evidence. He wanted a nice, convenient tableau to convince the Council that Stedman and I were guilty of *something*. With me and Cati dead, there would be nobody left to pin the blame on him."

"Except me." Barney shrugged. "Anyway, DeKurzak himself is dead now, so now no-one's left to mount a case against you."

"Maybe," Roads said, weariness sinking into his bones.

"Pessimist." Barney left his side to study the Mole. The silver balls didn't move as she approached; they hung unsupported in mid-air like Christmas decorations minus the tree. The angry buzz continued unabated. "We have to get back and help Roger, Martin," she said into the RUSAMC intercom. "But what about *this*? What do we do with it now?"

"I'm not sure," said O'Dell from below. "We can try moving it, if you like – although I wouldn't recommend it. It may look inactive, but it could be faking, playing dead. Even damaged, it's not defenceless."

"Have you tried communicating with it?" asked Roads.

"Yes. Still no response. Whatever it's doing, it isn't talking to us."

"Maybe it's thinking," suggested Barney. "Trying to decide whether to give up."

"Or not." Roads moved forward to stand at Barney's side. From so close, the Mole didn't look dangerous at all; just alien, incomprehensible. It was hard to believe that such an innocuous device had caused so much chaos in the last six weeks. "I won't relax until I see the damn thing in pieces."

Before either of them could react, the Mole re-appeared. An invisible force-field pushed Roads and Barney aside, spilling them bodily to the rusty metal several metres away.

Roads rolled as he hit, grimacing as his broken arm tangled under him. They came to a halt together near the edge of the hole in the platform.

"What the hell?" Barney muttered as she clambered to her feet. The RSD squad had turned their rifles on the expressionless Mole and fired several times.

Barney and Roads joined the squad. Each bullet vanished into the holographic illusion with a faint fizzing noise, audible over the echo of the shot.

"It must be draining power at an incredible rate to maintain that sort of field," said O'Dell via the cyber-link. "But why now? What does it stand to gain?"

Roads tensed as the Mole took a step forward.

"Any guesses, Phil?" asked Barney.

"I don't know," Roads admitted. "But I don't like it."

The Mole took another step, then began to change. The image blurred and swelled, ballooning into an upright lozenge two metres high. The light it cast was a deathly pearl-white, growing brighter by the second.

"Martin?" prompted Roads.

"I'm not sure, either," replied O'Dell. "I've never seen this sort of behaviour from any of the prototypes."

"It must mean *something*."

"True." O'Dell took a deep breath. "It's maximising its surface area, discharging its energy reserve at a dangerous rate. That could mean it's trying to overload its power supply."

"Which means what?"

"That the batteries will explode."

"It's going to self-destruct?" Barney took a step backward, away from the pulsing lozenge.

O'Dell hesitated. "You'd better get as far away as possible, just in case. Try to put as much metal between you and it as you can."

"Will that help?"

"Well, I've seen only one EPA malfunction before, and that destroyed a personnel carrier. The Mole has *five . . .*"

"Shit." Barney relayed the situation to the rest of the RSD officers on the platform, and told them to move away.

"How long do we have?" Roads asked.

"A couple of minutes. Your guess is as good as mine, I'm afraid. It depends on what the Mole hopes to achieve: complete annihilation of everything around it, or just enough damage caused to kill one person."

"Me?" Roads edged across the platform. The Mole followed him as though joined by an invisible string.

"Given a choice. I'd assume it's partly trying to erase all evidence that it ever existed, seeing it knows it's been discovered. If it can take you with it, all the better."

Roads exhaled as the RSD squad filed down the ladderwell. This was one threat he'd be unable to fight his way out of. He had to pass on what he'd learnt about DeKurzak's long-term goals. "You'll have to do me a favour then Martin. I'm about to transmit another feed. It's not long. Just make sure Stedman sees it and passes it on to Mayor Packard, with the recording you've made of all this. Do it now, before we lose contact again."

"But –"

"Just send it. You can look at it later." Roads concentrated briefly, then sent O'Dell the recording he'd made of his last words to DeKurzak.

"Phil?" Barney had waited until the last of the RSD squad was gone before turning to him. "After you. I'll bring Katiya."

"No," he said. "It's your turn, remember?"

"But you're *hurt* –"

"Exactly." He took a step to his left, and the Mole echoed the movement again. "It's locked onto me. If I go now, you'll be trapped up here, above it. You go first, then Katiya. I'll come last, when it's safe to follow."

Barney reluctantly obeyed; she knew the difference between good sense and blind heroics. "Don't wait too long," she called up at him as he watched her descend.

He waved and turned to Katiya. The woman's face was streaked with tears; her eyes hardly saw him as he indicated the ladderwell.

"Katiya?" He took her by the arm. "We have to leave now."

"No. There's nothing to go back to."

"Please, Katiya – for my sake. I'm not leaving here without you."

"I don't want to be saved."

Roads hesitated, caught between conflicting impulses. Did he have any right to force her to come with him? If she wanted to die, then that was her business, not his – especially now. There was little time for arguing.

With one last look over his shoulder, Roads swung his pain-racked frame into the ladderwell and began to descend.

The Mole, now a swollen, fuzzy sphere two metres across, followed. Roads heard the angry buzz grow louder as the Mole's power sources began to feel the strain. He tried to go faster, but was hampered by his broken arm.

"How long now, Martin?" he asked as he descended.

"I've spoken to the Cherubim team at base-camp. They reckon still a minute or two."

"Right." The angry light from the sphere became blinding as Roads found his footing on the second ladder. His scalp and neck registered heat blazing from above. The sphere descended close behind.

He reached the bottom of the ladder. To his left, the walkway stretched across the bridge. Below, he could see Barney and the squad; they had reached the first junction of the stairwell.

He paused to catch his breath. The Mole settled onto a junction of cables not far away, burning like a furious sun. To have any chance of surviving, he had to find a way to go faster.

"Martin?" Roads turned to look up the ladders to the top of the tower, not so very far away. "How will I know when it's too late to run?"

"If the safety overrides are still functioning, you'll hear a warning," said O'Dell. "It sounds like a siren, but it only lasts one second. When you hear it, the power systems are about to fuse."

"Good." Roads took one last look down, and then began to climb back upward.

"Phil?"

"Wish me luck, Martin," Roads muttered under his breath. As his good hand began to cramp, he added to himself: "God knows, I'm too old for this shit."

Katiya looked up in surprise as Roads emerged back onto the platform, closely followed by the Mole. Strange shadows wavered in the night air as he clambered to his feet and limped to join her.

"Take my hand," he instructed her.

"What —"

"Just take it!" Roads grabbed her left hand in his and dragged her toward the edge of the platform. "And when I say jump, do it!"

Katiya looked from him to the empty space facing them, and tried to pull away. "No!"

"We don't have time to argue, Katiya."

"But –"

A scream from behind them cut her off her in mid-sentence: the Mole's warning systems had been activated.

Roads braced himself to step forward. "*Jump!*"

He pushed himself off the platform with all of his strength, pitching himself into the air like an inelegant diver.

Katiya, tugged by his hand, had no choice but to follow.

Behind them, the Mole exploded. With a noise like the sky breaking open and a light so bright it dazzled Roads in the upper electromagnetic spectrum, the EPAs unloaded all their stored energy in one powerful blast.

The shockwave pushed Roads forward and out into clear space. Katiya was wrenched from his grasp. Pieces of bridge rained after him, some glowing molten-hot in low infra-red. He began to tumble end over end. A boiling cloud of smoke overtook him, blinding him for an instant in all wavelengths.

When it cleared, he tried without success to relocate Katiya. Flailing wildly with his good arm and both legs, he oriented himself against the growing updraught, and hoped that she was doing the same. If she wasn't, then there was precious little he could do to help her. He had time only to worry about himself – and that time was rapidly running out.

The cold, abyssal mass of water rose rapidly to engulf him. Fighting the giddy sensation of free-fall in his stomach, he assumed a rough diver's stance and judged his rotation against the passing microseconds. The fall wasn't as high as dives he'd performed during his training in the Army, but it was still risky. With his broken arm tucked firmly to his side, he closed his eyes and breathed one last gulp of air before giving himself over to the river's cold hand –

– which struck like the fist of a vengeful god. His neck snapped backward and he spun out of control into the depths. Stunned, he could only flounder weakly for the surface as the breath rushed out of his lungs.

Boiling rubble sank around him, burning him and making the water a mass of bubbles. Again, he thought he heard muffled screaming, but couldn't pinpoint the sound. He was surrounded by darkness – an icy, impenetrable hell from which he had little hope of escaping. His overcoat tried to drag him deeper, but he couldn't spare the time to take it off: he was already drowning.

If he could discover which way was up, then he had a reasonable chance of making the surface. *Bubbles go up*, he told himself, trying to focus on survival training he had received almost seventy years ago. But his lungs were empty, and only dogged will kept his mouth closed against the water trying to get in.

He called for Barney – for help – over the cyberlink, but there was no answer.

Then his outstretched hand touched flesh: a foot, kicking wildly. He clutched at it, tugged with both hands. It kicked back at him, tried to free itself of his weight, but he pulled himself relentlessly upward.

Katiya's eyes were wide and fearful when he drew level with her face; her head was still below water, not above the surface as part of him had hoped. Her last words drifted diagonally across her face, through her hair, and disappeared behind her.

Up.

Roads kicked himself in that direction, following the bubbles as well as he could with Katiya's forearm clutched in his one good hand. Oxygen-starved and exhausted as he was, he soon lost sight of the route to the surface, but he didn't let that bother him. He had no other option, now, than to hope he was heading in the right direction.

His thoughts became sluggish, but they held on to one with surprising tenacity: he couldn't survive assassins, Cati and even the Mole, only to drown in a few metres of water.

He began to feel distant from his body.

Then a hand gripped his shoulder. With a feeling akin to vertigo, Roads was pulled abruptly upward. He kept his grip firm on Katiya's forearm as he rose, understanding even as consciousness slipped from him that they were being dragged to safety.

The pressure on his chest and ears eased too rapidly, however, causing his respiratory reflex to kick in. Water gushed into his lungs despite his best efforts to keep his mouth shut. He writhed in agony, suddenly, irrationally, convinced that he was going to die within seconds of safety. Katiya slipped from his grasp and disappeared into the churning water. He struggled to find her again, but she had disappeared.

Then the hand at his shoulder let him go, and he was alone. Blackness enfolded him again, and he fell downward, ever downward, into the immeasurable depths below. And if he ever hit the bottom, he never knew.

POSTLUDE

1:35 a.m.

His fate was out of his hands. He was entirely at the mercy of gravity; there was nothing he could do either to arrest his downward plunge or to stop the river from striking him. He was falling, flying, *fleeing* . . .

And for one eternal moment, it felt like Freedom.

AFTERMATH

From the outside, it still looked like a warehouse. Its doors were rusted shut and its windows covered with boards. Its roof had seen worse weather and bore the rain with stoic indifference. An ugly black hole in one wall, where an explosion had recently ripped through brick and reinforced steel, had been curtained off with bright blue tarpaulins.

Kennedy Polis had many such buildings, but only one with a khaki RUSAMC jeep and an armoured personnel carrier parked in front of it.

"This is the place?" asked Martin O'Dell, peering through the rain-spattered window of the jeep. "Doesn't look like much."

"That's what I thought," replied Barney. She glanced at the time on the sophisticated dash. "He told us to meet him here at four."

"Then we'll be early." O'Dell swung open the door and stepped out into the blustery day. After a brief conversation with the driver of the personnel vehicle, instructing the squad to wait until he returned, he turned back to Barney. "Come on. You'll have to show me the way."

She did so, down a flight of stairs between two buildings, then along a short lane to an open steel door.

Inside the corridor, the air was humid and warm. Nothing searched them – none of the automated devices she had encountered the last time – and no-one asked for her weapon. The low counter where bouncers had waited to take ID was unoccupied. The only sign of life came from above: the lights were on.

"Maybe we've missed him," she said.

"He said he'd be here, didn't he?" said O'Dell. "Although it does seem a little quiet, I'll grant you that."

O'Dell edged past the counter to the entrance to the bar. "If no-one's around, maybe we should help ourselves to a drink. I know I could use one."

"Go for it." Barney took a deep breath and followed him inside.

The bar was empty apart from furniture and a large wooden crate in the centre of the floor. Judging by the lack of mess, the room had been hastily cleaned before being evacuated, although the air still stank of years of cigarette smoke and spilled drinks. The bar must have closed in the middle of the previous night, an event possibly connected with the explosion that had knocked such a large hole in the building. Exactly how, though, was a mystery.

Another one. She couldn't speak for the RUSAMC captain, but she was tired of debriefings and guesswork. Her only respite came when she was active, and all she really wanted to do was crawl into bed and sleep for a week.

Finding no sign of life elsewhere, Barney crossed the room to study the crate. It stood a metre high, a metre wide and two metres long. When she tried shifting it, it scraped heavily along the floor. The lid was nailed firmly shut. A black stencil along one side pronounced: "MiMIC Industries, 30/8/40."

"This is old," she said. "Whatever it is."

O'Dell prowled restlessly behind the bar. "And the drinks are gone."

"To be expected, if the bar is closing down." She stood up and wiped her hands. "This might be a test, a puzzle for us to figure out on our own. Or a trap."

"I doubt it. More likely he's just playing with us." O'Dell's watch chimed the hour with a single beep. Out of patience, he cupped his hands around his mouth and shouted: "Hello? We're here!"

"Yes, I can see that," said a voice from behind them. "There's no need to shout."

Barney turned to locate the source of the voice and caught movement in the row of cubicles along the far wall. Something flickered on one of the tables: a ghostly image dancing in the gloom, well-defined despite the distance.

"I told you four o'clock," said the head of Keith Morrow. "You're early."

"Sorry," she said, forcing herself to relax. "Things have been a little disorganised back at the office."

O'Dell stared at the hologram. "Is that him?" he whispered to Barney.

"Yes." She couldn't help but smile at his discomfiture. Just days ago, she had felt the same.

Stepping forward, she made the obligatory introductions: "Martin O'Dell, Keith Morrow."

"A pleasure," said the Head. Its angular features displayed a familiar crooked smile beneath a completely bald pate. "I'd shake your hand, Captain O'Dell, if I could."

"Likewise." O'Dell eyed the hologram warily, his face a mask of guarded fascination.

The trapdoor on the interior wall of the booth opened, revealing a bottle of vintage champagne and two long-stemmed crystal flutes.

"Please," Morrow repeated. "On the house."

Barney performed the honours, uncorking the bottle and pouring golden fluid into the glasses. Champagne of a twentieth-century vintage – the date on the label said 1976 – was to be treasured. A chance to sample such a delicacy might come only once in her lifetime.

"Tasty," said O'Dell, nodding appreciatively. "I'm honoured."

"As you should be." The Head regarded them both with an expression approaching envy. "Although I can simulate the taste of any wine with a fair degree of accuracy, nothing comes close to the real thing. I once knew people who would not have traded places with me, no matter what I offered them."

"And I'd be one of them." O'Dell tipped his glass. "Still, I'm amazed. I had no idea such things as you would ever be possible."

"They were, my boy, however briefly."

Barney put down her half-empty glass, keen to forestall Morrow's boasting before it got out of control. "But we mere humans have our strengths, right? You yourself just suggested as much."

"And your weaknesses." Morrow conceded her point with a wink. "I am trusting that the former will outweigh the latter, inasmuch as my future is concerned."

O'Dell just smiled to himself, and took another sip.

Barney could guess what he was thinking. Morrow had made the offer to turn himself in two hours earlier – a day and a half after the events on Patriot Bridge. In exchange for his surrender, he had demanded a fair trial before the Reunited States High Court in Philadelphia, plus a guarantee that he would not spend long periods disconnected from a power source.

Barney had seen the footage of the conversation. Towards the end, immediately after rejecting an offer of clemency if he identified the group of nomads he had been dealing with outside the city, Morrow had protested O'Dell's description of their arrangement as a deal.

"Deals become tiresome after a while," Morrow had sighed, his characteristic smile slipping. Underneath he looked much older than usual – certainly a deliberate affectation, since he no longer had a true face to reveal. "Even for someone like me, who thrives on them."

"Then what is it?" O'Dell had asked.

"Justice."

"I don't know about that," O'Dell said carefully, "but a trial I *can* guarantee you. The High Court will probably regard your processor as a form of life-support to avoid any unnecessary precedents. If found guilty, you'll be sentenced to one of our penal institutions – although exactly what amenities you'll have will be up to the judge. Hard labour is out of the question, of course, and I don't think we'll trust you with menial data processing instead. You'll be given something to do, though, or else we'll be contravening the human rights laws on sensory deprivation."

Morrow nodded solemnly. "That sounds fair."

"Does it?" O'Dell raised an eyebrow. "You're not really in any position to bargain."

"You misunderstand me. I have taken a great risk handing myself to you like this. If I didn't believe that I could trust you, then I would never have contacted you at all. That's what I meant by 'fair'. All I ask is that I be given a chance to repay my debts."

"If that's so," O'Dell had replied, "then we're going to get along famously."

"Indeed." Morrow had terminated the conversation shortly after that point, apparently satisfied with the arrangements.

Even now, Barney still couldn't believe it had happened so easily. Kennedy's most notorious underworld figure had turned himself over to the newly appointed government without so much as a fight. Of all the things she had guessed would happen, this hadn't even crossed her mind. As a coda to the events of the previous few days, it was surreal.

She frowned, wishing Roads was there to share the moment.

"Well," said O'Dell eventually, breaking the silence. "I'll organise the squad outside to collect your hardware and take it to base camp, where it'll be safe for the time being. When we head back to Philadelphia, you'll come with us."

"Whatever you wish." Morrow shrugged with his eyebrows. "My all-too-mortal remains, complete with original packaging, lie on the floor behind you. I advise you to treat it gently. Destroy the contents of the crate, and you effectively destroy me, too."

Barney glanced over at the box she had studied on her way into the bar. Roads' description of it in terms of a coffin portrayed it and its contents all too vividly.

"I wouldn't dream of doing such a thing," O'Dell drawled, with a certainty Barney could not have mustered.

"I'm glad to hear it," Morrow said. "And now, if you'll forgive me, I will spare myself the indignity of seeing myself hauled away. If you require my attention, I can be aroused by a short burst of white noise on the FM band. Otherwise, I will not speak to you until we reach base camp."

The Head closed his eyes, clearly for effect, and said: "Goodnight."

"Wait!" Barney held up a hand, and Morrow's eyes reopened. "I want to ask you about Phil."

"Yes?" Morrow inclined his head.

"Where is he? Do you know?"

"Answering that question would require breaking a confidence," said Morrow. "What Phil does, or chooses not to do, is his own business."

"But –"

With one last, enigmatic smile, the Head flickered and went out.

O'Dell exhaled heavily, then drained the champagne left in his glass in one gulp. "Thank God," he said. "I kept waiting for him to spring something at the last moment."

Barney forced herself to speak through teeth clenched tight with frustration. "He might still do that."

"Unlikely," said a voice from behind her.

She spun to face its source. O'Dell dropped the glass and drew his pistol in one movement.

Someone was standing in the shadows.

"Phil?"

Roads raised his hands and stepped into the light.

The first things Barney noticed were the mottled bruises on his face and the arm in a sling beneath his coat. He was dressed in jeans, boots and coat – clothes he must have borrowed from one of Morrow's ex-employees – and carried himself stiffly. But the most dramatic change was to his hair: it was cropped short to match where it had burned away in the explosion, and his moustache was gone. He looked like an entirely different person. Only his eyes, with their deceptive contact lenses, were the same.

A red dot of light wavered in the centre of his forehead.

"Hello, Martin," he said with a slight smile.

The red dot vanished and the pistol disappeared back into O'Dell' pocket. "Better late than never, I guess."

"Where the hell have you been?" Barney asked, hiding her relief behind a facade of anger.

"Busy," he said.

"Too busy to let me know you were okay?"

He winced. "I didn't want to run out on you, Barney, but there was something I had to do."

"Like convince Keith Morrow to turn himself in?" asked O'Dell.

Roads looked uncomfortable. "It wasn't that simple."

"I can imagine." The RUSAMC captain moved across the room to examine the crate. "But thanks anyway."

Roads frowned and wiped a hand across his face. To Barney he seemed slightly dazed, as though he had only just woken from a deep sleep.

"Are you okay?" she asked, concerned.

He looked at her. "Never been better, never been worse." For a moment, she thought he was about to move closer, perhaps to touch her, but he didn't. "We need to talk," he said.

"Here?"

"Alone, if possible."

She looked over her shoulder at O'Dell. "Martin, do you mind?"

"Not at all. I'll get the squad and organise the crate. You can talk outside while we do that, if you like."

"Actually, I'd prefer to go elsewhere," Roads said. "Away from here." He glanced at Barney. "Do you want to come for a walk?"

Barney studied him closely, searching for any sign of deception. All she saw was weariness etched bone-deep. For the first time, he actually looked close to his real age. Unlike Morrow, however, she was sure it was genuine.

There was something about him that made her think twice. A tension she couldn't fathom.

"I guess so," she said. "But no funny business. I haven't forgiven you yet."

"Understandable. At least give me a chance to explain." To O'Dell he said: "If we're not back before you leave –"

"Don't worry." O'Dell tossed Barney a key from his pocket. "Take the jeep. I'll hitch a lift with the squad. We can swap notes later, when you're ready."

Barney fingered the key apprehensively for a moment. "Thanks, Martin," she said, putting a hand on his shoulder.

"Any time." The RUSAMC captain smiled warmly. "I'll see you two later."

"Definitely," she replied, hurrying to where Roads waited for her. A slight limp didn't impede his progress as he turned and made for the exit.

"Probably," he said.

Ignoring the look of curiosity she cast at him, he led them out of the bar and into the rain.

Roads gave directions while Barney drove. She handled the unfamiliar controls of the RUSAMC vehicle cautiously at first, but with growing confidence. The powerful electric engine growled as she put her foot to the accelerator, propelling them swiftly through the wilderness of the harbour.

She could sense Roads' need to talk, but let him make the move. She knew him well enough – or hoped she did – to understand that he would talk when the time was right.

"I've been out of touch the last day or so," he finally said. "Have I missed anything exciting?"

"This and that," she said, thinking he was trying to lighten the mood. Then she noticed that he was serious. "How far behind are you?"

"Too far. Morrow's network crashed when the Mole exploded. You must have noticed that, because his version of PolNet went down too."

"We did wonder what was going on."

"So did I. Then Raoul contacted me on an emergency band and filled me in. That's when I discharged myself from the medical unit and came down here."

She pulled a face. "Have I told you how annoyed I am about that yet?"

"You don't need to." He half-smiled. "But you weren't around to talk to at the time, and I didn't want to leave a message. It was bound to have been mis-interpreted."

"Probably." She turned a corner he indicated. "I was at Mayor's House when you left, sitting in on the close of the emergency session. Have you heard about that?"

"No. They wouldn't tell me anything in the RSD medical unit, except to keep still."

Barney smiled at the image, then took a deep breath and began at the beginning.

The aborted assassination attempt and the siege of Mayor's House had dominated the news, of course. In the chaos that had followed Cati's attack on General Stedman, the Mayor had over-reacted disgracefully – a fact he had admitted in a special sitting of the Council, held an hour after the siege had been broken. A serious battle between RSD and the MSA had only been averted by the RUSAMC's second Cherubim prototype, which had confronted the Mayor in his private chambers and forced him to negotiate.

Barney had watched from the security control room while the Council, four of General Stedman's aides and every department head of Kennedy Polis had viewed O'Dell's recording of Roads' confrontation with DeKurzak. The liaison officer's confession, and his ultimate demise, had been played unedited from beginning to end, with only a small break midway to discuss the ramifications of the news.

The Mayor had sat through the recording with his hands tightly folded, his face pale. When it had finished, he had called an hour-long recess to discuss the situation with Stedman's aides.

It was during that time, O'Dell had told her, that he had been played the additional feed Roads had sent.

"I still can't work out how you knew," she said. "There's no mention anywhere in the footage you took of DeKurzak."

"No, there isn't." Roads looked at his hands. "I followed a hunch, and it paid off."

"A pretty big hunch, calling the Mayor a traitor."

"It worked, though, didn't it? DeKurzak couldn't have been working on his own. Yes, he was Cati's controller, and yes, he had his own long-term goals – but in the short term, he was just another pawn caught up in the Mayor's little game."

"Easy to say in retrospect," she commented.

"It didn't hit me until DeKurzak told Betheras Cati was needed at Mayor's House," Roads said. "The only messages crossing the city the night of the siege were Keith's, Stedman's, and the coded signals leaving Mayor's House by landline. The Mayor was communicating with him all the time, so the Mayor knew what he was doing.

"Once I'd made that connection, the rest fell into place. It explained Packard's sudden reversal of policy after the arrival of Stedman's envoy, and the siege of Mayor's House he instigated. The Mayor only let the Reunited States into the city in order to kick them out later, by force if necessary. And DeKurzak was an integral part of that plan. That's why the Mayor supported his every move."

Barney drummed her fingers on the steering wheel. "DeKurzak admitted that he was planning to shaft the Mayor, at some point."

"To assume control himself, I presume."

"I still can't work out *why*, though. He'd lose his power base the moment he opened the Wall – and he'd have to, just to survive. The city wouldn't last, otherwise."

"Did you actually see the second feed I sent?" Roads asked.

She shook her head. "No, but Martin told me what was in it."

"He obviously didn't tell you everything. You haven't brought up Betheras yet."

"I don't follow you."

Roads' eyes didn't leave her. "DeKurzak and Betheras were working together. Did you ever wonder what Betheras stood to gain?"

"I assumed he was an interventionist, as Martin calls it, gunning for military solutions rather than negotiation."

"He may have been once," Roads said, "but not this time. That would have put him and DeKurzak at odds. No, I think he – perhaps both of them – were wrecking the Reassimilation so that one of the Reunited States' enemies could move in instead."

Barney absorbed this in silence. The possibility made her head reel. "Fucking hell."

"That's what I thought," Roads said. "But it makes sense. Kennedy has enormous strategic value. It stands to reason that someone else would want it."

"Who? I didn't know there was anyone else out there."

"There are at least two other major nations," Roads explained, "and we lie midway between the States and one of them. I learned about the New Mexican Alliance from Martin's files, although I never suspected that hostilities had reached this point. Betheras had probably been spying for them for some time, and came to Kennedy with the original envoy specifically to look for allies. Whether or not he found DeKurzak then, and they worked together throughout the whole of Cati's spree, we can only guess. All we know for certain is that they came to some sort of agreement at the end."

"Both of them hoping to give the Mayor an excuse to throw Stedman out of the city," Barney said, continuing the thought. "Then, when the dust had settled down, and everyone had got used to the idea of opening the city, Betheras' friends could make a more tempting offer."

"No doubt DeKurzak stood to gain a lot out of it," Roads said. "Power, or money."

"No doubt both of them did." Barney shook her head. "And they deserved everything they got."

"Betheras is dead too?" Roads asked.

"No. He's still in intensive care, in a coma. Here's hoping the sonofabitch doesn't pull through."

Roads grimaced. "Is there any evidence he tampered with the Mole's programming, given he worked for Project Cherubim?"

"Martin doubts it. The specialists think the Mole's internal conflict was genuine, not faked. What's possible, though, is that Betheras gave advice, supposedly to fix the conflict, that actually made it worse, such as when the Mole was ordered to kill Cati."

"Logical," Roads said. "The more the Mole misbehaved, the greater the damage done to Stedman when its origins were discovered."

Barney nodded, remembering the events on Patriot Bridge. After the confrontation with Cati, the explosion that had destroyed the Mole had torn a large chunk out of the bridge. She, along with O'Dell and the rest of her squad, had been lucky to escape the hail of debris that had fallen from the maintenance tower. And luckier still that the section of the bridge below them hadn't collapsed under the strain.

"You haven't finished telling me what happened at the emergency session," Roads said, bringing her back to the present.

She forced herself to continue the story. Whatever he had to say was obviously going to wait a little longer.

The Mayor had returned from his discussion with Stedman's aides to table a motion that a number of judicial decisions be added to the public record. Given the timing of the crimes and the need to minimise public unrest, plus the fact that at least two of the suspects were known to be dead or dying, the need for a trial could be circumvented by the Council's emergency powers. That way, the cases could be closed, the trouble forgotten, and more important matters dealt with without further delay.

It was a shrewd move on the Mayor's part, even without the knowledge of the second feed taken into account. Between the Mole, Cati and the RUSA, the Council had suddenly realised how vulnerable the city was while the Reassimilation issue remained unresolved. DeKurzak's apparent betrayal – and his own involvement with the RUSAMC – had hammered home the fact that the sooner the situation was dealt with, the better it would be for everyone.

Knowing what Roads had said about the true relationship between DeKurzak and Packard, however, she could guess what had really happened in the private chambers. The Mayor hadn't been discussing options; he had received an ultimatum. Betheras was to be sacrificed in order to draw attention away from the person who had sent the Mole in the first place – which was Stedman himself. That way the RUSA could avoid a public backlash. If Packard didn't do as he was told, then the truth would come out about his relationship with DeKurzak, and he would lose everything.

Making DeKurzak a scapegoat allowed Packard a way out of a very sticky situation, even if it did mean letting the Reassimilation go ahead after all. To keep his own involvement secret, he rushed the motion past the council so quickly that no-one had time to ask themselves why they were letting Stedman off so easily.

The Council debated the motion for less than an hour. With the support of Senior Councillor Norris and the other Reassimilationists, it was voted in with a two-thirds majority. Half an hour after that, the *fait accompli* had become a part of official city history.

"And the motion was . . .?" asked Roads.

She knew it by heart: "Betheras and DeKurzak were found guilty of espionage, murder, conspiracy to commit murder and treason. Everybody else caught in the crossfire – including Margaret and Roger – were acquitted of all charges."

"And me?"

She took great pleasure in saying: "Innocent of murder and conspiracy to commit murder."

Roads sat in silence for a moment. His face was grim.

"Aren't you pleased?" she asked, disappointed by his reaction. "You're off the hook. You can come out of hiding any time you like, now."

He didn't reply immediately. Instead he pointed through the windscreen at the ruins of what had once been a row of shops and said: "Stop there. We'll walk the rest of the way."

Barney pulled the jeep to a halt where he had indicated.

"Why here?" she asked.

"Humour me."

Roads climbed out of the seat, feeling every sore bone from his neck to his ankles. The rain had eased, but the wind was strong enough to make speech awkward. The noise it made reminded him of distant times: of tents on battlefields, of nights waiting for orders, of the betrayals both small and large that his life seemed mostly composed of. The feel of cold air whipping across his exposed scalp made him long for freedom, for flight.

At that moment, more than at any time previously, he could imagine how Cati had felt.

It took them several minutes to reach the end of the freeway – time he was grateful for, to think. The area was sealed from the general public by Major Crime tape. A pair of RSD officers maintained a cursory watch from the shelter of an abandoned tollbooth. Seeing Roads and Barney, the pair waved them through. Slowly, cautious of the ribbon of pain down the muscles of his left thigh, Roads crossed the pot-holes and shattered tarmac of the freeway, and walked onto the bridge.

He brought them to a halt a hundred metres from the shore and leaned against the western guard-rail to watch the water rolling below. He couldn't remember being dragged from it, although he vividly recalled nearly drowning. But for the timely intervention of a RUSAMC soldier – whose name he didn't even know – he might well have joined the rubbish on the river's bottom. A fish's meal snagged on a rusted car-wreck; just another piece of flotsam left over from the twentieth century.

Barney stood next to him with her hands in the pockets of her new coat, not too close but not too far away either. He supposed that her old coat had been singed or torn, just as his had. The sun sank in front of them, dipping gradually through gaps in the clouds to

447

kiss the distant horizon. To their left and above, clearly visible as a dark, twisted scar in the superstructure of the bridge, was the place where the Mole had detonated. Several of the thick suspension cables that had once terminated at the summit of the maintenance tower had been severed by the blast. Most had fallen away from the roadway and into the river, where their truncated ends dragged into the river; two cables, however, had fallen into the infrastructure, causing considerable damage.

"You almost died this time, you know," Barney said, braving the wind with an echo of his own thoughts. "First Blindeye, then Danny Chong, then –"

"I know," he said. "But that's not the reason I brought you here."

"Why then?"

"They'll demolish the bridge for sure, now," he said. "This could be my last chance to see it relatively whole."

"I guess that's understandable." Barney glanced at him curiously, clearly uncertain where his mood was taking her. "It's always been fairly unsafe."

His eyes traced the path of the dangling cables. "Even if they do decide to rebuild, only the pylons will be salvageable. Construction from scratch is often more difficult than reconstruction – or reassimilation, if you prefer. And reassimilation is more difficult –"

"Than dissolution?" Barney interrupted, picking up the metaphor instantly.

"Always." Roads nodded. "I remember when I first arrived here. Kennedy seemed like heaven compared to the rest of the country. With Keith's help, I managed to forge an ID card and found a job in security. That earned me a regular food supply for the first time in over ten years, but it also gave me something to do. I had a *life*, Barney . . ." He turned to meet her gaze. "I don't know if I can make you understand how important that was to me. Everything I'd ever loved was gone. My home was ten thousand kilometres away, on the other side of an ocean that had once seemed insignificant. My implants were dead, and their very existence threatened to destroy me. I needed something temporary to fill the gap, and Kennedy was it. To watch it dissolve over the years . . ." He stopped to find the right words, and failed. "It's hard for me to talk about these things."

"I can imagine," Barney said. "The important thing is that you're trying."

He wanted to touch her, but didn't allow himself to. "Everything has its breaking point if you push it far enough," he said instead. "Patriot Bridge, Kennedy Polis, the Mole, Cati – and me. That's one reason I disappeared. I've lived the last thirty years alone and anonymous, and part of me prefers it that way."

The surprise in her eyes was obvious, but it didn't show in her voice. "Is this what you wanted to talk to me about? You're saying you don't want me around any more?"

"No. I'm saying that, after everything that's happened in the last month, I need a change of scenery."

Barney's face tightened further. "And you came to say goodbye?"

"No. Not necessarily."

"Then what, Phil?"

Roads squinted at the sun, trying to burn out the confusion in his mind. The western sky deepened slowly to red. In another time, the rumble of aeroplanes and orbital shuttles would have marred the stillness of the scene. Roads hadn't heard the sound of jet engines or even seen Kennedy's terminal for decades. The RUSA appeared to have concentrated its strength in land-based transportation, maybe from a shortage of aviation fuel.

He wondered how long it would be before any nation recovered enough to even contemplate international flights; years, possibly decades, would pass.

Sydney seemed as far away as ever.

"Did you ever find Katiya?" he asked, changing the subject deliberately.

She followed his gaze, then shook her head. "We dredged the river yesterday morning. Her body, and Cati's, must have drifted downstream. They'll turn up in one of the locks soon enough."

Roads nodded. "And the Reassimilation? Is that going ahead as planned?"

"More or less. Stedman has made a few speeches promising all sorts of things, but the changes will be slow coming. He's leaving a full squadron here to oversee the amalgamation with the MSA. RSD will continue as normal, as a local department of the States' police force. If all goes well, the Gate will be open permanently in a month or two."

"Slower than I thought," Roads mused.

"But still too fast for some."

"More demonstrations?"

"Not many. Just people talking. It still doesn't feel *real* – and probably won't for some time. That's the general impression I get."

"They'll catch up," Roads said. "They have to."

"Don't get me wrong, though," she added. "There are a lot of people – like me, I guess – who are curious. Stedman's had a lot to say about life in the Reunited States. It doesn't sound so bad." She forced a smile with some conviction. "I can see why Morrow was so happy to turn himself in. The States are clearly a more attractive option for someone like him."

"Infinitely," Roads said. "He really could live for centuries, so a stint in jail isn't going to bother him.

He'll be right where he wants to be at the end of it: in the heart of Philadelphia, ready to reconnect with the datapool around him. And once he does that, his potential for expansion is limited only by the size of the Reunited States itself. As they expand and spread, so will he."

"Unless they kill him, of course," Barney added.

Roads studied her for a moment. No, she hadn't guessed. That didn't surprise him: she still hadn't fully accepted what Morrow was – and part of him wanted to keep it that way. But he had no choice. It was crucial that she know the truth about him before he could expect her to make a decision.

Taking a deep breath, he said: "You don't really believe that's Keith in the crate, do you?"

At first she didn't think he was serious. He could see that in her face.

"Are you telling me it isn't?" she asked. "Because if you are, Martin's not going to be amused when he finds out."

"No, no. Keith Morrow is in the crate, in a sense. But it's not *him*." In response to a sceptical look, he explained further: "Look at it this way: Keith is a computer program. A very sophisticated one, of course, that has far outgrown its original specialised hardware. And a program can be *copied* . . ."

Barney opened her mouth to say something, then shut it.

"It's a copy in the box, edited to fit his original processor," Roads elaborated. "His current form is in a quite different facility on the other side of town."

Eventually she found the words she was looking for: "And you *let* him do this?"

"Worse than that," Roads said, before he could have second thoughts. "I helped him pull it off. *That's* the main reason I disappeared so suddenly, and couldn't tell you where I'd gone. I couldn't say no to Keith, and you wouldn't have approved."

"You're right about that," she said, scowling.

"What else could I do?" he protested. "I owe him at least as much as I owe you. Without each other, neither of us would have made it to Kennedy Polis intact. He would have been salvaged for spare parts, and I would have fallen to pieces."

"But you said you had nothing to do with him any more –" she began.

"I know," he broke in. "We drifted apart over the years, but we still kept in touch. There was always an agreement between us that whenever one needed help the other would respond. Hence all that business after PolNet collapsed – and earlier, when we went to him looking for information about the Mole."

"But what about after the Mole blew up?" Barney protested. "We almost lost you when Morrow's version of PolNet crashed. You couldn't call for help; it was purely by chance that someone found you drifting in the river and pulled you out before you drowned. What made him change his mind about helping you then?"

"He didn't have a choice, actually," Roads said. "When the Mole self-destructed, its central processing core went with it. The explosion destroyed a fair amount of Keith's auxiliary equipment in the bar, thus rendering him incapable of supporting the PolNet program any longer."

Barney's eyes, wide before, narrowed. The ramifications of this statement didn't elude her. "You mean he had it all the time?"

"Without knowing what it was, of course. It was just a puzzling piece of tech someone found in his territory weeks ago. He planned to examine it more closely when he had the time, but the Mole's own activities kept him preoccupied."

"And it almost blew him up as a result." Barney's lips whitened. "Perhaps there *is* a god, after all."

"Why?" Roads asked. "He wasn't really hurting anyone, not directly. If he'd had truly sinister motives, he would have taken over Kennedy long ago."

She turned on him. "That damned thing almost *killed* you –" she began, but cut herself off.

Roads waited for her to continue. When she didn't, he continued his confession.

"Anyway, that's why Raoul called me. Keith needed someone he could rely on to repair the damage after the Mole's artificial intelligence blew up. His back-up had to be assembled, tested, prepared for him to inhabit. The explosion ruined his chance of making a quick getaway. I was the only person he could trust to do the grunt work."

He tried to catch her eye, but she looked away.

"I was hoping you would understand, at least," he said, "and maybe even forgive me, eventually, if you could." He leaned closer. "What do you think, Barney? *Can* you?"

"That depends," she said, her voice soft but intense.

"On what?"

"On what you plan to do next." Barney turned to face him. "If you leave me here without telling me where you're going again, then I'll be justifiably pissed off."

"I understand that," he said, measuring every word with care. "But my options are limited. The city's in the hands of a puppet government with no real power, and a Mayor who's even more pissed off with me than you are."

"But what about Margaret?" Barney pressed. "She came out of this fairly well. She'll do everything she can to protect you."

"But she can't fight the law she's supposed to uphold. Remember: Packard's motion to the Council only clears me of murder and conspiracy; it says nothing about Humanity crimes, so they can still haul me in on that if they want.

"Besides, this business has just brought to a head what was building anyway; I couldn't go on pretending to be a well-preserved sixty-year-old forever. Even if I can clear my name completely, somehow, the rumours will persist in the upper ranks. I never wanted to be a hero *or* a villain, and here in the city I'll always be regarded as both."

"But if you leave," Barney said, "where will you go?"

"I don't know for sure. The original Keith is planning to move soon, to escape Outside via the old maglev tunnels we came in through. I could join him for a while. Or I could wander aimlessly like I did before I came here, until I find somewhere else safe to live. Or –"

"Or?" she prompted.

"Or I could take up Martin's offer, if it's still open, and travel with him to Philadelphia when he goes back."

Barney thought about it for a long moment. "That's not a bad idea, you know," she eventually said, stating what he had only half-admitted to himself.

"No?"

"Think about it, Phil. You'd be close to Morrow's duplicate, and away from all the scandal. I'm sure Martin could arrange for your implants to be kept a secret. He could probably even give you work to do, if you wanted it. You know how military service operates, having held a rank in the old days." Her eyes lit up as another possibility occurred to her. "No, wait. I've got an even better idea: if you don't want to work for the Reunited States, then the Mayor might be convinced to give you temporary status as a trade envoy."

"Just to get rid of me?"

"Yes, partly." Barney almost smiled in the deepening sunset. "But he'd still need someone to keep an eye on you, of course."

Roads felt a knot inside him slip loose. "And I'll always need an assistant."

"*Partner*," she shot back. "Keeping you organised and out of trouble deserves at least that much, don't you think?"

"Definitely." Roads reached out and placed his good hand on Barney's shoulder. She accepted the gesture with equanimity, neither moving closer nor pulling away. He opened his mouth to speak, but she pre-empted him again:

"Is *that* what you've been working yourself up to say? That you'd like me to come with you?"

"Yes." He couldn't meet her gaze. He felt as vulnerable as a schoolboy on his first date – which was absurd for a man in his ninth decade. "If you want to, that is."

She responded instantly: "Why wouldn't I?"

"Well . . ." He shrugged. "This is your home, for a start."

"And yours, too."

"Only for the last few decades."

"Likewise."

"But you were *born* here –"

"All the more reason to leave, then. It'll broaden my horizons." Her gaze remained fixed on him, undeterred. "I'm not like DeKurzak. Kennedy isn't the only city in the world that matters."

"But you've never been outside –"

"Exactly," she said, "and it scares the shit out of me, to be honest. But I can rise above that. I don't intend to pick a fight with anything like Cati without making certain I'm armed to the teeth first. I don't go for stupid machismo stunts like some people I could mention." She prodded him in the ribs, making him wince. "As for my reasons *for* going . . . they're a little more complex. I'm not a love-struck teenager infatuated with an older man. I think our relationship can be more than that, given a chance. If I do decide to go, it'll be for that reason. Because I want to explore that possibility. I don't have to justify my decision any more than that, so don't expect me to, okay?"

"Wouldn't dream of it." Roads met her intensity with a smile, admiring her bravado and accepting her feelings on the matter without questioning them, even though he was certain they weren't quite so clear-cut. His own weren't, especially about pressing the Mayor for favours.

"Besides," she added, "I haven't said I'm going to, yet."

"At least you're interested," he said, with genuine feeling.

"Just don't wait too long. Martin leaves in five days."

"So soon?" Roads raised an eyebrow. "I thought he'd stick around to make sure the Reassimilation goes smoothly."

"Why? It's not *his* problem. He came here to deal with the Head, and that's all. The paperwork can be left to the politicians."

"True," said Roads. Although he felt slightly guilty about abandoning the city in such a mess, it wasn't his job, either, to midwife Kennedy through its difficult rebirth. It had to do it itself, or fail trying.

He had only himself to worry about. His indenture to the city was over.

"Martin's missing his son, I think," Barney said. She stepped away from the rail and looked pointedly back to the shore. The wind had stiffened as evening fell around them. "And he's probably wondering where his jeep has got to."

Roads nodded, taking the hint. It was time to head back. There remained, however, one final issue to deal with before he could cut free of the previous week's events.

"You go on ahead," he said, giving her shoulder a quick squeeze. "I'll catch you up in a minute."

"You're sure? I don't mind waiting."

"No. I just need some time alone."

She hesitated, then nodded once. "I'll meet you at the jeep, then," she said. "Don't be long."

"I won't." He watched as she turned and walked unhurriedly along the pitted road. The wind tugged at the hem of her new coat, making it flap with every step. The material was much lighter than he was used to seeing in Kennedy, but clearly no less wind-resistant. The exchange between the RUSA and Kennedy Polis had already begun, it seemed.

When she had passed beyond the range of unamplified eyesight, he turned back to the rail and reached into his pocket.

Leaning forward with his good hand clenched into a fist on the rail, he peered down at the surface of the river. The grey water churned sluggishly, becoming darker by the second as night fell. What secrets it kept in its unfathomable depths would remain hidden forever. And perhaps, Roads wondered, that was a good thing, ultimately.

The doctors in the RSD medical unit had said that he had been pulled unconscious from the river and revived ashore. If he had been out cold at the time, he should have felt nothing. But he remembered a hand on his shoulder pulling him up through the water, the hand letting go, and a sinking sensation as though he had begun to descend again. And then he had blacked out. As far as he could tell, he must have been rescued sometime after that point – although on the surface of it that made little sense.

The only person who could shed some light on the situation was Katiya. If she had been rescued as well.

Wherever she was now, she was out of his reach forever.

He opened his fist where it rested on the rail and stared at its contents. Some questions required no answers, or were better left unasked. He was still alive, and that was what counted.

With a grunt of effort, he raised his good arm behind his head and aimed for the stars. A glint of reddish sunset reflected off silver as the object in his hand flew free – upward, far above him, turning as it rose – then fell down over the guard-rail and toward the water.

Roads turned away and headed back to the shore, to where Barney waited for him.

With barely a splash, the river below Patriot Bridge hid Cati's dog-tag from sight, as though it had never existed.